Vincere aut mori

CONQUER OR DIE

The Mafia King II

Series book no.2

S.H

Vincere aut mori

Vincere aut mori

trigger warnings

This book contains sexual content, mature themes,
description of torture and sexual harassments (not in detail
but mentions it) in the book a warning has been presented
during the sexual scene's along with sexual harassment scenes
to give readers a chance to skip over if they feel
uncomfortable reading such content.

Vincere aut mori

CONTENT PAGE

THE FAVOR

Isabella's POV

It's been a little over a month and I smiled watching Dante sleep peacefully in my lap, my entire nervous system was in overdrive staring at the angel that clung to my shirt and peacefully slept without a care in the world. I traced his chubby cheek with the back of my finger smiling with a heavy heart. Not able to shut off the guilt, I couldn't help but wonder if Vincenzo knew about his son.

Would it have changed anything? Would it somehow spark some sort of memory? Or was I just overthinking it all? It's closing to a full year since I last saw him, since I last swore to take a break from revenge. For the sake of this little boy in my lap. Hearing the door creek, I looked up and saw Lorenzo peeking inside "is he asleep?" Lorenzo whined, I rolled my eyes and immediately smiled waving him in. "He just fell asleep five minutes ago. Don't you dare wake him" I warned, as I slowly sat up and laid him down on the bed, I sat opposite him. "He looks so much like Vincenzo"

Lorenzo whispers, I nod my head examining my little boy. His tan complexion complemented his grey eyes, which was covered with the longest most beautiful eyelashes any baby ever had. I smiled looking at him, feeling an outburst of joy and pride rush through me I move his hair from his eyes. His gorgeous black hair.

"I love how it curls in the front" I whispered. Lorenzo nodded "he got that from Dante" he informed me in a soft whisper. Lorenzo started laughed softly I eyed him curiously not knowing what was so amusing, "he's in a dinosaur onesie" he childishly pointed out laughing harder. I suppressed my laugh and rolled my eyes, "the onesie you bought" I whispered pointing out the gift he got Dante.

"He looks sick" He bent down and grabbed his arm "Raw" he whispered.

I let out a laugh and slapped his hand away "let him sleep!" I whisper shouted "all he does is sleep. I want to play" he whined. I pointed towards the door, "out!" he shook his head 'no' crossing his arms over his chest and he laid down next to Dante.

"It's nap time" He waved his hand ushering me out.

I looked at them and lifted my hands up surrendering and leaving the room. I closed the door behind me and made my way into the kitchen, I grabbed a few things I had left in the fridge and got started on making something to eat before Dante wakes up and needs a bottle.

I turn on a live broadcast on my phone and hum along to the song as I start kneading the dough.

"We interrupt with breaking news" The host cut the song short piping my interest. "Following the Rossi Mafia being eliminated. The Salvatore Mafia seems to be next. Reports saying that the head of the Mafia King's is no longer playing around, making sure everyone knows his Mafia is still in charge and the true Kings of New York." I raised an eyebrow biting my lower lip as I waited for them to continue.

"This major act of violence was a display of authority reminding his enemies as well as all of New York who still has full control, reports saying after having his own murdered in an abandoned school that was set to be bombed, looks like V.K was tired of hiding in the shadows. Whoever he is after need's more than government protection. If you're listening hide! Please stay safe everyone and don't for-" I slammed my phone shut turning off the live broadcast. I wash my hands in the sink and my face.

I let out a shaky breath slowly lifting my head up.

"No matter how much I try to hide and forget you ... you always manage to find a way back in" I whispered to the wall-shaking my head. I wish I could rid you from my head as you did me. To forget you would be a blessing in disguise this guilt and anger would vanish leaving me at peace. I close my eyes sighing he has been going on a killing spree lately, every breaking news announcement has the King's name in it. It's like he officially went mad, something was triggering his murdering spree I just don't know what.

I saw Lorenzo come out of the bedroom on his phone, I look at him curiously trying to figure out who he is talking to. I walk closer to him on my tippy toes trying to hear whoever was on the other line.

"I'm on my way" He hangs up the phone and rushes out, I huff annoyed and rush out after him.

"Where are you going in such a hurry?" I ran out standing in front of the car blocking him from driving off.

"Isabella move."

I cocked my head to the side waiting for him to see how little effect his threat had over me.

Sighing a sigh of defat "Vincenzo called I need to run the numbers for the next shipment" he explained calmly. I nodded my head "what's with him?" I asked genuinely concerned.

"I have no idea" he breathed.

"I thought it was about the families questioning his authority and wanting to kick him out, but they are more confident in him than before ... he has been like this for little over a month and no one can figure out why" He explained. I nodded my head slowly trying to comprehend everything. Despite my hatred I couldn't help but worry for him, I let out a breath and stepped aside so Lorenzo can drive off. I heard a faint cry coming from inside the house I looked towards the door and quickly rushed inside to my bedroom. I tapped Dante on the stomach calmly singing to him to calm him down. I smiled singing the lullaby my mother use to sing to me and Maria when we were little. "A la nanita nana, nanita ea, nanita ea. Mi niño tiene sueño, bendito sea, bendito sea." **Let's sing a lullaby, lullaby, my bab's sleepy, bless him, bless him.** I laid down next to him and softly cuddled up next to his small body. "A la nanita nana, nanita ea, nanita ea. Mi niño tiene sueño, bendito sea, bendito sea." I hummed caressing his cheek with the back of my finger as I tapped his thigh softly. "Fuentecita que corre clara y sonora, ruiseñor que en la selva cantando llora calla mientras la cuna se balancea, a la nanita nana, nanita ea." **Little spring bubbling clear and loud, nightingale singing plaintively in the forest keep quiet while the cradle rocks to and for, lullaby, lullaby, lullaby -by.**

I smiled as I watched his body relax and go back to sleep. Letting a small smile appear on his cute little face as he heard me sing to him. "A la nanita nana, nanita ea, nanita ea. Mi niño tiene sueño, bendito sea, bendito sea." I kissed his forehead and watched him in awe. I looked over my shoulder hearing my phone ring. I raised an eyebrow this was a new phone and sim, so no one was able to track me and the only ones who had my number was Sebastián, Alex and Lorenzo.

Grabbing my phone and I saw an unfamiliar number appear; I hesitantly answered the call curiosity getting the best of me. "Hello?" I spoke up.

"Isabella it's so good to hear your voice Preciosa" I sighed a sigh of relief and immediately smiled recognising that deep voice.

"Garcia you don't know how happy it is to hear your sweet voice." I smiled.

"Isabella, I need a favour from you" he spoke getting straight to the point, I squinted my eyes and looked down at Dante who clutched my finger in his tiny hand.

"You know I would never refuse you, but if it's anything violent related I have to warn you I buried that side of me a long time ago" I answered him honestly.

"Why is that?" He asked, I chewed my bottom lip thinking about what to say "Isabella?" he called out softly.

"Uh … let's just say I have other priorities" I answered him as honestly as I could.

"Bigger priorities than when you were pregnant and doing all that running around?" he laughed on the other end of the line.

My eyes widen as I sat up straight "I wasn't-" I tried saving myself before he swiftly cut me off.

"Preciosa, you might have fooled everyone, but you can't fool this old soul" I smiled letting out a sigh.

"How did you know?" I asked him honestly.

"When I mentioned having children your eyes sparkled and when Vincenzo commented he didn't want. You protectively clutched your stomach. Besides, you can't fool an old soul who has been yearning for a child of his own for years" I smiled sadly hearing his attempt to cover up his pain with humour.

"I don't know if this makes a difference, but you already have children. You have Vincenzo for starters. The way he spoke about you and his childhood where you played and hung out with them made him feel normal and special. Like the only felt whole and a fatherly bond with you" I reassured him, he let a laugh and joked "then that baby you have there is my grandchild. I'm coming to see him" he hung up the phone without asking for my address and I looked at the phone screen my mouth hanging open as I let out a small laugh.

I turned my phone off thinking how did he manage to get my number? and how is this man going to find where I live?

I rolled my eyes remembering who he was and who he raised it was just easier not to question it. I got off the bed and placed pillows as barricades around Dante, so he doesn't roll off I stood up leaving the door open so if Dante cried, I would hear him while I tidied up the house before Garcia came.

I rushed into Alex's room "need you to watch Dante while I have a shower" I smiled at him from the doorway he looked up from his phone and nodded his head. He got up slowly and walked towards my room and laid back down next to Dante getting comfortable. "Thanks' for letting me borrow your laptop yesterday" he commented hesitantly.

I smirked and looked over at him "anytime".

"I think I didn't log out of my bank account do you mind if I just check th-" I cut him off laughing.

"Already cleared the browser history" I reassured him.

"You're a good woman" he announced relieved pointing his finger at me as he laid his head back on the pillow and scrolled through his phone relaxed.

I rolled my eyes laughing. I grabbed my clothes and got into the bathroom closing the door behind me, taking this rare opportunity to shower, I can tidy up after.

I quickly turn the water on feeling the temperature before stripping and getting in. My body relaxed as the hot water prickled at my skin, I quickly rushed to the shower to avoid overthinking every decision and my life.

Besides I don't want to leave Dante with Alex for too long. I stepped out and quickly got dressed when I heard a knock at the door, I squinted my eyes and shook my head he can't be here already, and there is no way he found me this quickly.

I finished changing throwing on a pair of grey sweatpants and a black singlet. I got out of the bathroom and saw Dante on the bed by himself as he tossed and turned wanting to play, I smiled and picked up slowly.

"Hey buddy" I whispered as I kissed him on the cheek, "my small little dragon" I laughed knowing that's what my imaginary friend would call him, I mean that was his nickname for me. I held him in my arms as I walked out to the living room seeing Alex anxiously sitting in front of a man "Alex?" I questioned him, getting nervous all heads turned to me "Isabella" Garcia greeted me.

I giggled "Hey old man" I laughed out.

Garcia let out a small laugh standing up to embrace me. I walked towards him and let myself be embraced in a tight hug I guess I never noticed just how much I missed his hugs.

Letting go he looks down at Dante in my arms, he looks at him mesmerised. "Is that him?" he asked in a soft whisper scared he might frighten him. I watched him with admiration as he looked down at Dante with pride and so much love just like a grandpa.

I nodded my head observing him he looked so excited not being able to relax his face, his strong facial expressions softening becoming like a little baby the longer he stared at Dante.

"My cheeks hurt from smiling so much but I can't stop" he softly cried as he looked up and then back down at Dante not wanting to take his eyes off him.

"Garcia, are you tearing up?" I whisper laughed feeling my eyes tear up looking at how emotional Garcia was getting. He nodded his head not even trying to deny it.

"He looks exactly like Vincenzo when he was younger, but he has a hint of mischievous in his eyes" he looks up at me "and that's all you" he laughed as I rolled my eyes smiling feeling a little proud. "You want to hold him?" I asked he looked at me and backed away hesitantly "I don't want to hurt him" he admitted I giggled softly and shook my head "You won't come on" I carefully handed Dante over who was now in Garcia's arms looking up at him with his big grey doe eyes and those thick black lashes that I'm extremely envious of.

Garcia laughed not being able to take his eyes off him "Oh you're such a handsome boy ... I promise I'll always protect you." He looked up at me and smiled "God help anyone who tries touching him" I nodded my head laughing.

"Oh, don't worry, I'm his mum they're not even allowed to look at him the wrong way" I winked and sat down next to them as Alex watched the two of us. He nodded his head for his men to wait outside they obliged and quickly hurried off turning his attention back to me and Dante.

"What did you name him?" He asked in a baby voice.

I raised an eyebrow and laughed.

"Now I know why you told your men to go outside" I smirked trying not to laugh at his sudden change in personality.

He ignored me and simply continued talking to Dante "your mum is annoying isn't she" he cooed, Dante gave him a smile and Garcia smile widened "I made him smile! Isabella look at him he's smiling! And he agrees with me ... oh you are just the most precious and smartest baby to ever exist" I watched him shocked never in a million years would I ever think to see a well-respected Mafia don act like this with a baby.

After a minute I finally answered his question "I named him Dante" he looked up at me slowly a sad smile took over his lips as he looked back down "Dante King. Oh, you are named after one of the most amazing souls to walk this earth" he whispered to Dante making me smile. "I just knew in my heart that was his name" he nodded his head staring at Dante who had now fallen back asleep in his arms holding onto his finger for dear life.

Garcia pulled Dante closer to his chest protectively, "I watched Vincenzo grow up ..." he suddenly spoke up getting my full attention at the mere mention of his name, "my wife and his mother were very close, his dad and I never got along but dealt with one another for work" I nodded my head seeing how that would play out. Vincenzo's parents are very hard to get along with especially his dad, "I didn't get along with him for obvious reasons and frankly I wasn't fond over my wife being so close to Anna but I can't tell her who and what to do but besides them, I enjoyed going for the boys" He smiled at me as he reminisced "I was there when they brought Vincenzo and Dante home from the hospital, they were so little so innocent" He emphasised how little they were with his hands before he wrapped them back around Dante hugging him close.

"Then me and their dad had a falling out and I never saw them again not until they were in their early teens, when my wife forced me to go see them, I much rather do anything than look at Giovanni's face, so I went outside and hung out with them. It broke my heart watching those two boys being turned into weapons by their power-hungry father. The first couple of times I didn't approach them just watched from afar ... I promise it's not as creepy as it sounds, a part of me loved them like my own and you could say I was just making sure they were okay. Then finally I got enough courage to approach them, I heard Dante and Vincenzo talking about never wanting to become like their father and how sad they were they didn't have any sort of relationship with neither their dad nor mum. So, I decided to step up" he explained in a calm tone as he looked at me with soft eyes.

"Anyone can be a biological father, but it takes a real man to be a dad ... to fix a heart he didn't break and raise children he didn't make" I whispered admiring his love for them, he would have made such an amazing dad.

"I loved those boys, and I made sure I was there whenever they needed me, I never had kids, but my wife and I always thought of them as our own."

"Vincenzo can be a handful and a pain in the ass" he laughed shaking his head smiling making me laugh a little, "but he has a good heart, sometimes I think it's too big for his body. I feel like I was privileged to witness that side of him, he hides it from the world because that's what he was taught to do, that heart of his was abused into hiding, but it's there I know it is ..." he drifts off looking back down at Dante.

"Just give him a chance ... a reason to use it" he whispers. I bit my lower lip feeling anxious, "how-" he shook his head "I know you haven't told him; I know I have no right to tell you what to do, but Vincenzo is like a ... is my son. He has a right and hey he might surprise you Bella".

"I know he would make such an amazing dad but, with his memories of me gone and everything that's happened in the last year ... my feelings have been so all over the place I don't know what to do" I admitted feeling comfortable enough to talk to Garcia about it. I looked up at Alex and nudged my head to the door hinting for him to give us a minute. He happily obliged and left us alone, Garcia stood up and put Dante down in his rocker. Giving me his full attention, he sat next to me and grabbed my hands smiling "Isabella, I say this because I love you. Don't let your feelings corrupt your son's relationship with his father."

"Give Dante a chance at having a dad... I know Vincenzo won't let you or his son down if you did" I slowly closed my eyes knowing he was right, I was being selfish and I knew it. I nodded my head "I'll let him now soon" opening my eyes again. He smiled and gently placed a soft kiss on my forehead "that's my girl" I smiled leaning in for a hug, his hugs always made me feel comfortable and safe.

"Know for the real reason I came here" he pulled back with an innocent smile plastered on his face "What?" I asked confused and curious looking at him with a raised eyebrow "what do you mean real reason?" I questioned.

"I need a favour" I decided to stay quiet letting him finish what he needed to say before I gave him my answer. "I promise it's nothing too dangerous, I know you have Dante, and I would never want to put you in a position where he could lose a mother and I would never put you in a position where you could lose your son" I nodded my head slowly taking in everything.

"I need you to accompany Anthony to a wedding tonight I need someone who will blend in with the rest of the guests and once he and my men capture the intended man, I'll need to interrogate him. He has information on a very important mole in my circle that I need intel on. No one has ever managed to get anything out of him, and I know for a fact that the only person intimidating enough to get him to talk would be you." I sat there looking at him with a poker expression taking in everything he said.

I didn't know if I should be flattered or taken back by his 'small' favour. Apart of me did miss the adrenaline of my past life and I so desperately wanted to get back into it, to both not forget who I am and to give me the confidence that If I go back and I'm still as ruthless as ever when it counted, that the side of me that made me who I am isn't completely dead.

Although a bigger part of me kept screaming Dante, I couldn't leave him without a mother. I cannot deliberately put myself in danger just to get a familiar high. I had someone other than just myself to worry about I had the cutest, innocent baby boy who is completely dependent on me.

Taking in a deep breath I finally speak up "Garcia, I don't think I can do it." He sighed nodding his head "Isabella, I wouldn't ask you unless I was desperate. The man I'm asking you to interrogate raped and killed little girls and boys all under the age of six and is keeping the man in my circle who does the same a secret. He also has knowledge of some very big human trafficking schemes and groups. I'll admit we are not saints, but I will not tolerate harm on innocent children especially babies. You know we mainly go after predators like them, which is why the feds are not completely focused on my Mafia or Vincenzo's".

My blood suddenly boiled imaging anyone attempting to touch a child like that, then my body lit a flame putting myself in the position of those victims' parents. "I'm in" I spoke up without thinking twice. "I have conditions" I pointed at him he nodded his head smiling waiting for me to continue "I want security around this house at all times but make it discreet, so it doesn't draw too much attention. I want Lorenzo, Sebastián and Alex inside this house with Dante while I'm gone. I need you to promise me that Dante will be safe and protected for as long as I'm not here."

"Isabella, I will have my best men around and in all the streets connecting to your house until and even a day or two after your arrival. I in fact will also stay the night to make you less hesitant." He calmly assured me; I smiled nodding my head. Knowing Lorenzo and Garcia were both going to be here with Dante gave me the reassurance I needed, I knew no one would be able to lay a finger on my son with them here. As powerful as the two individuals are together, I knew in the pit of my stomach that Vincenzo alone is more capable of protecting Dante but given the circumstances I knew that was just a dream at least for now.

"Okay, you have a deal, Garcia." I smiled nodding my head. "I'll be in touch" I nodded my head as he stood up gave me a final hug before he knelt to Dante giving him a kiss on his head "I'll always protect you, buddy, just like I protect your dad but maybe a bit more." I smiled trying to not cry from how sweet the scene in front of me was. "Okay my hormones are kicking in you can leave any time" I laughed trying not to cry. He laughed giving me a peck on the cheek and leaving.

I walked towards Dante and sat beside the rocker "I swear no matter what I'll always come back too you; I'll never leave you alone. I'll never leave you without a mum and I promise to do everything in my power to protect you." I watched his nose flare as he took in breaths, if I could kill every threat in this world to protect every baby, I swore I would even if I kill one every threat one by one I will. "You have such a cool mum. Just so you know" I pointed out. "If your aunty Maria was here, she would sarcastically agree with me, then proceed to explain how she's cooler." I smiled looking out the window "she probably is telling your uncle Dante right now just how much she's cooler she is, and he is probably arguing that he is in fact cooler" I laughed imaging the two of them bickering.

"I wish you got to meet them; you would have loved them so much ... They would have loved you with everything they had and more" I kissed his little hands resting my head on my arms as I watched him sleep.

Vincenzo's POV

Punching the boxing bag repeatedly, with every blow my head became more clouded not knowing what thought to focus on. It was like there were a million voices screaming at me at once and each voice took over my body. **She's pregnant!** I let out a grunt punching the bag with more force. **She kept it a secret.** Throwing my arm to the side of the bag hooking it **I had to watch my son's birth in secret**

like an outcast. I huffed feeling my muscles burning **I let Maria die** my veins bulging out the harder I went; I stepped back from the bag hearing the voices get louder and louder. The final voice that sent me over the edge in a low female voice yelled out **YOU LET ME GO VINCENZO, YOU LET ME GO!** I looked up at the roof then back at the bag gripping my head before letting out a shuddering scream. The room shook as my scream echoed in the small gym. The shouting was violence in the air, a way to take the anger and voices from my head and transfer it into the universe I don't care where it went as long as it went away from me.

"Boss, Senior Garcia is here to see you" I turned around and saw the new soldiers in the mafia standing at the door in a group.

"Don't travel in packs to tell me something" I spat looking at their fearful eyes as they watched me.

"Guide him to my office I'll be there in a minute" they hurried out shutting the door behind them. My previous state of guilt was washed over with anger and feelings of annoyance. She carried my son in her for nine months she kept it a secret and whets worse is she allowed Lorenzo to be part of it every step of the way and didn't bother to think I had a right to know. I stood up grabbing my towel and water bottle from the floor making my way out of the gym and headed upstairs to take a quick shower before going to see Garcia in the office.

X

Quickly grabbing a pair of grey sweatpants and a black tank I throw them on and make my way to the office. "Vincenzo my boy" he stands up extending his arms. He pulls me in a hug patting me on the back I suppress the urge to laugh and smile returning his hug.
"Been a long-time old man. To what do I owe the pleasure" I sit opposite him knowing this wasn't a simple visit. I watch his friendly attitude be replaced with a serious one his eyebrows lowering while his eyes turn cold. He turns around and nods his head towards the door. His two men bow their heads and walk out of my office.
"I've heard you've officially gone mad" he makes a comment and takes a second to analyse my presence.

Looking at my new scars and my stained and bruised knuckles.

"I'm just back to my roots" I shrug him off not wanting to get into it. He hummed unimpressed and not convinced "why?" he pressed I huffed and shrugged my shoulders. "I didn't go mad. I have been more myself the past month than the past year."

"How would you know how you were like the past year?" He asked sarcastically.

"You can try and convince me all you like that whatever is causing your outburst is unrelated to a certain 5-foot 4 psycho" my hands balled into a fist hearing him mention her. He paused for a second looking at my fists and shaking his head disappointed.

"Garcia, I've been like this since I was a kid. Nothing's changed" I pointed out that my violence has been threaded into me since I was born to this world.

"You did" he firmly spoke.

"You changed, and not because you had to, but because you wanted to you became who you truly wanted to be. Before the world forced you to become a weapon"

I sat there in silence watching him as he spoke, "son, never change be your true self ... and if you don't know who that is yet then go find yourself. Don't change to fit someone else idle match but" he paused emphasising the 'but', "never lose someone who accepts you for all you are all your demons and skeletons. It's easy to love a man in all his glory, his power, his good looks but it's hard to love him for the things that make that man human." Garcia smiled at me softly trying not to overstep but also wanting me to be aware of things he thought I wasn't.

I know all this; I know I lost her, and I know I'm the reason why. I know that I broke and now went mad because I never wanted to feel that pain again. I was looking for anything to hate her and I did I hate her so fucking much. Although at the same time I couldn't help the overwhelming feeling of wanting her, needing her. I couldn't help the foreign feeling that would creep up every time I would think about her ... but then I remember she kept my child a secret and everything goes dark even if a part of me understood her.

I needed any reason to hate her so I wouldn't crumble. I sit up straight fixing my posture realising I zoned out for a minute, "I did come for important matters. I need a favour from you" He starts off, knowing I wasn't going to discuss Isabella. I nod my head waving my hand indicating for him to continue "I need you to attend a wedding today with my employee Lilly. We have a man there that needs your kind of persuasion." He smiles indicating torture methods. I cocked an eyebrow as a devilish smirk overcame my lips.

"Right" I laughed "If this is some kind of way to set me up with another girl you got jokes Padre" I laughed. His eyes softened "padre?" he softly spoke up.
I looked up at him and smiled nodding my head. "You have been more of a dad than my actual father." I coughed clearing my throat not wanting this conversation to become emotional.

"Son, trust me if I was trying to set you up with anyone it wouldn't be my employee it would be Isabella" he sat back in his chair calmly "No." I responded firmly. He cocked an eyebrow and smirked "yes." he responded.
"No"
"Yes" he mocked I huffed Garcia finding humour in my annoyance bursting out laughing shaking his head.

"You may be saying no, but your eyes son ... they say a different tale. One I'm not comfortable repeating but it does show me you want her" he laughed at his own joke causing me to roll my eyes.

"Garcia, the favour" I pointed out trying to get him back on track. He cleared his throat and proceeded.

"The guy I need you to interrogate is a well-known child rapist he has information about a man and potentially an entire circle in charge of human trafficking they sell and keep some for their own pleasures" he speaks up disgusted suddenly my stomach turned hearing the information.

"I'm in" I spoke firmly. My hands balled into fists imaging anyone touching my child or anyone's child in that way, "you have always assisted in these sort of missions ... Thank you" he stands up. Following his actions, I stand on my feet and nod my head "these sorts of missions make a difference, save lives. It is the only non-selfish thing I'm proud to be a part of." Garcia smiles hugging me and stands back.

"I'll send a car today with Lilly. She along with my other man will discreetly kidnap the man without causing suspicion, you, along with another guest of mine will be there distracting the guests and having a good time at the wedding. Once he is captured and in a secluded room in my warehouse. You will be given the address and you will both be needed there to interrogate the man for answers."

I nodded my head "simple enough" I spoke then shot my head up "wait who's the other guest?" I asked.

He simply gave me a sly smile and walked out of my office "you'll find out soon enough" I stood there stunned for a second watching him leave my office as I watched him curiously. "Garcia, I want to know now" I called out chasing after him, "in time you will. Trust me son you're gonna love it ... even if you don't, I will get a laugh out of it" he jokes smiling at me getting in his car driving away. "Sarà una lunga notte" (He is up to something) I whispered to myself walking back inside.

"You're going to a wedding?" Ariana perks up behind me. I couldn't help but smile at her excitement over me simply going to a wedding ... unless she knows something I don't.

"Maybe I am... it's for work though" I quickly point out.
"I'm picking an outfit for you" she rushes to my bedroom
rolling my eyes I follow behind her already exhausted.
"Ariana, I need to work I'm just wearing something simple" I
point out. She shoots me a glare warning me to back off.
"You will wear what I put in front of you, because you have
to look good" she ruffles through my clothes.
"Why? Why do I need to look good?" I pressed.

She turned around facing me with wide eyes before slowly
turning back around and whispering "you're my big brother.
Is it such a crime to want you to look presentable" I walked
closer to her and kept pondering "you never seemed to care
how I look during work" she started chewing her bottom lip
"Ariana, I raised you, I know you're hiding something from
me" she turned around to face me.
"I can't say" she softly speaks up "just shut up and wear this"
she gets frustrated and pulls out an off black suit with a white
button shirt. She hurries off to my drawers and opens them
revealing all the luxurious rings, bracelets, and watches.

"You have nicer jewellery than me" She pulls a few out and places them on the bed "wear those shoes" she tosses out black ankle boots and smiles walking off.

"Lorenzo promised to take me shopping so I'll see you after you get back!" without another word she runs out of my room before I could press her for answers. I mentally rolled my eyes and sat on my bed. Taking in a deep breath I sighed and buried my head in my hands. My head was so scattered and as much as I hate her for keeping such a big secret from me. She is the only voice I want to listen to, the only voice I can focus on in the millions in my head. I still can't wrap my head around the fact that she and Lorenzo and most likely Ariana have kept it a secret for me. I stood up finally deciding to get changed, grabbing the outfit. Looking at myself in the mirror I fix my hair grabbing my glasses. I examine myself quickly before leaving "Boss, a car just pulled up with a woman waiting for you inside." I nod my head and walk outside seeing a black Rolls-Royce pull up and stop in front of the front stairs. I tilt my head seeing a familiar woman in a red dress sitting in the back.

X

Isabella's POV

Garcia left about an hour ago Dante was still asleep, and I was cleaning the house before the boys and Garcia and his men came to help watch Dante. I giggled at the number of men needed to watch a baby but also appreciated the overprotective attitude. I looked over to the side hearing my phone ringing I move to the side putting the vacuum away and grabbed my phone.

"Isabella" Lorenzo greets me I smile shaking my head "Lorenzo" I mimicked his tone. "I have someone who wants' to see you" he speaks up hesitantly. I narrowed my eyes "who?" I questioned putting the phone off speaker and to my ear. "Ariana" I sighed relieved. "You told her, didn't you?" I questioned. "She got it out of me when she saw me at the mall buying that Dino onesie!" he shouted. I rolled my eyes "as long as she doesn't tell Vincenzo I'm fine with it" I hang up my phone when I see his car pull up in the front. On cue I see Dante stretching and opening his eyes. "Aw hey, buddy. Look at those pretty eyes" I squealed excitedly. I bent down and scooped up his small body and held him close to my chest "no, no don't go back to sleep yet. Mummy wants to see you" I begged him when he started yawning again. "I'm gonna be gone for a few hours, okay? I promise I won't be long, and I'll be right back. Until then you have a million guys coming to take care of you ... because it takes that many to protect you like mummy does" I winked earning a small smile.

I laughed watching his small lips curl into a wide smile before it went back to a cute little pout. I heard a gasp beside me, I lifted my head turning towards the door "Is that?" she whispered softly. I smiled and nodded my head for her to sit next to me "Dante King meet your aunty Ariana Nicole King" I playfully introduced them.

She gripped my arm squeezing it in excitement "I was planning on attacking you for not telling me, but he is so cute I'm going to let it go for now" she speaks in a baby voice while she taps his hands playing with him. I rolled my eyes and laughed "do you want to hold him?" I asked she nodded her head eagerly I slowly handed him to her, as soon as she held Dante in her arms, she never took her eyes off him for a second, holding onto him as she watched him in awe.

"He looks so much like Vincenzo" she commented. I let in a deep sigh and exhaled softly I nodded my head "he could pass for his twin" I admitted. She smiles "his dark hair, tan complexion and the most beautiful grey eyes I've ever seen" her smile widened to the point where my cheeks started hurting on her behalf. Lorenzo sits in front of us on the couch "when do you leave?" he asks me slightly disappointed. I look up at Lorenzo and frown "Lorenzo".

"No, you promised that you were giving all of it up" He points out. I sigh and shake my head "Lorenzo, I said I won't put myself in danger and I'm not. I can't sit in this house for the rest of my life scared if Xavier or Vincenzo are going to do something. You can't expect me to stop being me ... whether you like it or not this is who I am. That promise of me giving it all up is like giving up on myself. Dante is the most important thing in this world and always will be, but if I can make a difference, I'm going to do it." I pointed out. He let out a sigh and put his hands up in surrender "Lorenzo we both knew that me becoming a stay-at-home mum was a stretch, we both knew I wasn't going to be able to sit still for long. I would never purposely put myself in a position where I couldn't come back home to Dante. Trust me on this, I can't explain it, but my soul is burning to go. It's like I'm supposed to be there for whatever reason." I explained this gnawing feeling I couldn't seem to shove off. I saw Ariana from the corner of my eye she was smirking like she knew something, I decided to focus back on Lorenzo for now, he finally exhaled and relaxed "Okay, just come back home" he begged me. I nodded my head smiling "Always will" I winked.

"You need a dress" Ariana chipped up, I turned to her shaking my head. "No, No. I don't need a dress whatever I have in my closet is what I'm wearing" I denied her offer to doll me up, "I'm going to interrogate a man. Not dance on the dancefloor with the man of my dreams" I laughed shaking my head. She smirked at me then quickly hid her smile clearing her throat, she did it again. She knows something, "you have to look good for-" she cut herself off and pursed her lips.

Lorenzo and I both raised an eyebrow looking at her "for who?" I fake amusement edging closer to her. She held

Dante closer to her chest like he would protect her "for the mission ... Yeah the mission. You're going to a wedding you need to blend in" she subtly regained control and nodded her head.

I hummed not believing her "even if I agreed with you the driver is coming in less than 30 minutes. I don't have time to go to the mall and find a dress." I shrugged my shoulders; she stood up and squealed excitedly still holding onto Dante. "I came prepared" she softly placed Dante back in his rocker and ran outside excited. I looked at Lorenzo he immediately shrugged his shoulders not knowing what was happening. "How did she even know about the wedding to bring a dress?" I questioned; he looked deep in thought for a second. "I really don't know ... maybe she overheard on the phone?" I pursed my lips to the side nodding my head ... that still doesn't explain how she knew to bring a dress and, on whose phone, could she have possibly overhead it on?

Ariana runs back inside holding a breath taking strapless red dress. My mouth fell open in admiration I stood up running towards her only seeing the dress in front of me, running my fingers through the beautiful silk material I was already in love with it. "It looks gorgeous" I breathed out.

"If only my body was like it once was" I joked and stepped back. Ariana slapped my arm and rolled her eyes "you look beyond stunning, your body snapped back quickly, you look fitter than ever! Now embrace your body and love yourself because your body just birthed a whole human, and you look fine as fuck" she lifted my tank and examined my abs that started to reclaim their spot. I

guess my body was coming back but it's been so long since I dressed up that I started getting a little insecure, her words of encouragement helped a little though.

"You're wearing it no if's or buts let's go" she grabs my wrist and drags me to the bathroom "LORENZO WATCH DANTE PLEASE" I shout out while being rushed out of the room, I huff when Ariana pushes me on the bed and instructs me to do my makeup while she curls my hair. She sounds just like Maria, but Maria wouldn't let me touch anything, "Ariana I'm going to get information out of a man through non-conventional methods. Don't go crazy please" I begged her knowing what that twinkle in her eyes means. She shushed me and heated the curler in the bathroom I sighed smiling accepting my fate. She started working on my hair while I started doing the bare minimum on my face.

Twenty minutes later we were done she cheered and demanded me to wear the dress, I laughed she was so excited that she basically helped me undress so I wouldn't ruin my makeup or hair. She looked at my bare chest and smirked "Vincenzo lost so much" she whispered hurt. I widen my eyes looking at her then laughing and shaking my head. "Just turn around" I laughed and quickly slipped on the dress she grabbed my red strap heels and assisted me zipping me up.

She stood up examining her work and smiled "you look breath taking!" she smiled.

I looked in the mirror and my draw dropped. The dress hugged my figure nicely and drew attention to all the right things. I shook my head smiling "thank you" I hugged her and walked out hearing a car beep outside. I slowly made my way to the living room fixing my bracelet and rings. I looked up and saw the men all with dropped jaws "Isabella?" Alex questioned getting up to get a better look at me I giggled and shook my head "shut up".

"You look hot" Sebastián muttered, I laughed and looked over at him "when did you get home?" I questioned he shrugged and kept gawking at me. "Sexy mama" Ariana commented I shook my head and rolled my eyes smiling a little. "Listen to me very carefully, I pumped breast milk and left it in the fridge, my phone is on me in case of any emergency, and he needs a bath today an-" I started listing before Lorenzo shushes me and tells me to relax.

I sighed "Okay ..." I started chewing my bottom lip looking at Dante asleep in the rocker. "Oh, but maybe I shouldn't go" feeling the paranoia creep up inside me and the mum guilt of going anywhere without him. Although this wasn't the place to take him to, "no, you were right to do what you do best and stop that disgusting fucker. Maybe you really need to be their" Lorenzo comments. I sigh "besides we and Garcia's men are all in the area and inside with Dante. He'll be okay" he whispered. I nodded my head and left before changing my mind. I got in the black rolls Royce and smiled at the driver, "I'm Anthony" I turned and saw the man sitting next to me who was going to be my date for the night, I smiled as he introduced himself.

I smiled back and shook his hand "Isabella".

He started briefing me and suddenly the car started moving an unsettling feeling sunk in my stomach ... my breath caught in my throat at the familiarity of the sudden feeling.

THE SYNC

Isabella's POV

I shook my head trying to push away every single voice that was screaming at me. I focused my attention solely on Anthony "we will both attend the wedding as each other's date, then after we have eyes on him. I along with the rest of my men will infiltrate and once he is in a secure location, we will take you to him." I nodded my head.

Seemed simple enough "you being Garcia's replacement have to interact and acknowledge the bride and groom. Play the role of a normal guest and you can play assassin again when you and Garcia's guest begin the interrogation" He informed casually.

I nodded my head slowly feeling an overwhelming dizziness come over me, maybe it was the fact that I had to work with an unknown guest, I just hope Garcia knows what his doing.

I laid my head back and closed my eyes for the duration of the car ride. I felt the car come to a slow stop opening my eyes slowly.

"You ready, Isabella?" I smiled nodding my head.

"As ready as I'll ever be" taking his hand as he led, me out of the car. He helped me fix my dress and intertwined our hands escorting us inside. I looked down at our hands and felt an unsettling sense like our hands didn't fit together, ugh my mind just won't let any moment pass without making my think of him. Like the way his hands felt in mine, how they fit like a perfect puzzle, how safe and secure it makes me feel.

I shook my head rolling my eyes, now is not the time to compare anything! I mentally scolded myself I needed to focus on the mission so I can finish and get home to Dante.

X

We arrived at the reception, and I'd be lying if I said it wasn't breath-taking, it was a rooftop wedding. The place was decorated in white and gold everything looked like it costed them thousands. I wandered off to the pictures on the wall and smiled seeing the couple's story being told in pictures. "Lilly who's your date?" a man behind me asked a girl. "This is Vincenzo King" my heart sank like a heavy stone in my chest, it's been a year since I last saw him, since I last heard his voice, since I last smelt his scent a blend of earthiness and warmth immediately intrigued my sensed. It was as if the very essence of nature's rawness had been captured and infused into this one man, the musky notes seemed to dance in harmony with wisps of smoke that lingered off him, it added an added layer of intrigue, creating a sense of nostalgia as I breathed in him trying my best not to look or sound like a creep. I slowly turn around and the mere sight of him completely knocked the air out of my lungs. He looks so handsome, I bit my bottom lip analysing him he hadn't seen me watching him yet, so I used it to my advantage.

I watched his body tense when she hugged his arm, smirking I sniffle a laugh watching his awkward state. My eyes rank over his body biting my lower lip in the process before Anthony snaps me out of it. "Isabella, our table is over there" He calls my name out reaching for my hand, I smile and nod my head as he intertwines his hand in mine. I couldn't help but look back to my surprise he was already watching me his eyes narrowed and cold staring at our interwind hands. I smirked and quickly looked away before he catches me staring.

"Remember to blend in we have to look like a real couple, play along, okay?" Anthony whispered in my ear. I giggled acting like he said something cute he smiled and shook his head "you're good" he confirmed. I fake gasped and flirtatiously slapped his arm "shame on you for thinking differently" both of us laughed as we took our seats. A part of me was enjoying this more than I should knowing it was driving Vincenzo crazy is a bonus.

I took a seat crossing my legs and looked around the reception, without me realising it my eyes weren't just looking at the décor they were looking for him and finally, they found who they were searching for. Vincenzo looked breath taking in his suit the sight of him somehow managed to melt away all the anger and hatred like it never existed. His charcoal grey suit complimented his white shirt along with his mouth-watering caramel like tan, all I wanted to do was lick it.

I licked my lips my eyes unable to stop staring at him after they've been deprived for a year without the man they wished to stare at, he was like an eclipse you shouldn't look directly at it, but you can't help but find yourself drawn to him. He

turned around and I quickly darted my gaze back to Anthony.
We started exchanging in a comfortable conversation when I
felt a presence behind me "looks like this is our table" his low
husky voice echoed in my ears, hearing his voice in so long a
burst of emotions exploded in me, while another type of
emotion followed a little lower. I kept my head straight
fixated on Anthony not giving him or his date any attention.
I felt a hand lightly brush the back of my neck, my body
reacting to his touch almost immediately a spark of electricity
shooting down my spine. I knew it was him, and I knew what
he was doing.

"Anthony" Anthony politely introduces himself to
Vincenzo's date.

"And this is my date Isabella" He draped his arm on the back
of my chair, pulling me closer to him in a protective manner,
I slowly turn around facing the two of them. Forcing myself
to put on a smile "nice to meet you" a deaf person could
hear the jealousy laced in my words. Vincenzo smirks looking
at me knowingly "I'm Lilly Vincenzo's date" she bit her
bottom lip placing her hand on his thigh, Vincenzo tensed up
but quickly covered it up.

My eyes darted to her hand tensing my jaw I sat up straight, "get your hands off his thigh before I jump over this table and snap it off" I threatened unintentionally, Vincenzo's eyes widen with amusement as he lets out a low chuckle. Lily quickly removed her hand looking at me slightly terrified. I coughed trying to cover up my outburst, "I just mean no one wants to start something they can't finish in a public setting" I quickly speak up trying to come up with a random excuse that didn't sound great, but it was all I could come up with under pressure.

"How long have you two been together?" Anthony chimed up saving me from this awkward tension.

"Oh, a little under a year" Lilly answered. My eyes shot up to Vincenzo "Oh, really?" I laughed out.

"Little under a year? Baby want are the odds?" I turned over to Anthony he laughed nodding his head.

"Same with us!"

Vincenzo's jaw tensed sitting up straight he subtly leaned in closer to me as Lilly and Anthony got lost in a conversation "If you call him baby one more time I promise you, you will be watching his body being wheeled out in a body bag" he harshly spoke up. I leaned in closer "and if she touches you, one more time she will be the one in a body bag" I remarked going back to my date, he smirked resuming his previous posture leaving me stunned.

I cleared my throat and focused my attention back on Anthony who was eyeing me suspiciously "so how is everyone's day going?" Lilly attempted to break the tension that suddenly rose in the air.

"Well, no one died." Vincenzo and I spoke responded at the same time; our heads turned to face one another a small smirk forming on his lips as a sly smile took form on my own.

"Those are your standards?" Lilly laughed. We both shrugged "it usually means it's a pretty dull day" I shrugged.

"Besides people can do worse things than kill you" I added grabbing a drink placing the tip of the glass to my lips taking a sip, putting the glass down I licked the reaming wine off my bottom lip slowly looking back at Vincenzo with dough eyes and an innocent smile. Knowing it drives him crazy when I bite my lips, seeing him twitch gave me the victory I needed.

"That makes no sense" Vincenzo spoke up frustrated as he

repositions himself in his seat. I laugh "I am under no obligation to make sense to you." I smiled feeling like I had the upper hand, "besides I'm sure you can **remember** things that are worse than death" He laughs dryly "don't tell me something cliche like the truth is worse than death" I eyed him rolling my eyes "yes, actually I rather be destroyed by the truth. I think it's such an enchanting way of having your soul torn apart. Because even in chaos there's an order, and in order there's peace, knowing the truth well most of the time anyway" I took another sip of my wine.

I watched Vincenzo looking deep in thought, if you had told me to stay, if you had told me the truth that you still want me. None of this would have happened we could have fought through the chaos instead you allowed it to become our undoing.

"Maybe this is what we're all looking for." Vincenzo chimed in, I looked at him curiously "maybe it is. To find peace within the destruction we created and can't control anymore. Unfortunately, the price is too high. Too painful for some to handle." He added.

With the truth you never know what it is, did he want me?

did he not? Did he believe me? did he think I was a rat? Does he remember me in any way? Or has he purposely shut me out forever?

"What about you?" he whispered, I looked up and laughed softly. "What about me?" I questioned.

"Are you afraid of the truth and the chaos that comes with it?" he emphasised.

"I'm not afraid of the pain that follows the truth if that's what you're asking. I just avoid feeling it so often. I know how long it takes to recover. And I have no time to waste." I recalled my months of sorrow when he forgot me and then faked my death because of his lack of trust. "So, Lilly tell me how did you and Vincenzo meet?" I asked her in hopes to change the conversation and wanting to get a feel for her. She smiled looking nervous before coughing "well we meet at a horse ranch actually" my eyes widened while my mouth opened slightly my hand bawling into a fist. I let out a dry laugh "horse ranch?" I spat she awkwardly nodded her head, "hmm, you don't strike me as a horse type" I tried to cover my jealousy Vincenzo looked confused at Lilly before he turned to me seeing my fist, he smiled using his thumb to brush his lower lip in attempts to cover up his amusement.

"Isabella and I met at a club, she was quite the eye-catcher." Anthony laughed I turned to him and smirked deciding to play along, "you're one to talk baby, the second I saw him I just knew I needed to make sure I took him home" I laughed and playful traced my fingers along his jaw. He bit his bottom lip and tucked a strand of hair behind my ear, he leans down to kiss me before Vincenzo loudly clears his throat.

I smirked looking up at Anthony who surprisingly looked annoyed, I turned to Vincenzo "are you okay?" I sarcastically asked him he eyed me and stood up from his seat, grabbing my wrist and forcing me up. I yelped as he rushed us through the crowd, suddenly both of us were cornered by important men. I looked at them as they kindly greet Vincenzo, turning their attention to me waiting for me to introduce myself, and I don't know if it was the fact that I haven't been in this type of environment in a while, or if I was just overwhelmed. I tried to speak up, but my nerves were killing me, I froze. I felt Vincenzo's hand trace my back before finding my hand intertwining it with his own, giving me a reassuring squeeze.

Such a simple gesture was all it took for my confidence to come rushing back, without saying a word he gave me the reassurance I needed. "Sono proprio qui bellissima" he whispered in my ear softly, **I'm right here beautiful.** I took a deep breath and looked up "Isabella, sorry men I was struggling to speak up with the amount of smoke in the air" I pointed to their cigarettes, they laughed approvingly nodding their heads.

"We haven't met before. Are you a friend of the bride or groom?" he piped up looking me up and down, making me slightly uncomfortable "Rodrick I don't appreciate you eye fucking my wife" I snapped my head towards Vincenzo in full shock, "oh i-i-im sorry I didn't know you got married Vincenzo. Congratulations" he congratulated the both of us. I forced a smile nodding my head, Vincenzo spun us around and he led the way until we reached a secluded area on the roof. "What the fuck are you doing here? and with him?" He spat, I narrowed my eyes and scoffed "Yeah, in this situation you're not allowed to ask that question." I turn to leave before he grips my arms and spins me back to him. "Wife?" I yelled remembering what he said a moment ago. He smirked

shrugging his shoulders, "don't act like you weren't flattered."
He winked. My body lighting up on fire I turn around in
another attempt to storm off, but I should've known by now
it's not so easy to get away from him.

Pulling me back by my waist, my body hits his chest before
he leans down my ear and harshly whispers "Isabella I swear
to god If I find out you've let another man touch you. I will
kill him and deliver you his head and we both know I. do.
not. fucking. bluff." I rolled my eyes at his behaviour, while
he was frustrating me and a part of me also enjoyed watching
him get so jealous.

Okay a big part of me was enjoying this just a little … okay
all of me was enjoying it I was loving this!

"You're one to talk" I muttered annoyed, he looked at me and
rolled his eyes. "I'm serious" I shook my head and went to
walk off. "I know a hundred ways to kill a man and I can
make one hundred of them look like an accident. Never.
Forget. That" his eyes darkened.

"What did you say?" I whispered.

FLASHBACK

"Vincenzo" I laughed pushing him off me, "come on be serious" I tried to focus his attention back to work. He gripped my hips and forced me to sit on his lap, I hummed in pleasure as I rested my forehead to his. His hands trailed down my back finding their home on my ass. I rolled my eyes and smirked.

"Comfortable?" I joked, he groaned squeezing me as hiking me up I gripped the back of his hair and tilted it up crashing my lips to his. Almost in an instant, everything went from playful to intense. "Oh fuck" I moaned softly into the kiss. He pulled back and watched me for a second, "you're mine. Only mine." He cupped my cheek his voice was stern and demanding. "Only yours" I whispered back leaning in to get another kiss. I licked my lips before Vincenzo's Office doors opened. "Cazzo" Vincenzo cussed under his breath. "GET OFF MY SON'S LAP" Giovani bursts inside the office yelling. I turn my head around "he has work he needs to do and you're no fucking help" he cursed. He looked drunk. I let out a sigh and went to get off before Vincenzo's grip on my waist tightened forcing me back down. "I'll tell her when to get off my dick." he harshly spits sending my feelings into overdrive. Oh, my if I didn't want him before. I widen my eyes and bit my lip trying not to let out a laugh. He stares at Vincenzo for a second then glares at me before Vincenzo let out another threat in Italian. He turns around and leaves without another word and Vincenzo stands up pinning me against his desk, "I don't care who's touched you like this in the past, do you understand?" his voice sounding so dominating, my breathing hitched as he cupped my pussy in his hands. "I don't share ever. If you let me touch you now, you're mine."

My eyes roll to the back of my head, my back arching as I gripped the desk. "Do you let me?" he whispered in my ear. I rolled my head back my eyes following shortly behind. I hummed nodding my head. "Say it Isabella" he demands. "I let you touch me" I breathed out.

"No other man touches you and if they do ..." his fingers dig into my upper thigh and with his free hand, he pulled me closer by my neck. **"I know a hundred ways to kill a person, and I can make one hundred of them look like an accident. comprendere?"**

END OF FLASHBACK

X

"Don't forget it" I shook my head ready to ask another question before he walked straight past me. I bit my bottom lip anxious and shook my head, I won't let him play mind games with me. I refuse to fall back in the same cycle, I grabbed a drink off one of the trays and made my way back to the table.

"You, okay?" Anthony whispered softly, I gave a reassuring smile and nodded my head. I took my seat and watched the people getting up to dance, "we should go say hi to the bride and groom now" he nudged his head my mouth forming an 'oh' I nodded my head and stood up, we made our way to the bride and groom and not far behind was Lilly and Vincenzo. I rolled my eyes massaging my neck, their closeness shouldn't bother me as much as it is. "Congratulations, we are so sorry Garcia couldn't make it. He however sends his best wishes" Anthony shook the groom's hand. I leaned in and kissed the bride on the cheek shaking her hand also.

"You look stunning" I complimented her dress.

"You look gorgeous, red is really your colour" she smiles being friendly, "your date is pretty good looking too" she winks laughing.

Her husband shoots her a playful glare as I giggle. Do you want to play Vincenzo King? let's play.

"Oh, if you think he is good looking now you should see him without any clothes on" I wink, she goes red and joins me in a small fit of laughter. I can feel Vincenzo's death stare on the back of my head, I smirked feeling victorious. I move to the side allowing Vincenzo and his date to congratulate the couple. I stand near Anthony who is scanning the room looking for the target, and the whole reason why we came to this wedding.

Seeing Vincenzo clouded my head I completely forgot why I was here. I looked up at Anthony and shook my head slightly asking if he found him yet. He looked down at me and leaned in my ear to make it look natural "Nothing yet, how are you holding up I know you haven't been in the game for a while" I smiled and nodded my head that I was ok. It scared me just how okay I was like I was back in my element my comfort zone. I went to speak before my eye caught Lilly making out with Vincenzo, I tensed my jaw and bawled my fist my knuckles turning white. Her arms wrapped around his neck; he rested his hand on her waist. If she doesn't step away from him in the next second, she can be the one to leave this wedding in a body bag. I grabbed another wine and walked near them, I fake tripped and tipped the glass of wine all over her back. She abruptly stepped back and gasped. "Oh no, I'm so clumsy sometimes" I quickly rushed out trying to pat her dry with a napkin.

She faked smiled "It's okay, it doesn't show. I'm just going to go wash up" she sighed and walked towards the bathroom. I looked at Vincenzo with doe eyes "oh I'm sorry did I disturb anything husband?" I sarcastically questioned him.

He looked at me with a frustrated expression "you may have one hundred ways to make a death look like an accident, but I have a hundred and one" I smiled and shoved the glass of wine in his chest and walked away. I sat down at the table and saw Anthony rush towards me "we have a visual, I'm going to need you to stay here. Keep natural until we send someone to grab you" I nodded my head he and a few other men and women headed out. I sighed and sunk into the chair.

I bit my bottom lip wondering how Dante was now, I grabbed my phone and called Lorenzo. "Hello?" He answered the phone in a whisper. "Hey, how's my baby?" I asked concerned and relieved Lorenzo didn't sound stressed. "Oh, he is fine" he fake cries. "What's with the voice?" I questioned. "Well let's just say, he wanted his mum. We had every hand on deck trying to feed him his bottle, burp him, change him and put him to sleep but he wouldn't stop crying and screaming." I sat up straight worry beginning to consume me "What!" I whisper yelled "I'm coming" I stood up and grabbed my purse "Isabella it's okay we handled it. He is safe and sleeping" I stopped and took in a deep breath "We printed a picture of you I put it on my face like a mask and cut a hole in my shirt to feed him the bottle and I kept it on until he fell asleep." I started laughing "Aw that's cute" I giggled. "Sort of creepy but I'll look past it for now" I added shaking my head, "thank you so much, I owe you one. Put the phone near Dante and put me on speaker." I felt a shudder come over me, my body tingled slightly. I cleared my throat and stood there stunned for a second. I shrugged my shoulders maybe it was just the cool breeze making me shiver like that. "Okay you're on speaker." He announced.

"Hi baby, I'm sorry I'm not home and sleeping next to you. Don't worry baby I'll be back before you know it. I love you so much mi amor" I kissed the phone and hung up. I turn around and slam into a familiar rock-hard chest, I groaned stepping back. "Who was that?" He snaps. I look up at him and roll my eyes, he takes a step closer to me closing the gap between us. I gulped looking into his eyes, his beautiful grey eyes with a mix of blue, the type of eyes you can easily get lost in... just like I am right now. "Who. Was. That" his eyes darkened, and his voice was dangerously low, the small hairs on my arm stood up following the goosebumps that rose. "Why do you care?" I bit back, he let out a throaty chuckle. "Isabella, do not test my patience." I raised my eyebrow smirking "No, I think I'd like to test it". He stared at me for a second, pulling out his gun he placed it in front of me on the table, I looked at the gun and let out a small laugh. Pulling out both my guns I had hidden in my purse I smirked "Mine are bigger" I rolled my eyes putting them back in my purse standing up to leave. A soft gasp left my lips feeling his hand wrap around my neck and pull me back to him. My back hits his chest, he slides his hands further up my neck tilting my chin up. My body was stunned, and my head was spinning a million miles per hour, I couldn't speak, I couldn't think, and I couldn't move I was paralyzed.

My lips parted, once his thumb reached my lip, I stared at him waiting for his next move and without warning, he turns me around and smashes his lips onto mine. I quickly reacted kissing him back, he spun me around and I grabbed his shirt forcing him closer to me, not wanting to feel any sort of space between us, he rested his hands on my lower back and pulled me in even closer. His tongue swiped my bottom lip leading to a soft moan escaping my lips involuntary. He smiled into the kiss lowering his hand further down giving me a firm squeeze. My body was on fire I would never admit this out loud but I'm craving him. Craving his touch that flames my inner desire, his soft lips on mine that completely devours my own taking ownership of what belongs to him.

We broke the kiss trying to catch our breath, I bit my lower lip still spinning from what just happened, "unless you want me to take you in the middle of this reception. Let. Go." He tugs at my chin so releasing my bottom lip. Suddenly coming back to reality, I step back and push him away, "who do you think you are!" I whisper shouted so we wouldn't draw any more attention than we already have, he smirked "You might say one thing cucciola ... but your body tells a different tale." he looked down at my goosebumps and then rested his eyes on my chest that was still rising and falling at a rapid pace than I would like to admit. I shut my eyes and turned my head. I was livid at the fact that he just kissed me to prove to himself and me how much I still wanted him he knew what he was doing he was reminding the both of us who we each belonged too. The kiss didn't frustrate me as much as his new nickname. "Don't call me that" I warned lowly, he eyes me "Cucciola" he purred once more. "Call me that again, and you will find my knife somewhere very uncomfortable," I warned him feeling the anger rising from his stupid new nickname. It's just another reminder that his forgotten me, he pulls me away and into a more secluded area "Cucciola" he teased, I grinded my teeth together my jaw tensing. He pins me against the wall and smiles condescendingly "You're cute

when you're angry" I rolled my eyes pushing him off me.
"I will slit your throat" I warned him, he laughed backing away he walks off I watched curiously that was it? He was just walking away. What happened to us? That wasn't the fight I was expecting. I gasped as a knife punctures the wall the blade was inches from my face. He smirks looking at me, his ego visibly inflating. I smirked there he is, I mentally cheered.

"A knife Mr King? Are you flirting with me?" I called out watching him walks over to the table on the opposite side of us picking up an apple. I pulled out the knife throwing it towards Vincenzo hitting the apple dead straight right in the middle. His eyes widened clearly not remembering just how crazy I am. "Next apple I hit will be an adams apple" I warned him, walking off.

Vincenzo's POV

I watched as she walked away, taking the apple out of my mouth I take out the knife and my eyes find their way back to her, she was breath taking in that long red dress. The way it hugged her figure and highlighted her chest, her beautiful lips smiling as she spoke to the bride, her smile painted with that dark red lipstick, that was driving me insane, she always looked like she knew everyone's deepest darkest secrets, how her confidence effortlessly beamed off her. I couldn't keep my eyes off her as she moved by the dance floor like she owned the world ... like the world owed her. A sick feeling found its place in my stomach ... she was once mine, but now it looks like she's someone else's. My jaw tensed thinking about her in bed with another man, touching another man, letting another man know her. Letting another man near our child. My blood was boiling I cracked my neck trying to distract myself. I saw Lilly approach me "we have eyes on the target, I need to leave but we will send a car to grab you in an hour." I nod my head and she leave's sharply.

I look over at Isabella, fuck it. I approach the table and sit beside her, while she tries to avoid my stare. Picking up her glass of wine I snicker "careful, I just discovered you're a bit clumsy" I mocked her, she smirked and turned to look at me. "Oh, I am. You wouldn't want me tipping this on you ... maybe you should go annoy another girl" she took a sip. "Oh, how about you go annoy your girlfriend she's probably looking for you" she spits jealously laced in every word like venom. I tried not to smirk at her failed attempt to cover up her jealousy, she stands up and turns around facing me. "I hate you" she speaks up her voice stern and low, but it was crystal clear that wasn't what she meant.

I turned towards the dance floor and heard a familiar song being sung. Isabella's face looked visibly sad when she heard them singing **so this is love**, she looked down at her heels and then slowly back up at the couple's dancing. "Dance with me" I whispered she looked confused and went to object "sorry love, I think you got a bit confused I wasn't asking a question" I intertwined our hands and pulled her towards the dance floor before she could hesitate or make a scene. We stood among the rest of the couple's and Isabella gave me a sour look, smirking back I laughed "you don't want to make a scene now do you?" I whispered in her ear as I pulled her closer. The singer began singing and I softly hummed along, she looked up at me with such innocence, my grey eyes melted into her green ones.

For the first time in such a long time, I felt serene, I pushed her out and spun her back into my chest. Her back rested against my chest as we swayed ever so softly "you're cute when you're jealous" I whispered softly, she turns her head and gives me a sour look. I chuckle and spin her.

"Jealous? If anything, you were the jealous one" she bites back, "I am jealous" I admitted without an ounce of hesitation. She looks taken back for a moment before she quickly recovered "what?" she asked like she didn't hear me properly. I laughed dryly "Isabella, I've been threatening every man at this wedding for simply looking at you, I never tried to be subtle about my jealousy." I smiled looking down at her.

"Do you want to admit something now?" I teased she shot me a warning glare causing me to laugh, she soon cracked and giggled. I couldn't help the soft grin that formed on my lips as we danced like we once did ... or at least I think we did. To this song, all I remember is getting a flashback in the middle of my office, I don't know if it was real or a daydream, but I guess I'll find out now.

We swayed for a few moments, I dipped her and dragged my

hand up her thigh, the slit in the dress giving me easier access. My hands stopped at the strap wrapped around her leg holding her knives. She looked at me smirking knowing exactly what I felt on her thigh, "Oh how I've missed you amore" I whispered. She smiled softly looking deep into my eyes allowing herself to get lost in the moment, and I for once allowed myself to just be present in the moment. "On a mission, are we?" I teased knowing full well she was here for the same reason I was. **"Son, trust me if I was trying to set you up with anyone it wouldn't be my employee it would be Isabella"** Garcia's voice echoed in my head, **"Trust me son you're gonna love it ... even if you don't I know I will get a laugh out of it"** that sneaky crafty old man I thought to myself. Two birds with one stone. "I'm on a date" she hisses, I huff and pull her closer to me closing the gap between us knowing full well that man was just one of Garcia's men.

"He isn't your type" I smiled she cocked her eyebrow looking up at me "really? Then what is my type?" she bit back, I pulled up from the dip and spin her around, "tall, handsome, smart, muscular, a King's crown tattooed on his hand and his name has to be Vincenzo King" I sarcastically answered her question. She leaned in closer "You just listed all the things I hated" she whispered in my ear, her lips lingering as she innocently teased me, she was driving me insane, and she knew it.

I raised my eyebrows "so you want him short, ugly, fat and dumb?" I laughed. She grunts and steps on my foot. I muffle a groan "Isabella".

"What is it you want from me? You told me to leave. I left, what do you want" she whispered softly after calming down a little. I sighed softly finally mastering the courage to talk "I may not remember you ... or our past but ... " I cleared my throat; she looks down with teary eyes before she looks back up at me with a stone face. I let out a sigh mastering the courage to keep going "after everything, all of this, I can't remember my own name. But you- somehow, I know exactly who you are, and I know what your name means ... What it meant." She continues looking at me with her doe big green eyes. "I shut you out ... because I thought that was what Vincenzo would do, the Vincenzo before he met you. I thought that if I acted like you didn't exist, then I'd be okay, that everything would go back to normal." I scoffed a little and continued "but it didn't. I didn't remember you, but my soul does. I look at any corner of my home and I'm reminded of you, like my subconscious is trying to unlock the memories my head shut out. I don't remember you, but my hands do, my soul and my body do." I tensed up and whispered faintly "my heart does."

She stopped dancing and stood straight up looking at me dead in the eye "does your heart hurt?" she asked dryly. "Does it hurt knowing the one person you cared for more than yourself turned his back on you so easily? Does it hurt knowing that the only person you truly connected with, your heart forgot? Does it still beat knowing that even though your heart forgot me, not on purpose, but it purposely didn't try to remember me ... and for what? to make new memories?" She shouted.

I shut my eyes listening to her speak. "Isabella ..."

"Because it hurts. When you're near me it hurts, when you're away from me, it hurts. Knowingly or unknowingly, you have caused my heart more pain than anyone else ever has ... and I wish I could understand why it still beats for you." She sighs and looks up with guilty eyes, she shakes her head turning around to leave but I grab her by her arm again to finish the dance. I let her go once I wasn't planning on doing it again, "Vincenzo" she whispers softly trying to leave. I hissed at the pain in my head, Isabella looked up at me concern written all over her face, I shake my head trying to get rid of the pain and assure her I'm okay. I shook it off quickly and pulled Isabella closer. I looked up at the singer's as they finally got to the bit of the song, I was waiting for recreating the memory or daydream I saw in my office.

"E' questo allor hmm" I hummed as I sang the song to her like I once did, she looked up at me stunned for a second. "Quel dolce ardor" by now the dance floor had cleared up as everyone stood and watched in awe, the singer had fallen silent and allowed me to continue. "L'incanto che si chiama amor" her eyes now began tearing up as she softly hummed along. "Adesso so hmm" I spun her and dipped her, "Che ormai non può" slowly lifting her back up. "Null'altro sognare il mio cuor" I finished off. Our faces inches apart her heavy breathing, I licked my bottom lip my eyes trailing down to hers then back up to her eyes.

We both lean in slowly before we stop abruptly as the guests applaud. I cough and smile firmly; Isabella takes a deep breath and dashes off.

I go to call for her, but she's gone. She disappeared into the crowd of people, I move through the crowd and find her near the edge of the roof looking out, "Isabella" I call for her she turns her head slowly then looks back out to the view. I move closer to her "hit me if it'll help you" I spun her around to face me she looked confused. "Hit you?" She repeats I nod my head.

"Right here." I hit my chest with a closed fist.

"A punch. Two punches. However, many you want. Do it!" she looks at my chest then back up at me, she's hesitating. "The offer only stands for 30 more seconds. After that, you can't get mad at me anymore." Without hesitation I felt her fist collide with my chest, I moved back stunned she actually did it and it hurt a lot more than I will ever admit out loud. She looked up at me shaking her head "your methods although bizarre surprisingly work" she lets out a deep breath.

"I'm sorry" she mummers, I look at her confused "sorry?" I question.

"I've spent so much of my time hating you for so many things ..." she looks up at me slowly "most of them out of your control ... I forget myself sometimes and the stuff you should hate me for" She whispers the last bit.

After finding out she was pregnant and gave birth to my child, knowing Lorenzo knows about it stung me more than anything. Whatever, Isabella's reasoning is we can figure out later, but my own blood kept such a big secret from me, it was the biggest betrayal from both, but I still could never hate her for it, and I couldn't hate him. I couldn't hate her for anything no matter what she did. "I need to tell you something and I should've told you a while ago, but I was scared" she shuts her eyes, her hands are shaking.

"We have a-" she gets cut off by a man "Sir, Miss a car waits for the two of you." she looks confused I nod my head excusing the man "what?" she questions "Garcia" was all I said she nodded her head as realisation overcame her features. "What were you going to say?" I asked she shook her head "I'll tell you later let's go?" she smiles weakly I nod my head slowly "you ready?" I asked frustrated. She was finally going to tell me about our baby and of course, fate finds a way to screw me over.

She took a step back and tripped I lunged towards her "NO!" I shouted, I gripped her arm and pulled her towards me her chest slammed into mine as she gripped my arms. She looked at me shocked. Then suddenly, my head started throbbing I let a small groan holding onto my head looking down.

"Vincenzo are you okay?" Isabella rushes out bending with me her hands protectively holding my arms.

I looked back up again with a pounding headache and saw myself, Isabella, Lorenzo and Xavier all on top of a roof. Isabella had a knife to Xavier when she slowly turned to me. "I might not know a thing about you," I hear myself speak up "but I know one thing, when you kiss me, I feel alive again and my whole world becomes something different. It was heaven and hell, brought together in my head. You're my very own secret world. And I intend to burn there" My own voice echoed in my head. She laughed looking at me through teary eyes, her dimples showing and her green eyes glistening. "I hate to break up this tender moment, but I gotta go." and within a second my world flashed before my eyes he pushed her off the roof.

"NOOO," I roared.

I gasped and took a step back the scene in front of me disappearing as I come back to reality, "what? what's wrong?" she rushed out looking at me then back to where I was staring. "Vincenzo, are you okay? Should we get you to the clinic?" she looked at me concerned. "This isn't the first time I saved you, is it?" was all I said, looking at her waiting for her response, praying to get some closure that what I'm seeing isn't me going insane.

She looks stunned before her gaze softens "no it's not" she spoke sincerely.

Isabella's POV

We got in the limo after saying our goodbyes to the bride and groom, I sat quietly deep in my own thoughts, did Vincenzo remember me? Or was that memory just triggered because I almost tripped? I look up at him and I tilt my head seeing him also deep in thought his mind is trying to remind him, to give him his memories back but he's shutting it out.

He isn't letting them come, **he needs a real reason for it to come back.**

"Mr Garcia informs me to tell you he had a good laugh" I roll my eyes grinning as the driver announced Garcia's approval of how everything went down. "I'm sure he did" I speak under my breath "Crafty old grandpa" Vincenzo speaks up. I look up at him ... grandpa? I whispered in my head. Does he ... No, no. If he knew he would have exploded in my face by now.

"Anthony and Lilly have told me they are waiting for you at the warehouse." I roll my eyes and cross my arms over my chest hearing her name, Vincenzo looks over at me smug "You're jealous, aren't you?" he teases me, "Yes" I blurt out facing him, I lean back into my chair "Are you satisfied?!" I huff out. He gets up placing both his hands on the seat next to me, closing me in. My breathing hitches but I continue to look unfazed by the sudden closeness. "No. Not at all." he breathes out, his teeth sinking into his bottom lip. I clasp my legs shut feeling my body immediately fire up. "You're not going to be" I smirked and pushed his chest back with my finger.

He gets up and sits back down in his seat "I wouldn't bet on it" he adjusts his hair and gives me a wink. I eye him "who's going to satisfy you?" I mocked indicating my little playtime with Roxy and Lexi "If you think those two are the only girls who are willing to have sex with me, you're delusional." He shrugs his shoulders. I rolled my eyes and turned my face to the window. "It's not like you're the only one with a more than willing group" I purred and traced my upper thigh with my finger. "I don't doubt that" he laughed but his tensed posture showed how much it pissed him off.

"I got someone tonight as a matter of a fact" I smiled innocently. "uomo morto" **dead man** he threatened under his voice I cocked an eyebrow at him and shook my head. My phone buzzed and I looked down at my phone and saw Lorenzo's name, I look back up and see Vincenzo with a pissed expression. Shit did he see my phone? I shook my head and moved my phone turning my back to him 'When are you coming home the King misses you?' I giggled shaking my head 'On the way to the warehouse shouldn't be too long!' I replied turning back around I looked back at Vincenzo his jaw was tensed his hands were balled in fists he was ready to kill someone. I look back down at my phone 'Go all dragon on that pussy! I'll see you soon don't keep us waiting' I rolled my eyes and smiled turning my phone off.

"Who messaged you?" I looked back up at him shocked and taken back. He spat in a hoarse tone his Italian accent became so thick when he was mad ... and right now he was livid. He saw my phone I mentally slapped myself.
"None of your business" I bit back trying to turn around, "Isabella, don't make me fucking do something I'll regret why is my fucking brother messaging you? And why does he miss you and want you home" He started shouting his accent getting thicker than ever and the veins in his neck and head started bulging out, when his accent got thick that's when I knew he was about to explode.

"My fucking brother Isabella! Your sister's-" I cut him off sharply matching his tone and demeanour "I advise you to choose your next words very carefully!" I shouted pointing a finger at him, "It's nothing, drop it" I bit.
"What else are you lying to me about?! I wonder what else you're going to hide from me" he snarled.

I edged back in my seat staring at him what did he mean what else? There was something else so I couldn't get too high and mighty.

"What's that supposed to mean" I sneered "I don't know Isabella why don't you tell me, why don't you tell me what you've been hiding for months!" he yelled emphasising the word months. The car came to a stop and the man informed us we have arrived, Vincenzo stared at me intensely before he stepped out of the car coldly and left me sitting there alone in complete shock and fucking guilt.

My head was buzzing with so many possibilities and emotions. My heart sunk my entire body was paralyzed with fear, anger, frustration, irritation, guilt and sadness. What pissed me off, even more, is I didn't know what emotion overpowered the other, and I knew I was so fucking wrong for keeping this from him.

I take a deep breath and step out of the car; wanting to just get this over and done and fix my mistakes, I see Lilly hanging off Vincenzo and Garcia standing next to Anthony. My eyes widened staring at him he put his hands up and reassured me to calm down.

He nodded his head slowly indicating his men were all still surrounding and protecting the house, I let out a relieved sigh and saw Vincenzo do the same, I looked at him then back at the floor. If there was any doubt in my head that he knows about Dante it was slowly being washed away, he knew.

"Isabella, are you ready?" Anthony greeted me and questioned. I let out a deep sigh and nodded my head "as you probably both guessed by now you two will be interrogating and torturing him together" Garcia chimed in, we both shot him a stare and shook our heads frustrated. "Tough crowd" he jokes and walks inside the warehouse wanting to watch us. It was full of shelves of boxes but in the middle was a man tied up on a chair, I raised my eyebrows and laughed it was the man that was flirting with me. The one Vincenzo informed we were married. "Something funny?" he snarled, I nodded my head still laughing "seeing as you're the one tied up, do you think it's wise to make snarky comments?" I tilted my head smirking.

He rolled his eyes "If it isn't the newlyweds" he mocked recognizing us, Garcia looked confused before rolling his eyes assuming it was something stupid. Vincenzo grabbed a chair and sat in front of him, "let's just cut to the chase, give us what we want, and I promise to be merciful. Don't give me what I want and then you're going to be facing something very unholy" his voice dropped a **satanic smile** formed on his face, his eyes darkened as he edged closer on the chair waiting for him to make a choice. "Fuck off" he spat causing Vincenzo to laugh, **goosebumps rose on my skin I haven't seen him smile like that in years and I forgot how terrifying Vincenzo can be.** "I was hoping you'd say that" he stood up and punched him square in the jaw repeatedly, I watched in shock and quickly stopped him.

"We still need him alive" I whispered, he shrugged his shoulder out from my grasp and walked back a little. I sighed and gulped I turned around and smiled, "Does it hurt?" I looked at his busted jaw.

"Wow, sarcasm how original" he spat blood getting some on my dress, I rolled my eyes. "I wore red on purpose. I knew it was going to get messy" I smirked. "Who pays you and the others? Who's the boss?" I asked him straight up instead of beating around the bush, he rolled his eyes and kept his mouth shut. I sighed and stood up grabbing my knife from my thigh ... I looked down at it and realised the engraving on the handle. **'V.K'**

I saw Vincenzo's eyes scan the knife then before he looked at me, I quickly looked away, "Is it one boss?" I sighed sarcastically and dragged a line on his forearm, he hissed and shut his eyes "or is it two?" I cut another line, "or maybe it's five?" I gasped and made a score of five on his arm. He stayed quiet I rolled my eyes and stepped back.

I looked up and saw Garcia putting his two fingers together, I looked at Vincenzo who looked at me. We both knew why he wasn't talking we both weren't trying, both of us off our game because we of our previous fight. Us fighting and hating each other right now was what was distracting and draining us. I sighed and gave Vincenzo a nod he turned back at the man coldly. "Awe are you two fighting?" He laughed. "Already trouble in paradise?" he laughed, he sensed the tension between us, he had the upper hand and we needed to reclaim it.

"Hey, while you both are trying to figure out your domestic issues. You don't have any kid's I can 'babysit' do you?" He laughed.

Vincenzo's tensed body lunged forward holding him up by his throat, the man struggled and I along with the rest of the men were in utter shock at his strength. "Touch my son and I swear I will skin you alive, I'll serve your meat to your family while I use your dick and every bone in your pathetic body as my dogs new chew toy. Touch my son and it'll be the last thing you ever do" he threatened.

The man gulped staring at Vincenzo with fear in his eyes blood staining his face, I heard Vincenzo went dark, but I never believed them. Not until right now, my guilt only worsened after hearing him defending our baby. I took in a deep breath my blood still boiling from the man's comment, I stepped closer.

(Tw graphic scene)

"Do you want to play a game baby?" I smiled and looked at Vincenzo, he smirked sinisterly sending a shiver down my spine. I licked my lips "you ask him a question and if he doesn't answer I get to cut off a body part!" I squealed excitedly I turned over and saw Garcia with a shocked yet satisfied look on his face. Giving us a nod of approval, I shook my head closing my eyes gathering all my energy and I opened them and stood behind the man.

"Go on ask him a question" I purred, and Vincenzo did just that he kept his mouth shut and I sighed, "seeing as you don't want to listen why don't I start with your ears?" I chimed up and place the blade to his ear he screams out in pain as the blade slices his ear clean off. Some of Garcia's men turn around and some leave unable to handle the sight and his horrifying scream. I smile satisfied seeing the ear fall to my feet.

I move to the other side and whisper in his ear "you still have one left" I stand up straight after he stopped screaming, Vincenzo edged closer and grabbed the knife from my hand he stopped for a moment seeing the engraving on the handle then quickly went back to what he was doing.

"You know right above the knee is a nerve called Guillain-Barré" he states out loud looking at me, I smile shocked "really? What happens if we damage it?" I questioned looming over the man.

"If damaged it continues to damage parts of nerves. Causing muscle weakness, loss of balance and paralysis" Vincenzo smirks knowingly as he placed the tip of the knife in a precise position and angle. He looked at the both of us and shook his head "I'm a dead man either way what difference does it matter" he hesitantly breathes out hopeful that we'll offer him some type of deal.

"You have one of two choices; you suffer a slow but painful death. Or" he stops letting me continue "a quick and easy death" I finished.

He gulps knowing there was no way out, within seconds he started spilling every contact's name, all the men he works for, and every single piece of information Garcia needed to take them down. Vincenzo smiled and tilted his head; I cocked my eyebrows up knowingly "If only you answered when we asked you" I purred watching the light in his eyes drain into nothing but darkness. Vincenzo piped up "also if you think that comment about my son was something I would forget you're sadly mistaken" Within a second Vincenzo stabbed his leg causing sharp pain and a horrified expression overtook his face.

He did the same to the other leg and proceeded take off his pants and cut his dick off, I widened my eyes in horror "that's for all the kids who couldn't fight back" he spat and threw it at him "vai a farti fottere" **go fuck yourself.**

"All yours bellisma" he winked standing up, I looked at him and smiled, an old tradition of mine popped in my head. "Say bye, bye." I winked, stabbing both his eyes with my knife, pulling them straight out I put it in one of the boxes from the warehouse, I can feed them to my secret pets when I get back, or I can let Sebastián take it and feed them if he has the balls.

(End of trigger scene)

We walked off and left Garcia's men to clean up, "Well done" Garcia chimed up. We both stood still staring at him, the both of us still livid and ready to kill each other. He rolled his eyes "You guys felt it right?" He questioned. "Felt what?" I asked him, "the power" he emphasised. "When the two of you interrogated him alone you got nowhere, he had all the power but when you joined forces you not only got him to expose every little detail. You also managed to scare and dominate every man and woman in the building with the power you two share together." I sighed knowing he was right and knowing damn well I felt it. Did Vincenzo feel it?

"Literally look around, none of my men had the guts to watch. I even had to turn around a few times" he admitted. "Alone the both of you are terrifying and dangerous. Together you possess more power in your pinkie than anyone does in their whole body. You two could rule the world ... but only together" He smiled at the both of us then lowered his head. He looked back up and teared up slightly "you kids be careful" he smiles and shakes our hands letting us go since we both clearly were not in the mood. "Oh, and thank Ariana for me, this wouldn't have been possible without her help." My mouth dropped, Garcia and Ariana both planned to parent trap me and Vincenzo? Okay now everything made so much sense.

X

We got back in the limo as the driver took each of us home, I sit in my seat uneasy Vincenzo stared at me coldly, "how?" I questioned he narrowed his eyes and looked at me "does it matter?" he replied coldly. "No" I whispered.

"You fucking lied to me for so long! You kept my own child from me Isabella!"

"I had every right to keep my child safe!" I yelled.

"SAFE FROM ME? HIS OWN FATHER!" He yelled.

"YES!" I shouted back.

"You tell me what you would do if the person who got you pregnant doesn't remember you! If he doesn't trust you!" I shouted.

"I PROTECTED YOU! I WANTED YOU SAFE AND AWAY FROM ANYONE WHO CAN HURT YOU BECAUSE I KNEW I COULDN'T DO THAT ON MY OWN WITHOUT MY MEMORIES" He erupted all his emotions were surfacing.

I pound the car seat with my fist. "Who gave you the right to protect me, Vincenzo?! The moment you forgot me I died! I no longer belong to you!" I hissed. In the second it took him to turn and face me, his expression had transformed back into anger. He leapt towards me his hands on the edge of the seat closing me in, leaning into my face.

"WELL, I BELONG TO YOU!" The veins in his neck bulged as he shouted, and I met his glare refusing to even flinch. He looked at my lips panting. "I belong to you," he whispered, his anger slowly melting as he realized how close we were.

Faster than I could comprehend he smashes his lips to mine, and before I knew it my body and lips immediately reacted, and I melted into the kiss.

We both pulled back out of breath, our chest rising and falling in perfect sync.

THE NICKNAME "LEONE"

Isabella's POV

Looking up at him he moved back to his seat not making a sound. His intense stare never leaving me, making my body shiver. I bit my bottom lip, letting out an ironic laugh he raises an eyebrow confused.

"It's just ironic the first time we see each other again all we did was fight" I shake my head.
"Was it always like that?" he asks softly looking at me. I looked back up at him sighing "yes, but that's just us." I explained briefly, he softly nods his head.

"I'm sorry" I whispered softly, he looked at me taken back nodding his head slowly unsure of what to say. I let out a deep breath "I'd love you to meet him ... officially " I trailed off "I'd love to" he speaks up after a moment of silence, I look confused "After watching his birth I want nothing more than to able to finally hold him" he elaborates further. I nod my head looking out the limo window before realising what he just said.

"You what?" I asked stunned, he was there? He watched the birth, but he didn't come inside.

"I wanted nothing more than to walk in that room and hold my son, but I wanted to respect your decision. I thought maybe you would eventually tell me or that my brother would want me to meet my son and would speak up. I was wrong."

I took in a deep breath feeling the guilt eat me from the inside out. The limo finally came to a final stop, outside the house. I sighed, "come on" I gestured him to follow me.

He looked at me with widen eyes "now?" he asked alarmed.

I looked at him sheepishly "I think you've waited long enough" I admitted sadly.

"What if-" I cut him off shaking my head.

"You're going to be the best dad" I emphasised, getting rid of any doubts I know he had. I nodded him along and walked towards the door waiting for him, I looked around seeing the cars surrounding the streets nodding my head before each car took off one by one. Vincenzo looked down at me shocked noticing how every car drove off after I allowed it, I shrugged my shoulders sheepishly "you didn't think I'd leave him without protection?"

I looked back at the door unlocking it and walking inside. "Where have you been! We missed you" Lorenzo shouted coming into view, before closing his mouth staring at Vincenzo behind me. "Why is he here?" Lorenzo harshly spat out, I looked at him confused at his outburst.

"Why shouldn't I be here?" Vincenzo matched Lorenzo's energy getting agitated. "Okay ..." I trailed off trying to think of something to say to calm everyone down, Sebastián, Alex and the rest of the men quickly left the house leaving me alone with the King brothers and my baby. "Cowards" I harshly whispered.

"No, tell me Lorenzo why the fuck shouldn't I be here? So, you can play dad to my fucking son?" He harshly spat protectively pulling me behind his tall frame, I went to speak up before Lorenzo got in his face.

"Why is this man in my house?" Lorenzo commented. I widened my eyes looking at the two of them ... didn't they fix their problem I thought they were back to being close what is happening. "This isn't your house, its mine" I reminded Lorenzo that Vincenzo built it for me.

"The better question is why haven't I been here all along"
Vincenzo snapped feeling isolated from myself, his brother,
and his son. I stepped in between the both of them.

"Okay stop, Lorenzo I don't know where this came from, but
Vincenzo is Dante's dad and like you pointed out he has the
right to see his son and as Dante's mum only I have the right
to make that decision." I pointed out firmly looking at him.
"Why should he be allowed back into your life after
everything he did to you?" Lorenzo hissed.
I looked at him confused "What?" I asked completely
unaware of how to handle the situation. "You know he had
no control over what happened" I pointed out feeling the
need to defend Vincenzo.
"All he did was hurt you, why should he be allowed here" He
repeated himself, he threw his hands in the air frustrated "Oh
and you fucking dropped your panties at the sight of him
didn't you?!"
I looked at him taken back, my mind struggled to
comprehend the words that just left his mouth, shock washed
over me like icy water.

I couldn't think to do or say anything I just stood there paralysed in disbelief. My pervious state of shock now slowly being replaced with anger, my vision narrowed, my eyes locking onto his, I felt my breath quicken, chest rising and falling rapidly as I struggled to regain composure. I wanted to scream and throw something at him, I wanted to go crazy at his low comment. Seeing my reaction it dawned on him, he just realised what he said, his eyes widened lowering his hands looking at me remorseful "Isabella I-" I put my hand up ignoring him "Isabella?" I taunted him "Isabella what?!" I shouted pushing him back.

"You out of all fucking people should know-" I started shouting before he cut me off, "know what? How fucked up the two of you are? How screwed my brother is? How fucking much he hurt you? I know it all" he shouted getting in my face. Next think I know Vincenzo lunged towards Lorenzo the two of them on the floor punching each other, "ENOUGH!" I shouted.

Both came to a halt, "I've been there for everything where the fuck where you? I'm basically his dad" He hissed, "how could I have been a fucking good dad if THE BOTH OF

YOU KEPT MY FUCKING SON A SECRET?" Vincenzo finally snapped, "It's one thing that I thought I would never be a dad, because I didn't want to scar him like dad to me. It was one thing that I thought I would be a bad dad but the fact that my own fucking brother kept him from me and tried replacing me ..." he shook his head trailing off, I looked at him guilty. "It was one thing thinking I was going to fail my son.

It hurts a lot more that you thought that as well. Especially since I raised you, does that mean I failed you?" he asked getting slightly emotional. I looked over at Lorenzo whose features softened, he looked remorseful not knowing what got into him he let out a breath, "Vincenzo I never thought-" my head snapped towards my bedroom at the sound of Dante crying, cutting Lorenzo off. I shook my head disappointed and Lorenzo for some reason took it upon himself to get Dante. He came in rocking him, but Dante kicked and cried even harder, I looked between him and Vincenzo both of them on edge but Vincenzo's eyes now locked onto Dante, he didn't care about anything or anyone else in the room. He looked at him with admiration and more love than I ever saw in his eyes.

Lorenzo started getting flustered when Dante kept crying, I took him off Lorenzo and Dante started calming down in my arms before he started screaming and crying all over. Vincenzo edged closer to me slowly looking down at Dante, he looked at me asking if he could hold him, I nodded my head handing him over to him.

Within seconds of being in Vincenzo's arms he went quiet, relaxing, and snuggling closer to Vincenzo's chest, like he was taking in his father's scent, that he recognised his heartbeat. "I think he just wanted his dad" I whispered softly edging closer to the two of them creasing Dante's cheek with the back of my finger. Vincenzo let out a proud chuckle looking at me smiling. I smiled back feeling a sense of pride, and like everything was hole again, I turn around and see Lorenzo staring at the both of us before he quickly left the house, slamming the door behind him. I go to chase after him but stop myself, I let out a sigh deciding to give him time to cool off. I'll check on him after an hour, hopefully by then he would have digested everything and be ready to talk about it.

I look back at Vincenzo who was rocking Dante, he played with his hands before Dante wrapped his tiny hand around Vincenzo's finger squeezing it tight not wanting to let go.

I let out a small laugh tears starting to fill up my eyes, I looked at Vincenzo my gaze softening I exhaled softly and put my hand on his arm "I never thought you'd be a bad dad" I whispered softly. He looked at me "I was just scared" I explained softly, "scared that you didn't want a baby, scared that you might've taken him from me, scared that you wouldn't believe a stranger ... I wanted to keep a part of you with me, I already lost all of you and the mere chance that I could have lost the baby scared me to death" I trailed off he looked at me his features softening, everything making sense to him now, knowing why I kept him a secret. He placed a soft kiss on the top of my head before turning back to Dante.

"Thank you ... for giving me a chance" he whispered, "thank you for understanding" I smiled looking at Dante. "Dante King ... god you look so much like your dad, but you have your uncle's hair and his dimples." Vincenzo whispered. Dante looked identical to Vincenzo. Vincenzo's brother had a dark oceanic blue eye colour while Vincenzo had a silver grey, and of course my baby gets his eyes and his features ... it's not like I carried him in my stomach for nine months god forbid I get anything that resembles me.

"He would have loved you so much" he whispered softly holding back the urge to cry, "I know his watching over you, and I know just how much Dante loves you. The lengths he would take to protect you." He took a deep breath. "Dante always wanted to have kids, but one thing he couldn't wait for was to be an uncle. He had stories he was preparing to tell, games he wanted to play, road trips he wanted to take and so much love he couldn't wait to give ... He would have been the best uncle and an amazing dad, I'm hoping I can be just like him, be that person for you" he trailed off, "you're my second chance Leone" he whispered. My breathing hitched at his nickname choice ... Leone, lion.

"Leone?" I asked him, he turned to me smiling "he's got a lions heart, and a Kings name" he explained softly not wanting to wake him up, "that nickname doesn't remind you of anything?" I asked him softly trying to make him remember without pushing, he shook his head softly eyes fixated on Dante. I nodded my head disappointed before letting out a breath, "I should go" he whispers looking at me, I bit my bottom lip "you could spend the night" I suggested softly not wanting him to leave. He looked at me nodding his head "I'd love that" he hugged Dante closer to his chest looking at me, the door creaked open turning around I saw Sebastián and Alex walking back in "did anyone kill each other?" Alex called out, I shook my head rolling my eyes "almost ... just go to bed" I pushed them towards their rooms before looking back at Vincenzo, "they all live here?" he muttered through a clenched jaw.

"Are you jealous, Mr King" I teased, he looked at me his jaw locked, eyes hard before he spoke up "Isabella" he warned, I smirked looking at him "yes sir" I purred and walked off to the bedroom, he followed behind. I waited for him to walk in closing the door behind him locking it, "you can put him in his bed over there" I pointed to the cot next to my side of the bed. He looks at him in his arms before slowly putting him in the cot watching over him protectively "you, okay?" I asked him softly, "I didn't know I could love this much" he admitted not taking his eyes off of Dante.

I bit my bottom lip wishing I could turn back time and tell him earlier and yell at myself for everything I feared because it was far from reality. I exhaled and edged closer to him "unzip me?" I breathed out he turned looking at with a shocked expression before covering it up quickly.

I spun around lifting my hair up, my breathing became rigid feeling his fingertips brush over my neck before trailing down my back unzipping me. Both of us letting out a shaky breath, he took a step back and I spun around slowly holding onto the dress "thank you" I whispered he gave me a sharp nod and turned around.

"Go get dressed Isabella, unless you want another baby" I let out a chuckle shaking my head while heading off to the bathroom to get changed. Grabbing a pair of black shorts and a tank I make my way over to the bed putting my hair up in a pony. I watch him lay on the bed without anything on but his boxers, I raised my eyebrow looking at him, "really?" I questioned.

"I'm not sleeping in a suit" he stated defensively.

"Besides it's nothing you haven't seen before" he smiled condescendingly. I shook my head getting into the bed, I sat up pulling the covers over my legs before looking at Vincenzo.

"Isabella?" he called softly.

I hummed looking at him "would you come back?" he asked turning his head to look at me. I sucked in a breath and turned to look at him.

"What?" I asked again thinking I didn't hear him right.

"You heard me" he confirmed me.

I looked unsure "I don't know..." I whispered drifting off.

"The whole reason we are staying in this house now is because Xavier found out about the-" he cut me off sitting up alarmed. "What?" I shut my eyes forgetting he didn't know about that.

He probably thought I did all this to hide the pregnancy and hide from him. "Why didn't you tell me?" he snapped, I sat up and edged closer to him, I went to speak before he cut me off again "I could've protected you a lot better than my brother. I could've protected you and our son, why the fuck didn't you tell me" I watched his anger unfold before I snapped myself feeling defensive over Lorenzo, he did what he had to do.

"Protect us?" I whispered harshly ... "Maybe you could have Vincenzo, but who was going to protect me from you?" I asked him to remind him of his unreliable mind. "The only reason we are getting along now is for that little guy" I whispered reminding him of our readiness to kill each other just an hour ago.

He slouches looking at me "I wouldn't hurt you or our baby you know that" he explained, "I knew that ... ever since the accident I honestly don't know what to expect" I admitted softly looking down, He edges closer putting his finger under my chin lifting it up to look at him. "Every version of me will protect you, even if it's from myself" he whispered reassuringly.

I nodded my head softly smiling feeling peaceful once more, a feeling I haven't felt in a long time 'safe'. "I'll think about it" I answered his question about moving back, he nodded his head and turned to Dante before he laid back down falling sleeping. I sighed looking at his body frame next to mine once more, how was it that he was so close, but it felt like he was seven seas away.

I laid down cuddling closer to my pillow feeling my eye lids close slowly before I drifted off to sleep.

X

I tossed awake hearing a crying Dante, I peeked my eyes opened slowly not seeing Vincenzo in the bed, I sit up slowly turning around to pick Dante up from the cot and jolt awake not finding him in his bed. I jump out of bed and rush to the living room seeing Vincenzo holding Dante trying to put him back to sleep obviously flustered. I sniffle back a laugh and watch him from the door frame, his back turned to me.

"Come on buddy take the bottle" he whispered trying to feed him his bottle, Dante kept spitting the milk and weakly pushing the bottle away, trying to latch onto Vincenzo's chest, I couldn't help the wide grin "Buddy my nipples don't work like that" he pulled Dante off his chest whining flustered and panicked. I couldn't help myself I burst out into a fit of laughter alarming Vincenzo to turn around, his cheeks flushed red looking at me. Rolling his eyes "okay, you can stop" he mummers trying to get me to stop laughing.

I straightened up my posture still laughing but desperately trying to be discreet. "Just give me my baby" I laughed holding my arms out, grabbing a hold of Dante I take a seat and take my breast out so he can eat, he immediately latches on. I look up and see Vincenzo watching intensely "how come he gets to do it?" he whined, I looked at him with an amused grin, my eyebrows rising to my forehead. "Seriously?" I asked him, he looked at me nodding his head. "You're jealous of your own son?" I asked him one more time to give a chance to spin this around, "am I not obvious enough?" I rolled my eyes shaking my head, "go to sleep" I giggled he shook his head no "as long as you're up so am I" he plopped on the couch next to me, I eyed him shaking my head "you just want to stand guard in case any of the guys wake up and see my boob, and you also just want to keep staring at my boobs" I cleared up, he nodded his head pursing his lips "well when you put it like that I sound like jerk" he pointed out. I went to say something before closing my mouth why bother.

I looked at the door then back at Vincenzo "what's going on with you two?" I asked him, he sighed "ever since Maria's death his found it hard to have any relationship with me,

probably blaming me for her death and for pushing you out"
he spoke up softly, I looked at him sadly "it wasn't your fault"
I whispered finally accepting Maria's death as a tragic
accident "she wanted to be the hero" I smiled softly
remembering her words, "she was ready to go, before she
died she told us to look up in the sky and rest assure that,
that's where she wanted to be" I looked down at the floor
trying to blink away the tears, "it wasn't your fault she died, I
don't know if she's going to haunt me for telling you this but
she loved you a lot." I laughed.

FLASHBACK (NEVER WRITTEN ABOUT SCENE)

I sat on the edge of my bed frustrated, "Isabella!"
Vincenzo yelled from my door "VINCENZO IF YOU
DON'T FUCK OFF, I PROMISE YOU I'M GOING TO
MAKE A FUCKING SCENE" I yelled, after a moment it
fell silent. Sighing he finally left I fall back onto my bed
looking at the ceiling, my door flies open, and Maria jumps
on the bed next to me, "You know China heard you
screaming right?" she jokes, I rolled my eyes "Maria, do you
remember the first time we ever met Vincenzo and you told
me to stay away?" I asked her, she nodded her head "I

should've listened" I hissed.

She giggled sitting up, "in a way I'm glad you didn't" she smiled, I sat up looking at her "why? We would have gotten the fresh start we both wanted, and life would have been less violent" I pointed out, she pursed her lips looking at me knowingly "Isabella, is this your first time living? We were never going to get a smooth ride.

Life was not going to do us a favour and let us have a fresh start without a single problem." She took a breath, licking her bottom lip trying to find the right words. "Vincenzo is a pain, yes. He is probably the most dangerous man to ever live and might even be the biggest challenge in your life but, if it wasn't for him none of this would be possible. I wouldn't be finishing off my degree, I wouldn't have met Lorenzo, and ironically, I don't think I've ever felt this safe, before Vincenzo we both were constantly looking behind our shoulder scared of who's going to find us or kill you" she drifted off.

"But Vincenzo took us in ... maybe it wasn't in the most ideal way, but he did it. He **protected** us, made sure we were always okay, and he did the biggest thing of all he managed to tame you" she laughed, rolling my eyes I slap her.

"No, seriously. Dragon has always been a side of you, I wasn't even sure you knew how to handle, knowingly or unknowingly he guided you through that just like you guided him. He did the best thing I could have ever asked for, he protected you from yourself. If you ever utter a word, I will kill you but ... I'm glad Vincenzo came into our lives, I will never admit this to him until I die and that's a promise, but I love him like a brother without him I don't know what would've happened."

END OF FLASHBACK

Going back in my bedroom I put Dante back in his cot, he was sound asleep I gave him a soft kiss turning back to Vincenzo who was deep in thought. "She did" he whispered, I looked at him confused not knowing what he was talking about. He smiled into the distance, "she told me". He laughed softly.

"I'm going to need a little more information over here" I looked at him completely confused, he looked up at me "she wrote me a letter, and in that letter, she told me she loved me like a brother, she told me other things I'm sure if I had memories of her would've made me cry harder than I did." he trailed off.

I looked down at him "you ... You cried?" I whispered not knowing just how much Maria's death affected him that much. He nodded his head, "I cried harder than I thought I would, it was like I was crying for two people" he tried explaining "the side who knew who she was and the side who was just getting to know her again."

I nodded my head listening to him go on, "she was a pure soul, too precious for this world. She was like this rare gem I couldn't help the urge to protect her at all costs. Not in a romantic way but in a big brother way she deserved so much more than what she got ... I hope she's at peace playing in the waves like she wanted" he laughed out softly. "You knew she liked playing in the waves?" I asked him genuinely curious "she'd beg Lorenzo to take her all the time, I got the hint" he laughed.

"She knew you would be a great dad before I did" I whispered, he looked up at me confused and flattered. "I saw her before she died and she saw my belly, she knew it was yours and told me you'd be an amazing dad if I gave you the chance. She also said it again when I gave birth, I had this delusion or hallucination when I passed out, her and Dante actually" I remembered the out of body experience I had, "my twin?" he asked. I nodded my head yes. We both spoke for another hour before feeling the exhaustion finally crept its way, we both drifted off.

X

I turn over to the side extending my arm out but having it fall flat on the bed, I peak my eyes open seeing Vincenzo's tall frame at the end of the room on the phone. I stayed laying down trying to hear what was going on, "are you sure? Did you get a solid lead?" he whispers, the person on the other end of the phone speaks but I couldn't make out a single word.

"No, I'm not telling Isabella. She won't be coming either, that's an order Hacker speak or utter a single word and you're dead" he threatened him in a hushed voice before hanging up.

I quickly shut my eyes acting like I was still sleeping, he placed his hand on my shoulder softly shaking me away "Isabella" he whispers, I open my eyes slowly. I sit up straight rubbing my eyes "you, okay? Is Dante, okay?" I asked worried looking at Dante. He shakes his head "Yes, yes. Everyone is okay, I just I have to go, I got a shipment coming in I need to go be there." I nodded my head slowly, my head buzzing with a million scenarios on where he could be going, what he could be doing and why he doesn't want me to know or be there. "Do you need some company?" I asked him to see what he'd say.

He shook his head no, almost immediately "I'll see you later ... think about what we spoke about okay?" He whispered softly, going to give Dante a kiss on the cheek before he left. I quickly stood up from bed grabbing a jacket and put on my black combat boots, running out to Sebastián's room "stay with Dante! Don't leave the fucking house I'll be back" I quickly rushed outside to my motorbike, I plugged the key in watching it pure to life, flipping my jacket of my shoulders putting it on, "where are you going?" Sebastián shouted out alarmed running after me, I looked up from the bike "I honestly don't know yet, but I'll be back" I assured him and quickly took off, looking for a King's car. Someone picked him up, I swerve past the cars looking into each window of a black range. Finally spotting a familiar face I slowed down keeping my distance but tailing them. They took a turn into a street I knew all too well he was headed back to the estate. I waited on the side street hoping he would come back out, whatever he is doing it was making me squeamish.

Vincenzo's POV

I yawn opening my eyes softly, extending my arms out stretching. I go to sit up but feel pressure on my chest, looking down I saw Isabella peacefully asleep holding onto me. I calmly laid back down watching her not knowing how long this moment will last. Trying to memorise every aspect of her, how her hair falls onto her face, the way her lips pout when she's asleep, how her long black lashes make her look like a doll. I turn my head to the table next to me grabbing my phone hearing it vibrate, 'missed call from Hacker'.

I sighed trying to slide out of the bed without waking her up, standing on the side of the bed I look at her watching her snuggle up to the pillow, I sigh in relief and walk around to Dante looking down at him.

A proud smile takes over my lips before I stand at the window at the end of the room calling Hacker back while I got dressed quickly.

"Boss" he quickly answers the call, "parlare" **(speak)** I respond. He clears his throat "I have a location on the matter you wanted to know about" he speaks up proud of himself, I'm stunned hearing him finally give me the news I've been waiting for.

"Are you sure? Did you get a solid lead?" I asked him seriously.

"I am, I've been tracking it for a while" I nodded.

"Nicely done, we will discuss details when I get home. Gather the men" I give him an order, feeling the familiar adrenaline, rush through my blood.

"Since you're back with Isabella does that mean she's coming along?" he asked me in the same tone Ariana would have. I shut my eyes shaking my head.

"No, it's too dangerous for her." I shook my head not wanting her to be in danger.

"Did you forget how fucking scary Isabella fucking is! She is never in danger she is the danger!" he yelled out forgetting that I did forget, "Hacker" I warned.

He coughed realising "huh I guess you did..." he laughed out. I rolled my eyes shaking my head. "You sure you don't want Isabella's help? If she comes, I don't think you'll need any of the men with you" he pushes trying to get me to bring along Isabella. I tensed up letting out a frustrated sigh "no, I'm not telling Isabella. She won't be coming either, that's a fucking order Hacker speak or utter a single word and you're dead" I threatened him in a hushed voice before hanging up.

Turning around I see Isabella changed her positions, I edged closer to her softly shaking her awake, "Isabella" I whisper not wanting to startle her, she slowly opens her eyes and looks up at me. She sits up straight rubbing my eyes "you, okay? Is Dante, okay?" she rushed out worried looking at Dante. "Yes, yes. I just I have to go, I got a shipment coming in I need to go be there." I explained praying she'd believe me and not ask any follow up questions. She nodded her head slowly. "Need some company?" She asked calmly, I shook my head no, almost immediately "I'll see you later ... think about what we spoke about ok?" I whispered softly, needing to leave fast before she figured it out. I walked around the bed going to give Dante a kiss on the cheek before I left. "I'll be back Leone" I whispered before straightening up my posture and quickly leaving.

I dash outside seeing Luca in the car waiting for me, jumping in I nod for him to leave to the estate. I sigh leaning back in my chair enjoying the calm before I got back home. I flip my phone out and hover over Lorenzo's name. Pushing everything aside I hit his name, placing the phone to my ear while it called. "What?" he asked groggy, "where are you?" I asked him worried. "Home" he breathed out, "good I'm coming" I informed him quickly, shutting the phone I look out the window and see someone on a motorbike near the car, I shrug my shoulders thinking nothing of it.

X

Taking the turn to our estate, I look behind us making sure the person on the bike wasn't tailing us. After seeing no sight of anyone behind us I shrugged my shoulders feeling overly paranoid for some reason, like I should be expecting someone to follow me. I got out of the car heading straight for the door, everyone moving out of my way nodding their heads out of respect. I pointed at Bullseye's, Hacker, Luca, and Franco.

"Office" I spoke ushering them. I turn the corner heading towards Lorenzo's room seeing him lying on his bed, I sighed walking closer to him, "Lorenzo" I breathed out, he turned looking at me. "What?" he asked irritated, I rolled my eyes "Office" is all I said and walked out. Not in the mood to fight or in the mood to discuss what the fuck happened at Isabella's house. I walked inside seeing everyone waiting for me around the meeting table, I walk around and take my stand at the head of the table, I look at the door waiting for Lorenzo to walk in, and he did. He stood next to Hacker annoyed but kept his mouth shut.

"Parlare" I ushered for Hacker to speak.

He cleared his throat "we all know why we are here and what the issue at hand is" He spoke up everyone nodded knowing exactly what was happening except for Lorenzo, who had no idea what, why or where we were going. I shook my head staying silent, if he spent more time at home, he would know exactly what was happening … if he knew me like I thought he did he would know.

"We must infiltrate a heavily armed home of 2,000 square meters. The house is double story, so we are going to need all hands-on deck for it work" He explained briefly.

I nodded taking it from here "this job needs to run smoothly and fast I don't want any of our men dead, so we need to be smart. The home is in the mountains, meaning lots of hills and higher vantage points also away from civilisation meaning no witnesses. Bullseye you and your most skilled men are going to be on the hills covering us from every angle, making sure to take out the men at the front gate first. Franco gather your best trained men in combat and get ready, when the men at the front drop, I want them to be collected and hidden I don't want anyone in that home to figure out what's happening until it's too late. Once we are in, we are disbursing-" I cut myself off grabbing a blueprint of the home from my desk draw.

"Fico, after that's done I need you and your men to make your way around here-" I circle the area on the side of the home covered in bushes allowing them to get close before being noticed, "take the guards out one by one, then the rest come up from the back of the house leaving the house completely unarmed, the rest of the guards that surround the home Bullseye will take out with a clean shot. The ones close to the doors of the home Fico you need to handle them quietly and discreetly." I intersected him nodding my head, he nods sharply.

"Lorenzo, Luca, and I will enter the house taking out whoever else is inside and getting to the desired target. Everyone clear on what they need to do?" I asked, "make sure to stay out of the security camera's way." I circled all the areas that are covered in camera, "Hacker will have them disabled but I don't want any what ifs so be sure to steer clear." Everyone nodded their heads sharply going to gather men and assume their positions.

"Gear up" I shout out, everyone rushed out of my office leaving me alone, I open my draw grabbing my handgun placing it behind my back. Walking outside my office heading, down to the basement. Opening the door smiling seeing all the weaponry on the walls and tables, I smile going closer to my holy grails neatly hanging on the wall behind glass windows.

I open it up looking at my revolvers, riffles, silencers, and handguns. I smiled like a child grabbing my silencer and a revolver strapping it on my hip, turning around I see Lorenzo on the frame of the door watching me intently "where are we going?" he asked, I looked at him my eyes narrowed "since when do you ask?" I questioned.
He shrugged his shoulders "since now" he spoke up firmly.

I straightened my posture and stood in front of him towering above him "just because you're my brother and I gave you the tittle of underboss doesn't mean you should forget who fucking runs everything. I ordered you to come, strap your fucking balls on and move" I brushed past him, his tone just reminded me of the fight and everything he said. I couldn't stand seeing him right now, but this meant to much, I needed my best men on the job.

Everyone climbed into their cars and drove off, a line formed behind us. I sighed sitting in the seat Lorenzo directly across from me, "where you with her?" he breathed irritated, I looked at him and simply nodded my head not wanting to get into it now. "Pathetic" he muttered under his breath, I shut my eyes closed feeling the anger rise up. Breathing in I opened my eyes and stayed calm choosing to ignore him, "didn't you hear me? I said you're fucking path-" cutting him off "Lorenzo" I called out his name. Immediately he shut his mouth rolling his eyes knowing not to egg me on.

"You don't even deserve her" he whispered pissed off, I turned to him "and you do?" I asked frustrated, he looked at me taken back for a second "that has nothing to do with it!" he shouted. I shook my head. "You think you're so much better than me, don't you? Lorenzo King the innocent one, the funny laid back one. The man who could do no wrong" I sarcastically praised him, "because he never had to do anything wrong" I hissed reminding him of how sheltered I raised him, never letting him go through what I had too.

"You were never under the influence of a father who

didn't want to raise a boy ... but a weapon" he looked at me analysing everything I said, and every movement. "You never had to go through a quarter of what I did, you never had to endure the pain and torture just so your power-hungry dad could guarantee that it would strip you of all emotions forcing all this rage in you. Traumatising you so you would become more power hungry than your old mad to prevent it from happening again. You love to point fingers and talk about how I'm the fucking monster, the dark cloud in everyone's life. You didn't have to do what I did, see what I saw, you never had to get use to the feeling of blood on your hands. You still jump and get squeamish when you see blood, when you watch me take a life." I pointed out, "just keep one fucking thing in mind, you never had to get used to it because I wouldn't let you!" I spoke out harshly watching his features soften. "If you deserve her, it's because I let you, because I protected you from becoming like me. I let the humanity in you stay alive, I didn't let you or dad make you selfish, angry, power hungry, blood thirsty. I didn't let it happen!" I shouted feeling my entire body light up.

"I didn't let anyone turn you into a weapon..." I breathed

out calming back down again, "I never said I deserved her" I whispered looking away, "and in my fucked up way I care about her, deeper than I can understand. I might not deserve her, but I deserve a chance... I deserve to be in my son's life the one you and her hid from me. I might be fucked up in more ways than one, but I deserve to be in my son's life, and he deserves a dad ... but you didn't think about that when you saw me did you?" I asked him, he stayed silent I nodded my head knowingly.

The car came to a stop, I looked out the windows sighing. Tapping on my earpiece pushing everything aside needing to focus on the task at hand, "everyone copy?"

"Copy" everyone responds in union.

"Bullseye, assemble positions on the hill's I want all bases covered. Franco get your men ready, after the men at the gate go down you need to be inside have three of our men remain at the front in case we have any outsiders. Luca, Lorenzo, and I will be waiting for your all clear?" I spoke. "YES, BOSS" they responded firmly, I watched seeing Bullseye and the men turn around in the car everyone going a different direction's up the hills.

After half an hour we get conformation from Bullseye that he and his men are ready waiting for my single, I instructed Franco and his men to be ready. Giving Bullseye the single I watch all six men at the front gate go down in seconds. Franco and his men quickly grabbing them and hiding them behind the bushes taking their places to not raise suspicion. "Franco, take the rest of the remainder men and go round make sure to stay hidden. Bullseye make sure you and your men have eyes on us, you're our eyes shoot to kill gentlemen" I nod my head ushering Lorenzo to follow me. "Luca" I call out from the driver's seat, we go through the back with the rest of the men.

"Hey!" someone shouts out, drawing his gun. I smile "how polite of you." I smiled grabbing my revolver from my hip drawing it at him, "Goodbye" I whisper shooting him square in the head. I nod the rest of the men to continue. Lorenzo, taking his anger out on one man pounding his fists into his face while the rest quickly kill and dispose of the men. I edge closer to Lorenzo and place my hand on his shoulder shaking my head.

He sighs getting up and like the rest disposing the bodies, placing my revolver back in my hip I pull out my silencer. Entering the house looking around, pressing my back against the wall I peak behind the wall seeing two armed men talking. I wait for them to get closer to me, I see their shadows on the floor they turn to the hallway I'm in. Having my gun already drawn I shoot both in the head, dragging their bodies out of the way and into a random room.

I watch seeing Luca, Lorenzo and Franco's men taking out everyone inside. Everyone nods their head giving me all clear, "how did you all get so many men dead, theirs only three of you?" I questioned. They all shrug also unsure. I raise an eyebrow and shake my head, I have a knowing feeling who was here, I look out the window squinting my eyes, seeing something next to our car. I storm closer towards the window seeing the same motorbike that was on the road earlier. "We have company" I speak out.

"Be aware" I warn everyone and continue my way up the stairs.

Looking at the master bedroom, I burst the door open wanting to fucking kill the bastard for everything he's done. "Fuck" I shout, empty. I turn around quickly hearing footsteps running, I quickly get out chasing the sound, I stop in the middle of the hallway listening. I turn to my side and see someone peak behind the wall. I run towards them, but they quickly run off, pulling out my gun I chase after them. Looking around I cursed "fucking hell" I lost him. I look around the basement, I turned on a light and examined everything.

It all looks normal, surpassingly very modern. A seating area along with a fire pit. Everything looked well placed except for a bookshelf in the far back, I edged closer to it examining everything, it seemed out of place, like it was randomly placed, it was stacked with books, but it was isolated from everything else, no reading chair, no rug not even a light. I grabbed the bookshelf and smashed it down on the floor, I stood back surprised.

A door knob?

I drew my gun and slowly opened the door. My mouth dropped seeing a couple huddled up looking very distraught.

"Mum? Dad?" Turning around seeing Isabella behind me, tears welled up in her eyes. "Boss, you all need to get out of there. Someone alarmed Xavier now his coming back and bringing re-enforcements" Hacker rushed out.

"You'll be outnumbered, I got his location and am tailing him through street cameras, you have approximately five minutes to get out".

"Everyone GO!" I shouted alarming everyone to leave through the earpiece. I looked at Isabella who still stood their shocked, it went without saying she was the one on the bike and the one I was chasing. Hacker's words taunted me while I rolled my eyes, so she really is dangers.

The feeling I had that something was off was probably my older self-knowing she would follow.

THE NEW HOME

Isabella's POV

I stared at the sight in front of me, moving closer slowly pushing past Vincenzo I stood in front of the two people I cried over my whole life, the two people that left me broken … the two people I thought were dead. The two people I went through hell and back to find and here they are right in front of me and all I could think to do was stare at them.

Unsure if this was reality or a cruel twisted dream, "Mum? Dad?" I whispered, they looked up at me their eyes opened wide upon seeing me, I kneeled in front of them seeing their bloodshot red eyes, and fatigued bodies I cried out and pulled them in a hug they flinched making my heart shatter into pieces but within a second, they hugged me back slowly I felt them starting to calming down placing their heads on my shoulder inhaling my scent.

I tightened my embrace crying out, feeling my body shake and the tears falling out like a waterfall. "We need to move now" Vincenzo spoke up sternly, I turned to him tears still streaming down my face, I stood up quickly untying my parents and Vincenzo's men came over to help quickly escort them out of the building.

Everyone ran out of the building, one of Vincenzo's men taking my motorbike back while I quickly jumped in the car with Vincenzo, Lorenzo, and my parents. Each car took off speeding, I looked at my parents still unsure about everything, I edged closer to them my dad squeezed my hand weakly, my mum wrapped her arms around my waist. Both of them hugged me with little to no strength, I looked at the two of them my head racing with possibilities of what they had to endure. My heart skipped a beat imaging if their torture was like mine.

I sighed trying to calm myself down, feeling overwhelmed not knowing what to do with so many emotions flooding me all at once my breathing slowly becoming heavier. I let go of my parents and placed my hand over my chest, suddenly it become harder to breathe. "Isabella?" Vincenzo calls out worried, "Bella?" Lorenzo then calls my name with an equally worried expression as Vincenzo.

Sweat began trickling my forehead, my heart was pounding against my chest. I felt my throat start closing, "Isabella"

Vincenzo calls out panicked. I lean down trying to breathe, my chest tightened, as a rush of dizziness overwhelmed my senses. My heart pounded relentlessly, threatening to burst through my ribcage. Each breath became a desperate struggle, as if the air had turned to a heavy fog, choking me with every breath I took. My thoughts spiralled out of control, a chaotic explosion of fears and worries. My mind raced from one worst-case scenario to another, each one more terrifying than the last. I knew the only person who could help me, and he was already extending his hand out looking at me full of worry. I leaned forward slowly Vincenzo knowingly took his seatbelt off along with my own and pulled me towards him. Sitting me on his lap in the passenger seat, he softly rubbed circles on my back, whispering comforting words in my ear.

"Just like the thunder it'll all fade in the background. Listen to my voice" he whispered, I felt myself calming down his soft-spoken words reminding me of the night when he rushed into my room to help my panic attack from the dark.

I slowly let out a shaky breath, feeling the tight hold on my throat and chest begin to ease. I take a deep breath and bury my head into Vincenzo's chest, needing to escape and calm myself down for a second. I inhaled his scent, my breathing slowing down listening to his deep voice as he kept whispering in my ear. I calmed down and solely focused on listening to his heart beating.

As much as I hate to admit, Vincenzo was the only one who could calm me down so quickly and effortlessly and right now all I needed was to lose myself in him even if it was just for a moment.

We arrived back at my house, I looked up from Vincenzo's chest and he looked down at me concerned, I nodded my head and got off his lap and out of the car. He followed me out closing the door behind him he stood in front of me, studying my face making sure I was okay. "Maybe you should come home" he spoke up worry evident on his face.

"I am home" I whispered back scared of what it would be like if I gave in and came back.

His features hardened he took a step back and got back into the car leaving me standing alone. Lorenzo comes out of the car walking past me and inside, Vincenzo rolls down the window "I'll send a car for you to come and see your parents, they'll be at the clinic on the estate undergoing check-up and therapy if needed" He assures me before closing the windows and driving off.

I watch as the car faded off into the distance, why did I say that. I wasn't home, home was wherever he is. I closed my eyes shaking my head regretting how I handled the situation, before rushing inside to see Dante, "there's mama's boy" I picked him up and rocked him in my arms, "you're going to meet your Abuela and Abuelo" I whispered tapping his little nose he smiled wide looking up at me with his beautiful big grey eyes.

"Hey Isabella, can we talk?" Lorenzo whispers walking into my room. I nodded my head smiling, "I just wanted to apologise for what happened, I don't know why I lashed out the way I did. I think I just built this fantasy in my head and seeing Vincenzo come into the picture it all came crashing down." He admitted softly. I bit my lower lip placing Dante back in his cot. I stood up straight and ushered him to sit on the bed with me.

"Vincenzo is Dante's dad but that doesn't make you are any less important. You're his uncle, his fun, crazy, stupid, childish, and most importantly sarcastic uncle. Dante's going to need you in his life just as much as he's going to need his dad" I grabbed his hand giving it a tight reassuring squeeze.

He smiled calming down again, "I watched him come into this world, I saw you transition into a very gusty mum to a responsible one" he paused to laugh, I shook my head rolling my eyes. "I just ... I didn't want that all to go away. I already lost Maria, I didn't want to lose the two of you ... and whenever you're involved with Vincenzo it always ends with you leaving" he admits in a soft cautious tone.
I sigh knowing he was right "you'll always find us" I nudged him laughing.

He shook his head smiling, knowing he would "are you back to being the sarcastic little shit I've come to know and tolerate?" I teased, he rolled his eyes standing up "I do not have to condone such disrespect" he walks towards the door and turns back "actually I do, I have nowhere else to be" he pouts. I laugh shaking my head and tapping the bed once more, he rushes and jumps on the bed making me jump a little on impact.

I squeal laughing, "Dante's sleeping" he hissed. He takes a peep to a very awake Dante, "well not anymore" he shakes his head at me disapprovingly picking him up and laying him down on the bed. "Hey Leone" I sang softly making him laugh at his dad's nickname. "Leone?" Lorenzo questions, "is that how I sound when I try and talk Spanish?" he laughed, I nod my head yes laughing with him.

"Are you ready to go see daddy?" I pick him up and hold him like in the lion king. "Leone?" Lorenzo continues to mock.

I roll my eyes "can you not be such a puta for one day" I hiss getting up to grab Dante a change of clothes and pack my mum bag.

"Do you really want your son to be so much like you? You gave him the same stupid nickname Vincenzo gave you" he mocked jokingly. I turned my head to face him "first of all the sound of your voice is starting to irritate me" I pointed at him.

"Second of all, your brother gave him that nickname. Even with his memories gone when he says stuff like that, he really gives me such high hopes. Even said the same thing he did when I had that panic attack during the thunderstorm and the lights blew out" I sigh zipping the bag, "you know he's been getting a lot of these headaches, sometimes I'd catch him just staring into space ... what if" I cut him off "what if it's his memories coming back?" I finish his sentence off.

"This isn't Disney bitch stop finishing my sentences and let me talk" he bites before continuing "if it's coming back shouldn't he have remembered it all by now?" he questions, I pout thinking about it. "Not really, I think his memories are just triggered whenever something happens that triggers a past event. However, he could also just be fighting it off maybe a part of him doesn't want to remember everything" I sigh knowing that maybe he just rather leave me in the past. Maybe he missed who he was before me.

"Maybe he took it as a way to go forward without distractions" I continued before he cuts me off, "I think Vincenzo just needs a reason to remember" he speaks up. I eye him sceptically "A son isn't a good enough reason?" I questioned.

"No, as much as he loves his son. That doesn't correlate to you, you're the boys mum but that isn't a reason to remember you. He needs a reason specifically from you" I eye him raising an eyebrow before I sigh. "I don't know what to do" I threw my hands in the air frustrated.

"Look after the fight, and we had a small argument in the car. I really saw it. I saw what Maria saw. The love in his eyes is a genuine form of love. The love where he will burn this world to the ground but won't let a flame touch your skin, it was the first time I ever saw it, he spoke about you and Dante and finally, I understood him" he sighed.

"If he is pushing away his memories or fighting to block as many as he can it's not because he doesn't love you" he whispered, my breathing hitched at the mention of 'love' did I love him? Did he love me? How could we even know if our entire time of knowing each other we never said it all we did was fight.

"Then what?" I whispered. "Guilt" he answered sure of himself.

"Guilt?" I questioned unsure of his answer.

"Don't give me that tone. Yes, guilt." He snaps sighing.

"Think about it before his accident, he would have never done what he did to you or treated you the way he did. If his memories come flooding back, then so does his feelings and the old him. The him that would've shot Roxy and Lexi the second they came with that bullshit accusation, the Vincenzo that would of never left you alone not for a second. The Vincenzo that would've attacked you the second he saw you again, the Vincenzo you got is the Vincenzo I've known my whole life. Cold, distant, that version of himself decided everything with his head, and only makes decisions based on facts not emotions."

"Guilt" I whispered realising it, maybe that's why. Maybe he just doesn't want to feel it all come crashing down at once. "Give him a reason Isabella" he nods his head and walks out, "now get changed and hurry up I'll be in the car waiting."

X

I shake my head and quickly change into something more comfortable, locking up behind me. Sebastián and Alex already beating us to the estate. I quickly put Dante into the car making sure the seats secured. I walk around getting in the car rolling down the windows as the car takes off.

"Excited?" Lorenzo chimes up. I smile nodding my head "it's a moment I thought would never come, but how did you know where they were?" I questioned. "I didn't" he admitted, I looked at him confused "to be honest I gave up, I didn't know how to find them or even where to start. Little did I know Vincenzo was doing his own thing." I nod my head smiling like a child. Vincenzo was like my guardian angel.

X

We parked the car at the front of the stairs, I got out and everyone in the yard fell silent watching me. I stood there for a second looking at everyone with a grin, I couldn't help but feel happy. "Isabella!" They all shouted rushing towards me, I shouted excited as they formed a group hug around me. "I've missed you guys!" I admitted laughing, "bitch came back from the dead" I looked at Bullseye with my eyes wide open "or did I?" I questioned. They all took a step back and eyed me, I burst out laughing.

"Are you all drunk already?" I questioned half of them said no the other half said maybe. I shook my head "you want to catch up?" Fico begged, I pouted "those days have come to a small stop. I gotta be responsible now" I informed them. They all look confused, "ah" I spoke up snapping my fingers knowing they probably have no clue what's going on. "Give me a second" I walk to the side of the car and take out Dante's seat turning it around showing the men the baby. They all jumped back scared like I was holding a bomb before stepping forward again this time they all looked excited. Their faces all formed sly grins.

"YOU HAVE A BABY?" They shouted I nodded my head, "Men meet Dante, Dante say hi to your bodyguards" I laughed looking at them.

They all came closer smiling looking at him, all six of them crowded his seat towering over him "okay we got it from here be gone" Hacker grabbed the seat off me, and they all ran away with my son. "WHA- HEY!" I shouted, hearing the faint giggle coming from Dante as they ran with him. Lorenzo laughed shaking his head "you're never getting him back" he pointed out. Laughing I shook my head "I don't know what's scarier, the fact that mafia men took off running with my son or the fact that I let them" I tilted my head watching them from a distance, putting Dante in the shade all talking and playing with him. You could see Dante reaching his tiny hands out trying to grab one of their faces.

"You know his dad is the don, right?" Lorenzo laughs out looking at me, I glare at him "oh shut up" I bite back. Turning around I stare at the familiar doors my heart twisted into a knot, letting out a deep breath I walk up slowly. Looking around nothing much has changed, "Isabella?" Ariana calls out, I smile giving her a hug.

"When did you get here?" she asked shocked and surprised to see me. "Oh, about the same time you managed to trick me and Vincenzo into both being at that wedding" I commented. Her eyes go wide smiling innocently she looks at me "me? Psh wha- Is that Dante?" she cuts herself off looking at the men holding his car seat. "IT IS!" She shouts pushing me to the side and dashing outside. "STAY AWAY!" The boys shouted grabbing him in his seat running away from Ariana, "GIVE ME MY NEPHEW!" She shouts, "LEAVE OUR NEPHEW ALONE" They shout in return. "Wait ... nephew?" Hacker shouts, "THIS IS VINCENZO'S SON!" they all yell out. I look at them dumbfounded who else is it going to be? "OH MY GOD" They shouted getting even more excited than they were before. "WE ARE HOLDING THE FUTURE BOSS OF THE KINGS" they shouted making me laugh out. They looked down at Dante full of pride the same look Lorenzo had when he first saw Dante.

"You know that they're never letting him go now" Lorenzo laughed. "They just figured out that that boy is their next boss, and the son of the two people they love most in the world" he looks at me serious.

I smiled shaking my head "did the kings just kidnap my boy?" I asked, he nodded his head walking away. "I WANT HIM BACK IN ONE PIECE STOP RUNNING AROUND!" I shouted watching them desperately trying to doge Ariana. I shook my head laughing fucking idiots … I missed them. I walked up the familiar staircase walking past Vincenzo's office my feet took me to my old room, walking inside I take in everything nothing's changed my bed is still the same as I left it, the sheets were ruffled. I close my eyes shut and walk towards Maria's room. Taking in a deep breath I opened the door slowly, looking at everything my eyes start to tear up.

I walk closer looking at her bed smiling at the memory of us talking and watching movies, laughing at the time Lorenzo jumped in joining us watching a horror movie. Then he spilled the popcorn all over Maria. I laugh tracing the side of the bed, where she would normally sleep, I walk towards her nightstand and see a photo of the two of us I smile picking it up. Tracing over her face with my finger a tear manages to escape my eye. What I would do to go back in time, to have you so close again. I miss you so much butterfly.

I hear a soft knock I turn around and see Lorenzo looking at me with a sad expression, I smile nodding my head "it's hard coming in here without her" he admits looking around the room, he smiles looking at the photo in my hands. "Oh god, I remember that day" he laughed. I laughed nodding my head "we were so drunk" I commented laughing at the memory. "You two were hammered, Vincenzo and I were stuck on babysitting duty. I remember you got drunk after watching Jennifer's body, the two of you started filming and copying that iconic scene with the lighter. Both of you almost burnt your fucking tongues off" he yelled.

I laughed nodding my head "OHHH YEAA" I cracked up remembering that "she begged me to take her to get that printed out and framed, after an hour of her begging I caved. She was so wasted and trying to figure out how to print it was hilarious. She was yelling at the computer thinking it's a robot" he laughed out. I smiled shaking my head looking back at the photo "it's days like those that make me feel human, and grateful having shared a moment like that with my sister" I sigh smiling "I miss her so much" I admitted. Looking at the photo of the two of us holding lighters in our hands laughing while trying to hold onto each other so we don't fall. Lorenzo nodded his head pulling me in a hug "I miss too" he whispered softly. I put the picture frame back in its spot and take one last look before leaving, "I think I should go see Vincenzo now" Lorenzo hissed and stood in front of me "maybe you should go sightseeing" he said trying to steer me from Vincenzo's office. I eyed him sceptical "you not wanting me to go see him just makes me want to go."

"Okay, then go see him?" Lorenzo tried reverse psychology, but he just sounded so unsure of himself, "now I don't want to" I pouted, he looked at me shocked "really?" he questioned proud of himself. I smiled and ran past him "nope!" I shouted and ushered his men to move aside, they hesitated but knew I was going to get my way anyway. Glad to know nothing has changed, I open the door and see a woman completely naked in his office, my mouth drops to the floor. I turn on my heel and storm out of his office, "Isabella" Vincenzo shouts out. "Hey, hey! Where are you going" Lorenzo stops in front of me trying to block my way, I duck under his arm and stomp to the kitchen "what are you doing?" Lorenzo asks scared of my answer. "I'm going to relax" I smile at him "honey that smile is the same smile you get before setting someone on fire" he points out looking me up and down.

I continue smiling at him "what's more relaxing than setting someone on fire?" I chimed up grabbing a lighter and walking past him again, "a lot of things!" He shouted sacred running after me. "Isabella!" he shouts snatching the lighter out of my hand "you can't set her on fire" he tries to rationalise.

"Who said I was setting just her on fire?" I asked him trying to get it back out of his hands. Just before he could reply the girl came downstairs looking very offended, I raised an eyebrow at her, and she looks me up and down before walking off. "The fuck is that bitch looking at?" I yelled getting her attention, she stopped in her tracks and spun around. She stood in front of me about to say something before she was cut off "Get. Out" Vincenzo warns her from the staircase, she closes her mouth rolling her eyes.

She turns around to walk off before I grab her arm, applying pressure I whisper, "if I see you near Vincenzo again, you'll be walking out of this estate in pieces." I threaten her, letting go of her arm. She gulps fear evident in her eyes before she rushes off, I spin on my heel.

"Really?" I waved my hands up. Walking up the stairs I go into his office waiting for him to follow me, he walks in watching me with a smug look. "You're fucking proud of yourself, aren't you?" I yelled not finding the humour behind this situation. He watches me while I throw a fit, I huff pissed off.

"If you wanted to fuck other girls don't invite me to stay" I coldly snapped walking off, he stops me midway holding onto my arm pulling me back so now I am facing him. "Isabella" he tried to rationalise with me, but the thought of him with anyone else sent me over the fucking edge.

"If you wanted to fuck some slut, then don't invite me over, DON'T send a car for me and DON'T you dare do it with our son in the same fucking house!" I shouted punching his chest.

"I hate you" I whispered aggressively and slowly letting the words sink into his head. His stare hardened, the veins in his forehead became more and more visible the harder he clenched.

"No" he denied shaking his head.

"Yes" I confirmed nodding my head.

"From the moment I fucking met you, I should have run the other way." He looked down at me hurt, granted he had no idea how we met and when he first saw me but still, he looked hurt.

"Then leave" he hissed, still holding on to my writs. I looked up at him with glossy eyes not expecting that reaction.

"What?" I whispered taken back.

"Leave" he spoke up in a rather aggressive low tone. He let go of my wrists and stepped back, tears threatening to fall I stayed looking at him. "Is that what you want?" I asked, he shook his head frustrated "Isabella isn't that what you wished for? To never have met me?" he yelled clearly agitated by my choice of words.

"If that's your desire you can leave me but know this. The feeling of my hands on your body, the feeling of my breath on your neck. The goosebumps you get when we are close, the way your soul feels safe with mine. Those feelings... they'll never leave you" a tear escaped my eye hearing him speak, I bit my lower lip looking up at the roof. "So go on, leave. If that's what you want, you can go. Live your life free of me, free of the thousands of shadows that follow. Just don't be surprised if you see a shadow lurking behind you." I look at him not saying a word, I shake my head taking in a deep breath. That shadow lurking behind me was his shadow, the one shadow that even if given a choice I wouldn't shine a light on for it to go.

He stood in front of his mirror, the exact same broken mirror that has taken a fair share of the blunts of our relationship, over the years. I stood behind him staring at him through the broken reflection smiling ever so slightly, a million emotions rushed through anger, sadness but somehow power. I felt powerful knowing that a simple sentence could send Vincenzo spiralling. It made me powerful to know that I had the same effect he did on me, maybe even more than him.

"Did you figure it out yet?" I whispered, tilting my head looking at him through the mirror. He looked at me through the mirror hands in his pocket his facial expressions remained stone cold. "What?" he clenched.

"Who you're looking at, the man staring back at you," I emphasised, his stare fixated back on himself his eyes darkened looking at his reflection. I nod my head slowly, "I'll take that as a no" I spoke up, my eyes still burning at the tears I refuse to let fall.

"I could've killed you" he whispered; I shook my head remembering that day. "I should have, that's what I'd do.

What the boss of the Kings does to traitors." He continued, shifting his eyes to look at me.

"That's who I am. I don't do nice" He continued. "You wouldn't" I whispered. Knowing no matter what he would never hurt me, not intentionally. He turned around fast, before I could comprehend, he had me pinned up against the wall. "I could've easily murdered you without hesitation." He spoke up, I gulped looking at him, my chest rising and falling matching the fast rate of my heart.

"Then why didn't you" I hissed, not wanting him to know how much his words make my heart twist and break.

"Those angelic eyes made me all dizzy and weak" he whispered looking down at me, his eyes resuming their usual grey. I looked up at him still visibly sad. "Clearly" I scoffed referring to the girl who was here earlier. "I didn't know she would be here" he answered my unasked question looking at me, I rolled my eyes.

"That doesn't make the situation better" I started feeling the steam coming out of my ears. "Isabella, I haven't touched another woman since I woke up from the accident" he admits.

My eyes snap up to him, his hands trail down my frame until they find their usual spot on my hip. "You haven't?" I whispered my breathing now in sync with his. He nods his head slowly.

"Why?" I asked, he stepped closer towards me leaving no room for the air to get in between, his body towering over me as he looks down at me. I look up at him the bridge of our nose just touching. My back arched the second his hand trailed down my spine, it was like my body was under his command, it knew exactly what he wanted with a simple hand. "Your memory loss was a way out for you, you could've had any girl you wanted, started over and found someone with less demons … so why me? Why pick me?" I questioned needing to hear the answer. "Why anyone else when you exist?" His husky Italian voice sent me spiralling not letting me think straight.

"You asked me if I figured it out, if I recognise the man in the mirror" I waited to hear him continue.

"I'm more fucking confused now than I ever was before" he stepped back looking at me, I wanted to comfort him "your parents are probably waiting for you" he stated looking away and going back to his desk. "I-" I went to speak up, but he kept his head down frustrated, confused and hurt. I didn't even thank him for never giving up on finding my parents, Instead, I came in attacking and yelling at him.

I sighed walking towards him his head still down, I bent down slowly and placed a soft kiss on his cheek "thank you" I whispered and walked off.

X

I rushed into the clinic "where are they?" I quickly rushed out looking around frantically. The women pointed to the room across the hall, I rushed in stopping at the doorway. Both my parents were asleep in individual beds resting. "Are they, okay?" I asked softly, the nurse nodded her head "surprisingly no physical or emotional damage was done to them. Whoever held them hostage took care of them, although due to the years spent in captivity, they are jumpy and paranoid. They are going to undergo therapy and whatever else they may need." I nod my head tears threatening to spill.

I walked towards them grabbing a chair placing it in between the two of them. They both slowly open their eye's jumping back seeing me, "sorry, sorry" I rushed out in a whisper not meaning to startle them. "No, no. It's okay mariposa" mama whispered softly, "we just" I cut her off nodding my head knowing what she's going to say. "I'm so sorry, I'm so sorry you had to go through that. I'm sorry I never found you, I'm sorry I gave up. I'm so sorry I let you down" I was shocked feeling the tears streaming down my face, my dad opens his arms slowly.

I rush towards him burying my head into his chest, he stiffens but quickly recovers slowly wrapping his arms around me and easing into the hug. "It was never your job, Mariposa. You thought we had died, you ... you thought what you saw was the end." He whispered into my hair, Mama got off the bed and cuddled towards us.

"I'm sorry our death made you spiral and landed you in the hands of Xavier" he whispered. I lifted myself up looking at them whipping the tears from my eyes, "you knew?" I whispered. They nodded their heads shutting their eyes.

"We heard everything" Mama cried softly. "That's why he attacked us. Not for our empire but for you, kidnapped us to get to you. He knew you'd find him eventually" Papa spits. "You heard?" I cried softly, my heart shattering into a million pieces knowing they were under my nose, knowing they heard my screams and cries for them. I shook my head "no" I begged them. They looked at me and widened their eyes, both using their hands to cover their ears like they were trying to block out the screams. They started shouting making me jump back scared, the nurses came rushing in as they quickly pushed me out.

I stood at the door watching them, I turned around my back against the wall sliding down crying. "No, no" I kept repeating over and over as I started banging the back of my head on the wall. "NOOOOO" I shouted feeling myself reach breaking point, my anger was finally at its limit. I tried, I tried to put everything behind me. I tried but now. Now I want them all dead. Xavier and his men, every last one of them. I was going to be the one to put an end to him and his fucking line.

"Isabella?" Vincenzo calls out looking down at me, I look up tears stained my face, my cheeks flushing red. "They heard" I whispered. He looked down at me confused. "They heard my screams, my pleas. They heard him torture me" I shouted, "Isabella get up come with me" he grabbed my arms lifting me up. I turned around seeing my parents yelling "let her go! ISABELLA IM SORRY"

"NO" I shouted, guilt consuming me.

FLASHBACK (TW! MILD SEXUAL ASSAULT)

"NO" I shouted trying to shuffle away, my hands and legs bound my chains. "FUCK YOU" I spat at him as he tried climbing on top of me. I kept shuffling and thrashing my body trying to make it impossible for him to get onto me. "Please." I cried out feeling so hopeless and defenceless, never feeling as weak as I did right now. "You're mine Isabella, like it or not. I've marked your soul in one way or another, you're mine" He mocks laughing at me.

I shake my head crying. He slaps me across my cheek. My face hitting the cold metal floors as a cry escaped my lips, "I will burn you alive for everything you did" I threaten him, holding back the tears that threatened to fall. My cheek stinging as I watched his face grow cold, "I will make you fucking burn as I set you on fire like you set my soul on fire." I yelled trying to get him off me.

"You will one day be under my power, and it'll be too late for you. I just need to break you, break you to the point of no return" he yelled like he was trying to make someone else hear what he was saying. I shook my head "you'll never break me" I hissed determined "you might think you broke me, but I'll fix myself. I'll be back and when I am you're dead".

He slaps me across the face, punching me repeatedly in the stomach. Ripping my pants off, I let out a scream. A cry of panic, screaming, shouting, yelling, screeching. "PAPA! MAMA! HELP ME PLEASE" I cried looking up, hoping they could hear my cry for help. I shook my head my eyes shut, "look away please" I cried out. Not wanting them to see this hoping if they can hear me or see me. They would look elsewhere. Protect Maria, it's too late for me now.

END OF FLASHBACK

Vincenzo hugged me close to his chest, I clung to him like a baby. My whole body trembled. Vincenzo took me out of the clinic and sat me on the grass outside, he calmly hugged me closer to him. Tightening his embrace around me, "I've got you." He reassured me putting his cheek on my head, "no one can hurt you as long as I've got you" He whispered. I cried out holding onto him feeling relived, calm, and grateful for Vincenzo.

X

After a while I finally calmed down, I eased my grip around Vincenzo but still hung onto him not ready to fully let go. "I want him dead" my voice coming out horse, but stern. "Just name him" he quickly responded. I lifted my head up looking at him.

"You would really kill for me?" I asked shocked at his fast response. "I would give you the world all you have to do is ask and its yours" he whispered. I sat there looking at him clinging to every word, "You want someone dead? Done." He kissed the top of my head.

"You want to explore the world? Done." another kiss, "You want to be the only three people alive? Fucking done." Another kiss.

"If you want to watch the world burn?" I smiled "You'd burn it?" I asked him. He leaned back still holding me, he smirked looking down "No. I'd hand you the match and watch you set the world on fire as it did you. I'd proudly watch you become queen of all that has fallen." He smiled looking down at me, and for once for a split second. It felt like I was back, back at the horse ranch. "Give me the name" he sternly spoke cutting me out of my daydream. "Xavier" I spoke out, he nodded his head. "Done" he stood up, "where are you going?" I questioned running after him. "To get him for you, because you're going to be the one to end him that was always the plan" he stated.

I stopped in front of him causing him to come to a halt, "the plan?" I questioned. "I always planned to bring him to you, to make him cower at your feet. No one touches you and gets away with it ... But this one, I'll let you deal with" he puts his anger and thirst for revenge aside letting me take full control.

I smiled "don't be silly, we can set him on fire together" I smirk. He looks at me shaking his head "what a plot twist you are Isabella Knight".

I go to reply before my eyes land on the men now chasing Ariana around the estate garden trying to get Dante off her. I laughed shaking my head, Vincenzo turned to see what I was laughing at. His eyes widened seeing them running around with Dante. "ARIANA" He yelled, they all came to a halt "Vincenzo it's okay, look Dante's laughing" I pointed out Dante's wide grin. "I don't think I have ever seen him that- and he's gone" I throw my hand up looking at the smoke coming out of Vincenzo ears.

I rush after him, his men and Ariana stand still watching him holding Dante, he takes him out of the seat holding him in his arms "Hey buddy did you get bigger?" he asks him analysing him as he held up him. I stood there watching him. "Isabella, does he look dizzy to you?" he asks me.

"He looks like he's going to throw up. Maybe we should take him to the doctors" I shook my head rolling my eyes.

"Vincenzo, babies spit up its normal and Dante is looking at you with the biggest smile on his face." I point out, he looks back at Dante smiling.

"You're bored back at home with mum, aren't you? You like the action like your dad huh?" He laughed. They all watched Vincenzo in awe, "who knew?" Hacker cried out, whipping a fake tear from under his eyes.

"Our boy's a dad, AND A FUCKING GOOD ONE" He buried his head in bullseye's chest fake crying. The rest of the men joined all hugging bullseye fake crying at the sight of Vincenzo being a dad. I laughed shaking my head, Dante turned his head towards them and let out a giggle. "OH MY GOD," I squealed hearing his laugh. I stood in front of him, "they're silly huh?" I baby talked, "a little stupid but funny" I smiled wide nodding my head, "do you wanna stay here for the night?" I asked him, he smiled slightly jumping back. I laughed, looking up at Vincenzo he looked at me with a wide smile, "really?" I sighed nodding my head.

"I think he likes it more here" I admit smiling. "It's just for the night, I'll see how I go" I quickly point out. He nods his head. "OH MY GOD! Dante is having a sleepover with the guys" the boys cheered, I raised an eyebrow at them "he's sleeping with me, but in the morning you're more than welcome to take him while I sleep in" I shrugged my shoulders.

"Fine but if you see a shadow ... or two ... or eight creep inside the room in the middle of the night. Don't scream you'll wake up the baby" Hacker scratched the back of his neck sheepishly smiling at me.

I shook my head "and if I stab or shoot at these 'shadows' don't scream you'll wake up baby" I whispered in a hush mocking tone.

"Okay, so no sleepwalking" Bullseye snapped his fingers. I shook my head smiling "Isabella is definitely back on the estate." Hacker smiles shaking his head at my threat, "you all missed me don't lie" I smiled.

"Isabella!" Lorenzo yelled rushing towards me, I turned to look at him. "What's wrong?" I rushed out, he came in between me and Vincenzo indicating for the both of us to look at his screen. It was the surveillance cameras for the house, my eyes widen seeing Xavier and his men surrounding the area, "I KNOW YOU TOOK THEM, WHERE ARE THEY?" He roars, I look at Vincenzo worried then back at the screen.

"I'm coming for you Dragon, you and dragon junior" He smirked holding up one of Dante's shirts.

My chest rose and fell, my hands balled into a fist. "Burn it" he instructed his men, and within seconds his men went to the house to lit it on fire burning it to the floor. Lorenzo shut the iPad and looked at us "Isabella I'm so sorry" He apologised knowing how much that house meant to me. I shook my head "Fuck the house right now, he knows about Dante".

I never saw Vincenzo this mad in my years of knowing him, his body completely tensed. His jaw clenched. His eyes were as dark as the night. His face ... his face was dangerously tensed you could see his veins popping out from his neck and forehead.

"You both stay here from now on." He ordered, I nodded my head knowing it was the safest option. "Men." He called for his men, soon enough we were surrounded "our main mission." He handed Dante over to me to not scare him, Vincenzo was still fuming at the idea of anyone touching us.

He looked back at everyone who gathered around, "Kill Xavier and wipe out his entire fucking line" He spat.

THE SANCTUARY

Isabella's POV

It took Vincenzo three months to find us a new sanctuary, a new home and I couldn't believe it. I stood there frozen almost not wanting to believe what I saw on the security footage, not wanting to believe that we weren't safe. Not wanting to believe that the only shred of the old Vincenzo I had left was burnt to the ground. I refuse to believe any of it.

I looked around watching everyone running around to secure their safety everyone packing up their belongings and ridding any traces of our next destination, getting rid of any existence the King's once had in this home. I felt a whirl of emotions rushing through me, but denial seemed to be the strongest form of emotion. I didn't want to believe we were simply forgetting all that we went through in this estate, every inch of this land held a story, held a memory, held a burst of emotion. The secrets the walls hide and keep safe, now gone to keep another's secret hidden. I looked in my lap seeing Dante sleeping softly after a long eventful night I sighed sliding back into the bed. I put him down beside me and walk towards the window. Looking out I couldn't help but feel bitter.

Everything was always being taken from me and it was always due to him, he took my parents away from me, they're alive yet I wished I never saw them in the state they were in. Alive but traumatised. My son was now his next target, my life was his final destination, and it terrifies me the lengths he might go to in order to get it.

What settles my mind is the lengths I and Vincenzo will go to protect Dante … would Vincenzo go to any length to protect me? I fluttered my eyes closed reminiscing about all the good memories I once shared in this home, in this very room. "Isabella?" I turned to the door and saw Lorenzo peeking in, I smiled and waved him in. "How's Dante adjusting?" I let out a small puff of air ruffling my hand through my hair. "Better than I expected, I think his tried form all the running around" I laughed.

Lorenzo looks up at me "how about you?" He cautiously asks. I turn my gaze from Dante to Lorenzo, I bite my bottom lip before nodding slowly, "I can't believe I'm back, and I can't believe I'm already leaving." I state.

"Vincenzo wants to make sure all precaution is taken, he wants Dante, you, and the rest of his men safe. They managed to break in once before …" he winced recalling the painful memory. "He won't take that chance again, and quite frankly neither will I." I nodded my head in agreement, "where is he?" I asked, he looked at me and nodded his head towards his office. "Can you stay with him for a minute?" I asked softly. He nodded his head and took his place next to Dante. I thanked him and quickly made my way towards Vincenzo's office. After everything we've been through, I knew him well enough to know he doesn't like feeling cornered or helpless, and Vincenzo hates. Making. Mistake's and his been wallowing for three months.

"Vincenzo?" I knocked on the door softly calling out his name, his back turned to me as he was ruffling through a bunch of papers on his desk. His back muscles moved intensely with every movement, sweat was visible on his back and his stressed state could be seen from a mile away. I stepped closer edging slowly not wanting to set him off, "this isn't your fault" I whispered. He grabbed the glass of bourbon and viscously throwing it against the wall. The loose papers he had in his hand now scattered on the floor as he swiped everything off his desk. "Vin-"

"Don't." He warned still not turning around to look me in the face, I went to say something, but he cut me off again. "Isabella don't" I let out a defeated sigh and turned around to walk away before something caught my eye. A baby's desk in a box, I smirked softly and bent down towards it "what's this?" I whispered softly. I opened the box seeing all the parts to build a mini desk for a little kid. "Is this desk for Dante?" I laughed softly, the smile on my face becoming impossible to wipe off. I turned to look at Vincenzo, his back still turned, hands gripping the edge of the desk his back muscles tense keeping his head down. I let go of the box and walked towards him, I stood behind him and without hesitation hugged him from behind, my arms wrapped around his waist protectively while I nuzzled my head against his back.

"Listen to me this isn't your fault" I whispered. Under my touch he relaxed slightly, his white knuckles going back to its original shade his tense stature now calming down his body immediately reacting to my touch. "Yes. It is" he insisted. "Until I entered your life again, you and Dante were safe.

You are getting out of this house was the greatest gift I could've given to you and our son. Now I selfishly took it from you and now your back in a live or die situation." He vented feeling defeated.

I stood back offended on his behalf, "Vincenzo look at me" I demanded, "Vincenzo, it's unwise to piss off a Hispanic women who hasn't had a decent sleep in a year." I warned him lowly, he let a small laugh escape his lips before he finally turned around to face me.

"My life was already in danger long before I met you. I was in a deep hole and the more I ran the more I dug myself deeper. Our meeting wasn't conventional but without it I would've been dead a long time ago … or back in that basement." I bit back tears as I looked up at him.

"When you were lost … and everyone thought you died." I took a shaky breath and moved my hair out of my face, "all I remember was thinking that you can't be dead, you promised me to insanity, and we haven't reached it yet. You promised me you'd be back, and you don't break promises." His eyes softened as he hung onto every word I said, "even though when you came back, you didn't know who I was I didn't care

I was just happy to have you back again. The fighting and the lack of trust could be fixed but if you weren't in my life nothing could fix it." I took a small step closer, "Dante is lucky to have a dad like you, a dad that will go to the end of the world to protect him, a dad that wants his son next to him at all times that you bought him a mini desk" I laughed looking behind me at the box that stood next to the door.

"Xavier isn't your fault. Its mine and it always has been mine. He is after me and I should've known he would use what's dearest to me to get me. He killed Maria, and now he will kill you and my son to secure me. This isn't your mistake its mine" I admitted my eyes glazing over.

"No. He is just as much my enemy as he is yours, and together we will get rid of him. He stole Dante from me once, I won't give him touch my son" I nodded my head smiling, he pulled me into a protective hug and I stayed there for a second, it's been a long time since I felt like we were back to what we once were. That small moment we had that vanished as fast as it came. "ISABELLA DANTE'S HUNGRY AND MY NIPPLES DON'T OPERATE LIKE THAT" Lorenzo shouted across the hall, I sniffled a laugh and shook my head. "Duty calls" I saluted and made my way out of his office.

X

I looked over at Dante who was wide awake, trying to get my attention. I giggled and sat up right grabbing him, "you're getting big huh?" I baby talked, "you're becoming a big boy" I sang, he laughed looking at my facial expressions. "Oh, you got your aunties cheeky laugh" I blew into his stomach, he gripped my hair and let out a baby chuckle. I kept doing it until his grip eased slightly, "oh mummy's going to have no hair" I frowned to which he giggled. "Cheeky boy" I glared him.

A knock on my door snapped me out of it. Ariana peeked her head in followed by Lorenzo, "we heard talking and laughing and wondered why we weren't apart of it" I rolled my eyes laughing.

Inviting themselves in they plopped on my bed and took Dante and started playing with him. "Do you mind watching him for a little while I go check on my parents and the move." They nodded their heads empathetically. I quickly slipped on my slippers and made my way to the clinic.

"Isabella" the nurse greeted me, I smiled and nodded my head "how are they?" My voice cracking trying to keep it together. "Better than yesterday, they went through physical as well as mental therapy.

We have them on appropriate medication as well, but they are aware of everything they went through but are making promising progress accepting it." I nodded my head. "They've been through worse together, I don't think it was their hostage situation that made them lose it, it was hearing me in the other room crying for them and then them witnessing me break." I thought aloud. The nurse looked at me with sympathetic eyes, I shook my head and went to see them. "Mum? Dad?" I called softly, they turned and looked at me smiling. "mariposa" Mama chimed up. "I'm sorry for scaring you yesterday" she softly whispered. I shook my head "no it's okay … I can't imagine what you went through all those years." I whispered lowering my head feeling guilty.

"I'm sorry I gave up" I whispered, referencing so many things, giving up on avenging them, giving up on my family, and on myself. My dad edged closer and hesitantly embraced me in a hug, he sighed easing into it "that wasn't your fault, were sorry we couldn't save you when you called out." He whispered trying not to break down, I shook my head whipping a tear that escaped. "No. I could take it. You did raise me to be tough" I smiled. He weakly smiled back knowing that was a lie, that I took it, but I broke down eventually that I became numb to everything and everyone. "Isabella … is it true?" My mum chimed up, I turned to look at her and judging from her facial expressions I knew exactly what she was referring to. I gulped and lowered my head "Oh my god" she whispered holding her hand to her mouth, "my flower died?" She softly cried. I bit my bottom lip shutting my eyes closed, nodding my head slowly. "She made me promise her something." I whispered softly.

I let out a deep breath before getting the courage to look at them, "She wanted me to tell you that, she missed you both and loves you both more than anything." They both held nodded their heads smiling through the tears that escaped their eyes. I cleared my throat before continuing "Maria wanted me to tell you Mama that she still checked up on the flower shop and that she planted the seeds you gave her. She didn't want anyone to mourn her passing.

She wanted us to bathe and remember her life for what she was to remember that even though she's gone now Maria will always be around. She told me to tell you both that when you miss her look at the flowers or the waves at sea and know she's there." I took another deep breath wanting to just break down and cry, but I cleared my throat. I promised Maria, I'd tell them when I found them, I reminded myself and looked at Dad. "She wanted me to tell Papa that she tried to keep me out of trouble and that she loves you so much. That you were her rock and her role model the man she wanted in a husband and the man she knows is going to be the best Abuelo" I finished. Their eyes winded, "Abuelo?" They both questioned. "You both became grandparents a month ago." I smiled softly, "you and X-" I quickly cut off my mum not wanting her to finish that name. "Vincenzo" I corrected them. They both nodded their heads relieved. "What did you call him?" She whispered, "Dante" I whispered.

They both awed, Vincenzo tapped on the glass softly letting me know it was time for us all to go. I nodded my head and helped my parents leave the room.

The nurses assisted, "Get Dante and all your things I'll meet you in the car" I nodded my head and rushed back to grab my boy and our things. That consisted of Maria's things that was left behind and Dante's baby bag.

"This is where it all started, can't believe it got taken from us" I whispered holding Dante on my hip, he gripped my shirt biting his bottom lip looking around cluelessly. I laughed looking at him "Oh how I wish I could be as clueless as you right now amor" I kissed his forehead and made my way out of the room closing the door behind me. Vincenzo grabbed Dante from me holding him up giving him a kiss, "Leone" he boosted holding him up full of pride. I shook my head looking at the two, Dante was giving his dad the biggest grin ever, "careful his drool might fall in your mouth" I laughed. Every man was now locked and loaded the estate looked like no man's land, I let out a bittersweet sigh and got inside the car. I jumped in the back of the range rover putting Dante in his seat, then taking my seat in the passenger's seat next to

Vincenzo. Ariana and Lorenzo joined us and sat beside Dante in the back.

"Where are we going?" I questioned.

"Somewhere safe" he replied taking off.

X

What felt like days on the road we finally arrived at the location. I looked out the window and saw an unfamiliar ground. "We're here" Vincenzo spoke up, I looked at him with an eyebrow raised "we are in the middle of nowhere. It's all trees" I pointed out. He looked at me and sarcastically smiled, "that's the point." He took a sharp turn and the further into the forest we got the trees began to clear and revealed a gorgeous mansion smack in the middle of the land. My eyes widened looking at the beautiful scenery in front of me, the mansion was black, and a gorgeous fountain was centred in the middle of the estate. It was big enough to fit all his men in the one house, it was two stories high and wider than the eyes can see. Accompanied with two pool houses along with an onsite clinic like our previous home. We all got down from the cars and rushed inside excited to see the new home. Vincenzo grabs my upper arm and leads me to the master bedroom, in the room was an ensuite a massive bed in the middle and a baby's crib on the side of the bed. I looked back at him with a raised eyebrow. "We are sharing?" I questioned.

He shrugged his shoulders "not enough rooms" he responded. I laughed "this big ass mansion doesn't have enough rooms?" I sarcastically responded. "Ironic, isn't it?" he sheepishly smiled at me standing in the door frame. I stared at him slightly frustrated at his distant behaviour.

"I don't want to share a room with you" I speak up knowing damn well I did in fact want to share the same bed with him I just wanted to piss him off a little.

He doesn't even acknowledge what I said and continues to unpack his things, I roll my eyes and snatch the top from his hands and throw it to the other side of the room. He looks down at me hovering above me, backing away I hit the edge of the bed, I fell on my back and Vincenzo climbed over me. I feel my chest tighten at the sudden dominance and at the mere inches between us. "I don't want to share a bed" I repeat myself, still saying nothing he just looks down over me his hands cornering me in. Waiting for me to cave. "Are you listening?" I bite frustrated pushing him away, "No." He finally breaks his silence I groan frustrated "I-" before I could finish my sentence, he harshly cuts me off.

"Isabella enough." He warns lowly his voice becoming deeper than usual and his Italian accent becoming a lot heavier which use to be my indication to shut the fuck up. Not this time, If I'm dealing with the old Vincenzo, I need to be the old Isabella the one who didn't know him. "No. You don't get the right to Isabella me anymore!" My voice stern as I watch the veins in his neck beginning to poke through, "the days of you ordering me around are gone." I warned him knowing full well it was going to set him off. One thing the old Vincenzo could never do was give up or lose power, "You're staying in this fucking bedroom I don't care if you like the fucking idea or not. You don't to share the bed? Sleep on the couch" He responded clearly trying to keep his cool.

I scoffed "how noble of you" I bite, he scoffed. "I'm not exactly a beacon of good behaviour doll" He stood up and walked towards the door I groan frustrated "don't fucking call me that!" I yelled throwing a pillow at his head. He dodged it easily making me even more agitated "Stop. Fucking. Dodging. IT!" In between every word I threw whatever I could get hands on, pillows, clothes, hats even Dante's bottles.

"Listen. You don't have much of a choice. You either stay in this bedroom or you can go back to that burnt down house doll. Up to you" he spat visibly reaching his limit. "You'd rather send me to ashes then let me have my own room?" I argue logic my breathing becoming heavier like I just ran a marathon. "YES, ISABELLA YES I WOULD." He shouted finally giving me the satisfaction that I was still the only one to get him to reach this level of anger.

"Yelling? That's very amateur of you … boss" I mocked him enjoying it more than I probably should, standing up getting in his face, "Isabella." His voice deep and rigid.

When he speaks, his deep voice, his Italian accent the way his authority twirls around his words is magnetic to the core of who I am, as if he's able to resonate with all of me when others can barely achieve a fraction of it.

I stared back at him blankly not saying a word, both of us stayed like that for a moment staring at each other and in that moment behind his cold Icy stare was a mountain of pain yet extracting it would bring pain and instability. Either he'll remember and our souls can once again be reborn, or he would lash out and it would be forever over. But staring at his hard gaze that held no emotion, this was the moment I made the unconscious decision that he … we are worth a real attempt.

"Get out" he finally whispers looking slightly defeated like he was trying with every cell in his body not to yell and scream. "No" I stood my ground, "you want to yell? Yell. You want to fight? Fucking fight me, but don't you dare shut me out or push me to the side like I'm not real because I'm fucking real!" I started losing control feeling like no matter what he was always ready to shut me out, to turn his back on me.

"I can handle you" I harshly whispered standing my ground. Faster than I could comprehend he had a tight grip on my arms slamming me into the wall "Don't!" He yelled. His mismatched eyes bored in mine.

"Don't ever. Try to get inside my head," he snarled, slamming me against the wall. I didn't move, not even flinch at his outburst instead I continued to stare into his eyes, watching his internal battle. He moved his hands from my arm to my neck his grip on my neck was never tight, and it didn't hurt. I knew what he was doing, I knew he was trying to scare me, but little did he remember I don't scare easily. Ironically it was turning me on.

We stayed like this for a minute, finally his eyes softened ever so lightly. "It's too dark for you" he trailed off. "You're doing it on purpose aren't you?" I whispered realisation settling in, he looked at me his eyes telling me he knew exactly what I was talking about. "What?" He questioned trying to act coy. "Don't fucking do that" I shouted pushing him off me, I shoved him back grabbing the lamp on the bedside throwing it at him. He dodged it quickly the lamp shattered into pieces colliding with the wall behind him. "You don't want to remember me, do you?" I shouted, "You can't stand the fact that I knew you. I FUCKING KNOW YOU!" I yelled. He sighed ignoring me and walking off, "Don't fucking turn your back on me" I warned him. He stood in the doorway for a second before he walked off anyway. I let out a frustrated yell, losing all control. I stormed out of the room following him to his new office, his new men stood in front of me stopping me from going inside. "Vincenzo, I swear I will unleash hell on earth if you don't make them Move." I warned him lowly my voice now matched his from earlier. Dangerous and daring.

His men immediately moved aside after seeing the other men indicating for them to get out of my way. "Do not let her in!" He shouted, "are you my men or hers?" He roared both of us clearly reaching our limits. "I wasn't finished" I yelled, he smirked and shrugged his shoulders "I was" he slammed his office doors shut. "Isabella … I usually don't bud in, but boss has a meeting with the five families soon, and they shouldn't see his authority being tested by you" I looked at hacker confused "what?" I snapped, he flinched stepping back "We all know you, your past, who you are. The family doesn't they won't see you as his equal they'll see you as a member who stepped out of line" I rolled my eyes huffing.

"Fine. This isn't over" I shouted making sure he heard me,
I looked at Hacker confused "wait shouldn't you go in?" I
asked knowing the boss, underboss and capo had to be
present during the meetings. He whined slightly and gave me
my son back. I watched Hacker get Vincenzo and walk off
towards a new meeting room. He stands in front of me the
both of us not breaking eye contact, none of us willing to
bow down to the other. I never have and I never will be a
weak sensitive girl, this conversation was not over. Hacker
cleared his throat forcing Vincenzo's eyes to leave mine. I
followed behind them slowly towards board meeting and
every trusted member of each family stood at the door
guarding it while their bosses walked inside. Vincenzo
ordering the men to close the doors behind him.

I let out a frustrated sigh, "Isabella" Ariana calls out my
name, she comes towards me playing with Dante's cheeks as
he lays his head on my chest. He should be due for a feed
soon, "do you mind holding him for a second while I go
make his bottle?" I ask without wasting time she snatches
Dante from me and ushers me off.

"Hi cucciolo" she cooed kissing him repeatedly on the cheek. I smiled quickly rushing off to get his bottle ready before his happy mood turns into a mini-Vincenzo.

X

Shaking the bottle, I walk around trying to find Ariana when I spot her, she's trying to get him to stop crying, I smile gesturing her to give me him. "Can I feed him please?" She begs giving me puppy dog eyes. I handed her the bottle letting her feed him. Looking up I wonder what they were discussing inside, if it's got to do with Xavier I should be inside. I huffed and stood up, since when the fuck did, I wait to be invited in. I walked confidently towards the office doors ignoring Ariana's harsh whispers calling me back. "Excuse me ma'am you can't come in" One of the men speak up, I raise an eyebrow at him and Vincenzo and Garcia's men sigh knowing exactly where this was headed, especially after hearing mine and Vincenzo's screaming battle. "Here we go" the whispered and took a step back knowing better than to get in my way.

Vincenzo's POV

We all stood for a moment as a show of respect exchanging nods, we take our seats. my mind couldn't wrap around the fact that she laughed in my face. Her laugh vibrated against my hand that was wrapped around her fucking neck … and she laughed. Her laughed ringed in my ears, she was pressed to the wall, and she fucking laughed. "I hear congratulations are in order" Samuel speaks up first, I smile giving him a firm nod snapping out of it. "Grazie Samuel" soon everyone joins in congratulating me "you had a son and didn't invite the families for his baptism" John speaks up offended. I clear my throat looking at the five families.

"Gentlemen, I myself have not had the time to baptise my son due to the threat hanging over my head." I finally address the issue of our meeting.

"Usually, I would handle business on my own, as we all take care of our individual families to how we see fit. However, this issue unfortunately is a threat not only to my family but to each family here" Getting their attention they all edge closer looking at me waiting for me to elaborate further. "The threat that is Xavier, who was a meaningless pity street gang has since evolved without our knowing." I admit that I may have overlooked his growth. "He was only a threat to Isabella Knight, until I discovered he was the man who killed my twin brother Dante." I revealed letting the news sink in.

Mummers were heard among the table everyone sharing the same shocked and enraged expression. "Through my informants it's been exposed to me that Xavier has joined forces with the Salvatore's and is ultimately trying to take over. Not just the Salvatore's but my city and spot on the five families." I balled my hands into fists trying to contain my rage.

"This is not just an insult to me but to all sitting before me. Since our decision to terminate Sammy Salvatore, Xavier has promised the family revenge against us all." If no one was paying attention, they all are now. "How can they possibly take on the five families. We individually all outnumber them" Garcia being the first to speak up. I nod my head agreeing, "Si, we do however he is planning a sneak attack. One that won't be expected and judging from his new status he can make that happen".

"Why did he even come to New York?" Samuel angrily voiced his frustration. I sigh because I couldn't remember the reason for his presence in my city. Lorenzo sees the confusion on my face and speaks up "he came to retrieve Isabella" My head snapped towards him "She is not her property" I whispered lowly, realising we are in a board room I quickly fix my posture and turn back towards the group.

Garcia giving me a smug smirk trying not to laugh as the rest stared at me slightly confused, I cleared my throat once again and looked up at the board regaining composure. "As I was saying the promise, he gave to the Salvatore's of revenge against the biggest mafia families and specifically me has gained him a lot of followers and respect for his bold promise. Stupid promise but nonetheless" I continued explaining how this matter no longer involved my family alone. "If this Xavier person came for Isabella, why should we all be dragged into this mess." Samuel speaks up, I inhale deeply trying to remain calm, "Correct me if I'm wrong Samuel but since when did we ever offshore a woman to solve our problems?" The board all looking towards Samuel.

His underboss and capo remained silent keeping their hard gaze fixated on me. "She started this mess. It's her responsibility to clean it up." He spits getting enraged at my comment slamming his hands on the table as he stands up. "Samuel, do you know who Isabella is?" Garcia piped in calmly looking at Samuel.

"No. Nor do I care" he replies smug, Hacker and Lorenzo giving him a hard stare clearly not impressed by his comments about Isabella. I cleared my throat "She's someone you do not want to cross" I responded equally as smug, despite my anger towards her right now it was true, she was the only person who I ever saw as my equal, the minute I saw her I knew why I would have been intrigued by her. He shoots his head towards me "I think I might" he threatens. I chuckle amused, "be my guest." Gesturing to the door knowing full well Isabella has somehow managed to eavesdrop on the meeting and gotten through all the men guarding the door.

If on cue the doors opened wide with all the security behind her on their knees, their belts used to restrain their hands all bowed before her aside from my own and Garcia's men, probably knowing best to just let her be. Even with my memory I know Isabella is not someone who easily backs down. She smirks widely proud of herself, "for someone who has been on maternity I still got it" she smiles looking at Garcia before taking her place next to me. She glares and I match her energy knowing her little show was about to make one hell of a fight. Hacker and Lorenzo look as though they are about to burst out laughing. I gave them a hard look warning them to remain professional which was hard to do myself.

The heads of the families all stand up shocked and frustrated, "tying our men is a sign of disrespect" John shouts looking embarrassed that Isabella was able to control and restrain all the men solo.

Isabella smiles calmly looking at John "No. What's disrespectful is trying to find someone to blame. For a problem that was created by many" she comments, I look at her confused. "You all assigned the death of Mr. Salvatore" she smiled looking at everyone in the room. They all looked at her shocked at her knowledge on the matter. I shoot her a glare, gripping her upper arm I harshly whisper in her ear "stop it" She snatches her arm out of my grip continuing her speech. "It was common sense really, only the elite families can authorise and carry out such an assassination it was too precise and well executed to be a rival gang. The mafia Don's don't die unless they break one of the commandments, meaning only someone of a higher rank could get a hold of such information." She elaborates, I looked at her shocked and amused at her knowledge of how we conduct business.

"I know this because no petty gang has feds on their payroll, it didn't take much to figure out. Being the five families only you could attain such information so quickly, besides being involved in crime all my life I picked up a few things" she cockily smirked looking at everyone, but I knew that last sentence was a dig at me. **I can handle you'** Her voice echoed in my head like a taunt. "The kill was also very clean, that's how I know Vincenzo personally executed it" She smiled looking up at me, I looked down her at her. Her eyes sliced through mine and the way she flicked her tongue to the edge of her mouth sent a chill down my back.

She was right and she fucking knew it. "How did you?" Samuel speaks up after a minute of silence his surprise visible on his face as he tried to decipher her. Huh yea good luck with that, I mentally thought to myself.

She ignored him and continued. "When I had a target, I wanted dead, especially if he was a higher rank. I wouldn't kill him straight away; it's too easy law enforcement would clearly focus on the first victim. Believing it was the intended target" she elaborated, "as an experienced assassin myself you learn to account for timing, after the first shot, no one moves." She stops midway and looks up at me waiting for me to continue. Like by being able to know my train of thought she was proving she's already been inside my head. "People are stunned looking to see where the noise came from trying to figure out what just happened" I elaborated further like she planned her satisfied smirk making my entire body tense at just how well she knows me proving her point.

"Exactly everyone's reaction is to look for the source of the sound, after the second shot it takes the average person-" she waves her hand "one and a half seconds to cognitively process that they're in a death like situation".
"It takes another seven seconds for a physical response to kick in. By which time the sniper already would have shot for

the third time. The ability to kill certain people will send an immediate message to Mr. Salvatore that those hits were meant for him. I know that Mr. King would have targeted men within his inner circle to seal the deal guaranteeing that Mr. Salvatore will get so scared he will think he survived by some miracle because Vincenzo King never misses. Forcing him to go into hiding in which he would be in a need-to-know spot secluding him from social contact and law enforcement. That's when Vincenzo took his time watching the fear in his eyes as he held his life in his hands" she smiled into the distance like she was reminiscing. "How do you know all this?" John questioned, "Because that was also my own method" she smirked proud, "Do you know who I am yet?" She whispered tiling her head towards Samuel with a devilish spark twinkling in her eyes.

The don's men slowly backing away as realisation overcame them, Isabella's smile widened like she missed those reactions, missed seeing the fear in people's eyes as they finally dawn on who she is and what she can do without thinking twice. "I thought you died in Spain" Samuel's underboss speaks up, she tilts her head the tip of her tongue tracing her teeth "Don't blame them, it wasn't from a lack of trying" she pouts. Before she laughs, Lorenzo looked at Isabella cautiously almost knowingly. "She's back" he mouthed to Hacker and me.

I looked at him confused 'she's back?' I knew Isabella was capable of many things, I witnessed her first hand when she was interrogating the man about her parents. My body shivered like it sensed danger, like my unconscious self knew exactly what Lorenzo meant.

"WHO IS SHE!" Samuel grew frustrated slamming his fits on the table disliking being kept out of the loop. "Dragon" she whispered coming out more like a threat. Fear immediately sinking in every man sitting on the board even Garcia had goosebumps rising on his skin and he knew who she is. "You not scaring anyone" John gulped, she smiled "There is nothing scarier than an eternity on your own, nothing and nobody to talk to. Eventually I asked for the pain just to feel something." She bit edging closer to the desk resting her palms on the table. "You'd ask for pain just to feel something" Michele asked softly, "Countless months of torture and solitude will do that to a person." She clarifies.

"It forces you to unlock a side of you, you never thought existed. No compassion, no remorse, your soul turns to the dark side without an ounce of hope. Some fight it and some accept the darkness allowing themselves to become one with it rather than letting it take your life." She looked into the distance most likely picturing herself back in that time. Knowing exactly what she meant I spoke up on her behalf, "so why not join the dark side? Why choose to be alone in your madness? Let the darkness show you the pleasure of cruelty, the joy of power. You'll find it so pleasurable. Inside you are one of us, we've seen it in you. You aren't pure enough to make it through the gates. So why live in-between the light and the dark? After all, what is there to be afraid of when you are the monster?" I looked at her, she looked up at me stunned. I knew exactly what she meant.

She smiled before quickly looking back at the board. "I don't play games, I know you are discussing Xavier and being his main target, I want in, but only Vincenzo and I decide how we kill him and if that means burning him so be it" she makes her conditions clear as crystal.

"You may have power in Spain b-"

"She has power everywhere" Garcia cuts Michele off swiftly.

"It's a mistake to underestimate her" I add in looking at her, she looks up at me surprised before regaining her composure. "I would have loved to handle him on my own, but seeing as though he now made a threat to each individual here making your own power unsteady, I suggest you let me help and agree to my terms." She takes her seat next to me knowing they had no other choice but to accept.

Everyone sits back down still on edge "I have been in meetings like this, done business with many Bosses much scarier than any of you and have done many things to make my name so well-known and feared. So, let's throw out trying to mansplain everything and let's talk business head on." She warns the group her comments more specifically targeted to me.

X

After about thirty minutes of the two of us and the board exchanging deals, we finally come to an agreement. We get to dispose of Xavier as we see fit and the rest of the men can do what they please with Salvatore's son and his men. "What do you need from us?" John asked the both of us.

"Men, if what we are planning is going to take effect. We need more manpower than before." I explained the men all nodding their heads in agreement.

"We are with you Vincenzo just say the word and you'll have as many as you desire" Garcia graciously speaks up.

"Just make sure that son of a bitch suffers" Garcia looks towards Isabella, she smiles giving him a wink "that's one thing I can guarantee" I turn my head to look at her, her face still facing Garcia and the rest of the board. I sigh trying to keep my head straight before turning to the rest of the gentlemen.

X

Isabella's POV

I knew he wasn't going to be happy with how I conducted myself, or how I tested their authority. Especially for my show of disrespect if I wasn't who I am I would have been shot dead without a second thought. The only thing that saved me was that side of me. I lay back in my seat, leaning my head back trying to mentally prepare for the battle to come. My body jumps up hearing the doors slam shut, "What the fuck was that?" He yells grabbing the arms of the chair swinging me out. He corners me in both his hands gripped the arms chair.

"What was what?" I raised an eyebrow acting dumb, "Isabella don't act oblivious, that was the stupidest thing you could have fucking done. Making their men kneel!" He roared obviously reaching his limit.

"They kneeled to their superior" I bit back, my eyes narrowed staring into his refusing to back down. "What about you?" He whispered looking at me. I raised my eyebrow "me what?' I questioned.

"Are you going to kneel?" He playfully asked taunting me, power laced in his words just like before. My breathing hitched "what's wrong doll?" He purred, I looked away furious that's not my fucking nickname. "Call me that one more time, and I promise I'll have your lucky knife in a very unlucky position" I threatened trying to push him away but failing miserably. His eyes bored into my own, his body stiff and still. Refusing to move an inch, "kneel" he demanded, I looked at him in disbelief scoffing I rolled my eyes. "Never gonna happen Italy".

He smiled stepping back like he was waiting for me to object, he bent down lifting me up by my chin, "Why don't you ever listen?" He asked looking at me then his eyes trailed down to my lips, "it's like you enjoy making me mad, making me violent" he grazed my bottom lip with his thumb before his hand found its rightful spot on my neck.

My breathing started increasing as the moisture in-between my legs started. I clenched my legs shut trying to stop the oh so familiar feeling, his face inches from mine he leaned in.

His lips inches from my ear, "do you like it when I start to get rough amore?" His deep Italian accent was enough to send me over the edge letting out an unconscious moan. I looked shocked at him as he looked at me pleased. "Kneel Isabella" he demanded.

I gulped and looked up at him, slowly kneeling. He smirked satisfied before he kneeled himself, I looked shocked "we are equals" he whispered. "You're the only person to ever make me kneel before them." I continued to stare at him shocked that he was on his knees. This was a surrender of power. He was putting us on the same level.

"However, I have more of a dark side than you may think amore" He stood back up and went to walk away leaving me on the floor.

I looked off wondering, I never actually knew what Vincenzo went through, what his dark side was. I was as blind as he was, I smirked knowing the game his playing at.

Grabbing the gun, I slipped out of his pants, and I aimed it at the wall, pulling the trigger a loud gun fire echoed throughout the estate. He slowly turned back to me "do you think our previous conversation was over?" I teased. "Men shut the door" I shouted as they closed the doors Vincenzo locked the door turning around. "Why?" I questioned allowing myself to finally explode.

"I don't want you" he answered simply "I don't want the memories back. I don't want the thought of you back. I am fighting with every fibre to rid them completely" he explained all to calmly. I bit back tears keeping the gun aimed at him.

"You're lying" I whispered. "Why would I lie?" He whispered back matching my tone of voice. "Because the you I know is fighting to break through. I see it everyday" I add confident in myself he licks the inner corner of his lip proving my theory. "His dead Isabella, the faster you accept that. The easier, the only connection that remains is our son and our need to burn Xavier to the ground" he goes to turn around again.

Before he heard the click of the gun making him turn around amused, "I'm not finished" I threatened through my teeth, my jaw clenched and my face hard. "Why? And I want the real answer not a half assed one" He looked at me staying calm, "You want an answer that doesn't exist Isabella." He explains, "What are you gonna do? You gonna shoot me?" He teases, I roll my eyes my grip on the gun tightening.

"They told me you were gone!" I shouted, finally letting him know how it felt to lose him, not by threats or anger or violence but by the truth. "I screamed. I wailed, I cried, and I screamed. As loud as my lungs allowed me." I admitted my eyes tearing up remembering that awful feeling. His eyes softened looking at me, "I hoped that if I screamed loud enough, you'd hear me wherever you were, and you'd turn around and come back to me." I shook my head biting my lip to fight back the tears. "But instead, you came back but not to me. Watching you, seeing you and not being able to hug you, smell you, feel you! Was worse than death itself. And you have the balls to ask me why I care?" I looked at him in disbelief. "Maybe I should shoot this gun, maybe it will-" before I could finish my sentence, he cuts me off.

"You think knocking me out will miraculously bring my memory back?" He shouts, his voice bouncing off the walls. "DO YOU?" He shouts. I flinch slightly not expecting his sudden anger "Well it won't" he snarls. "I tried" he whispered softly. My eyes tearing up I looked at him swallowing my pride "what?" I asked out of breath.

"I FUCKING TRIED ISABELLA" He roars, "but it doesn't work. Do you really want to fucking know why?!" He snaps I stand keeping my arm steady. He laughs pulling out another gun aiming to my head, I widen my eyes in shock. He smirked like I should've known he carried more than the one gun.

"Why?" I asked, he scoffed looking me dead in the eyes "because you are my biggest weakness, If I remember you, I don't know what'll happen, I don't know what will overcome me. I never want someone to have so much power of me that I chose to fight off the memory of you".

I suck in a breath he pressed the gun to my temple, and I do the same. Was this how it was going to end? Our death at the hands of each other? An unsettling smile overtook his lips his eyes darkened like I've never seen them before "I could easily kill you without any hesitation" he whispered. The hairs on my body standing up looking at him. "Then why don't you?" I questioned not letting him scare me. He smirked "those angelic eyes, they make me weak" he looked deep into my eyes. "Even without any memory of you. I will still let the world around me burn but never let a flame touch you." He admitted.

(Sex scene)

The adrenaline rushing through my body sends me over the edge giving me the confidence I needed. I throw the gun to the side pushing his arm out of the way I smash my lips to his and within an instant his body quickly responds to mine.

His groans into the kiss cupping my face I felt the cold metal on my cheeks. He pulls back lust in his eyes, he drags the gun over my swollen lips "cazzo" he groans out, quickly he picks me up I instantly wrap my legs around his waist. Only Vincenzo King can make me weak in my knees, the only man that can make me dripping wet at the sight of him, the only man I will kneel for.

He bit down on my bottom lip, I arched my head back letting out a low moan, the sound of my moan sent him over the edge "Fuck" he breathed against my lips. In that split second every nerve in my body and brain electrified. He pushed me against the wall, I groaned on impact and quickly found my way back to his mouth.

I grinned against him desperate for friction, "I need to feel you" I whispered against his lips. A deep growl escaped his lips he turns pushing off all the files on the table I excitedly watched it fall to the ground. The tingling sensation erupting in my lower stomach, his lips claim mine again laying me flat on my back against the old glass table.

"Mmmm your already so wet for me amore" he taunts. My chest rising and falling fast he points the gun at my head with a playful smirk.

"Take it off" I watch him my eyes showing the innocence his looking for. "Yes boss" I whisper, he bites his bottom lip shutting his eyes.

"Look at me, I want your eyes on me as I do what you command … please boss" I innocently beg him as I slowly start unbuttoning my blouse revealing my red lace bra.

He sucks in a breath watching me crease myself, "what do you feel baby?" He asked looking down at me not touching me, I pout "hatred" my lips curl tauntingly. He shakes his head he lowers the gun to my pussy pressing it against me. I let out a gasp arching my back grinding into his gun. "I know you feel it." I open my eyes looking at him "feel what?" I asked breathless.

"That hot, pounding pulse between those pretty little thighs" he smirks.

"Your body is just begging me to fill it up." His eyes now alight with nothing but desire.

He smirks knowing he was driving me insane, "Vincenzo Please" I begged him needing to feel him. He tore off my jeans and pressed the gun against me over my wet panties "such a good girl for me" He whispers ripping my panties off, I moan out as the pistol slips inside of me. "Keep your eyes on me" he demands.

I try to open my eyes to look at him, but he picks up speed, towering over me I clench the edge of the table, my body getting hot all over feeling the pistol hitting my G spot. "Look at me Isabella" I forced myself to open my eyes as a loud moan left my lips "Oh fuck".

"If you look away, I'll stop" he whispered against my lips, moving back to watch how my face looks when I moan, I kept my eyes open and on him "I want those pretty green eyes to watch me claim you" Fuck, my toes curl "I'm so close" I whispered breathless "I didn't give you permission to cum Isabella. Wait" he orders, I arched my back further gripping his towering body "Oh god" I cried out. "Don't you dare call for god," He snarled.

"It's my name you're going to be crying".

That was enough to make me explode. I clenched griping him as I let loose, he takes his gun out of my throbbing pussy, it was dripping wet. He presses it to my lips "tell me how you taste" he whispers. Pleasure immediately overtaking my body as I slide the gun all the way in tasting myself.

His lips moved to my own hungry for my taste, his tongue slides over my bottom lip, before he trailed to my neck sucking it, and overwhelming sense of pleasure overcame me as I moaned out for him, he sucked hard making my nails dig into his back. Claiming me as his, after he was satisfied, he licked over the fresh hickey. He leaned down pulling my tits out of my bra taking my nipple in his mouth he sucked on it, his tongue teasing it as his free hand grips my free tit.

My pussy pulsing, I moaned out gripping his hair. He grabs my hand and places it over my pussy, I start playing with myself. He trails kissed along my stomach and with every kiss he raises my legs high and higher, rolling my hips kissing my inner thighs until finally his lips meet mine. He teased it barely kissing it.

I groaned frustrated "Vincenzo fucking take me" I begged him, that was enough to make him finally claim me. His tongue entered me sliding deeper, I gasped out holding his head in place, I arched my back grinding my hips further into him. "Oh fuck" I let the pleasure of his tongue claiming my clit take over.

He picked up speed, before I had time to process, he slips his three fingers in me. I lean forward unable to let the moan out, I shake slightly "that's right baby" he moans against me. I hold his head with both my hands, his fingers picking up godly speed I finally Lean back arching my back.

"Oh Fuck, fuck, fuck! Just like that boss." I moaned out, I was close, he sucked on my clit thrusting his fingers deep and slow, my body shaking as I let loose, my breathing heavy as he looked at me with a satisfied grin, I just orgasmed twice.

I sit up and pull him closer through the loops on his belt, he watches me eagerly, "intoxicating" he comments sucking my juices of his fingers. He leans down smashing his lips to me, not wasting any time I kiss him back undoing his belt and tugging at his pants. "Off" I commanded, "so bossy" he smirked.

He slipped his pants off I knelt in front of him roughly pulling his boxers down, his length bouncing up. "So hard for me" I whispered against it, I held his cock in my hands spitting on it.

I looked up at him with my innocent big green eyes, as I slowly pumped him enjoying watching him moan at my touch. "Isabella" he warned softly and that's all it took for me to take him in my mouth. I pumped his length taking him whole in my mouth, feeling his tip hit the roof of my mouth. I gagged slightly pulling back to take a breath, I moaned "mmm" I laughed softly keeping up my pace with my hand.

I licked his length trailing my tongue all over it, playing with his balls in the process, my tongue traced the tip of his head circling it claiming it as my own. I felt his length grow harder under my touch, he grabbed a fistful of my hair and thrusted in my mouth not being able to take the teasing any longer.

"Oh fuck" He groaned out throat fucking me, bouncing my head on his length while simultaneously thrusting claiming my pretty lips as his "that dirty mouth of yours is mine" he groaned out he took his cock out of my mouth letting me breath, I took in a deep breath letting out a laugh grabbing his length and taking it in my mouth one last time, I played with the top of his foreskin using my lips and tongue to please him.

Hearing his harsh moans and groans only encouraging me further, he roughly picks me up bending me over the table, he extends my arms out in front of me stretching me against the table. My stomach makes contact with the cold glass making me gasp, he spits on my already wet and throbbing pussy.

I squeal when his hand comes in contact with my ass cheek, he slips his cock in me. His cock completely filling me up. I moan out, he doesn't move for a second "what do you want?" He purrs close to my ear. I bit my lip and grind myself against him needing friction. He slaps my cheek again making me jump "say it, Isabella." He punishes me. I let out a loud moan on contact "oh fuck." He stays still, before I finally plea "Vincenzo, I need you to fuck me. Remind me why I crave you" I cried out. He thrusted in me hard making me arch up "fuck" I breathed out.

He starts pumping in and out picking up the pace and getting rougher each time, my pussy throbbed harder than it ever did before. He was proving something he was proving that no matter what I was his and my obedient pussy knew who it belonged to obeying his every move. He picked me up by my throat squeezing while he kept fucking me, "Oh. My. G-" I moaned out unable to finish my sentence a series of moans, and gasp leaving my mouth. Unable to keep up with his pace, I bounce my ass against him needing more wanting more. "So needy" he whispered against my ear his hot breath sending me over the edge. "I'm close" I breathed out. "Cum for me baby" he ordered my pussy. Like an obedient slave my whole body shuddered, unable to stand on my feet feeling my legs turning into jelly about to give out. One last, deep, hard thrust. He took his cock out forcing me to kneel down. "I want my cum on your face" he ordered, he placed his cock in between my breast, thrusting in and out quickly. I stuck my tongue out his head hitting my tongue with every thrust, before he let lose all over my tits. I hummed pleased, massaging my now extremely sensitive pussy using my index finger I pick up the cum from my nipples and suck on my fingers. "Such a good girl"

(End of sex scene)

THE GAME PLAN

Isabella's POV

Dante's little cough snapped me out of my daydream, that was something else. I … we never. Woah, I let out a cough tucking my boob away burping Dante. I rock him for a minute before the milk drunk state takes affect putting him to sleep.

I put him in his bassinet next to my side of the bed, Vincenzo walks in the room wearing nothing but grey sweats that hung dangerously low exposing his sharp V line.

I gulp looking away, my pussy was still sore, but it was always so obedient, always so ready for him. "Isabella" he calls out, I look at him trying to avoid my eyes trailing down. He smirked his arrogant behaviour peeking through, I rolled my eyes grabbing my clothes to change.

"Where are you going?" he questions, I looked at him confused, "the bathroom" I sated the obvious. "I think after the meeting, you can just change here" he sat at the edge of the bed gesturing me to come closer. I looked at him hastily but my feet having a mind of its own making its way to him.

I stood in front of him, he stayed seated on the edge of the bed. The back of his fingers trailing up my thigh then hooking his fingers in my belt loops. Slowly pulling them down, his forehead rested on my stomach, his breathing was slow and heavy even though he just saw me completely exposed.

I knew this was different, it was tender. My breathing hitched when my pants passed my ass, once again completely bare from the waist down. I looked down at Vincenzo his head still resting against my stomach. My hands rested at my sides.

I stood completely still anticipating his next move.

"Off" he whispered against my skin, I kicked my pants off swallowing hard. He dug his fingers gently into my ankles slowly dragging his fingers up to my upper thigh. "Let me" he spoke quietly. He stood up and grabbed a pair of his boxers from his draw resuming his position, I eyed him sceptically before putting my feet threw the holes. He was dressing me … it was the most tender and softest thing he has ever done for me. He stood up now towering above me, he looked down at me never breaking eye contact like he was trying to prove something to me.

His knuckles grazed up and down both arms leaving goosebumps in his wake. "Up" he spoke up softly, I lifted my hands above my head my eyes never leaving his. He took my shirt off, I was now let in nothing but a bra and his boxers.

He looked down unclasping my bra with one hand, "I want you to be comfortable" he breathed out, sliding my bra off my chest. Grabbing his black plain shirt, he puts it on me.

He lifts my chin up with his index finger, "I'm trying" he breathed out. I looked at him softly, I leaned my forehead to his holding his hand tight. "I know" I whispered softly.

He didn't want to remember me because he doesn't know who he became, how his new self-acts. Vincenzo is dealing with the most difficult dilemma we all face. The person you know you should be and the person you want to become, the difference being Vincenzo was so close to crossing that line once. Now he has to start all over again with missing pieces.

He gestured me to the bed. I sighed knowing there was no longer any real point to me having my own room. I think it would be better for all three of us if we just settled into our new normal.

I missed sharing a bed with Vincenzo, the feeling of security and serenity I would get when I would listen to his breathing feeling his heartbeat against his chest. I got comfortable my head hitting the pillow, I immediately fell into a peaceful sleep.

X

I slowly opened my eyes, adjusting to the light before the memories of last night came crashing back. The meeting and what came after that. I exhaled deeply brushing my fingers through my hair. I look over and find Vincenzo and Dante gone. I shuffle getting out of the bed and finding a simple outfit for today.

I grabbed a pair of black high waisted leather shorts and Vincenzo's plain black distressed Tee. Tucking the left side in, I look around for my combat boots tying them up and rushing out to find my son and my ... well my Vincenzo? I questioned to myself before shrugging choosing not to go over that brain teaser today.

It was game day, Vincenzo, myself, and Lorenzo and the

rest of the intimate team were discussing strategies and our official plan to finally take down Xavier. I step out the mansion looking around, every man was in an area training. Hand-to-hand combat, gun practice, self-defence, knife, and sword fighting even Bullseye had a group of men up in the mountains teaching them how to be a professional sniper. I looked around and Vincenzo and Dante were nowhere to be seen. "Hacker" I call out.

He swiftly turns around "Isabella" he greets me warmly with his signature big smile. I laugh shaking my head, always putting me in a good mood when I see his charismatic smile. "Have you seen my son?" I asked. He shrugged shaking his head "No, I've been prepping the technicalities for the meeting later. Check near the pool around the house?" He suggests.

X

I turn the corner and see Vincenzo staring at the pool holding Dante protectively in his arms. He viscously shakes his head, like he was trying to get rid of a bad memory. I quickly approach the two of them. "Where did you two disappear this morning?" I question looking at a very cheerful Dante.

My god he is getting so big, I whine in my head. "We didn't want to wake you" Vincenzo mutters, I nod my head staying quiet. The awkward silence dawns on us before he mercifully breaks it. "Come with me" He states walking further into the bushes and trees.

"Vincenzo!" I yelled out, after his silhouette disappeared into the forest. Catching up to him, he hands me Dante and leads the way. "Where are we going?" I eyed him suspiciously before complying and aimlessly following him to God knows where. He walked through the backyard and into the woods, "is this were you murder me?" I questioned looking behind me noticing how far we know are from the house. He kept walking straight but even though he stayed silent I could still hear his eye roll.

"Daddy's going to punish me" I whispered softly to Dante, I look up seeing Vincenzo freeze in his tracks. Oops he heard. He cleared his throat and continued walking "you, okay?" I innocently asked catching up to his speed. "If you don't stop talking in a minute you won't be" he groaned. My eyes widened a sensual sensation erupting in my lower stomach and that familiar feeling between my legs crept its way back. I let out a throaty cough and caught up to a very smug Vincenzo. He points ahead before I could say anything, I eyed him sceptically following his gaze, my mouth hung open.

"NO FREAKING WAY!" I squealed handing him Dante as I ran towards a familiar white horse in the barn, "hey baby, I missed you" I petted it softly putting my head to his, Vincenzo caught up holding Dante with a satisfied grin on his face. "I thought you'd like him" he adds. I turn to look at him disappointed realising he didn't remember our first date.

I quickly shook my head and looked back at the horse "why'd you think I'd like him?" I questioned still petting his head.

"It's stubborn and keeps its distance from everyone. Once you gain it's trust however, he slowly starts warming up and once that happens you never want to go back to the previous distance" he truthfully spoke keeping his gaze fixated on me for longer than I think he intended. Dante reached his hands out trying to grab the horse's nose, I giggled softly "sorry buddy this one's for mum, this one is for you" he gestured towards the black pony to match Vincenzo's horse. I laughed looking at Dante's excited face, watching his hands clench and unclench trying to jump towards the horse. "I'm no genius but I think he wants to see the pony" I point out, Vincenzo says nothing and makes his way to the pony putting Dante on top of it my mum heart explodes into a million pieces at how adorable my baby looked, such a big boy on a horse.

"Can't believe you're already three months" I pout looking at him sucking his bottom lip completely in his mouth drooling, Vincenzo looks up at me "three months?" He questions I smile nodding my head. "I still can't believe it's already been three months" he adds shaking his head feeling like it was just yesterday when we finally got to the house. I clear my throat trying to change the subject, "you wanna go for a ride?" I asked playfully watching his eyes light up slightly. We climbed on our horses Vincenzo holding Dante securely as we rode off, keeping a steady pace.

"Be careful not to go to fast last thing I'd want is for you to fall off" he comments looking at me, I turn my head to face him "excuse me?" I questioned slightly offended but more amused he thinks I don't know how to ride a horse. He looks at me with a cocky expression, I lick the inner corner of my lip "I know my way around every deadly weapon you own, and I single headedly interrogated and killed men while pregnant ... but I don't know my way around a horse?" I tease never breaking eye contact.

"Don't overcompensate, it's okay not to know how. I can always teach you 1:1" He teases playfully, I bit my lower lip positioning my body getting ready to Gallop. I look at Vincenzo one last time giving him a wink I kick the side of the horse twice remembering that was its command to get it to run.

Within seconds I was off, leaving Vincenzo and my son behind me in the dust I laugh feeling the wind blow through my hair, tickling at my skin, I felt free like no one, and nothing can touch me.

Vincenzo's POV

I pulled the horses leach back coming to a stop as I watched Isabella dash off on her horse, she looked like a natural rider. I looked down at Dante in my arms who was looking up at me with those big grey eyes.

I looked down at him scared, what do I do? What if he starts crying? What if he vomits … Cazzo what if he does a shit? I looked back up in the distance "Isabella help!" I shouted out, Dante giggled at my frightened state. I looked back down at him and cocked an eyebrow "you really are a King" once again he let out a giggle before looking forward leaning down trying to grip the horse's hair, I let out a huff and sit him back up "come on bud" I laugh and continue a steady pace.

"So … do you like horses?" I asked him looking down at his little head, he didn't even look at me just kept staring ahead. I rolled my eyes "ignoring me?" I questioned, again no response. I huffed refusing to cave in.

"I won't do it" I stuck to my ground.

He turned around and gave me a wide smile playing with his fingers as he patiently waited for me. I looked around making sure no one was around. Clearing my throat, I looked down at Dante I let out a sigh.

He continued to look up at me smiling, "Bello come tuo padre, mio leone e altrettanto testardo" I gave in talking in baby talk. **(Just as handsome as your dad and as stubborn as your mum)**

He laughed out clapping his hands as he leaned back into my chest getting comfortable. I laughed and shook my head defiantly a mini version of his mum. I continued strolling on the horse slowly holding onto Dante, we stopped at a little pond, hopping off the horse letting it have a rest and drink of water.

I walked Dante over to the ducks in the pond "Dante guarda le anatre" I pointed out. **(Watch the ducks)**

He clapped his hands before holding onto me for dear life, I looked over at the ducks then back at Dante. "Don't be scared buddy, it won't bite. If it does, I'll just shoot it" I shrugged my shoulders, he leaned his head against my neck.

I smiled looking out into the pond I was proud of myself I was proud that I proved myself wrong, but most of all I'm proud that I fulfilled my promise to Dante, that I was going to break the cycle of our parents that we'd be different and if he was alive, I know he would have made the best dad and the best uncle. I looked down in both happiness and sadness looking at the little boy in my hands, who became my redemption. I felt like my heart was about to explode, how can I love someone so much?

For a second, I thought back to Isabella, did I love her? Did I experience the same feelings with her? Was this how she felt about me? I let out a frustrated sigh, "This whole thing is fucking bullshit." I groaned out before slapping my mouth shut.

I looked down at Dante "You heard nothing, if Isabella heard me right now shed chop my balls off" I scowled, and face palmed. "This stays between us" I looked at Dante sternly, he gave me a smile before continuing to squeeze my face, his nails digging in my skin. I laugh and pull his hands off before giving them a kiss.

Do I allow it all to come flooding back? Do I allow her back in or do I push it all away and focus on what I know best … and to be honest lately I don't even know what that is anymore.

I looked back at Dante and laughed. He was chewing on my shirt. I took it out of his mouth and held him in the air "My big boy". I sang out.

He giggled making my heart melt. I sound like a fucking girl, thank fuck no one's here to hear me. I sat him on the horse and grabbed my phone wanting to take a picture. "Smile Dante" I called out, he just looked at me with an unimpressed expression. I rolled my eyes and huffed "Smile Leone" I cooed out, he laughed and began clapping his hands. So, fucking stubborn.

After taking a few pictures and a few selfies we hopped back on the horse and made our way back to the house. "This isn't so hard, being a dad" I commented talking to myself. Speaking too soon I gaged at the smell.

I looked down at Dante and he looked forward completely unfazed.

"What does she fucking feed you?" I grunted.

"I mean- Oh fuck it this shit smells too bad to give a fuck about proper language." Okay time to pick up the pace I mentally yelled out holding my breath. I started seeing the poo escape his nappy and slowly reach his back. "LETS

GOOO" I kicked the side of the horse picking up speed holding Dante close.

X

Reaching the house, I jumped off the horse and instructed one of my men to take it back. I held Dante up and gaged seeing that it erupted and is now on my shirt.

"I thought we were friends?" I cried out. "Your mother can handle this" I looked up and saw Isabella approaching, I looked at her pissed off and Dante ironically mimicking my expression as he wants his diaper changed now.

Isabella's POV

After about thirty minutes I decided to turn back, coming up to the ranch I see Vincenzo and Dante waiting for me, both ironically had a scowl on their faces. Fucking hell talk about like father like son. My son really is his father's twin, I hop off my horse and let it go inside the barn, taking off the saddle and getting some carrot to feed him.

"So, you can ride a horse?" Vincenzo questions annoyed, I smirked looking at him "that's not the only thing I know how to ride" I winked grabbing Dante off him and beginning to make my way back to the house. Vincenzo snaps out of it catching up looking at me with a lustful eye.

"Boss, Isabella. Everyone's ready for you" Hacker calls for us. Taking in a deep breath we all make our way to the meeting room, flashbacks from last night flash back sending me into a coughing fit.

Vincenzo looks at the men with a smug smirk, I roll my eyes and put Dante in his little play pen Vincenzo had installed in almost every room in the house. Taking my seat next to Vincenzo we start the meeting.

"We are all aware why we are gathered and what's going on" Vincenzo states aloud looking around the room, everyone nodding their heads waiting for him to continue. "Xavier's death is long overdue. It's time we burn him like he burnt us. We will attack at the Salvatore shipment that is said to be going down tonight. I want every inch of that area covered, Bullseye I want you and your men surrounding and watching our backs from the high ground. Hacker, I need you to hack in to their systems and redirect their shipment to our secret facility so they don't know it us." Vincenzo gives the guys a run down, his authoritative tone had everyone on the edge of their seats and me drooling subconsciously. "Xavier is not tactful nor brave, the second he sees a threat he will run be aware and do not let him escape. If he does, he will go underground" I nod along knowingly.

"Marco you and your team will apprehend the south wing, Fico I want your team to cover the west wing. Luca, I want you and red to cover the North and East wings. I do not want a section of the docks to be empty. Our men need to cover all grounds and most importantly I need you all to prepare for what's to come." His men nod along knowing this mission may result in injury and potential death.

"Show him and the Salvatore men no mercy. I want everyone to suffer, for even considering going up against the Kings. Let alone going about it like scared gattinos. (kittens) "More importantly everyone stays alive." He looked at them with pride, like a true leader. "No mistakes"

FLASHBACK

I stood at the head of the meeting looking around the room. "No mistakes" I warned the men before they all scattered, Xavier approached me from behind placing his hand on my lower back. "Amore" he whispered in my neck. I cringed standing very still. Pushing him away I looked up at him "the meetings over we will be apprehending tonight" I announced to him trying to avoid what he was trying to do. "Is everything always business with you?" He groans frustrated, I roll my eyes and straighten my posture turning to look at him.

"I'm just living up to my end of the deal" I remind him of our deal. He leaves me alone in exchange I work and rise his gang through the ranks.

"You say that like it was such a difficult deal" he scoffs offended, I look at him suspiciously.

"Your gang was the biggest joke in all of Spain." I spit looking at him. "It was the laughingstock among every high crime family. Until I took over" I reminded him of how far he has come thanks to me.

"If it wasn't for me taking that deal. You would still be a

joke" I bite lowly. He steps in front of me blocking anyway for me to escape. "If it wasn't for that deal. You'd be dead doll" he purrs against my ears.

I cringe shutting my eyes pulling my head away from him. "Either way you were a coward in both scenarios" I yelled out pushing him off me.

"Do not make a mistake you will regret Xavier. Get that close to me again and I promise I will torture you in ways that still haven't been invented yet." I warned him my voice low and threatening venom laced in every word.

"I'm not that girl in the dark cell anymore".

"The girl that had emotions!" He yelled out before I could walk out the room, I put my hand on the door frame smirking before turning around slowly.

"The girl that loved going to the beach with her family to watch the waves. The girl that lovedz to laugh and smile at any given chance … that girl?" He questions trying to undermine me, to get me too crack to break.

"That girl is dead, and I killed her" I answered him. The sly smirk never leaving my face, "Killing, torturing, you're an assassin" He looked up at me. "Oh, but I'm so much more.

I'm the boss" I laughed. "I'm everything you couldn't be …
everything you wished to be".

He balled his hand into a fist stepping closer to me, "you're
living your worst hell, but you won't admit it." He tried again
to get me to show any kind of emotion. "It's not hell if I like
the way it burns." I purred. Leaving him in an empty board
room.

"No mistakes." I reminded myself quietly.

END OF FLASHBACK

"Isabella?" Vincenzo looked at me, I shook my head and
apologised for dozing off.

"Sorry continue" I nodded sitting up right.

"Xavier his men along with the Salvatore's are hungry for
power. They want revenge me dead and Isabella a prisoner,
their lack of rational thinking will leave them open and
unprepared focusing solely on anger and hate will only get
them so far. In tactic we have the upper hand. I know we are
more than capable of taking them down once and for all.
Their hunger makes them weak" he looks around the table.

"Hungry dogs are never loyal." He concludes. The

statement sending shivers down my spine. "We attack tonight go" he orders everyone to leave. They all stand and go out to prepare and train their men for tonight everyone ready to kill. I looked over at Vincenzo sighing "what's wrong?" He questions. I shake my head softly unsure of why I have this bad feeling in the pit of my stomach. "I just don't have a good feeling about tonight" I tell him honestly. He looks at me curiously "what do you mean?" He questions. I shrug once again struggling to find the right words to describe this feeling of doom. I let out a huff and smile "nothing I'm probably just worried about going out into a dangerous situation and leaving Dante behind" I whispered… maybe that's why I was worried.

Vincenzo shrugged his shoulders "that's why you're not coming" he states simply. I shoot up looking at him "excuse me?" I scoff out. "You're not coming" he calmly states once more.

"What about you?" I asked, he looked at me like I had officially lost my mind.

"Of course, I'm going I have to be on the field with my men, what kind of leader would I be if I send my men out in danger while I remain at home safe." I shake my head scoffing.

"This is my fight just as much as it is yours" I poke his chest.

"Dante needs his mum" he firmly sticks to his guns.

I nod my head "he also needs his dad" I remind him.

"If we are both out there, we risk him losing both his parents" he persists.

I shake my head "Vincenzo we are stronger when we work together. I need you with me just as much as you need me with you on that field. This is not up for discussion. I swore to make him burn just like he burnt me. Besides I think you learnt by now that I don't take the word no very well." I stood up to leave the room before he says another word.

"Isabella. It's dangerous what if you get shot? What if you die!" He shouts, I spin around looking at him softly "then take care of Dante" I whisper looking at him.

"This is something I need to do. I owe it to myself" I paused for a second "I owe it to her" I whispered referring to the girl in the dark basement. The girl who got tortured to breaking point, the girl that lost everything because of him. I owe it to her. I owe it to my innocence the innocence he robbed me of.

"I can't let you go Isabella" he states sticking to his word, he pushes past me to go to his office. "Italy!" I called out, he stopped in his tracks like he remembered something.

He turned around slowly, "I'm coming. I don't just owe it to myself, or my parents or Dante. I owe it to Maria" I remind him that because of him I was left without a sister.

"He broke me, he broke my parents, and he took Maria's life from her. He deprived me of my sister, my son's aunty and my parent's daughter. Don't make me stay behind" I choked out looking at him, his men watching us intently. "Okay" he nodded his head.

"But you need to do something for me" he adds conditions. I nod my head waiting for him to continue. "Dimostra a te stesso" (prove yourself) He firmly states in Italian I eye him sceptically.

X

Vincenzo stood in front of me in nothing but grey sweats, "seriously?" I breath out my eyes shamelessly ranking his body.

"You want to go out into the field? I know you're crazy, but I need to know your capable" he states.

I laugh to myself, his seen me interrogate and burn his two girls alive. Crazy was generous, "Okay" I agree.

"What do you want me to do?" I ask waiting for instructions.

"Fight me" he calmly says.

I look at him dumbfounded "What?"

"Fight me Isabella" he stands in his stance waiting for me to get in position.

"Vincenzo" I breath out ready to argue before I fall flat on my ass. He just kicked my legs from underneath me.

"Get. Up." Vincenzo sternly spits.

I huff and stand on my feet. "You wanna dance Mafia? Let's dance"

I get in position and throw a jab. He professionally steps away from my punch grabbing my forearm and hitting the side of my stomach making me bend down. He pushes the back of my knee making me kneel and hovers over me pointing his fingers at the back of head. "Dead" he announces.

I huff irritated, I grab his wrist from behind and push his

hand away from my head. Grabbing his forearm with my free hand keeping a steady grip on his wrist. I stand up and twist his body in front of me, hearing the satisfying impact his body had with the matted floor. I quickly hovered above him and pointed my fingers to his forehead. "Dead" I repeated his words.

He smirked proud nodding his head, he thrusts upward feeling his member as he thrusted up, on impact it forced my body forward. I place both my hands next to his head to keep me from head butting him. "Dirty player" I comment, he cocks an eyebrow "once you're on the field everyone's a dirty player." He flips us over now his on top of me. Pinning my hands over my head leaving me helpless, "Now what do you do?" He asks, I bite my lower lip trying to figure out a way out.

"Head butt me Isabella" He answers his own question. "Your key tactic to get out of this is your head. With the right amount of force, you can break my nose, or wound me enough to shock me to let go of your hand. Then you can push me off you." He explains.

He stands up offering a helping hand, I take it gracefully.

"You can't rely solely on your gun or knives. Your head is always your most important asset. If you can think quickly on your feet, you'll never lose a fight" I nod my head slowly, not use to seeing this side of Vincenzo.

Serious and strategic.

"Let's go again" he states.

X

We spent what felt like hours sparing until he was satisfied with my combat skills. I've been out of the game for a year now since Dante. I'd be lying if I said it didn't feel good to be back though. "Catch" Vincenzo calls out. Throwing me a prop knife.

"My favourite" I smirk, holding the blade I get ready. Vincenzo steps forwards going for my chest, I block his arm quickly stabbing him three times along his stomach. Stepping out of the way, he rushes forwards.

"Good" he complements, I look at his neck wanting to go for that next. "No" he comments.

"Keep your eyes on me." He explains, "never let your

opponent know your next move." He steps forward grabbing my wrist mid-air, twisting it behind my back and placing his prop knife on my neck. "Lock your eyes with his, watch him, study him. Our body, our behaviour, our slight movements give away what our next attack will be. If you focus your eyes on his everything else comes into your peripheral vision. You see things that are not in your direct sight, leaving you ready for anything." He explains sternly.

Vincenzo sounds so professional and in control. Truly like a real Mafia Boss. I nod my head slowly "so if you were in this situation what would you do Isabella" he whispers. I lean my head back softly tapping his nose with the back of my head.

He lets go of the knife playing out the scenario, I spin around and pin my knife against his neck pushing him up against the wall. We stay like this for a moment. In a calm silence, our eyes fixated on each other. Our harsh breathing perfectly in sync.

Being here with him in this crazy situation that is my life allowed me to really understand myself in a way I never did before. Maybe I've always been more comfortable in chaos,

I'm comfortable with the violence of it all.

I break away and take a step back from Vincenzo. He clears his throat nodding his head "okay" he whispers. I nod my head mimicking his movements "okay" I confirm.
"Are you sure?" He asks me one last time, I nod my head. This was freedom, as dangerous as it was. It was my version of freedom, and I prefer dangerous freedom over peaceful slavery.

X

Everyone is running around the estate preparing and making sure in our absence everyone will be safe at the manor, I quickly change into my black leather romper, strapping my throwing knifes on my upper thighs and zipping up my combat boots. "Your mum is a badass, and she looks good while doing it as well" I giggle talking to Dante who was watching me from his little cot.

"You will never be doing anything like this though" I sternly point at him, picking him up and holding him close to my chest. "I want a better life for you Leone" I kiss his little cheek. "My life was already written to go down this path, that doesn't mean your life has to follow mine or your dads".

"You get to pick what you want to do" I wink smiling at him, he laughs holding onto my chest burying his face in the crook of my neck. I giggle smothering him with kisses, the sudden fear sinking in my stomach, what If I don't come back from this? I sigh looking at his little body, this little boy whose life was dependent on my own. "I can't give you a chance if I don't kill that bastard" I whispered reminding myself why I'm doing this. He will always be a lingering threat on my life, Vincenzo's life and my sons. He must die.

Ariana walks in the room smiling reassuringly at me, "you sure you want to go?" She questions softly, I nod my head firmly "I have to" I stand up and give Dante one last squeeze. "Mummy loves you" I whisper in his ear and hand him to Ariana. "Keep him safe" I softly whispered. She nodded her head firmly "With my life" she assured me.

X

241

I walked out the manner and found my way to the clinic, I peeked my head through the window and watched mum and dad with their doctor. I smiled weakly slowly opening the door to go inside, "Butterfly" mama whispered as papa turned to look at me smiling as I approached.

The doctor stood up and smiled "they are improving rapidly, but the nightmares and PTSD like behaviour will forever be present psychologically" he gave a reassuring pat on the shoulder and walked off leaving me alone with them.

"How are you feeling?" I asked softly, they nodded their heads smiling. "Better knowing you're safe" Mama spoke up, I bit my bottom lip. I'm safe for now. "Knowing our girl, she'll be running after danger soon enough" Papa made a joke even though I don't think he was trying to be funny.

"Either way I'm a lot stronger than before" I tried reassuring them, but the mere mention made them cringe. "What exactly happened?" I asked him cautiously.

Papa sighed "I don't know how much of it I can relive before having an episode or if it will trigger anything but" he took a deep breath before patting the bed ushering me to sit next to him.

I hesitantly obliged and sat next to him, unsure if I really wanted to hear what happened. I looked up at my father anyway and waited for him to continue. "After that day … the day you saw him do what he did" he paraphrased it trying to remain calm. "Dad, you don't have too" I reassured him once more that he can stop if it was too uncomfortable for him. "It's okay it's good if I can talk about it. You have a right to know" he assured me taking in another deep breath he continued.

FLASHBACK

Mario's POV

I knelt in front of the bastard, Sofia kneeled beside me giving me a reassuring squeeze. "You'll never get away with this" she shouted at him. He laughed smug pressing the gun further into her forehead "oh dear, I already have" I grunt and push him away from her.

"Don't touch my wife" I warned him, he cocked an eyebrow up looking at me before rubbing his chest where I had pushed him. "Fine, I won't have too anyway. What I have planned for the both of you will be much worse than death."

He threatened.

I rolled my eyes "what you will do won't be anything new. We have dealt with much worse from more powerful people than you" I smirked. You either fear what's in front of you or make it fear you.

I do not fear anything. "I don't want the two of you. Don't flatter yourself Mario" he laughed out, looking at his watch like he was waiting for something. "What are you waiting for?" I asked analysing him.

"My desired target. If she is the girl, I think she, is she won't sit waiting to see what happens, she will run through those doors with a gun wanting to save her precious parents. Like she did that night" My eyes widened realising what he wanted.

"If you so much as look at my daughter, so help me god I will burn you!" I shouted standing up. He took the gun off safety pointing it, Sofia. "Sit down" he warned me. I hesitantly kneeled back down, "what do you want from Isabella. She's only fifteen" Sofia looked helpless. I never felt more ashamed than I did right now, a man threatening my wife and my daughter's life and I can't do anything to stop it.

"That day she shot my men, she got me excited. I never met or seen a girl with so much potential. So much power in her little pinkie than most people possess in their whole bodies. That night was the night I made the decision" He explained proudly like he somehow was responsible for Isabella's power.

"What decision?" I spat.

"To make her mine" he laughed out, "I feel in love with her from that night, and I won't rest until she's mine. She will single handily grow my gang with her influence, strength, and unmatched power. Then once I break her enough, she will fall for me like I have for her" he smiled off into the distance.

"You'll have to kill me before I ever let that happen" I warned him, no one was to touch Isabella or Maria. I don't care if I have to die to protect my girls, if so, much as a single hair is moved from their angelic head, I will raise hell on earth.

"I plan on it don't worry, but slowly. If my plan is to work, she will come looking for me after I fake your deaths. Once I have her in my possession I will break her, I will torture her and the two of you will hear and witness it all. I won't let you see it, but I will make sure you hear her screams. Knowing she's going through all this to avenge the two of you, and when she rebels because eventually, she will. I will reveal the two of you to keep her in control." He further explained.

Fake our deaths? Break Isabella? Torture her? Diego do not let Isabella go. I prayed she is somewhere safe before my heart shattered into a million pieces seeing her burst in with a gun in her hand. "Isabella get out!" I yelled she stood there frozen in place shaking her head no, my heart tugged looking at her crying.

The man snickered never looking at Isabella he extended his arm and aimed a gun at myself. "This empire will be mine" he mumbled. "I'll be nice ... any last words?"

I didn't know what to do. To warn her, either way I know my daughter I know the fight and power she possesses I know she won't rest until she avenged us.

"Isabella, our sweet girl. Our absence will be strong and warm, and it will hold you. It will teach you how to miss, how to be without and how to survive anyway." I spoke out, "Cry if you must, then let your grief be taken over by love.

Remember the love we had for you and Maria, let it guide you. Let it comfort you and never let it die. We might be leaving you now, but we will always ... always be right there. Watching over you, protecting you and watching you become who you were destined to be." I looked at her hoping she would take my advice and move on with life.

"No, because you're not leaving me" she cried out.

"Isabella baby, never forget how much we love you. No matter what we'll always be by your side, watching over you and your sister. Throughout the rest of your life, we will be right behind you. You may not see us but be sure we will be right there, watching you grow, hugging you when you're sad, kissing the pain away and protecting you for all eternity. Nothing's changed! The only thing that will be different is we will have wings while we watch over you and Maria ... and no matter what we are proud of the both of you." Sofia spoke up trying to instal the value of letting go.

"We love you" we both spoke up in together. He snickered shooting the gun at both of our chest.

"NO!" Isabella's shriek was the last thing I heard before it all went black.

I'm so sorry Isabella.

END OF FLASHBACK

Isabella's POV

I jumped back when my dad suddenly started screaming as he got to the end of his story, "ISABELLA, NO IM SORRY" He screamed out hitting himself as he screamed out, Mama watched in horror trying to calm him down. The doctors rushed back in and sedated him and my mum as she started screaming because of dad's outburst. I was rushed out of the room unable to speak, unable to hug my parents and tell them it's okay. That everything that happened wasn't their fault. I narrowed my eyes and marched out of the clinic. This was his fault he may not have killed my parents, but he took them from me.

His death is long overdue and its game time. I rushed back seeing everyone loading up and getting ready to go, I quickly jumped in the range with Vincenzo and Lorenzo. "You ready?" Vincenzo asked me, I nodded my head and kept my head straight. He eyed me sceptically but chose to stay silent. "Bullseye, I need you and your team in position once you give us the okay, I want everyone to move in from different entry points." Vincenzo spoke into the earpiece.

"Marco you and your team will apprehend the south wing, first like discussed. Fico, I want your team to cover the west wing next. Luca, I want you and red to cover the North and East wings. Once each wing is covered and secure my team will apprehend myself and Isabella will go straight after Salvatore and Xavier the rest of you … you know what to do. Stay safe and remember no mistakes" he looks at me giving me a sharp nod. I nod taking in a deep breath trying to ignore the sick feeling I had in my stomach the closer we got to the estate. We parked the car on the side of the road waiting for the okay from bullseye.

"In position. Marco you're set to move in, just beware of the three guards at the front." I looked out the window and watched Marco and his team go in taking out the three guards while three of his men take their places, Marco gestures for Fico to move in. Fico, along with his men slides through taking position around the manner, this seems all too easy.

After everyone is in position, we finally exit the car and go in, "Hey!" one of the girls call out I looked over at her and saw Vincenzo put his hands up. "I don't hit girls" he informs me, I shake my head and quickly rush to her before she exposes us. She goes to punch me in the nose, quickly ducking I hit the side of her stomach. She loses balance kneeling down using the back of my gun I hit her in the back of the head.

I huff dragging her body to the nearest bush, dusting myself off I walk back to Vincenzo and Lorenzo. "Welcome back Chica" Lorenzo smirks.

I shake my head and wait for Vincenzo to take the lead. We move through the bushes trying to get to the main manner, but our bodies stiffen hearing the alarm blaring. "Everyone out now!" Vincenzo orders through the earpiece, "Bullseye cover us" he snaps as everyone tries to leave without shooting their guns. A fantasy if we thought we were leaving without a fight. We turn to retreat before spotting Red getting caught, "Cazzo" Vincenzo curses under his breath.

"Don't do it!" He warns me before taking off to save his men. He shoots the man who held Red in a choke hold.

And before you know it, we were at war, everyone came out of the bushes Xavier's men joined with the Salvatore's outnumbered us. Fuck, I get out of the bushes and shoot at one of the men who was about to shoot Vincenzo from behind.

"Ah so lovely of you to join us amore" Xavier shouted from the Terrance, I grunted and ran inside.

"ISABELLA NO!" Vincenzo screamed wanting to run after me.

I ignore him and take off before he has the chance to grab me, I shoot my way inside killing anyone who tried to stop me. Fuck I curse running out of bullets. **"You can't rely solely on your gun or knives. Your head is always your most important asset. If you can think quickly on your feet, you'll never lose a fight"** Vincenzo's voice echoed through my head.

I charge for one of the men who drew his gun aiming it at me, twisting his arm around I smash his head through the wall knocking him out, hearing the sound of his nose crushing sent a rather satisfying chill down my spine I smirk and rush upstairs.

Grabbing the blade, I had strapped to my thigh, "I'm going to have so much fun with this" I smiled looking at Xavier. "Isabella please, you're outnumbered. You and your 'team' don't stand a chance" he mocked. I looked over the Terrance a lot of our men laid on the floor injured or dead, but so did his men.

It was hard to tell who was winning but I put the favour on the King's. I looked back at Xavier, "outnumbered or not. You will die today even if I die too" I warned him, I was not leaving here until I had his head on a stake.

"All I wanted was you so if I can't be with you, I'll take dying together" he smiled pulling out his gun aiming it at me.

I threw my blade hitting him in the shoulder, I kick him my foot coming in contact with his face. He falls to the floor grabbing his gun and shooting. I yell like I was realising all my anger out in that scream, grabbing him by his collar I pin him up against the wall and knee him in the groin.

He pushes me off him, groaning as he pulls the blade out of his shoulder blade. He tosses it aside and grips my throat pulling me up, "do it" I choke out. He tightens his grip around my throat and just as I was about to give up Dante's little face flashed in front of me. "NO" I scream, pushing my thumb all the way into his eye. He screams letting go of my throat, I grab the gun off the floor and aim it at him.

"You fucking bitch" he yells out placing his hand over his eye, he turns his head to look at me. "WHY?" He yells out, and suddenly everything went quiet, the fight below stopped as I felt everyone's intense stare on us. He charged for me. My back hitting the edge of the terrance.

"Why don't you love me back?" He asked looking hurt, I scoffed "Love?" I yell ironically.

"YOU KIDNAPED ME, TORTURED ME, RAPED ME! YOU BROKE ME AND YOU BROKE MY PARENTS, YOU KILLED MARIA AND YOU ASK WHY I DON'T LOVE YOU?" I yelled. Grabbing my other blade, I had attached to my thigh I stabbed him in the stomach repeatedly.

I stood over his bloody and barely conscious body feeling tired, I place my hand over my stomach and look at my now blood-stained palm. "Wha-" I breath out when did I get shot. I looked at Xavier who had a smile on his face, "I shot you and you didn't even notice. My dragon" he breathed out trying to stay awake looking at me in awe.

I look up and see Salvatore aiming the gun at me, "NOOO" Xavier shouts but it was too late he shot me. I stumble back losing balance and consciousness.

Xavier stands up, barely able to walk he goes to grab me, but he was too late my eyes roll to the back of my head my body fell back, "NOO" Xavier shouts trying to grab me mid fall but he failed he hovered over the terrance as he watched my falling body. I feel the air embrace me in a tight hug.

THE STORY BEHIND
EVERY VILAN

Isabella's POV

I slowly opened my eyes and was blinded by the bright light, I looked around trying to find familiar surroundings, but everything rushed past me in a blur, the sound of panic was all I could really hear. The exhaustion over taking me I couldn't but close my eyes and once again surrendered to the darkness that welcomed me home.

X

My slumber is short lived hearing mixed voices in the room, I slowly flutter my eyes open putting a face to the various voices, except for one voice. His voice was engraved in my head like a song on repeat a blissful sound.

"I don't want sneak attacks. I don't want ambush I want to tear him down until his nothing but ashes" Vincenzo roars looking at his men. "I don't just want him dead I want him to slowly deteriorate as I drain every ounce of energy. I want him to suffer" chills shivered down my spine as the hair on my arms stood up. I cough struggling to sit up, everyone's eyes dart toward me.

"Isabella?" Vincenzo calls out surprised. He rushes to my side helping me sit up, he moved to the side and poured me a cup of water.

"Are you okay?" He softly whispers, I nod my head before groaning from the excessive pain. I grip my head and shut my eyes trying to rid the pain, "I'll call the nurse" I gripped his arm and shook my head "I'm okay" I reassured him.

"Where's Dante?" I asked, he smiled telling me he was sleeping in Ariana's room. He looked at me hesitantly like he wanted to say something but was debating on whether it would be a good idea or not.

I looked at him curiously "what?"

He cleared his throat "It is not my place but, what were you and Xavier?" I widened my eyes at the rather strange question.

"We weren't an item if that is what you're insinuating" I reassured him, he looked unconvinced. I watched him curiously "what?" I questioned softly. He cleared his throat moving back "when you fell, he tried to jump after you, but the stab wounds didn't allow him."

I looked away cleaning my jaw, "Isabella?" He questioned. I shook my head softly before turning to look back at him. "I never loved him back, and I never will" I confirmed once again.

"Then why didn't you kill him?" He asked. "As far as I've known you, you're quite ruthless when it comes to finishing the job. From what I know about Dragon, she never leaves a witness and never leaves an enemy breathing. From what I saw in the basement with Diego, it was destruction at its finest, so why not Xavier? Why is he still breathing?" I looked up pondering his question.

A question a lot of people were curious about finding out, I let out a sigh and looked over at him again. "I felt bad for him" I whispered softly, "even after he did what he did?" Vincenzo spits out.

I nod my head softly "every villain has an origin story no one is born evil. They're created" I simply explained.

"That doesn't excuse him for what he did to me, and it never will, but it foolishly made me feel sorry for him. Every time I go to kill him, I see this damaged broken little boy and then my younger self flashes next to him. If he deserved to die for what he did then so did I?" I questioned softly.

Vincenzo shook his head looking at me "that's different he made you do all that he turned you into a villain" he explained trying to justify it all. I shook my head "just like someone turned him into the villain he is" I reminded him.

"You did all you did because you wanted to escape the mental and physical abuse, it was your only way to survive. You did what you did because if you didn't you would be dead" I nodded my head softly.

"He was right" I sighed softly. He looked at me confused **"Just like the moon half of my heart will always love the dark"** I quoted him.

FLASHBACK

I looked at the boxing bag in front of me, trying to reach mental exhaustion so I can sleep without the reoccurring guilty nightmares. I let out a grunt as my fist collided against the rough texture. I can't fucking keep doing this, I kicked the bag making the chain snap. I watched in satisfaction as the bag fell to the floor, catching my breath I looked up and saw Xavier in the door frame.

I kept my guard up as he approached me slowly, "I mean no harm" he put his hands up surrendering. I rolled my eyes "you have done enough" I reminded him. I stepped back looking at him uneasy. I was already seventeen and still stuck with him, stuck in the same twisted fate. This man was the reason why my hands are forever stained with blood, why my heart and soul have darkened and why I have become numb to the sight of violence, and why I'm terrified of the dark and spending too much time in my head alone.

"I just … I wanted to talk to you" he cautiously spoke up, I looked him up and down, not wanting to hear a word that comes out of his mouth. "Xavier. Just leave" I'm so tired. So, fucking tired, "I just … I need you to hear this. Please" he begged.

I looked at him taken back, he looked the most vulnerable I have ever seen him, I let out a sigh and gestured for him to continue. "I wasn't always like this." He looked at me guilty, "I wasn't always a bad person" he continued. I didn't move, I didn't blink I just kept staring at him with the same cold stare.

"I didn't have the best upbringing. I grew up without my parents, so I went in and out of the system a lot. It's ironic how a lot of people's criminal stories start with that." He joked trying to lighten the mood, but all I could do was just stand in place frozen, unable to comprehend what was happening and why he was doing what he was doing. Why after all this time after everything he did is he know trying to explain why ... did the guilt finally make its way to his conscious, or was this just another mind game? He, saw my cold exterior and coughed awkwardly before continuing.

"It's no excuse for what I did or what I'm still doing. But when bad things happen to you all you tend to do it focus on it and mimic what you know. All I know is pain, so inflicting it on others isn't a bad thing in my head its life. It's the life I grew up with."

He took a deep breath looking away "I was ten years old when I first got rap-" I cut him off putting my hand up feeling sick to my stomach.

"I was at an orphanage and the headmaster took a particular interest in me. This went on for two years, along with torture and beatings when I did something wrong." He barely spoke out, his voice dropping below audible. I was so torn in this moment I looked at him with genuine sadness, no one deserves that ever. For the first time in meeting and knowing him, I emphasised with him. It made me want to console him, but then my head reminded me of all he did making me haul in place.

"I ran away when I was twelve the abuse became so bad that if I stayed another day id be dead at his hands or my own. I was on the streets most of my life surviving on what I could steal, or what strangers would give me." He kept his head down like he was back in that very moment.

"A couple took me in when I was fifteen, it was amazing. They treated me like their son, I was well feed, well dressed. They did everything for me, then one day I figured out why … they were prepping me to be sold. Over and over. The people who took me in who I thought would be my redemption my second chance. Turned out to be the reason I became what I am. When id refuse advances or bash and fight my way out of that red room, I'd be beaten until I was blue. I'd be chained to the heater for hours. I can't tell you how many times I passed out from exhaustion. Eventually, I stopped eating I refused to take care of myself. So, I wouldn't be sold or desirable for anyone." His voice cracked, I swallowed the lump I had in my throat and watched him.

I felt the urge to tear up, but I couldn't, I was so numb I forced myself to be like this and now hearing something as inhumane as this was no longer affecting me as much as it would have. Xavier did not deserve any of that, but I didn't deserve any of this either.

"They would bring kids in from the streets and do it over and over with others. Then one day I decided I had enough, with every strength I had saved I snapped my wrist. I had to bite down on a cloth to stop me from screaming and alerting everyone that I was now free. I freed my wrist from the hand cuff. I unlocked all the room doors and helped the boys inside leave. I grabbed the gasoline outside from the shed and spread it all over the house, walking into their bedroom I hovered above them. It was in that moment my fate was sealed, I poured the gasoline all over their bodies they woke up screaming and scared. I felt like a god, I was finally on the other side I was no longer on the receiving end of being in fear I was now feared. The power that surged through my veins left me with no hesitation, I turned my lighter on and dropped it on their bodies." He smirked proud of himself.

"I stood there for a minute or two watching them scream at the top of their lungs. That blood curling scream that's been engraved in my head like a song on repeat. I laughed at them finding a satisfying feeling watching their skin sizzle and melt until they were nothing but bones. I was merciful but it was a sweet revenge." He smiled looking up at me, he was met with an expression he was not expecting.

My eyes were slightly wide, my breathing became heavier. As I stared at him, I myself was unaware of how to feel or process any of this. "I wasn't always a bad person Isabella, I just … I don't know what normal is." he quickly tried to make the situation more justifiable.

It sounded like he was trying to explain why he did what he did to me, like it was going to make it all better. I cleared my throat and walked past him before he called my name and made me haul once more. "Isabella. Let me finish … please" he pleaded softly.

I didn't turn around merely I just stood there waiting for

him to finish once he knew I wasn't going to face him he sighed. "I thought I'd never feel human again, that I'd never be innocent?" He questioned trying to find the right word to explain what he meant. "Then one day I was twenty-five, and I was on my walk when I saw this little girl who was no older than five years old stand up for a stranger, she didn't know he was being bullied for how he looked." He laughed out admiringly.

I looked straight ahead not turning to look at him, as I bite my bottom lip my eyes staring hard at the door in front of me slightly watering. I listened intently feeling my chest rise and fall at a faster pace.

"This little girl stood in front of the boy shielding him with her body from the bully, she was so mad fuck she made the bully nervous. Even though he was a few years older, she yelled at him and made him apologise to the boy. Once she was satisfied, she shooed him away and gave the boy a hug to make him feel better." I can hear the smile in his voice … is this the moment when he-

"I couldn't stop admiring you, not in a creepy way but in a feeling, I still cannot describe right now. I was infatuated by you, your bravery, your innocence, your compassion for others but also the power you possessed. When he asked for your name, and you replied. Isabella it was like that was the word to re activate my heart." I felt sick to my stomach I was fucking five years old.

"I- I just needed to make sure you were what I thought you were. So, I monitored you when my men came to the estate one night. You were sixteen, you saw my men about to kill your dad and with no hesitation you pulled the trigger your aim was something out of a movie so precise and so clean. You killed them without any ounce of compassion because you wanted to protect the one man dearest to you. After you killed them, you felt bad, you showed compassion. It was in that moment that I knew I wanted to be the person you do that for. The man you would kill for, and I hoped one day you will love me back." He whispered the last part, but I heard him.

"So, I killed your parents, the people who stood in my way. So, I could replace them, but you were so fucking stubborn I knew I had to break you first. Now that you're here and know my story I just hope you can see why I did what I did. I did it for you, Isabella I've been in love with you for so long before I even knew." I spun around so fast and pinned him up against the wall my forearm pressed against his neck.

My eyes and head narrowed staring him down I looked at him with pure hatred. "You loved my power not me. You killed my parents for your selfish gain not for love." I pressed against him harder and harshly whispered "Nunca vuelvas a confundir a los dos" **(Don't ever fucking confuse the two again)**
I realised my grip on his neck. He dropped down rubbing his neck soothing it while catching his breath.

"No one deserved a shitty childhood, and no one should ever have to deal with what you did but that doesn't excuse you to do it to others. Instead of protecting those around you from going through what you did you became your worst enemy. Maybe it's time you set yourself on fire" I spat.

END OF FLASHBACK

"He loved the power I had, my ability to not think or bat an eye. He didn't love me it was just a pretty word he could use to cover up the ugly truth. I never loved him, but I did feel sorry for him. His mind was so twisted and knotted from everything he'd been through. That I went through I had it worse because he came up with so many different torture methods that I completely split my personality. I took on Dragon as an alter ego to survive it because Isabella couldn't. I numbed myself so much that nothing mattered so nothing will ever make me as vulnerable as I was in that fucking basement." I looked deep into Vincenzo's eyes and for the first time in a while I saw a glimpse of the old Vincenzo shine through.

He looked away quickly before turning back to me with a mixture of sadness and vengeance in his eyes.

"I never killed him because even after all he did, I couldn't help but see that scared ten-year-old boy staring back at me. It was another fucking mind game. He only told me that story so I could sympathise … empathise. Even now he fucks with my head." I cried softly feeling defeated, he quickly embraced me in a tight hug rubbing comfortable circles on my back.

"Isabella, you are the strongest most fearless person I have ever met, you say what you think, and you do what you must. You don't mind being the bad guy and you don't mind doing the dirty work if those you love don't have to, I may have lost a year's worth of memories but it's not hard to notice this about you. You fight for who you love, and you do what you need to, you take on the villain role so it's you at the firing end not a loved one." He spoke resting his forehead against mine.

"You did what you did for survival Isabella and think back to it really hard, the people you tortured and killed who were they and why did you do it? Dragon is known for her kills and her torture she was more inventive than any fucking don past and present. She was so fucking feared not because she was scary but because of the people she hunted, you never hurt an innocent and you never killed anyone except for bosses, dons high scale vile scums. You killed and tortured people that are untouchable. Think about it, are you really a villain or someone's hero?" He added genuinely making me think about what he said.

I moved back looking at him, with teary eyes I really looked at him. Not just with my eyes but my soul, what was frustration was now replaced with admiration. Like when you stare out in the darkness and you see the sun rising, the warmth that sores in your soul the hope that rises. I knew now that no matter what, no matter how much I fight it, its him it's always been him.

Getting lost in each other we didn't realise another person entering the room, she cleared her throat looking between us unsure of what to do. "How are you feeling Isabella?" She whispered softly going around her boss. Vincenzo stepped aside but not too far, "better" I replied out of breath for some reason.

"Do you feel dizzy?" She asked me casually while doing some routine checks. I shook my head no, "miracle that fall did not do more damage. You're free to go but even though I know it's to good to be true but please get some rest." She smiles warmly I laugh and nod my head.

X

Back in the bed I felt serene, I had Dante next to me sound asleep, it was late, and Vincenzo wasn't back. I shook it off trying to get some sleep, cuddling up to Dante I shut my eyes.

But we all know that's too good to be true, I jumped out of bed securing Dante in his cot I walked around the massive house looking for Vincenzo, I walked past his office and heard murmuring.

"This means war, no more rushed plans no more strategic basic ambush when we do it. It's going to be the end, I'll set him up in flames and burn his world to ashes like he did to Dante, Maria, and Isabella." My heart skipped a beat hearing the names.

I stayed put against the door listening carefully. "I want all higher-ups training the soldiers and get Luca to get more recruits. This is going to be a life-or-death situation, no one outside of this circle is to know a single detail. For this to work out no one can know what's happening we need to minimise the chatter, once Hacker has a scheduled routine for both Xavier and Salvatore, we can begin to pick apart their lives bit by bit. I'll have the girls at the clubs keep an eye and ear out any chatter or mummers in regard to baby Salvatore and Xavier come straight to me. Same goes towards my men underground and in high office, with our contacts with the mayor and federal agents we can cut corners finding out what they know about us and them eliminating anyone and anything that will stop us from getting to our end goal." He paused for a moment.

"Hacker is going to be in charge of talking to the higher ups as he can do so in code and in a manner that's untraceable, Luca once you recruit people, I need you to spread the word to our workers in the clubs I want to know everything. Bullseye you're in charge of strategy and technique get your men up to a level that is lethal. Once we have what we need I will let everyone know about the plan including all of you, I need to first perfect it before letting anyone in, this is our main priority." He empathised to them, I can imagine his stern face and stiff posture as he talks and gives orders, his left hand is most likely gripping the edge of the table. While he does gestures with his right, the veins in his neck and arm bulge out when he is serious.

"This isn't a battle anymore. This isn't just an enemy I want abolished off the face of the earth. This is war and I won't stop until he is nothing but ashes."

Silence … I back away from the door and dash back to the room before he notices me snooping. I got under the covers and laid awake, my mind replaying the conversation I overheard before I couldn't help but overthink it all or wrap my head around how I felt about it all the door creaked open. Vincenzo saw me lying awake, "are you okay? How are you feeling?" He spoke softly checking my forehead for a temperature.

"I'm okay" I spoke up out of breath, he looked at me suspiciously "Why do you sound like you ran a marathon?" He questioned looking at my chest, I cheekily widened my eyes smiling innocently. "Whatever do you mean?" I asked acting oblivious.

He squinted his eyes looking at me, before shaking his head and walking to the bathroom closing the door behind him.

I sit up in the bed and rest my head gently against the bedrest, after a minute the door clicks open, and Vincenzo is walking back out … fucking shirtless and in a pair of his black boxers.

I let out an unsteady breath quickly looking away before he caught my stare, I felt the bed dip looking towards him slowly he settled himself on the bed getting in a comfortable position. I turned off the lamp on my end, the only light now shining was the lamp on his bedside.

I stared off into the distance, the accident was yesterday, and I still couldn't burn the memory from my head. Everything was blurred together and yet is crystal clear. I just didn't want to believe it all happened, his confession and his plea to love him back, my fall. We lost a lot of men yesterday and I couldn't help but feel responsible.

"Isabella?" Vincenzo softly calls out both of us still staring straight ahead lost in our heads.

"Hm?" I hummed in response.

"I know you were at the door" he replied in a smug voice. I winded my eyes and looked over at him smacking him in the chest.

"You knew!" I whisper yelled so I don't wake up Dante, he chuckled "I could see your shadow under the door, and from what I know you are not one to sit still Isabella Knight" he joked smiling.

I smiled shaking my head "were you serious?" I asked softly. His soft exterior now replaced with his normal one. Tense and stiff, "yes" he replied short and sweet.
"He has taken too much not to pay for the consequence of it. He took your entire childhood from you. He stole Maria's life from her, and he did the same to Dante. My fucking twin brother" he chocked out pointing at his chest. It was the first time I saw any true emotions displayed on his face.

I sighed nodding my head "then its war." I confirmed "but let me be a part of it" I added. He shook his head instantly "absolutely fucking not, what kind of parents would we be if we both go into this. I won't leave Dante without his mother. Especially after what happened yesterday." Vincenzo quickly rushes out.

"I won't leave him without his dad" I sternly responded "I am not letting you go into it alone.

I owe it to you, the mafia, my parents, Dante, Maria, and our son to fucking end him. Let me help, I know him better than anyone and more than what Hacker can find out. Let me help you, let's finish him together … please" I pleaded, I wasn't planning on letting this go without a fight so it would be easier for him to just agree with me now.

"Okay" he breathed out.

X

I opened my eyes slowly to the sunlight peeking through, I looked around and felt a pair of strong arms wrapped around me tightly. My head rested on his chest as my arm wrapped around his waist, I wiggled out of his embrace slowly to not wake him.

Grabbing Dante, we both made our way to the kitchen, "good morning" Lorenzo calls out walking in scratching the back of his head, "morning" I replied.

"You hungry?" He asked, I nodded my head "same. You know how to cook?" he asked sitting at the table.

I looked back at him rolling my eyes "for god's sake" I laughed grabbing Dante some baby food to eat, "I can't believe you're on solids" I cried out. He just stared back at me, "okay talk about moody definitely your father's son" I called out putting him in his highchair. Lorenzo chuckled settling down beside me, "so how are you?" He subtly tries opening up the topic of me and Vincenzo.

"Oh, look at your nephew, he wants you" I baby talked pointing at Dante. He turns looking at Dante who stared back at him with an annoyed expression, Jesus I birthed a mini version of Vincenzo.

"Uh huh" Lorenzo commented looking at me unimpressed.

"It's just his way of showing love, a King's trait" I shrugged my shoulders, he rolled his eyes "ouch" clenching his chest to mimic a broken heart.

I shooed him aside and started feeding Dante, "so how has it been with you and Vincenzo?" He tries once more, "ooo hot damn dana nana na na na" I start humming a song, "I'm trying to have a serious conversation with you!" He bursts. I shrug my shoulders "and I'm trying to subtly avoid it".

"Isabella" he calls out.

I sigh "Lorenzo its complicated enough without me trying to despair and explain to someone else, its only confusing me more" I whined, "Your brother is … complicated I don't even know what he wants." I gave in a little letting him in on my frustration.

"Did you know Vincenzo's gone to the doctors to see if there's anything he can do or take for his memory loss" Lorenzo speaks up after a long pause. I snapped my head in his direction shocked "What!" I whisper yelled.

"Good morning" Vincenzo speaks up walking down the stairs, Lorenzo looks at me and gives me a look to keep my mouth shut about it. Dante starts squealing putting his hands out, what the fuck. "He was just- now he hey man that's cold" Lorenzo greases Dante at his sudden mood change after seeing his dad.

"You happy to see me bud?" Vincenzo picks him up and Dante places his head in the crook of Vincenzo's neck. Lucky little shit.

I huffed shaking my head "I wish you were a girl" I hissed, Vincenzo laughed "girl or boy nothing would change" he condescendingly replied shrugging his shoulders.

Rolling my eyes, I stood up and grabbed Dante off him so he can finish eating. "It's just a phase, your mummy's boy, aren't you?" I baby talked watching his eyes light up after he starts clapping, "that's my boy" I cheered looking up at Vincenzo victorious, rolling his eyes he walked further into the kitchen to get something to eat.

Lorenzo sat back next to me and looked back making sure Vincenzo was far enough for him not to hear us.
"He is trying some new things they're testing for short-term memory loss. He wants to remember you I know he loves you. I know it's real for him because he managed to fall for you twice." Lorenzo whispered.

My heart skipped a beat love.

I don't think I've ever loved anyone. Fuck we haven't even said it to each other. I couldn't help but feel on a high hearing the news, he might be taking meds to remember me.

Before I could reply to Lorenzo, Vincenzo comes up towards us and places a plate in front of me. "Eat" he instructs me taking the baby food from my hand and moving Dante's seat to face him as he takes over feeding him. "Hey what am I chopped liver? I'm fucking hungry too" Lorenzo yelled out, I punched him in the arm "don't curse in front of the baby" I yelled out.

He groans holding the side of his arm "oh sure because punching me in front of him is fine, he doesn't understand what the fuck I'm fucking saying." He yelled out gesturing towards Dante.

I punched him three times again, he jumps up and storms off somewhere deeper in the kitchen mumbling under his breath. "Fucking can't even curse in my own fucking home, stupid strong bitch punching me. Dumb annoying brother won't make me food".

I rolled my eyes laughing at him, "idiota" I mumbled. Looking down at my plate, freshly made chocolate chip pancakes. "Thank you" I smiled up at Vincenzo, he nods his head smiling before ushering me to eat again.

X

After food Ariana took Dante out for some fresh air, while I went upstairs and got dressed, Vincenzo walked into the room admiring my figure. I turned looking at him "What?" I questioned softly.

He shrugged his shoulder "it's time for your training get ready" he answered my question "Gym in ten."

I huffed fucking great.

UNKOWN POV

I snuck around the back of the clinic opening the back door slowly, "I'm here for the short-term memory loss pills trial don't fucking know" Vincenzo blurts out.

The receptionist laughs nodding her head, "just sign this form and we can enlist you as a subject" she smiled "what's your name?" She smiled looking at him. "Leonardo Garcia" smart not giving her his real name, but I knew him I knew him too well. I was going to fuck his life like he did mine, I'm going to make her hate him and come to me.

"You know what let me think about it a bit and I'll come back next week for the pill box." He nodded his head the receptionist smiled looking up at him "you can call and confirm your participation and once you do, we will have a labelled box for you" Taking the forms he put his shades back on and stormed out. If your smart Vincenzo King do not come back for those pills because I'm going to make sure it leads you to insanity, then death. I'm getting her away from you and my revenge once and for all, this is war.

THE EL DRAGÓN

Isabella's POV

I ran downstairs in the gym and was met by an unimpressed Vincenzo, rolling my eyes I got ready for three hours of fucking hell.

He instructs me to do some stretches before our hour workout and then I get a few minutes break before we start training today was knife tactics. A weapon I consider Vincenzo's favourite, I stretched out and got ready.

"Go over to the assisted squats, I'm going to start it off with light weights. It'll get heavier the more we train." He gestured for me to go and get ready, getting in position he added the weights and guided me.

"Four sets forty seconds each" he ordered and started his timer; I squatted down and slowly got back up focusing on my form in the mirror. After around ten my legs began to shake, fuck I cannot be this out of shape. Vincenzo saw my struggle and smirked, I rolled my eyes "don't be a condescending asshole" I hissed. He rolled his eyes and came to assist me. Standing behind me closing the gap between the two of us thinking we couldn't get any closer he proved me wrong as his hands slowly make their way to my waist then down gripping the side of my hips pulling me further into him.

"Take your stance" he whispered against my ear.

I gulp fixing my form. "Bend your knees and lift with them not with your back" he guides me down into a proper squat.

His hands behind my thigh then down to my knee to demonstrate what he means by lifting with them and not my back. We stayed like this for what felt life hours and I forgot all about the pain I was in, I forgot about the burning sensation in my thighs, because I was feeling a whole different sensation in between my thighs.

I staked the weights back breathless as I watched him move around the machine and in front of me, while I was trying to catch my breath Vincenzo looked rather smug. He leaned his wrists on the metal rod and looked down at me, our hight difference once again leaving him to tower above me, I rolled my eyes "condescending ass, I had a baby come out of me I can be unfit if I want!" I hissed crossing my arms over my shoulders. "You want to call it a day? Or do you want to get into combat?" He genuinely asked me, I cocked an eyebrow and thought about it.

Combat meant hands on hands training, and he had to be even more up close and personal, in various positions. "I made a deal. Let's do it" I smirked suddenly determined to finish what we started, I took a small swing of water and was guided over to the mat.

"Get ready" he throws a punch at me I quickly duck and push him back "what kind of fucking training!" I yelled.

"I told you get ready" he retorted. I rolled my eyes noticing my unamused facial expression he gets serious again.

"I know you're good with your hands, now I need you to be able to do both a calculated hit and also using the other persons strength against them" He got into his stance nodding his head for me to mimic his actions.

I got into my stance myself and waited for his instruction, "Block and control the punch" he explained. "Punch me" he states I look at him confused "Isabella punch me" I shrug my shoulders, and do as I'm told he swiftly slips and moves my arm to the side, trying to use my opposite arm he blocks and puts me in uncomfortable stance my arm reached out behind my back.

"Okay you made your point asshole" I grunt out, he lets go looking both amused and smug.

"When you see the attack coming lock and control it".

"I'm going to punch you slowly and do as I say" he instructs nodding my head he throws a punch very slowly guiding me how to lock and control it.

"Slip and quickly carry the attack with the front hand" he instructs, I slip to the side his arm going just above my shoulder, using my left I push it aside stopping it from nearing my face. While my right hand rests on his left fist. "Control the movement with both arms and redirect any cross attack using the opponents force against him." He goes to throw a left punch my right hand that was rested on his left, now clutched his wrist redirecting him to the side.

"Twist my arm up and put pressure on my neck. Make sure you have control over your arm and lock the elbow." I smirk feeling satisfied with his new position.

"Okay" he informs me to let go but I just stay like this for a minute.

"Isabella!" He grunts, I smirk letting go mimicking his previous smug expression.

"Cazzo" he curses under his breath before moving aside. "Come on" he waves me over "now that you caught on. Let's do it for real. Ready?" He asks.

"Yes" I answer waiting for him to throw the punch, but he just stood there looking at me I got up from my stance and put my hands up "what are you doi-" Cutting me off he throws a punch, quickly slipping aside I move it away, he swings his left faster than I thought but I redirect it aside.

I twist his arm up putting pressure on his neck and locking the elbow. "WHAT THE FUCK WAS THAT" I yelled at how he abruptly thew the punch. Letting go of him he straightens his posture and shrugs.

"If someone is going to try and punch you Isabella they won't ask if you're ready. You need to be alert" he grabs his towel and water bottle taking off his shirt he walks over to the treadmill.

"You're done for today, but tomorrow be ready. This was your first gym session since the baby you learnt one technique today don't worry, I plan to work you out tomorrow get rest" he smirked knowing how that would sound. I rolled my eyes turning around before he saw the smirk that made its way to my lips.

Dashing off I go upstairs and jump in the shower quickly stripping and stepping foot underneath the hot water, I sighed as the water fell onto my skin, I took a moment feeling the hot water land on my arms making my body shudder at the sudden heat.

I looked up at the shower head my eyes closed as the water fell over my face smiling feeling somewhat peaceful, "Isabella! Dante's fussing" Lorenzo shouted from the bedroom door I laughed shaking my head "give him to his dad I'll be out in a minute" I shouted from the shower and quickly rushed to get clean.

Can't imagine Vincenzo and Dante alone … what a disaster I mentally teased laughing.

X

Going through my closet I hummed trying to figure out what to wear, I ranked my eyes through the various clothes and smirked pulling out a black crop corset and light blue ripped denim jeans. Pairing them with my white and grey Jordans.

As I'm walking out of the bedroom, I let my hair loose from its previous ponytail and make my way to the living room, "Lorenzo where's Dante?" I asked concerned.

"With his dad like you said" he mocked like I should know the answer "yes ..." I huffed taking a deep breath "but where-" cutting he off he shoots up and gasps.
"What!" I jumped back alarmed he gestures to my body and does another exaggerated gasp.
"Lorenzo what!" I scream looking down dusting myself off in case there was a spider on me.

"You're ... dressed" he explained, I looked at him eyes wide and irritated. "THATS WHAT YOU-" I cut myself off grabbing a pillow I chase after him hitting him with it repeatedly.
"Son of a bitch" he curses trying to block the hits.
"Okay. OKAY!" He yelled out grabbing the pillow from my hand giving me a death stare that couldn't hurt a puppy, but I faked scared "ooh scary" I shudder rubbing my arms.

"Idiota" I mumbled under my breath.

He looked at me cheeky with a wide grin, "come on I didn't mean that you looked ugly before but we gotta admit you let yourself go honey." He pointed at me.

I widened my eyes, my mouth slightly hung open with a humorous after tone. "Excuse me" I breathed out, "you look hot now though glad to have you back" he winked. I blew the loose strand of hair out of my face and rolled my eyes, crossing my arms he widened his smile "come on smile" I looked at him like he lost his mind "it was a compliment I promise" he smiles crossing his heart.

I continued staring at him with the same expression, "come on smiling is contagious" he whined throwing his hands up I rolled my eyes "don't worry I'm vaccinated against it" now it was his turn to roll his eyes "honey just before you go ... who you dressed up for? A certain stubborn ass perhaps?" He scratched his chin deep in thought.

I looked at him like he had gone mad "I just felt like getting dressed" he burst out in the most sarcastic condescending laugh "denial looks so bad on you" he continued laughing.

I let out an exhausted huff and wandered off.

"The two stubborn men are in the gym" he called out.

I raised an eyebrow making my way to the gym "what could he do with a baby in a gym?" I wondered aloud to myself, turning the corner I stand in the doorway staring at the two of them.

I stand there invisible to the two of them as they entertain one another Vincenzo standing behind the bar as he slowly let's go of Dante while my baby grips the steel bar hanging off of it, Vincenzo protectively standing close behind his hands under him in case he lets go.

"That's my boy!" He cheers him on as Dante giggles and let's go of the bar catching him, he holds him above his head and kisses his temple. "Come on you can spot me" he baby talks, I covered my mouth quickly to muffle a laugh, I have never heard him speak in a baby voice I don't know if it's cute or plain comedic watching a Mafia boss act like that.

Vincenzo spots me at the door with my amused expression "You do realise I'll have to kill you now" he states looking at me I shrug my shoulder, "I will happily let you kill me if you do it in that voice" I smiled back wide and stepped inside going towards Dante.

Vincenzo goes to speak before staring at me in shock, I looked at him worried "what?" looking down at myself and behind me in the mirror to see if I had any stains. He exhaled and rubbed the back of his neck with his free hand, I smirked realising what was happening and shook my head.

Grabbing Dante out of his arms I held him close to my chest and looked back at Vincenzo who was shamelessly ranking my body up and down "you might want to go" he whispered out, I looked at him confused "because if you don't I might have to pay for Dante's therapy" my eyes going wide, looking up at him my eyes full of lust like his beautiful grey eyes.

"Go Isabella" he warned me, I smirked and walked out getting the exact reaction I intend on, I slowed down my pace as the realisation that I dressed myself up to get a rise out of Vincenzo … huh maybe I am in denial? I paused for a second looking at Dante who gave me a confused look "Nah" I denied it.

X

I wandered into the new clinic we had on the estate and saw my parents talking, they looked so deep in conversation that when I walked in, they jumped up like they were scared if I heard what they were saying, or like teenagers getting caught smoking by their parents.

"You, okay?" I asked feeling uneasy, they both smiled nodding their heads, but my dad looked very off, I edged closer to mum and sat beside her, "are you feeling, okay? Is it being stuck in this hospital environment making you get PTSD?" I questioned feeling genuinely concerned.

They shook their heads no, but no one was saying a word, and a very sick feeling began settling in the pit of my stomach. I looked at them both uneasy but before I could say anything Vincenzo's voice cut me off "Isabella" I looked at him and then back at my parents before slowly standing up and leaving the two of them alone once again.

Before approaching Vincenzo, I walked by the nurses designated for them specifically "keep a closer eye on them" I nodded my head at her, she understood and nodded her head yes "Yes, boss" and with that she walked off.

I haven't heard someone calling me boss since the time
Vincenzo ... I shook my head not wanting to think about it.
I approached Vincenzo who looked at me weary "what was
that?" He asked and nodded his head in the direction of my
parents. I looked up at him as we started making our way
back to the house "I can honestly say I don't know" I drifted
off "if you need time with them yo-" I shook my head
sternly.
"No, come on let's go" I took the lead and made our way
upstairs into his office.

I smiled widely seeing Garcia sitting in the chair "Marcel!"
I cheered and ran towards him giving him a tight squeeze
which he gladly returned "my sweet girl" he whispered
admiringly into the hug. I pulled away smiling, I turned seeing
Vincenzo giving me a weird look before he moved me aside
and gave the old man a hug.

"Nice to see you again old man" Vincenzo smiled
welcoming him. "I may be old, but I can still kick your butt"
he warned pointing his finger at him. I sniffled a laugh and
looked up, the office was full of Garcia's trusted inner circle
and Vincenzo's most trusted men. "I thought the five families

were supposed to be here?" I question looking in between the two of them.

"They will be informed when they fit the picture" Vincenzo chimes up, "besides you learn not to trust anyone. Not even the five families, every mafia is for themselves the only one I trust with my life is Garcia" He turned to look at Garcia giving him a grateful smile.

Garcia smiled nodding his head a look of sympathy washing over his features, telling me he knows something deeper about Vincenzo than anyone else. Which would make sense since Garcia has known Vincenzo since he was a little boy.

"Okay let's begin" Garcia claps as he sits down in his chair, he ushers for his men to join him by sitting. Vincenzo also gives his men a nod indicating it's okay for them to take a seat.

"We have underestimated them, as hard as it is for me to say it. It's time we start planning for the real war, properly and a lot more precise than our previous attacks. No more sly attacks, I want this place to go up in flames." Vincenzo began looking over at me to cue me to chime in.

"Xavier is anything but brave, but what he is, is conniving and very good at brain washing people. He managed to get the Salvatore's under his command, making this whole game a lot harder than we originally thought" I spoke up, looking at Vincenzo.

"That's why this time when we attack it won't be child's play because we are dealing with a mafia that is literally threatening the King's, now it's time to remind them what and who the Kings are." He explained to the room moving over to his desk and grabbing a blueprint.

"Recently I have contacted my moles in the Salvatore mafia along with requiting more of my workers in the strip club, bars, restaurants and so forth to keep an eye and listening to everything they say. After giving them a photo of how they looked and how his inner circle looked, Isabella informed the ladies to place a mic on a table and keep it open only seating those in the photos on it. Recording many conversations" He smirked feeling proud and I couldn't help but smirk with him.

Lorenzo rolled his eyes and drew a heart in the air only for me to see, I squinted my eyes at him acting like I couldn't see him. Vincenzo looked over at me and ushered for me to continue, "After the mics were implanted in specific private rooms, restart tables, poker tables and so forth we have gathered very useful information. For example," I extended my hand out to Vincenzo, he gave me one of the blueprints and stood next to me.

I smirked and opened it on the table gracing my hand over it, "we got the exact blueprint of their hideout, a hideout they believe to be completely safe, hidden and most importantly impossible to find. Especially because it's in Italy we believe they are planning something soon" I pointed my finger up "in their defence it would have been impossible to find but thankfully Xavier and Salvatore's inner circle of men gossip more than us females" I shrugged.

"With this we can infiltrate within the walls, roofs and so forth. This is our ticket to give an attack none of them will see coming. When the time comes" I smirked looking at everyone in the room who had a very interested facial expressions plastered on their faces.

I stepped aside allowing Vincenzo to finish off "I don't want to make any moves until we have all the information I need, all the training I see fit and most importantly until I know we can do this with as little deaths. No pre-mature moves, Garcia myself and Isabella will be in many meetings to discuss the depths of what our move will be. This blueprint is only our first step, there will be many more to come. As of right now I want everyone to start getting ready, sharpen your training along with the trainees, Lorenzo and Bullseye I need the two of you to make sure all the recruits we have do the work we need, scooping, and getting small jobs we need done to strike a little fear in their hearts." He started giving off orders.

"Hacker, I need you to work with Garcia's tech Alex and begin getting into their systems, I'm talking about everything from their phones to their houses if you can." He looked at Hacker who had a smug look on his face "if I can?" He retorted making Vincenzo roll his eyes.

"The rest of you, you know exactly what to do. I want to see everyone training and getting ready. This time no fuck ups."

X

After about another twenty minutes the meeting was over, Garcia dismissed his men telling them to go outside by the car or mingle if they pleased while he spoke to myself and Vincenzo.

"Now I want to see my boy" he smiled rubbing his hands together, Vincenzo looked at him confused while I knew exactly what he meant I rolled my eyes laughing "excuse his confused expression I think he forgets sometimes he has a boy" I walked out to get Dante before Vincenzo stopped me "I'll get him" he ushered me to stay as he went out to look for where Dante was.

"How are you dear?" Garcia spoke up ushering me to sit next to him, I smiled and nodded my head "I'm okay... a little confused but I'm good" I smiled reassuringly he edged closer to me with a curious look as he furrowed his eyebrows, "confused?" He questioned, "is this a sex change confused or a preference confusion?" He asked.

My mouth fell open as I stared at him, bursting out in a fit of laughter he looked at me taken back before he leaned back into his chair and watched me laugh with the biggest most admiring smile plastered on his face. "So beautiful when you laugh el dragón".

I slowly stopped laughing and smiled looking at him. *'el dragón'* the way it came out sounded all too familiar. It was soft and safe. How can a word or nickname be safe? I questioned myself shaking my head.

He saw the puzzled look on my face and smiled "It was a nickname I gave someone a long time ago" I nodded my head slowly, "your wife?" I questioned he smiled sadly and shook his head "she passed away years ago" he confirmed. I looked confused, "My wife and I wanted children, but she passed away pregnant. I was grieving two losses, and that's when I really bonded with Vincenzo and his brother Dante." I nodded my head understanding.

I rubbed his shoulder with a sympathetic smile "I'm so sorry" I whispered he looked at me and smiled "it's been a long time, I'm okay. Anyway, why don't you finish telling me what's wrong" he ushered for me to continue.

I leaned back in my chair and sighed feeling selfish continuing my problems after discovering his wife was dead, "go on" he urged me, I shrugged my shoulders and continued to explain my dilemma to him.

"I meant my parents have been acting strange, like they're hiding something, or they know something. I just can't shake off the feeling that whatever it is it's bad" I confided in him and truthfully said what was bothering me.

"I mean, have you taken into consideration that maybe it's just part of what they experienced being trapped for all those years?" He suggested. I sighed still not feeling that the two coincided "it's different this time, it's like they've changed? I can't explain it but somethings going on and its more than just PTSD … it's like they're getting certain memories back or just realising things … I don't know it's just a feeling I can't shake off" I whispered the last part drifting off.

He looked at me with a smile and nodded his head "when I get a gut feeling like the one you have it's usually always right trust it." He advised me, as he was about to say something else Vincenzo walked in with Dante.

"There's my boy" he cheered standing up, Dante laughed getting all excited as he tried to jump out of Vincenzo's grasp and into Garcia's. I giggled and watched as Garcia held Dante close to his chest and rocked him back and forth. "Cómo estás cachorro?" (How you doing puppy?) He asked him holding him up in the air, Dante clapped his hands and went to pinch Garcia's cheeks, "how cute" I awed watching the two of them.

Vincenzo looked at the two of them with admiration and some sadness probably because he never got this as a child, I looked at him my eyes softened watching as he looked at the two of them with yearning.

Garcia turned to look and caught Vincenzo's expression "Your dad is not use to sharing the spotlight when it comes to the old man" he mocks earning a chuckle from Vincenzo.

"I may not have had any kids, but you my son I'm so proud of and I love you far deeper than you can imagine" he reassured him "maybe not as deep as Dante but still pretty deep" he commented making me laugh out.

"All the attention is for him now" I shook my head watching my spoilt son get all the love.

X

Garcia left and now I was bathing Dante after Garcia insisted, he would feed him chocolate … 10 minutes later my son is now covered in chocolate. I washed him off and now I was watching him play with the bubbles in the bath. I leaned my chin on my arm "oh if your aunty was here, she would be so obsessed with you" I smiled weakly at my son.

It's not fair, she didn't deserve to go so soon.

"If she was here shed also side kick me and play with you and tell me to leave because the fun one came" I laughed imaging how Maria would be with Dante, she always loved kids and I know if she was here, she would die over Dante.

"Isabella?" I looked over at the door and saw Vincenzo, Ariana, and Lorenzo standing in the doorway surprised I ushered them in. "We wanted to watch" Ariana claps, I sniffle a laugh and they all take a seat around the bathtub.

"You sure we shouldn't put a pillow or something for him?" Vincenzo anxiously spoke up.

I rolled my eyes smiling "No if you have the guts, I dare you to disturb him right now" I laughed daring him, "Oh you don't want to get in the middle of Dante and his bubbles" Lorenzo spoke up from experience.

"He looks so much like Vincenzo" Ariana commented, I looked up my eyes making their way to a very proud Vincenzo who watched his son with so much love it made me melt.

"He might look like his dad, but he has his mum's attitude" I laughed out wanting to get something out of the human I held in my stomach for nine months. Laughing we all watched him splash away soaking us and the bathroom floor in the process, it's funny how such a little person had so much power that he brought us all back together.

"Isabella?" Ariana spoke up softly, I hummed looking over at her "are your parents, okay?" She asked curiously, I furrowed my eyebrows "what do you mean?" I questioned. "Me Sebastian and Alex decided to go check in, and we heard them arguing like really bad." I straightened my posture and looked at her "did you know what about?" I asked. She shook her head "the second they saw us they went mute" she shook her head slightly apologising for not having much more information.

I nod my head softly "everything okay?" Lorenzo now questions while Vincenzo looks at me concerned "I don't know" I answered honestly, "is that why you were weird when we left them at the clinic this morning?" Vincenzo recalls piecing it all together.

I shrugged my shoulders "I don't know … I sensed something was off like there hiding something but I just I don't know what that is yet." They all nodded their heads softly I shook my head wanting to change the topic.

"You know Dante's going to be four months next week" I smiled looking at Dante who looked up at the mention of his name, "stop growing please" Ariana begged tickling his exposed stomach.

He giggled shying away then splashing the water getting Ariana in the process. "Shouldn't you get him out?" Vincenzo laughs out I shook my head no, "his tiring himself out, plus his quiet why would you want to disturb that?" I questioned.

"Believe me when he is finished, he will let me know" I added.

"A lot like you in that sense" Lorenzo commented looking at Vincenzo.

"What's that supposed to mean?" He asked offended.

"He is thick headed and stubborn he has a scheme he won't steer from and if anyone dares disrupt him, he will throw a tantrum" Ariana and I laughed aloud and watched Vincenzo's face change from pride to a scowl.

"Case in point" Lorenzo motioned to Vincenzo's grease and Dante's grease that he was giving Uncle Lorenzo. "It's like he knew you were insulting them" Ariana pointed out watching Dante's unimpressed little face.

I shook my head laughing, and before I knew it Dante held his hands up and began squeezing his hands open and shut indicating he was now finished and wanted to get out.

"See" I motioned to Dante, Vincenzo laughed "that has to be the funniest and cutest thing I've seen in my life." He smiled watching Dante, I stood up as Ariana threw me a towel to wrap him in. Picking him up and quickly wrapping his wet body in a towel I walked out to the bedroom. Drying him off I started dressing him up, buttoning up his onesie.

Out of breath I put my hands on my hip and watched him try to roll over to his side. "Oh my god" I screamed excited. Vincenzo, Lorenzo, and Ariana ran towards me to see what happened looking panicked.

"He is trying to roll over!" I commented, Lorenzo slapped me and let out a sigh of relief. I picked Dante up and put him on the carpet flat on his back waiting for him to roll over, "Come on!" I cheered him on and soon everyone started cheering him on with me.

"Come on leone!" Vincenzo cheered when he saw Dante start rocking himself to the side.

"Come on you, stubborn little man" Lorenzo cheered earning a scowl form me. I looked over at the door and saw Hacker and Bullseye watching and many more men behind them trying to get a peek. I looked back at Dante who rolled on his arm, the men getting excited held their heads chanting. "Come on! YOU GOT THIS GO DANTE!" They all started chanting, jumping up and down as the excitement sunk in.

Laughing I shook my head and turned back to Dante, who had rolled back on his back. "NO!" They yelled, all of them including Vincenzo were on all fours cheering Dante on.

"Come on, one more time bud" Vincenzo spoke up.

"Come on baby" I smiled clapping my hands he looked at me then at his dad.

"Come on! Come to me" Vincenzo spoke up extending his hand out. With all the strength in his little body he flipped over rolling onto his stomach, lifting his head up his eyes grew big while he sucked on his bottom lip.

"YESSSS!" Everyone erupted in a very loud cheer, jumping up and down clapping.

I burst out laughing "oh my god and I thought I was the over excited parent" I commented watching everyone's reaction. Vincenzo picked up Dante cheering "that's my boy!" He kissed his cheek and lifted him in the air like his most prized possession.

I laughed watching Dante get surrounded by his dads' men, uncle and aunty. I smiled at the sight, knowing he was so loved and treasured not just by me but by so many people warmed my soul in a way I never knew possible.

After a few minutes Vincenzo noticed Dante getting sleepy, "okay bedtime for the big boy, everyone out" he ordered, one by one everyone kissed Dante goodnight and exited the room.

"One for you!" Lorenzo baby talked kissing Dante and then looked at his brother "and one for you" he squealed out kissing Vincenzo on the cheek "ok bye" he quickly rushed out before Vincenzo could reach him.

I laughed shaking my head before sighing in self-pity, God I fucking miss her. I wish she was here.

"I'll get him to sleep" Vincenzo whispered noticing my sudden switch in my mood, I nodded my head and stepped outside on the balcony. Leaning on the edge I took a deep breath closing my eyes allowing the wind to prickle my exposed skin.

Feeling refreshed and serene, I opened my eyes slowly looking up at the night sky. "I miss you so fucking much" I whispered. "Not a day goes by where I don't think of you, you're with me every single second" I emphasised just how much I think of her.

"I miss our talks, our hugs, hell even our fights. I miss every moment I had with you … I would give anything to just be with you again to go to the beach and watch the waves crash" I sighed closing my eyes a tear managing to escape.

"I don't know what to do, I don't know what's going on with mum and dad and my gut keeps telling me that there's something bad and maybe that nagging feeling is you giving me a sign that there really is something … I love you hermosa" I lowered my head back down.

"I miss her too" Vincenzo's soft voice breaks the silence.

I looked behind me weakly smiling at him, he made his way next to me looking out at the view. "I may not have known her for long and everything I knew I forgot but, she was so special. So, forgiving, caring, loving and protective. She was the type of girl that would do anything to protect the ones she loves." He smiled shaking his head.

"I can't tell you the number of threats and curse words she threw at me when she thought you were gone" he let out a soft laugh.

I shook my head laughing softly "she was always a feisty one when she wanted to be" I smiled.

"She would've been the best aunty" he looked over at me.

"I'm sorry you won't be able to share those experiences

with her" he apologised looking guilty. I shook my head "It wasn't your fault, Maria did what she did because she wanted to protect the people she loves and who have been protecting her and me. She saw the look in your eyes and knew in her heart what she had to do" I commented remembering the words she told me in the hospital.

"Her death won't be in vain, don't worry we will burn him to the fucking ground for everything his done" he reassured me, I smiled nodding my head, "I'm going to make sure he wished he burned himself in that fire." I commented.

"Come on" Vincenzo ushered me inside, I nodded my head and walked inside. I walked inside and felt like I needed to check up on my parents right now, "I'll be back" I spoke up and walked towards the door.

"You, okay?" He questioned I nodded my head "I just … I need to check something" he nodded his head slowly watching me leave.

I made my way towards the clinic a gut-wrenching feeling twisting my insides, I held my stomach and walked inside quietly trying not to tip them off that I was in the room.

"You fucking betrayed me! And now look where we are! If

they fucking find out what we did Vincenzo will have our heads that's if Isabella doesn't get to us first" My dad screamed out.

I stayed back my eyes widened shocked, holding onto my stomach feeling my breathing becoming more rigid "she won't find out! Besides it's your fault Mario! You're the one that wanted revenge against the girls ... against me!" Mama shouted out hurt.

"ME! IF YOU DIDN'T SLEEP AROUND, WE WOULDN'T BE IN THIS FUCKING MESS." He shouted out.

Cheated? What the fuck is happening. I looked around confused and in denial at everything I was hearing "IF YOU KNEW THE GIRIS WEREN'T YOURS YOU WOULD HAVE KILLED US ALL" She shouted.

What? "Well good thing I found out before our supposed death and kidnapping" he mocks.

"I just wish he didn't let her escape."

"If Isabella finds out what you did, she'll kill you!" Mum whisper yelled he growled and slammed his hands on the bed "she'll kill us both. You didn't object to any of it when I told you, you said it was your way of making up for your cheating".

My breathing picking up pace as I listened to the horror that was unfolding "and whose idea was it to kidnap-" before he could finish his sentence my senses went into overload and everything around me turned black.

THE TAJO DE RONDA

Vincenzo's POV

I quickly got out of bed making sure Dante was okay and sound asleep, heading out of my bedroom I shout "Luca watch Dante I'll be back" I called out and quickly made my way to Isabella.

I know she wants to be alone, but something was telling me to follow her, like if I didn't something bad was guaranteed to happen, I walked in the clinic slowly and saw Isabella crouched down against the wall. She had her hand over her chest she looked like she was having a panic attack.

Exactly like I expected her arm fell to the side and her body collapsing from underneath her. I quickly jumped towards her catching her mere second before her head hit the floor. Not wanting to make any noise I quickly carried her out, "come on Isabella" I whispered as soon as we were out of the clinic, I looked behind me and couldn't help wondering what the fuck she heard that made her collapse.

I carried her back to the estate and up to our bedroom and laid her down grabbing a glass of water I sat next to her as she slowly regained consciousness. Slowly opening her eyes, she looks at me relieved "was I dreaming?" She asked desperate for me to tell her that that's all it was. I sighed and shook my head "it's okay slowly" I whispered helping her sit up.

I handed her the glass of water which she took with appreciation, I sighed looking at her I didn't know if I should ask her what happened I mean do I even have a right to know? On one hand they're not my parents but on the other if she found out something that could threaten my mafia and especially our son, I have the right to know.

I decided it was best to just let her rest, and not push her just yet. "Isabella are you okay?" I whispered moving a strand of hair away from her face tucking it behind her ear. Her state wasn't settling, she's shaking and whispering to herself like whatever just happened triggered a mental episode.

"Nothing I'm okay" she whispered trying to come back to reality. I shook my head "something's made your eyes go dark." I pointed out looking into her eyes, her once emerald, green eyes now looked back at me hollow and dark. She slowly looked up at me, and in her state her eyes somehow softened when they connected with mine, she let out a breath nodding her head slowly.

"Promise me something" she whispered. I nodded my head immediately "anything" I spoke out. Biting her lips, she looked over at Dante with a longing expression "if anything happens to me, you won't turn your back on our son. You won't stop loving him and you will never let him forget me" her voice cracking as she spoke.

I stepped back looking at her, "Isabella don't talk like that please" I coughed shaking my head not wating to so much as imagine a life without her in it, memories, or no memories. "Vincenzo … please" she begged like she knew there was a chance she might not be here in the future. "I promise" I reassured her.

She nodded her head slowly taking in a deep breath, "are you okay?" I questioned softly she shook her head no. "Do you want to talk about it?" she shook her head again looking down, I nodded my head and sat next to her.

Pulling in her shaking body as she eased into me slowly calming down. "I think you need some rest, lay down" I ushered her, but she clung to me scared shaking her head. I sighed holding her tight, I looked down at her, her eyebrows furrowed, her eyes looking back and forth not being able to focus on anything while he nervously chews on her bottom lip. Her grip on my shirt was also deadly.

I laid down lying her with me, starting to hum. Knowing the one thing that might work in helping her calm down and take her mind off everything. "I know you haven't made your mind up yet" I classically sign out, keeping my voice deep and low with a hint of softness to it. Her head flies up looking at me shocked not expecting me to sing to her, "but I will never do you wrong" I rub circles on her back resting the side of my head on top of hers. "I've known it from the moment that we met" placing a soft kiss on her head, "no doubt in my mind where you belong" I hummed before continuing feeling a little nervous suddenly. "I'd go hungry, I'd go black and blue. I'd go crawling down the avenue. No, there nothing that I wouldn't do". I finished off smiling at the sight of her asleep, so calm and peaceful with a small smile dancing on her lips. She felt warm and familiar, solid, and safe. I wanted to hold her tight bury my face in the curve of her neck and never let go. Focusing on her breathing and listening to her heart beat I knew … I was screwed she would drive me to insanity and id happily allow her.

X

Slowly opening my eyes, I look down seeing Isabella in the same position when we fell asleep, rubbing her leg up and down I widen my eyes looking at my already grown erection. "Cazzo" I curse under my breath moving her off me and rushing to the bathroom.

Splashing myself with cold water I look at myself in the mirror, after all this time still unsure of who was staring back at me. I sighed picking up my phone and calling the clinic "I made a decision I want to remember" she spoke about the drug and gave me an appointment to come in. Hanging up the phone huffing out "spero di aver preso la decisione giusta" (hope I made the right decision)

"Vincenzo?" I looked out the bathroom door and saw Isabella waking up, I finished up in the bathroom and made my way to her. She let out a stressed breath and ushered me to sit, "I need to talk about something." I nodded my head sitting down slowly not sure if I was ready for this conversation, I looked at her anxiously waiting for her to continue, "it's about my parents. There uhm-" her voice cracks, pulling her into a hug "it's okay take your time Bella" she closes her eyes taking in a deep breath.

"I think there the reason I was kidnapped, and I think they intended for me to be killed by Xavier. Also, my mum cheated on my dad so the man who I fought for and went through my most traumatic time not only isn't my father but is the man who deliberately put me through it." She went to look up at me, but I pushed her head back on my chest because the reaction on my face is probably not one, she wants to see at the moment.

I need a second to take in what she just said because that must be the most mind fucking thing I've heard ever. I took in a deep breath and calmed my facial expressions as she slowly rose to me, "is that what you heard them say?" she nodded her head "and there the reason you passed out?" I asked my tone getting more aggressive, she hesitantly nodded again. "Okay" I shot up ready to walk out before she jumped in front of me "wait!" she rushed out, "move Isabella" I warned her. "It may not be true" I looked at her confused waiting for an elaboration "it can be the drugs there on, it is possible its messing up their memory along with ability to tell what's true and what's not" I shook my head "how would such statement make any sense in any hallucination, a scenario like that wouldn't even be said if it wasn't true. Isabella what if what they said is true?" she chewed on her inner cheek visibly stressed.

"There's only one way to know for sure" she looked at me, a look I haven't seen in a long-time determination. "What are you up to now?" I asked cautiously, "were going to Spain." Laughing I shook my head "no" smiling she looked up at me "yes" shaking my head "did you forget about your son?" she shook her head "Ariana and the thousands of armed men can watch and keep him safe. This is something I must do, and I prefer not to do it alone." I sighed shaking my head again "no"

X

Isabella's POV

I sigh buckling my seatbelt looking out the plane window, "I kept saying no how are we here?" Vincenzo blurts out abruptly, smiling I turn to him "no one ever tells me no" I wink. I sighed looking back out the window feeling the air being knocked out of me.

"Okay what exactly are we planning on doing in Spain?" he looks over at me waiting for some sort of plan, I looked out the window avoiding his question "hello?" he called out, I hummed keeping my eyes on the pretty clouds. "You don't have a plan, do you?" he sighed exhausted shaking his head as he rubbed his temples with his fingers. "Not exactly, but I've been known to do things on a whim, and when have I ever let you down?" I smiled.

"How about the time-" I put my hand up immediately "it was a rhetorical question mafia" He huffed a subtle laugh and leaned back into his seat, "we are going to die" he breathed out "always thought I'd be the one to kill us" he smiled, "just when you think you got it all figured out life throws a pink knife straight at you" I rolled my eyes "are you done?" I called out rolling my eyes, smiling he shook his head no.

"A loaded pink bomb" his eyes were closed with that stupid smug smirk on his face that I always shamelessly found attractive.

X

Finally landing in Spain we made our way to our hotel room, putting our stuff in the room we decided to plan for what I needed tomorrow seeing it was too late to do anything now. I called Ariana to check up on Dante, my stomach was in knots being this far away from him. "You okay" Vincenzo's voice snapped me out of my daze. I nodded my head softly admiring the moon from our balcony, joining me he put a blanket over my shoulders. "The view is gorgeous huh?" I whispered, nodding his head he smiled looking at me "breathtaking" I looked over at him smiling sheepishly.

"There's always something about the moon that draws me, it gives me serenity in the mist of chaos." I smiled admiring everything about the night sky tonight, "I think I know why you romanticize the moon" Vincenzo speaks up, I hum interested in his theory "go on" I encourage him.

"I've noticed when you get sad or go through a bad time you turn to the moon, because it is the one thing that never questions you or begs you for answers to problems you have no solutions for. You never had to prove yourself to it, it was always just there, shining and in most ways, humans can't understanding and listening to you. Reminding you that to be hole again we must go through phases of emptiness, and even in those phases the moon always rises providing light in the mist of darkness." He smiles in the distance admiring the moon.

While I stand completely stunned admiring him and his ability to read me like a book, I shake my head slightly looking back at the moon. "How'd I do?" he whispers, smiling sheepishly I nod my head slowly "you never disappoint Italy" I smirk at the old nickname I use to call him.

"So, what's your plan for tomorrow?" I sigh nodding my head "I have a few contacts with Xavier's ex men the ones who left when I left. If there is any truth to my parents' involvement there the ones who will know" I started explaining my thinking. "I'll call them in the morning and arrange a meeting, it's time to let my hometown know Dragons back" I eyed him mischievous "this should be fun" he smirked pulling me in for a side hug.

X

I slowly opened my eyes seeing Vincenzo's muscular arm wrapped around my waist holding me tightly pressed against him, I lowered my head back on my pillow slowly smiling to myself. I wish this could be an everyday thing, not sharing a bed but feeling like one. I missed him, I missed Vincenzo on an emotional level. As much as I thank God for bringing him back to me and I know his trying to remember … I just wish he was mine again I want him so damn much and sometimes it feels like I have him and then it vanishes in an instant.

Vincenzo woke up and slowly removed his arm, he leaned over to see if I woke up and I quickly shut my eyes faking sleep, I heard him sigh relived trying to get out of the bed without waking me up. Feeling a shadow above me my bedside dipped, "I'll get there eventually Isabella, I'll remember you and I'll make everything right … but truth is" he takes a deep breath, obviously nervous. I wanted to open my eyes and hug him but the only reason he was talking was because he thought I couldn't hear him, so I decided to keep up the act, it'll good for both of us if he gets this out, maybe it'll finally shine a light on everything.

"I'm scared Isabella, I'm fucking terrified I've done a lot of messed up shit when I woke up from that coma because I didn't know you, the moment I laid my eyes on you I was taken back, and when I met you, I was even more shocked, at how someone like you could've ever been with me. After everything I put and continue to put you through, you always manage to understand me, even if I don't understand myself. You never gave up on me even when you really should have. Now if I remember you every fucked up thing, I did is going to gut me, if not kill me and I'm so fucking scared for everything to come flooding back at once …" I felt myself start tearing up as he spoke.

"I promise you this Isabella, memories or no memories I'll fix everything, and I'll make it right." He stood up placing a tender kiss on my forehead. I stayed still for a few moments until I heard his footsteps start fading away. I opened my eyes as a tear flowed down my cheeks "you already made up for it" I whispered to myself quietly. He may have not remembered me, but I knew he was always there for me, and seeing him with our son made every doubt and hateful thought vanish. I yawned stretching out my arms before slowly sitting upright, "Vincenzo?" I call out softly, "bathroom" he yells back. I grab my phone and call up Mateo, he along with Alex were the only ones I was very close to in the gang, but of course the line goes dead.

I try one more time and get sent to voicemail, "hey Mateo, it's drag- uhm it's Bella. I know it's been years, but I really need to see you, if by any chance you get this message meet me at our spot, es importante y sobre la mano que mis padres tuvieron en todo llámame por favor" (it's important and about the hand my parents had in everything call me back please)

I hang up the phone and start calling up the only remaining men I know who would know if my parents had a hand in everything.

"Hola Samuel hablando." He answers his phone, "Hola Samuel es dragon" **(it's dragon)** the only person I could be myself with was Alex and Mateo, if I said my name, it would show weakness and right now, I needed them to be fearful that I'm back not that I have softened.

Dragon had the fear and respect that I needed so it was time to welcome my old self back … temporarily.

"No hice nada!" (I did nothing) I roll my eyes, idiots. "Lo sé, pero tienes información que necesito. Trae a Ángel y encuéntrame en el Viejo esconditie." **(I know but you have information I need. Bring Angel and meet me at the old hideout)** "Si, como quieras dragon" **(yes, as you wish dragon)**

"Samuel no me hagas esperar tienes una hora" **(don't keep me waiting you have one hour)** I hang up the phone and look over at Vincenzo who was now fully dressed and ready for the day, "you're not coming" I pointed my finger at him waving it back and forth before getting up to get ready. "Yes, I am" he insisted, I huffed closing the door to the bathroom, "when I made you promise to take care of Dante if I'm gone, I meant it, how is that going to work if you die with me?" I grabbed my toothbrush brushing my teeth.

"You insisted on me coming with you, and now you don't want me with you?" he calls out confused, I roll my eyes "you came because I needed you for the private jet" I spat in the sink and rinsed my mouth out. Opening the door, he stands in front of me "These are my contacts and it's risky they won't speak with an outsider, the only reason they agreed to see me is because if they didn't my punishment would be far worse than what Xavier would do if he found out" I pushed passed him going straight for my suitcase.

Rummaging through the clothes I finally found my outfit. I fling my loose cargo pants my bodysuit lace singlet along with my combat boots. "Turn around" I swirl my fingers around indicating for him to spin. He rolls his eyes turning around while I change.

"I'm coming with you and don't waste your breath trying to stop me. You're not the only one who can be stubborn" he shrugged his shoulders and I'm assuming that arrogant smirk also took place on his features.

"Fine but don't say a word!" I moved past him fixing my hair in the mirror, "as you wish, I'm only going to make sure you're safe" he whispered probably so I wouldn't hear him. I smiled to myself choosing to stay quiet, "if the meeting isn't for an hour why are we going now?" he questioned, I turned around smiling "I thought since I dragged you out the least, I could do is show you around."

"Oh really?" he mocked. I rolled my eyes smiling sheepishly.

"This doesn't mean I like you" I pointed out and grabbed the rental car keys on my way out. "Vamos!" I shouted out, hearing his low chuckle made me smile like a little girl with a crush. Shaking it off we both get in the car, I turn the key hearing the engine come to life, I smirk mischievously looking at Vincenzo who gives me a weary look in return, "what are you do-"

Hitting my foot on the accelerator I speed out of the garage, reversing back and taking a sharp turn to get on the street, zooming and swerving past cars I smile at the familiar feeling creasing through my veins.

The adrenaline rushing back to me, being back home in my element and knowing I was back to doing what I use to do it brought back nostalgia, I missed it so much, I missed the interrogation, the fights, bullets flying everywhere the rush it gave me and how it made my heart skip a few beats the sparkle id get in my eyes.

It's ironic how you can feel most alive when your facing death on a daily basis, once you get into it and I mean really get into it, it is an adrenaline, like nothing you've ever experienced before, a high so addictive that once you get a taste of it, it's very difficult to not want more and wanting more is where things begin to get dangerous.

I eased my foot off the accelerator and the car came to a steady safe speed as we drove past my old hunting ground, once people got a proper look at me, everyone began whispering, pointing, recording, and calling everyone and anyone. Dragons back and that was something my people loved, but the crime world hated. Even if my stay is temporary, they know I can do a lot in a short time.

X

After a long drive we finally arrived in one of my favourite cities in Spain. "Welcome to Ronda, Málaga" I cheer looking over at Vincenzo excited and giddy. He chuckles shaking his head as he admired the beauty of the city. I unbuckle my seat belt jumping out of the car like a child going to Disney land "vamos" I laughed out ushering him to hurry up. We started walking through the city and with each passing moment, I was emersed in the views of my old safe haven. This city is by far the most beautiful in all of Spain.

"The agriculture is beautiful" Vincenzo speaks up breathless. I smile nodding my head admiring the old buildings. "The detailing in the carvings is gorgeous, it was during the invasion that such building was built by the Arabs" I smiled.

"When people say invasion, it has such a negative relation to it, but truth be told the Muslim invasion of Ronda brought a lot of good, thanks to them Ronda became a city that was in control of an entire region." I pointed out as we walked pasted various restaurants and flower gardens.

"Ronda became the Taifa 'the nation', an independent kingdom, and it was said that during that time, was when the city flourished and was developed greatly." I explained the history behind this beautiful city, Vincenzo looked around absorbing the beautiful sight as well as my speech.

"Speaking of. This is known at the Arab baths" we walked into the old historic building seeing the architectural structure that was left behind and well preserved for us to see, the stone floors and tall arch's made out of what looks like stone but could be something else.

"Woah" Vincenzo breaths out looking around, smiling I nod my head "they invaded back in 711, to think this place is still standing is crazy" I point out the very big gap.

"Come on I want to show you another building they did the Mondragón Palace!" I squeal excited grabbing his hand and rushing him out.

"I wonder why you'd be excited for that" Vincenzo calls out sarcastically "it's the dragons palace and your sarcasm is overlooked!" I exclaimed guiding him through the busy streets. We stopped in front of the palace, out of breath but excited. "This is one of the town's most visited and most important monument in Ronda." We walked inside seeing the exhibits all around, this palace houses the municipal museum.

"You have to see the courtyard, Maria loved it she used to

spend hours sitting and admiring the structure, said it was extremely clear it was from the Arab period. It's truly a beauty the Arabs have gorgeous taste" he smiled sadly at the mention of Maria, before nodding his head. I smiled at him nodding my head letting him know I'd be fine visiting the garden without her.

As we made our way I looked up at Vincenzo with a sheepish grin, rolling his eyes he laughs "go ahead" he ushers for me to talk. "Okay! Legend has it that this building was the residence of the King Abbel Malik or Abo Malik. The son of the sultan of Morocco." I spill another fun fact feeling all giddy, Vincenzo eye roll turned into a sheepish smirk he couldn't help overtaking his features.

"Say what you want Italy, but you're enjoying this" I point out he shrugs his shoulders muttering a "maybe" but I was to entranced by the gorgeous garden to listen or care.

"The garden as it is today would have been part of the Arab period as would the gallery on the front. The most important work was carried out on the building. It is a unique courtyard in many ways" I pointed out as we walked around looking at everything the way a triple series of low arches which stand on some web-built brick walls and marble columns and capitals.

I moved towards the small water fountain in the middle and smile sheepishly gliding the tips of my fingers along the water.

FLASHBACK

"Maria mira que linda" **(Come see the fountain)** I shouted at Maria to come see the water fountain, "dios mío que bonito" **(oh my god how pretty)** I ran my fingers through the crystal-clear water, getting an idea. I smirked looking up at Maria before splashing the water on her completely soaking her. "Isabella!" she shouted, laughing I bent over holding my stomach.

"Isabella! No hay postre por salpicar a tu hermana" **(no dessert for splashing your sister)** Mama yelled but I was too busy laughing at Maria and her death stare to care, "valió la pena" **(it was worth it)** I laughed, finally starting to calm down. Maria lunges for me both of us falling in the small fountain.

Looking at each other we both burst out into laughter as

Mama and Papa shake their heads exhausted. "te tengo" **(got you)** Maria smiled, rolling my eyes I laugh. "no está mal niña de las flores" **(not bad flower girl)**

END OF FLASHBACK

"Isabella?" I snapped out of my trance and looked up at him "sorry, I just remembered something" I smiled at the bittersweet and distant memory of us being innocent ten-year-old's not knowing what life was about to hit us with.

"I have one more place to show you" I smiled grabbing his hand and guiding the way to the Tajo de Ronda. Standing on the edge of the bridge I smile looking out at the view and the water beneath us crashing against the rocks. "I've always loved this spot, it holds so much history including destruction and yet it is the one thing that makes Ronda unique, popular and special." He leans against the stone barrier admiring the view.

"What destruction?" he questioned looking confused, I smiled nodding my head "when this bridge was first built it couldn't withstand the traffic and weight of the two cities being co linked. So, it collapsed taking fifty innocent souls with it" I explained briefly.

"The town wanted to rebuild it, so they did in 1759, they made sure to take their time and not leave a thing to chance. The bridge we are now standing on took roughly 34 years to build, and it is now stronger and even more breathtaking than before".

"Sounds like someone I know" he whispers looking at me, I turn to face him moving the hair out of my face as I let a smile overtake my lips, "It's strange to connect and have so much in common with a bridge but whenever I come here it gives me hope, that everything takes time whether its healing or rebuilding yourself. Whatever it is this bridge is a symbol of rebirth for me. I always felt calm when I visited it" I take in a deep breath, really letting myself enjoy the moment.

It's been years since I was here last, and my soul was yearning for it without me realising it. "We should bring

Dante here." Vincenzo piped up.

I looked over at him surprised at his statement "I want him to connect with this place as much as you do. To look around and feel as safe and serene as you in this very moment. Then one day you can explain everything to him as you did to me" I don't know why I was getting emotional, but I nodded my head fighting back tears, "ok" I whispered nodding my head.

"We'd bring Ariana and Lorenzo as well something tells me they'll love it … and maybe a few of my men to make sure Dante is safe" I narrowed my eyes at him shaking my head. "I'm his mother, he is the safest baby in Spain" I pointed out.

"His mum is the reason I want full time protection, you crazy bitch" he muttered sarcastically making me burst into a fit of laughter.

"I would expect that tone from Lorenzo." I slapped his arm shaking my head "where do you think he got it from" he gave himself a sharp nod visibly proud of himself.

Rolling my eyes and shaking my head I couldn't help but smile to myself, this was the first time since his memory loss that I felt that connection with him again. I looked at his side as he looked out at the view, while I admired him.

I miss you Vincenzo King, I really fucking miss you.

X

After our trip it was time for the meeting, I walked into our old hideout back when I was in the gang, I had both feelings of nostalgia and anger at the memory of being here. It was not so much my acts that made me sick but working for Xavier.

"Isabella" I turned around, as my eyes bulge out of its socket. "Mierda" (fuck) I cussed under my breath ... so much for a calm day.

THE REVEAL

Isabella's POV

In front of me stood someone I never thought I'd see ever again, a man I thought I left behind in Minnesota, our adoptive abusive father. "Miss me?" he smirked waving his gun around. "Sabes cómo usar esa cosa?" **(You know how to use that thing?)** I mocked pointing to the gun.

"Who is that?" Vincenzo whispered, not tearing my eyes from stepfather "Someone who I should have killed" I mummer back as stepfather smirks tightening his grip on the gun. "Is that anyway to talk to the man who put a roof over your head Isabella" he smiled cunningly.

"It is the way to speak to someone who spent two years abusing and scaring my body" I bite back.

"What!" Vincenzo grunts from behind me, if he bites down on his jaw anymore, I'm scared it will crack. "You did what?" He aims his question at him, "how else could I have relived the sexual tension I had pent up for her … I mean look at her. It was either take her or scar her so no one else would" He breathes out his eyes ranking over my body making me extremely uncomfortable.

"Besides if Xavier found out I touched you he would hang me by my balls" at the mention of Xavier my head shot up "what?" I spat now connecting everything. Why he took us in, why he seemed like it was an order to take us, why it seemed like he had no life and why he kept saying we ruined everything. He was ordered to take us in, so Xavier can keep an eye on me so he can get me whenever he wanted.

"Yes! Yes! Look at her eyes widening she's figured it out" He laughed out, "and when you and your bratty sister ran away, I was facing very bad punishments!" he roared pulling his shirt up revealing multiple stab wounds, and markings.

"You ruined my life twice!" He put his fingers up, "now it's time to ruin your life, everything ends right here right now!" He moves to step towards me before Vincenzo stops him.

"Take one step near her and I promise it will be a step towards your death" Vincenzo's icy tone sent a shiver down my spine, I shook my head slightly trying to stay calm, this was not the time to get turned on.

"What are you going to do pretty boy?" he remarked. I

smirked looking over at Vincenzo who had that exact same smile on his face the same one I saw when we first met the first and only time, I was genuinely scared. Such a simple move his sinical smile that let everyone who saw it, know he out for blood.

"Well, you pointed out you didn't like your scars?" Vincenzo questioned he nodded his head confused "well when I skin you alive it won't matter would it?" my mouth dropped open looking at him. Damn, I want to do that. "You can help Isabella" Vincenzo winked seeing the disappointment on my face, smiling I turn back around to a very disturbed man. "What? Some people bond over food, art, or sports. Torture, knives and guns have really always been our thing" I shrugged my shoulders.

"You forget killing" Vincenzo chimed in, I pursed my lips pointing at him nodding my head "how did I forget that".

"Hello? Man with a gun" he waved his gun around. I laughed shaking my head, on cue Vincenzo and I pull out our own guns from the back of our pants.

"Our ones bigger" I smirked recalling the conversation me and Vincenzo had at the wedding.

I faintly heard Vincenzo let out a throaty chuckle, "if you pull that trigger, I'll kill you!" he yelled, I looked at him irritated at his genuine dumbness. "You do understand that if we pull the trigger, you die … so you can't actually shoot us … right?" I tried slowly breaking it down for him. He stood there for a moment before fully understanding what I said.

"You know what I mean!" he cursed out, shaking my head.

"No. No, we really don't" Vincenzo sighed exhausted. "Ok give me the gun" I roll my eyes extending my hand out, he smirked looking very confident for a man in his situation. "I don't think so" he whistled, and men emerged from behind the walls entering the space we occupied.

"You proud of yourself?" Vincenzo mocked him at his dramatic reveal, "we may be outnumbered but that doesn't mean we can't kill all of you" I slyly smirked watching his demeanour deflate, "why can't you just surrender like a normal person?" stepfather sighed exhausted. Did he really think I was going to just lay on my back and wave a white flag?

"She prefers dangerous freedom over peaceful slavery. She

will never surrender" Vincenzo pointed out, "as you wish. Get them" there was about ten men behind him all storming towards me and Vincenzo some holding a bat, others a crowbar. Clearly none of them are from or were a part of the gang, but since none held a gun, I put mine back.

One thing I will never do is fight an unfair fight, I like my wins to be genuine, also love to point out they got beat up by a girl. I turned seeing Vincenzo do the same. Everything suddenly felt like it was going very quick, five men charged towards me while the others charged for Vincenzo.

Oh, baby it's good to be home.

The man went to swing the bat at my face, skilfully ducking down I uppercut him in his stomach grabbing a hold of the ends of the bat I twist our positions around firmly pressing the bat against his neck. Back kicking the other man in his groin, letting go of the bat he passed out on the floor. Swinging the bat upward hitting him on his jaw, immediately knocking him out.

I turn around seeing the remaining three watching me worried, "come on boys" I purred egging them on. "I'll even make it easy for you" I mocked throwing the bat to the other side of the room. Tensing their jaws all three charged at once, I punched one square on the nose, but the other idiot grabbed me from behind.

Fuck! I tried wiggling out of his grip, but the men smirked both punching me in my stomach, it felt like my intestines were going to come out of my mouth. "Isabella!" Vincenzo shouts out, fending off the two he still had on him. I grunt and slam my head backward breaking the man's nose.

Letting me go on impact, I drop to the floor gasping for air. "Oh, this gives me flashbacks doesn't it baby?" stepfather cooed standing over me. Smirking I looked up catching my breath "sure does old man" I grip his ankle pulling his foot off from underneath him.

Immediately loosing balance, a loud thud echoed in the abandoned room as his back made contact with the hard floor. Climbing on top of him I pound my fist into his face multiple times, his men pulled me off immediately flinging me to the side.

I wipe the blood from my lip, they looked at me worried seeing I picked up a dropped crowbar "let's have some fun" I smiled wide.

My smile clearly making them nervous, swinging it in my hands I charged for them.

Stabbing the end of the crowbar in one of the man's eyes before taking it out along with his eye still penetrated on the bar. Kicking him in his stomach with all the force I had in me, he flies backwards crashing into the window. I throw the crowbar at the two men who reacted exactly as I predicted "DOS MÍO, EN REALIDAD ES SU OJO, OH. ME VOY A ENFERMAR" (my god it's actually his eye oh I'm going to be sick) they shouted.

Smirking to myself at their distracted and clearly disgusted states. I pushed them back officially breaking the window on impact I looked over at missing eye and pushed him out the window as well with my foot.

I turn seeing Vincenzo holding stepdad and looking at me very proud, "I did good?" I smiled proud of myself.

He laughed nodding his head amused "you did great princess" he praised me making me blush slightly. "Nice touch with the eye" he laughed nodding his head in approval.

Vincenzo looked down at stepfather and smiled "well I did warn you, didn't I?" he smiled, a smile that will always catch my attention and my heart. This entire trip is just making me realise how much I missed him. I tried denying it all I really did. I made myself busy with Dante, and trying to keep him safe but the way my heart hasn't stopped beating and my stomach hasn't settled I knew … I'm screwed. Vincenzo tied him up to a chair while we stood over him.

(TW GRAPHIC SCENE descriptive torture scene! Ends after the x)

Vincenzo's demeanour sent a shiver throughout my body, this was the most intimidating I've ever seen him. He was so mad that he was dangerously calm and composed. I looked back at Vincenzo who pulled out his favourite knife with his initials engraved.

"Woah woah!" stepfather screamed trying to get out of the rope's tight grasps around his arms and legs, if he didn't do what he did to me, and Maria id feel sorry for the old man.

"Have some mercy! Wait! Wait!" he screeched. Vincenzo scoffed placing the blade on his shirt.

"Mercy?" Vincenzo mocked pulling the knife down cutting his shirt in half.

"You took in two girls who were only seventeen, you saw how broken they were. You saw the pain Isabella went through and you knew the very detailed torture she had to endure. Where was your mercy?" My eyes stared watering hearing him speak, I think I'm getting my period because that made my heart explode and my eyes fill with fucking water.

"I was under orders!" he yelled trying to defend himself, "you were under orders to keep them under your eye not to torture them" he calmly explained as he used his knife to tear his shorts as well leaving him sitting in nothing but boxers.

"Instead, you abused what little power you had and tried to make yourself seem superior. Where was the mercy in that? While you were hurting them you never thought about getting hurt yourself? Well, I hope you're thinking about it now because for every scar you left on my girls is a patch of skin that's going to get torn off." My heart swelled doubling its size hearing him speak about us like that especially about Maria seeing how protective he is over her even if she's dead and never once complained.

He knew how much he hurt her, and he was more than ready to make him pay for it.

"I had to! They ruined my life!" he tried to fight his case

and failing miserably, Vincenzo gave him his signature sinical smirk and tilted his head slightly "now it's me who 'has to' old man" Vincenzo made quotation marks with his fingers before pressing the blade on his inner thigh delivering a straight cut cutting the meat.

Stepdad let out a scream as Vincenzo put his finger in the wound and began cutting his skin off from the muscle. Careful and precise "something tells me you've done this before" I commented over his screams watching Vincenzo intensely. "Well obviously this isn't my first time" he rolled his eyes like I just said the dumbest thing ever. I huffed and pushed him out of the way. "My turn, this is for all the scars you left of me, internally and physically" I snatched the knife out of his hands and pushed him out of my way.

"Isabella … please" stepfather puffed out, visibly exhausted and in dire pain. "Please?" I scoffed. "Where was your mercy when you would beat me every day? When you would burn my skin? When you would drown me until I passed out? I never punish the innocent and I will never harm a soul who doesn't deserve it. You did a lot to me, and maybe I deserved it for past sins, but what did Maria ever do?

She was innocent. Why did you do it? To feel powerful?" I scoffed. "How powerful do you feel now?"

I focused my attention on the flappy skin continuing Vincenzo's work, taking my time and being very through, "how did you get so good with a knife?" Vincenzo chimes in watching my work visibly impressed. I smirked looking up at him "Oh, you know. The usual way" I winked.

X

(End of tw scene)

I skinned his right thigh while Vincenzo did his left. Due to the body not having a protective layer and the amount of blood loss he died after a few minutes, but we decided to finish the job anyway. Both of our hands covered in blood, I laughed "are we toxic?" I questioned. Vincenzo shrugged his shoulders "we are the type of people, girls love reading about and listening about. You know true crime stories, once this hits the news people would say wow that's fucked but kind of cool. The bastard deserved it for everything he did" I giggled shaking my head.

Yeah, were mentally screwed, covered in blood from skinning a man alive and laughing about it.

"What do you want to do now?" Vincenzo looked at me, I sighed and nodded my head looking at him intensely I smiled. "What dragon would do" he looked confused and very intrigued. "Your thing was engraving your initial on them. Mine is hanging them upside down with two of my trademark knives in their eyes." Vincenzo's eyes went wide, "that's sick … remind me to stop pissing you off" he added making me burst out into laughter.

This place being our old hideout I had a lot of stuff hidden in here. This is where I use to do my interrogations outside the gang, so there is a lot of shit in here. I walked up to the end of the room in the far-right corner. Vincenzo looked ahead curiously. I looked back at him smiling like a child.

Banging on the top right corner of the wall and bottom left, I banged once more on the wall with both my hands and the hidden door cracked open from the side, holding on the side of the door I opened it wide revealing chains and weapons. "That's so pretty" Vincenzo commented suddenly behind me making me jump a little.

"Gorgeous right?" I spoke breathless, "Okay let's do it!" I grabbed my chains and two signature red knives, walking back towards stepfather I opened his eyes and stabbed both right in the middle. "Heavy lifting is on you now Italy" I smiled after I finished chaining his legs, he rolled his eyes as I gestured to dangle him in front of the window for everyone to see ... I was back.

Doing as I said he watched his lifeless body dangle and looked at me "psycho" he breathed out and stepped back. "That is the sweetest thing you have ever called me" I awed and stepped back.

"Joder gragones realmente de Vuelta" (fuck dragons really back) I heard an old crow behind me mutter, "Samuel" I greeted him smiling. "Sigues siendo la misma chica, perso esta vez no te ves entumecida" (Still the same girl, but this time you don't look numb) Ángel commented, I smiled and nodded my head.

"esta vez tengo el control" (this time I'm in control) I smiled nodding my head, the reason why I was so numb before was obvious but I was taking orders, I wasn't allowed to have friends and I was mentally and physically abused to the point of complete darkness there comes a time where humans just need human interaction I was so starved I became numb and did what I was told to avoid going back to that basement, I practically killed Isabella to do so.

Both nodding their heads smiling genuinely happy for me, "Este es Vincenzo King, líder de los reyes de la mafia. Vincenzo Samuel, Ángel. Samuel, Ángel. Vincenzo." (This is Vincenzo King, leader of the Mafia kings. Vincenzo, Samuel, Ángel. Samuel, Ángel. Vincenzo) I introduced them as they exchanged friendly nods. "I didn't scare you too much on the phone, did I?" I teased, laughing they nod their heads.

"Truth be told when I saw your name on my phone, I did get some PTSD" Samuel commented, I laughed and shook my head. "I think we should find another spot" Ángel commented on the body dangling behind us.

"Oh no it's fine. No one will notice him for hours this area only gets people at night, now I called you in here for a reason" I added getting serious, nodding their heads they urged me to continue before I completely stopped talking seeing who just came into view.

"Mateo?" I called out softly overwhelmed that he was actually here. I ran for him jumping in his arms easily catching me in his arms he held me tight letting out a sigh of relief. "Isabella" he whispered. I got out of his arms looking at him shocked but so fucking happy. "Cómo? Donde? No responsiste. No pensé que vendrías" (How? Where? You didn't answer. I didn't think you'd come.) I cried softly.

"No iba a venir, pero te extrañé y cuando escuché tu voz en el teléfono supe que algo andaba mal." (I wasn't going to come, but I missed you and when I heard your voice on the phone, I knew somethings wrong) He quickly added looking at my face making sure I was okay a concerned look over taking his features just like the old day.

"Estoy bien, solo necesito respuestas y realmente te extrañe." (I'm okay, I just need answers and I really missed you.) I embraced him one more time before making our way back, to a very pissed off Vincenzo. Oh no, I mentally cursed.

"Who's that?" he harshly whispered in my ear, "old lover" I lied watching his entire demeanour change. "Isabella my hands are already covered with blood, I don't mind staining them even more" he harshly whispered in my ear sending a wave of butterflies in my stomach.

"He was one of the men that was there for me, and his married" I added. Rolling my eyes, turning to the group who are giving us weird looks.

"Es complicado no preguntes" (it's complicated don't ask) I added shaking my head smiling like an idiot.

"Okay. You gathered us here to discuss something. We haven't seen you in over eight years, and suddenly you're back and bloody." Mateo gestured to my hands stained in blood and the bodies lying around including stepfather hanging upside down.

"Ok, we all know we rescued my parents from Xavier little over a month or two ago." I started filling them in on the news, they all nodded along "now Samuel and Ángel use two were apart of Xavier's inner circle, so the only people who can give me an answer to my questions are the three of you" I slowly started informing them giving them time to process the seriousness of this sudden meeting.

"When I recently went to check up on my parents, I

received core shaking news. I'm unsure if it's the medicine there on that is making them go crazy or if there fine and just exposed themselves when they thought they were alone." I took in a deep breath my stomach feeling like it's going to explode from stress.

"They mentioned that I was … they purposely had Xavier kidnap me and where apart of the whole thing" I blurted it out, they all looked at me shocked and stunned no one saying a word as they took in what I said. "Isabella" Ángel drifted off. Oh my god, no. It can't be true please someone fucking say something! I'm begging you.

"I'm begging you! Do not say the people I called out for when I was being tortured and raped were the people that put me in that position. Please! Samuel say something … Ángel?" I started pleading they say it was a lie that it was just the drugs making their head cloudy.

"Mateo?" I looked over at him my eyes watered tears ready to fall out with one blink, "I'm so sorry Bella" he whispered conforming my one true nightmare. "No" I whispered shaking my head taking a few steps back while I processed everything. "NO" I shouted when they tried to come confront me.

"Why did no one tell me!" I yelled feeling completely betrayed, "why?" I spoke through my teeth, "if we told you back then you would not have believed us especially in the state you were in. You would have killed us without a blink and if you didn't kill us Xavier would have. I'm so sorry you had to find out like that Isabella" Samuel spoke up, and as much as I wanted to scream and shout and yell and hit them for keeping this from me. I knew they were right. I wouldn't have believed them, and I would've killed them instantly.

I nodded my head slowly pointing to the door dismissing them. "Isabella" Mateo spoke up softly, I looked up at him feeling every little bit of energy I had left fade away, "we all heard whispers about a big kidnapping Xavier did, we don't know who, but we are sure it's somehow connected to you someone you know or knew." I nodded my head gaining some control in my emotions again.

"Find out who and once you do this time, I want to be the first to hear it." I warned them about hiding things from me, "also … thanks" I whispered they smiled sadly and nodded their heads knowing exactly what I meant before all three men left.

"Thanks?" Vincenzo questioned looking at me concern visible on his face.

"They knew my parents betrayed me and were the cause of everything that happened, so they stepped up and became my family. For that I owe them a lot." I explained my eyes roaming around before landing back on stepfather. "Looks like you were the only one who had the balls to hurt me and own it" talking to myself I step back and sit on the floor staring at his body dangling.

"Isabella?" Vincenzo calls my name and from his tone I cringed the one emotion I hate with every cell in my body. 'pity'

"I'm fine, at some point you start to become numb to the betrayal, at some point it's so common it borders on overkill" I spoke never taking my eyes off stepfather, for some reason watching his body hang there like that made me feel better about myself, in a very sadistic way it reminds me that I once and for all ended a darkness that consumed me and now a question hung over my head, was I going to end another darkness that consumed me?

Am I going to end the two people that specifically put me in this position.

"I know your hurting, and I know what it's like to be betrayed by a parent like that." I tore my eyes from the body and looked up at Vincenzo confused, "for as long as I've known you, you've never said or spoken about anything from your past." I pointed out, he nodded his head looking around the room. "Let's get out of here yeah?" I sighed and stood up slowly, "we can go visit anywhere you want" he tried cheering me up.

I smiled softly nodding my head "okay let's go" I spoke up gesturing for him to follow me as we made our way downstairs to the car. Speeding off I saw from the corner of my eye, Vincenzo staring at me intensely like he was staring down a ticking time bomb and honestly? He had every right to look at me like that because I'm too calm right now.

"Where are we going?" he questions softly trying not to trigger me, I smiled to myself "to a prison that was used to imprison the most dangerous thing to ever exist in all of Spain history." I explained knowingly getting his attention "some say it's a historical monument, they imprisoned something so feared and dangerous they needed to tame it somehow. So, they chained it to the metal pipes, and did anything they could to break it and bend it to their will. For its power to become their own so it can become they're protector and win all the wars" I explained looking straight ahead.

"Did they?" he questioned if they succeeded if they broke its will, I nodded my head "oh yeah it broke, but after a while they regretted breaking its soul because without its soul it was incapable of knowing who the true enemy was, it became so violent and viscous it was sent away. It became the monster they wanted it to protect them from … When it was sent away it was also the worst thing for Spain, as what was protecting them from the monsters disappeared and they were left to fend for themselves once again" I parked the car right in front of the place, seeing many people surrounding the area, some placing flowers or notes even paintings.

Vincenzo looked onwards intrigued in the creature's dungeon, "where it all began" I whispered looking ahead. As soon as I approached it the people turned to look at me, some relived some frightened and some were both.

"Vete" (leave) I announced lowly, everyone quickly finished what they were doing and vanished leaving the place empty.

Except for one girl and her mother who approached me slowly and cautiously "Sé que la gente dice que eres malo y aterrador, pero no creo que te hayas deshecho de las personas malas haciendo cosas malas, eso no significa que seas malo, gracias, dragón." **(I know people say your bad and scary, but I don't think that. You got rid of the bad people by doing bad things that doesn't mean you're bad thank you dragón)**

I bent down to the little girl, pulling her in roughly and whispering in her ear "ser peligroso es ser libre no todos lo entienden … eres una chica especial" **(being dangerous is being free not everyone understands it … you're a special girl)** keeping a persona in front of her mum to show no weakness even for children, while at the same time reassuring the girl. I gave her a wink and she smiled back understanding.

I stood upright she looked up at me smiling like a child meeting their hero, I kept a straight face the entire time, but I honestly just wanted to smile, but I can't show any sort of emotions. It will turn ugly. They will think the monster went soft and will try to abuse it all over again. Turning I looked at her mother "vete" (leave) I spat roughly she immediately grabbed her child and scattered off.

Vincenzo looked at me and then back at the entrance, we walked pasted the flowers and notes and made our way inside.

"This doesn't look like a prison" he whispered looking around, "this isn't it … follow me" I ushered with my hand for him to follow me, walking down the stairs until we reached a bolted door, looking around I grabbed the first heavy thing I saw a brick. Slamming it down on the lock snapping it open, I grabbed both door handles to the underground prison taking in a deep breath I opened the doors. Walking down the stairs inside Vincenzo looked for a light, and only three lights dangled from the ceiling pulling on the chain the prison lit up very dim nothing much was seen grabbing his phone he used his flashlight.

"You said this place was used to imprison something right?" I nodded my head "yeah" I breathed out feeling my insides turning "what was it?" he whispered examining the chains still attached to the metal pipes. "Me" I spoke out firmly, trying to keep my cool.

"What?" he directed the flash towards me, "this is where it all began" I spoke up feeling sick to my stomach, I walked towards the chain bending down grabbing ahold of it.

FLASHBACK

"You can't leave me here!" I screamed tugging against the chains that bounded my hands and feet, "XAVIER!" I yelled out, he spun around looking at me intensely "you will stay here until I say otherwise, you will stay here until you break and come the monster, I need you to be. You will burn here if you refuse" he threatened. "No one but you will burn here, one day I'll have you in this same position but unlike you I'll have the guts to set you a flame." I threatened.

"You will break darling, it's inevitable you may take longer than the average, but you will break" and without another word he turned on his heel and faded into the dark, "hello!" I called out trying to get anyone's attention before I heard the door violently shut.

I looked up at the dark roof imagining the skies above my head "I hope you're watching over me … something tells me I'm going to need your help" I whispered to my parents in heaven.

END OF FLASHBACK

My jaw started to hurt from how hard I was biting down on it, I tugged on the chain and screamed, feeling the chains snap from the old rusty pipe feeling like my inner self needed to break free from them. I was only fourteen when he took me, I was only a baby when my parents sold me to the wanna be devil.

Vincenzo immediately grabs a hold of me pulling me in his arms, "I don't want to do this anymore" I sobbed against his chest, "don't talk like that, never let them win. Isabella, use it.

Use every bit of anger every bit of rage and every bit of pain to your advantage don't go numb don't shut it out, embrace it and use it to tear the guts out of your enemies. Be the one in control don't give them the satisfaction they so desperately crave".

"You're a women use it! Bring everyone and every man you meet to his motherfucking knees bare your teeth and show them they fucked with the wrong person".

X

After Vincenzo calmed me down, we got out of there, walking back to the car my feet immediately froze in front of the memorial site. They knew I wasn't dead, but the fact that I wasn't here stopping or going after the human trafficker's and the worst of the worst in Spain they considered all hope dead … therefore I was metaphorically dead.

I looked at the paintings some had just my face from what people remembered when I was merely sixteen and seventeen, others had me in my signature red leather jacket with dragon wings, but every painting had one thing in common they all said "en el amor y la memoria Dragón" **(in love and memory dragon)** I read out loud smiling sheepishly to myself, Vincenzo smiled "grab them" he gestured to all the flowers, notes and paintings.

"They are for you and when you go to break again read what they have to say about you."

X

Putting everything in the trunk of the car we took off, my head was buzzing, so much was happening my head was in chaos. I was still too calm for finding out that everything was in fact planned by the two people you should never fear, the two people who should be the ones protecting you from the scars of the world we live in, not be the people who push you toward every single scar the universe had to offer.

(tw talk of explicit childhood trauma)

"I was ten when my dad took me to a meeting, little did I know it wasn't an ordinary meeting" Vincenzo randomly spoke up.

"Dante and I never got along with our father, and after that day any hope of love was sentenced to death. We all sat down in chairs, looking around and like any normal ten-year-old boys we were scared. So, fucking scared all the men were old and all looked scary to a child, scars on their faces, guns attached to their hips and worst of it all everyone had fresh blood stained on them" Vincenzo spoke up never looking at me, I decided it was best to keep my eyes on the road seeing how this entire conversation was making him extremely uncomfortable.

"Five minutes into the meeting my father was in extreme debt to these men, and he decided to use me to pay off his debt. My dad said since I was next in line to take over because I was always the more aggressive one that it was perfect if I was the one to pay his debt. I was ten Isabella I was so confused on what I had to do, why I needed to pay for his fucked mistakes. They forced Dante to watch just in case this experience broke me, it would toughen Dante to never fuck up and take over for me. The men wanted both to sit and watch as they raped me. All at once" he took a breath clenching his fists, "Vincenzo you don't have to" I whispered feeling my insides turn into a giant knot.

He shook his head fighting back tears "I stood there nude and scared, I was screaming so loud it felt like my soul was leaving my body with every thrust, every punch, and every gag. I was fucking ten years old, and I looked at my dad and I screamed for his help, I screamed and cried and begged and all he did was say I'm doing this for the family. He had no emotion on his face, not even a slight cringe. I pleaded and begged and screamed and cried I fucking did everything in the book to get my dad to be a fucking dad." His Italian accent getting thicker something I haven't heard in a long time, the angrier he got the more noticeable the accent.

I blinked rapidly trying to blink the tears away unable to imagine Vincenzo in that position never wanting to imagine him in such a position, defenceless vulnerable and a fucking child.

"After they all finished, I was lying on the floor unable to move every inch of me ached and felt like my skin and body was torn from my bone, I felt disgusting and so mad I wanted to grab a knife and tear my skin off." He took in a deep breath and continued.

"The men walked to my dad shaking his hand telling him the debt has been paid and we can leave but my father decided a gang rap wasn't enough to toughen me he wanted me tougher, so he asked them to shoot me in the leg. I have no fucking idea what that was supposed to do but this became an annual thing until I was twelve years old, that day I decided I wasn't dealing with it that was the day I made my first ever kill."

I looked at him shocked that went on continuously for three years. And it only ended because he killed them? "Funny enough the debt was paid so my dad was just taking me there to stay on good terms with the heads of some traffic ring even though that's against the mafia code. Anyway, that day I had enough, they began unbuckling their belts and I remember screaming and grabbing one of their guns and shooting all of them in a swift motion all head shots. They died instantly and I looked at my dad gun in hand and do you know what he said?" he whispered, "I did it. You're a man now your training begins." He spat recalling his father's words.

"He did all that so I can become emotionless to kill and feel no remorse and to use that situation for everything when I took over as the mafia king".

(end of explicit talk)

I slammed my breaks looking over at him people behind me beeped until I spun around, seeing my face all fell silent and the traffic went around me. "Why didn't you kill him as well?" I questioned not wanting to step over any line. How didn't he kill him why his dad is still alive is unbelievable.

"I thought about killing him so much, oh fucks sake I wanted to kill him every cell was screaming at me to end his life, but I needed him alive. I vowed that day that I will never allow what happened to me to happen to Dante or Lorenzo and the baby mum was pregnant with at the time".

"Ariana" I whispered, he nodded his head and gestured for me to keep driving, I sat back in my seat and drove off again.

"For me to protect them I needed to take over and I needed to wait until I hit the appropriate age, for the power to be passed to me I had to prove myself to the five families and my father I need to be suggested in by the higher ranks.

It's not always about birth especially since our mafia wasn't known and or feared. Once I took over, I thought about killing him a lot, but I couldn't do it to Lorenzo and Ariana they lost Dante and last thing they needed was to know the truth about him. So, he survived on the mercy of his children minus me. So, when I told you earlier, I know what it's like to be betrayed and feel like you have no one in this big world, trust my word. I know the feeling and I know what's going on in your head and whatever decision you make I'll support you and be there through it all, I promise you that Isabella. Memory or no memory it's me and you against the world".

I parked the car in the garage and immediately jumped into his arms holding him tight, "I'm so sorry Vincenzo. I'm so fucking sorry" I cried into his chest feeling so much at once I couldn't control the tears anymore.

"It's okay bellisma I'm okay" he whispered in my hair holding onto me so tight like he was still that scared ten-year-old and all I wanted to do was go back in time and save him, take his pain away but all I could do now is be there for him. No matter what.

No matter what I promised him.

THE TEASE

Isabella's POV

We got back on the plane and started making our way back home, I couldn't even begin to describe the anger that was spuing in me. I was livid but confused, I didn't know how to comprehend the information that was given to me, and I don't know how I will react when I'm back at home. Will I forgive them and send them on their way? Will I lose my temper and kill them for doing that to me? All I know is I'm pissed.

I looked over at Vincenzo who was deep in thought himself, I wondered what he was thinking about before he turned to look at me, "you okay?" I sigh nodding my head "I will be" I reassured him, I've been through worse, and I always bounce back.

"I just miss Dante" I commented not being able to handle being away from him for this long, "honestly me too, I miss how he would start hitting my chest when I'm not giving him the attention he wants. Like mother like son" he joked.

I gasped offended and slapped his chest "Hey!' I laughed shaking my head "I have other ways of getting your attention" looking at his bulge before I slowly licked my bottom lip trailing my eyes back up to him. "Really? And how do you plan on doing that?" he questioned teasingly, smirking I unbuckle my seatbelt and cradle his lap making sure to slowly grind myself against him.

Sucking in a breath he grips my hips and stops the movement "do not start something you cannot finish" he warned me slowly, I cocked my eyebrows up "I always finish what I start" I flicked his hands away from me and pushed them to the side of the chair while I continued grinding myself on top of him teasingly. "No touching" I whispered softly as I untied his tie using it to restrain his hands using the arm rest to assure myself, he wasn't moving very far.

(sex scene)

"Isabella" he trailed off slowly knowing he wasn't going to be able to keep his hands off me for too long. Smirking proud of my handy work I stand up tall slowly pulling off the panties I had on from under my dress careful not to reveal anything just yet. I spin around leaning forward as they slide off my ass and down my legs, pulling it out from under my shoes I wave it around. Slowly walking back to Vincenzo, I teasingly sit on his lap sideways I trail my panties along his mouth biting down on it he pulls it out of my hands.

Standing back up I continue by strip tease, swaying my hips trailing my boobs before I finally sit down right on the seat in front of him leaning back, I slowly pull up my dress revealing myself to him my hot and very wet self. I smile watching his Adams apple bob up and down unable to contain himself much longer.

I stick my middle finger and ring finger in my mouth sucking on it getting it wet, slowly pulling it back out I lean back putting my right leg up and start playing with myself tracing my clit I let out a soft moan keeping my eyes fixated on him, "oh fuck" I moaned out watching his already intense gaze turn hungry and desperate for me. "I did this for months thinking of you between my legs" I whimpered as I inserted one finger inside myself keeping my gaze on him. "For months when I was alone in my room, all I could think about was your big cock in my mouth … in my hands … in me".

I purred watching him squirm.

"Isabella" he spoke up almost begging me to finally untie him, although I'm sure if he wanted to, he could get out of that tie on his own. I shook my head no "I had to go months without your touch to help me, and I could never finish. Today is the day I cum from my own fingers and you get to watch" I inserted my rig finger in as well using both fingers to pump in and out as fast as I could, my juice splattering around the wetter I got and the more intense I went.

"Oh just like that" Vincenzo groaned out watching on the edge of his seat, "slow down" he instructed me and I obliged slowing down my pace "good girl, now with your left hand rub your clit but don't stop fingering yourself" doing as he said.

I continued pleasuring myself leaning my head back I let out a moan feeling my senses about to erupt "look at me Isabella!" he groaned out frustrated. I slowly lift my head and open my eyes meeting his stare, "if you're going to cum you will do so under my instructions and voice" I bit my bottom lip nodding my head slowly.

"Yes boss" I whispered out breathless always finding his dominating personality so attractive.

"Deep breathes" he reminded me, my chest heaving up and down as I looked at him submissively. "Go faster" he instructed me "imagine my fingers in your pussy pumping in and out of you, my hot breath on your neck my cock hardening with every thrust every pump and every look. Imagine me fingering you while I hold you by your throat so I can feel every scream and every moan" I sucked in a breath letting out a supressed moan.

"Because as soon as I get myself out of this restraint that's exactly what I'll be doing, my hands all over you my cock inside of you pounding your sweet tight pussy until you climax screaming my name so loud that it will shatter the mountains and send a disturbance through the plane." If on cue I felt a surge of pleasure wash over me as I cummed all over my fingers, I smiled letting out a breathless laugh looking up at him, as I went to lick my cum off my fingers, he gave me a stern look.

"Come" he ordered me, I cocked my eyebrow up slowly making my way towards him, sitting on his lap I sucked on my fingers first before giving him a taste, he sucked on my fingers licking them clean "so fucking delicious amore" I stood up teasingly pulling my dress back down and taking a seat "thanks for the help Italy" I teased looking away not giving his the satisfaction of touching me himself.

He scoffed and tugged on the armrest completely pulling it off from the seat then pulling his hands apart tearing off the tie. My mouth fell open watching him.

"Did you think you could put on your little show, and I was going to only watch?" he questioned condescendingly kneeling in front of me he roughly pulled me towards him my back arched, and my pussy perfectly displayed in front of him. "You want it? Claim it." I teased.

He separated my legs apart pulling it behind me as he

positioned his face between my legs his hot breath hitting my clit. I was so fucking wet and throbbing like mad I needed friction I needed to feel his mouth on me, but he waited.

"Say it Isabella" he probed wanting me to beg him, "I have nothing to say" I whispered lying through my teeth watching his eyes grow dark, "Isabella" he warned me. I sucked in a breath and leaned my head back not wanting to give in and admit how much I wanted him, but my pride was standing in my way growing impatient he stood up tall pulling me up with him.

Positioning himself behind me he roughly pulled my body back into him my ass firmly planted on his erection, biting my bottom lip to supress a moan, "you're so fucking stubborn Isabella" he whispered in my ear, sitting down he laid me on his lap my ass perked up against his knee. Rubbing his hand on my cheek "say it Isabella" his tone stern and low biting my lip I shook my head no. His hand connected with my right cheek I jumped up supressing a moan, letting out a squeal instead.

"Say" he paused for a slap on my left check quickly rubbing his palm against what I assume was his hand print on my ass, "it" he finished slapping both of my cheeks making me jump and squirm against him "I want you to fuck me Vincenzo I want you so bad I need you" I caved in moaning out how badly I wanted him and how badly I craved him.

Smirking victorious he pulls me up by my throat smashing his lips to mine, the kiss was hungry, but also full of passion. Sliding his tongue in my mouth we fight for dominance him winning of course, biting down on my bottom lip I let out a soft whimper my eyes rolling to the back of my head.

Pulling him closer to me by his waist band "you know when you do that it drives me crazy?" he whispered in my ear his hot breath on my neck sending an excitement shiver down my spine. "I missed the feeling of your hard cock in my mouth" I whispered back matching his energy.

Going down on my knees I unbuckle his pants pulling it down along with his boxers his cock flopped out hitting my mouth. I take his dick in my hand slowly pumping up and down sticking my tongue out I slap his dick against it teasing him. Using his thumb, he pulls my mouth open nodding his head, "if you tease me anymore today, I will punish you again" he warns.

Smiling innocently, I look up at him acting clueless, "me a tease?" I mock but before he could say a word, I take his cock whole in my mouth my tongue swirling the tip. Pulling my hair up in a ponytail Vincenzo bobs my head back and forth, mouth fucking me.

As he pulls out, I gasp for air, pulling me up to my feet by my hair he picks me up holding me on his shoulders wrapping my legs around his neck lightly.

Pulling me closer to him as his skilful tongue meets my throbbing clit.

"Oh fuck" I moan out threading my fingers in his hair as his tongue plays with my clit, tugging at it each time he sucks on it my clit being already very sensitive. Going faster I felt myself reaching climax again, I start tugging harder on his head, while crossing my legs around his neck tighter. Not putting me down or moving to breath he kept going his tongue hard at work taking me whole I gasp out cumming all over his mouth. He moves back letting out an airy laugh slowly allowing me to come down as I straddled his waist, he kisses me softly. "Taste yourself on my tongue".

Still holding me up he positions himself sliding his cock in me, I let out a gasp as it filled my tight pussy. He grips the V-neck of the dress pulling down making my boobs fall out free as they bounced back and forth matching Vincenzo's thrusts. "I'm gonna cum" I moaned out gripping the arm rest, "cum for me" he softly groaned in my ear sending me over the edge pulling himself out of me he spun me around putting his cock between my boobs thrusting a couple of times before finishing.

Licking my lips, I swipe the cum from my chest and suck it off my fingers, watching him out of breath for some reason sent a sensational feeling to my stomach, it could be the cum dripping but who knows anymore. He pulls me up to my feet cupping my cheeks softly pulling my face to his he places a soft kiss on my lips taking his time savouring the kiss like it was the last.

(End of sex scene)

X

Thank God this private jet had a shower we quickly washed ourselves off before landing, once we got back all I could think about was getting home to my son, jumping in the car Vincenzo's driver took off while I sat anxiously waiting to see him God knows how much of Lorenzo that boy can take.

"You, okay?" Vincenzo asked analysing me up and down, biting my lower lip I nodded my head yes. "Just thinking about Dante" I admitted honestly, he nodded his head understanding "I think this is the last time we stay away from him for this long" Vincenzo commented looking as anxious as I am. I giggles shying away "I wouldn't say last time maybe just not for that long" I winked.

He let out a low chuckle "in that case anytime Bella anytime" he smirked.

The car finally pulled up to the estate I ran out of the car before it came to stop seeing my boy waiting for us at the front door in Ariana's arms. His little wave making me melt.

"Hi baby" I whispered grabbing him, he immediately melted into my chest resting his head and grabbing the strap of my dress, "I missed you to my big boy" I kissed his forehead watching Vincenzo approach us "Leone" Vincenzo called out admiring his fucking twin you know it's not fair I had to carry him for nine months then proceed to push him out of me all for him to look like his fucking dad I swear his first words better be mama or I'm killing his dad.

Dante lifted his head upon hearing his dads voice, he starts jumping up and down trying to get out of my arms leaning and extending his arms out for his dad "traitor" I hissed as Vincenzo laughed taking him from my arms "that's my boy!" he cheered proud rolling my eyes I look at Ariana giving her a hug "thanks for watching him" I smiled she nodded her head.

"Honestly wasn't a problem I love this kid" she smiled squeezing his cheeks "THAT'S BECAUSE YOU DIDN'T CHANGE A DIPAR YOU FUCKING SPOILT DUMB BITCH" Lorenzo came screaming, I slapped his arm for cursing in front of the baby "fine! But that baby can unload a fu- fudging bomb!" I rolled my eyes trying to sniffle a laugh.

Lorenzo turned to Dante "I better be your favourite human being on earth! Or so help me God" he warned him before walking off "MIA RUN ME A HOT BATH WITH BUBBLES MAMA NEEDS A BREAK" he yelled for the housekeeper I laughed rolling my eyes again something I do often when it comes to Lorenzo.

"Okay! Time to go inside" Ariana clapped her hands and stepped aside letting us in, walking upstairs into our bedroom I looked around deep in thought. Mateo kept playing on my mind what he said in Spain.

"We all heard whispers about a big kidnapping Xavier did, we don't know who, but we are sure it's somehow connected to you someone you know or knew." His voice echoed in my head who could it be? I ranked my head trying to think of someone, could it be Sebastian? I haven't seen or heard from him in a while … or Alex? My head racing trying to think of who it could be, while the other part of my mind was about to explode from anger. Once again trying to fucking manipulate me by kidnapping someone closest to me. "Isabella" I turned around seeing Vincenzo look at me, I hummed looking at him. "I want to tell you something" he takes in a deep breath and ushers me over to the bed. I sit down slowly my stomach doing flips as I start feeling very nervous. "I've been thinking for some time now, that I want to … I want to remember you I want to remember us." My eyes went wide finally hearing the words I've been aching to hear for a year.

"There's an experimental drug I enrolled in, and I just wanted to let you know that I'm starting it soon." I sighed feeling relieved.

"Vincenzo, I have been waiting to hear you say those words for the longest fucking time … but I'm not sure you should do this." I admitted sadly. He looks taken back waiting for me to elaborate "Memory is a tricky game. I don't think it's something you should mess with especially an experimental drug what if something goes wrong and you forget Dante or yourself. What if something goes terribly wrong?" I let out a sigh before looking back up at him "if you were meant to remember me it would've happened by now naturally not forced by trial medicine" I whispered softly looking down playing with the bed sheets.

He tilts my chin up with his finger then cups my cheek creasing it slightly holding me tenderly. "Life is full of risks, and its full of fucked up shit but if we don't take the risk will never know. If you didn't take the risk to stay here instead of leaving me, we wouldn't have Dante or each other." I smiled softly letting his words sink in, nodding my head softly despite my gut feeling telling me this was a bad idea.

"Do what feels right, I'll support you no matter what. I mean it no matter what" I put emphasis as he takes me into his arms squeezing me tight.

X

Walking out of the bedroom hand in hand with Vincenzo and Dante in Vincenzo's arm everything finally felt right again, like it was supposed to be us against the world. Ariana looked at our hands and back up all giddy jumping up and down clapping "FINALLY! All is right in the world again" rolling his eyes he ushers her to move, I giggle watching him become all flustered.

"Ariana leave" she shakes her head no "fuck off I'm not moving anywhere I've been waiting for this since break up 0.2" looking at her confused "you know first break up, was when Vincenzo got intel that your life was in danger and the spotlight was being shined on you due to dating the most feared mafia boss in New York and the rumour of dragon coming back. Then the second breakup which happened when he faked your death, I lost track of your on and offs after that shit show" she shrugged her shoulders.

I nodded my head knowingly "yeah don't blame you that's when I stopped as well" I added agreeing with her. Vincenzo shoots me a look I shrug my shoulders "what it was" I called out defensively, rolling his eyes we made our way outside all his men upon seeing our linked hands stopped what they're doing and began cheering making Dante jump before he joined in and began clapping.

"Aww amore" I laughed out pinching Dante's cheeks, after the men finished congratulating us on finally getting back together, we made our way to hacker.

Opening his door we walked in his tech office "what can I do for y-" cutting himself off his mouth drops looking at us "NO!" he yells in shock "Dante I know you're not one yet but you don't understand the severity of this situation that's happening before your eyes" he exhales holding his hands to his chest "I just witnessed a historical monument and Dante when you get older I'll explain how breath taking this was" rolling my eyes I let go of Vincenzo and push Hacker on his chair towards his computers.

"Less talking more typing" I usher him, "fine but I'm tweeting about this" Vincenzo looked over at him with a look I can only describe to be confusion and a little judgement.

"I found out some information recently and it was confirmed at Spain, but before I do anything Isabella like … or more precisely dragon like. I have one more thing I want you to do for me so I can be a hundred percent sure. What you find out determines what I'll do" I gave him a knowing look.

"Oh fuck. Life or death" he elaborated on my statement I nodded my head "life or death" some might judge me fuck some might condemn me for even thinking about murdering my parents but once you go your whole life thinking they're dead and praying for them to save you only to find out they were the cause of everything. The sleepless nights, the abuse, the torture the mental and physical exhaustion, the nights I debated to end it all to see them in heaven only to find out they were in another room watching and instructing for a petty revenge that didn't concern me but him and my mother.

"Okay tell me" I let out a sigh "search for any activity under the names Luna Gonzalez and Romano Gonzalez" my parent's alias they would use to hide their true identities from government officials, rivals and the names they would use when they were off the grid. "There they are" hacker pointed at the screen their names pinned off, "go back ten years that's when I was kidnapped" he nodded his head typing away. "Going back that far will take me a few minutes go and I'll find you with the files." I nodded my head "thank you" I smiled he winked giving me a sharp nod. "Go".

"Vincenzo I'm going to go see them, one last time before Hacker gives me the news. I just want to see them one more time before everything changes more than it already has." I bit my bottom lip anxiously.

"Do you want me to go with you?" he asked rubbing circles on my back.

I shook my head no "I think this is something I want to do alone. Go spend some time with Dante and your siblings, I got it." I smiled kissing Dante on the cheek before going on my tippy toes and giving Vincenzo a peck on the lips.

X

I walked up to the clinic taking in a deep breath trying to calm my nerves, I walked inside with a smile acting like nothing's wrong, knocking on the door I open it slowly.

"Mama … Papa?" I croaked out trying not to get emotional.

"Mariposa are you okay?" dad or should I say Mario spoke up. He ushered me to come closer, I reluctantly walked up to him sitting next to him on the couch they recently added in the room. "Were okay no need to get emotional" he pulled me close giving me a kiss on the head.

I let out a breath trying to contain my anger, my disappointment but most importantly I was trying to contain the part of me that wished this was real the part of me that yearned for so long to have my parents back just to find out it was all fake.

"Isabella are you okay?" Mama speaks up softly, I looked up at her not realising that a few tear drops managed to escape, "I'm okay. I was just thinking about Maria" I lied trying to cover up my emotional state. If she was here and learned all this, I don't know what she would've done, or how she would have reacted.

I shut my eyes trying to control my breathing. As much as I'm glad she's shielded from all this pain as much as I really wish she was here so I can hug her so I can have her by my side through all this.

"We miss her too, not a day goes by we don't think about our little flower." Mama smiled sadly looking at the ground, I nodded my head "in a way its good she's not here to witness this, the pain the hurt the betrayal" I began listing a few things purposely to get them nervous. Which worked immediately Mama laughed nervously while Mario eased his grip on me, I could feel him gulp.

"What pain? Betrayal? What are you talking about?" he questions looking at me. I shook my head "about how I was alive when she thought I was dead she must've felt so betrayed" I diverted their nerves they both let out a sigh of relief.

"I'm sure she forgave you. She was always a forgiving person." Mario added.

"A trait I never managed to obtain. Forgiving … I believe if someone wrongs you, then they deserve to deal with the consequences that follow the betrayal" I foreshadowed their fate, playing on their nerves. Unable to detain if I know or don't know what they did.

"Maybe it's something you can learn to do as a tribute to your sister" Mama spoke softly unable to hold eye contact "exactly maybe you forgiving the unforgivable would be like Maria living through you" Mario chimed in.

I shook my head no. "No, I don't think so, what made us different were our traits yes? I may have been the unforgiving one out of the two of us, but I always got rid of the nightmares, the pain the sorrow. I took all the darkness and ate it, fuck I became it so it couldn't hurt us ... so it would never hurt her, everything was for Maria, I didn't want her to experience what I did, and I never wanted her innocent nature to get tainted so while she was forgiving by nature I was not because I knew what forgiving the unforgivable meant. Forgiving the unforgivable only dims your light, and I would rather slaughter everyone and anything than allow her light to be dimmed" I began explaining subtly that they will face the same fate. They will be slaughtered like animals!

"If you had forgiven Xavier than your fate would have been different! Forgiving the unforgivable isn't a sin more a sign of braveness" Mario added, I let out a dry laugh "no it wouldn't have, he killed the two of you in front of me. He mentally scarred me forgiving him wouldn't have erased the image of you bloody bodies from my head, forgiving him wouldn't have magically made me happy and full of rainbows.

Forgiving him wouldn't calm the rage in my heart nor would it erase the image of that day. It may not be healthy, but everyone has their flaws mine is I don't forgive I take revenge" I smiled looking up at the two of them "and don't worry I will have my revenge" I threatened softly.

"Isabella maybe it's time to forgive him and end this war focus on your son" Mama tried to convince me to change my mind showing a guilty conscious "My son? That's who I'm thinking about. I can never rest or stop looking over my shoulder until his gone. He won't stop until his dead. He will do anything and everything to get me back and if that means killing someone close to me or kidnapping my son, he will do it. I don't want Dante to grow up without me but if I die killing him and those who helped him then so be it because that will be my sons only chance to live his best life. He will grow up knowing his mum did everything to protect him not use him to take as revenge for some petty conflict" I hinted once more that I was aware of them.

Just as I finished talking Mario shot up from beside me and stood next to mum, "you-" getting cut off as Hacker walked in "I have everything in here" he breathes out handing me the file quickly rushing off. I look at the file in my hands and back up at my 'parents'.

"Funny, isn't it? In this file is the outcome of life and death. I wonder which way it'll go"?

Vincenzo's POV

I left the estate and headed to the clinic to pick up my meds all I prayed for the whole ride was that it was a miracle drug because I fucking need a miracle. I fought so long to avoid remembering her thinking it was fate giving me a fresh start but everything, every decision, every move, every thought, and every breath is consumed by the thought of her. So, fuck fate I want her, and I know it. I want our future, but I want our past and even if I have to go to the end of the world to get it.

Parking my car in the parking lot I make my way towards the clinic, before opening the door my phone started buzzing in my pocket taking a step back, I look at the area code "Spain?" I questioned maybe it was someone trying to get through to Isabella. Answering the phone "Vincenzo King"

"Vincenzo where the fuck is Isabella!" a man screams on

the other line, "excuse me?" I spat out "its Mateo" he quickly added, not necessary making the situation better but whatever.

"Why do you need her?" I questioned confused "she's not answering her phone and I have information on the person who Xavier has hidden and she's not going to fucking like the answer! I need to go off the grid after this call because Xavier's men are starting to track me down from hacking into their surveillance, I need her to pick up".

"She's talking to her parents tell me who is it and I'll let her know now, I'm on my way back to her."

"It's Maria. She's still in a coma and unaware of everything happening but they got Maria" He hung up straight after leaving me shocked, furious, happy and fucking livid. I dropped my hand down as the air got knocked out of me, while I was thinking it was from shock, I started to feel a sharp pain shoot its way from my head down my spine. Everything around me suddenly turning blurry and before I knew it, I was on the floor, a pair of old boots standing in front of me.

UNKOWN POV

Slamming the wood against his head I watched him fall over hovering above him I watched satisfyingly as he finally came to the realisation on what was happening. "Hello boy".

THE REVELATIONS

Vincenzo's POV

I hissed at the sharp pain coming from the back of my head, I went to rub it before feeling chains around my wrists "what the fuck" I groaned out looking around the room everything was slightly dimmed but not enough for me not to see my surroundings.

Not that there was anything much to see, the room was completely empty except for the chair I'm sitting and restrained on and to my right was a table full of injections.

This is going to be so fucking fucked up. I mentally sighed for what's to come. The sound of a man's voice snapping me out of my train of thought and getting my attention "I see you woke up boy" I looked up to a shadowy figure "and I see you … actually wait no I can't see you" I squinted trying to get a good look at him.

"Good" he replied relieved.

"Gattino" **(kitten)** I called him mocking his cowardly behavior, "Vincenzo you're really not in a position to make fun" he remarked only making me roll my eyes. "Tied up or not I'm always in a position to mock especially when the enemy facing me is hiding and has me tied up out of fear."

His voice was so familiar I know I've heard it before, but I just can't place who the voice belongs to, I definitely know who he is which means this wasn't just a kidnapping it was revenge.

"Time to have some fun now boy" he snickered his figure starts appearing as he stepped slightly into the light his black silhouette holding a syringe "you're going to hate it boy" he laughed completely shutting off what little light there was knocking me unconscious, so I don't see his face.

X

Isabella's POV

I watched as hacker left immediately after hearing the threatening tone in my voice. I looked back over at them and smiled "let's have a peek, shall we?" I went to open the file before mum snatched it out of my hands, I looked up at her my eyes narrow full of hatred and pain. I really don't think this is the best time for her to test me.

"If you do not pass the file back I promise you that the person in front of you won't be Isabella but dragon and she hasn't been woken up to her full extent since Spain, unless you want me to literally unleash all hell on the two of you I suggest that file be in my hand in the next ten seconds" my tone was icy I was daring them to piss me off even more than they already have.

"What is this file going to prove?" she pleaded trying to make me gain some sympathy for the situation.

"ten" I started the countdown,

"Isabella please" Mario begged.

"Nine"

"Will it be worth it? If what you're looking for is in this file will you feel better?! Will it bring you peace or more pain" Mario kept trying to get me to be reasonable and understand the situation and its ugly outcome. What they don't know is I already was aware of the outcome, and I knew exactly what I was planning on doing.

"eight" my tone becoming harsher the closer I got to one.

"Isabella for god's sake! You don't know anything and whatever is in this file is lies!" mother shouted getting anxious.

"seven"

"Okay enough!" Mario shouted he spun looking at me more directly his facial expression was meant to threaten me but all it did was infuriate me even more. Does he honestly think he was the least bit threatening? I never feared him as a child let alone now.

"Six" I spat in his face showing him his little show did nothing.

"You are not getting that file back and you are going to let us out of here" he laid out his rules cocking a smile I raised my eyebrows up making a 'tsk' sound.

"five"

"Isabella!" he yelled.

"four"

within a second the file was placed back in my hands I smirked victorious, "why did you give it back?" he yelled at mum getting angrier with each passing second knowing that their lives as we know it was in the palm of my hands. Literally.

"Because if she didn't, we all know exactly what would have happened" I answered his question, opening the folder not having much of an expression already knowing that my worst fears came true.

"So, Mario, Sophia … or should I say Luna Gonzalez and Romano Gonzalez" I smiled looking up at their terrified expressions, "Isabella" I put my hand up silencing them "No! You don't get the right to Isabella me, you as a matter of fact you get no rights what's so ever, you have officially lowered your rank from fucked up parents to scum! You deserve nothing and will be shown no mercy" I made their fate crystal clear,

"Do not expect the slightest kindness from me because I will show you none! I much rather show Xavier kindness than you in this moment" I calmly explained making sure to keep my cool tapping back into my old self.
"The man who tortured and raped you?!" Sophia shouted
"Yes Sophia that man, because if not thanks to you and your husband than he would not have been able to do any of that, if not for the two of you handing me over to him. None of this would have happened. I will however say one thing

expect the same mercy you have showed me."

I turned around preparing to call the guards in to take them to the basement and imprison them down there until I wrap my head around everything, "Isabella you can't kill your own mother" Sophia shouted desperation laced every word as she pleaded for her life.

"Why?" I cocked my head looking at her.

"It's inhumane!" she shouted failing miserably to plea her case. "Just as inhumane as throwing your daughter into the hands of a man who will deliberately torture her both emotionally and mentally! Forcing her to feel so numb and desperate for any kind of human touch and affection that she works side by side for the very man who broke her. All because of some stupid revenge that began long before she was born. What's even worse is you were in the other room, watching, witnessing, and hearing every scream, every plea, every prayer, and every soul crushing cry ... and chose to do nothing. That's. Inhumane." I spat standing up straight.

"Take them to the basement now" I ordered the guard dropping my tone of voice dangerously low feeling all my emotional rational sides fade away.

"You both were never emotionally scarred or sick … but you will be" I threaten smirking at the two of them as their faces completely drop.

Making my exit hearing the commotion from behind me as they struggle against the guards dragging them out.

X

I somehow found myself driving to Maria, something I often find myself doing whether it be because I'm facing crisis or because I simply just miss her. I need her more than ever right now and if she was here, she would know exactly what to do, and if she didn't, she would go through every possible step alongside me, so I wasn't facing it alone. I parked the car and started making my way slowly to the grave Dante in my arms eagerly wanting to get to his aunties grave "I miss her too baby" kissing his cheek.

Getting closer to the grave I saw a man lurking in the far shadows, I tightened my hold on Dante looking out into the distance before the figure vanishes. I shake my head looking back out "I think I've officially lost my mind" I sigh exhausted. Sitting in front of her grave I smile tracing the engraved stone with the tip of my finger 'Maria Knight.'

"Hi flower, Dante and I were missing you … thought we would visit you" I spoke softly as Dante rested his head on my chest his hand out trying to reach the headstone. "I did what you made me promise, I bring Dante over all the time, and we always tell him stories about you before bed, it's Lorenzo's favourite thing to do. Maria nighttime adventures he calls it" I sniffle a laugh shaking my head, "we all miss you so much hermona" I bite my bottom lip to stop myself from crying.

"There is so much happening, it's so overwhelming and I'm literally caught between a stone and a wall with those body piercing spikes. I know what I want to do, what I would always resort in doing but then I know what you would want me to do, or at least what I think you'd want." I let out a deep breath.

"You were always such a forgiving soul, but when it came to someone hurting me you saw red, but what would you do if you knew the person who caused all the pain, hurt and distance between us were the very people we called mum and dad … what would you say then?" I looked at her headstone imagining she was sitting here with me, "would you forgive them because they're our parents … or would you see red?" I started chewing my inner cheek getting lost in my own train of thoughts.

I want them dead, I want them to suffer for everything they caused me, for everything they made me endure … but then I think of Maria if she were here alive, and healthy would she forgive me for killing our parents? For depriving her of them? Or would she see them in the same light as me? I lower my head down getting a headache as this overwhelming pressure start's building up inside me.

Just then I see Dante giggling reaching his hands up at the sky, my eyes tearing up I look up letting out a happy sigh "hey sis" I smile looking up at the sky as Dante continues to giggle and play with whatever he seems to see in front of him.

X

After a peaceful hour, it started getting chilly as the wind picked up, I hugged Dante to my chest and made our way back to the car. Opening the door and buckling in my baby I gave him a quick peck on the forehead, "I love you, mi Leone." I whispered before closing the door making my way to my side of the car before something caught my attention on the windscreen whipper. "What the …" I reached over picking up what looked like a polaroid my eyes widening seeing who was in the picture. I crumble it in my hand feeling my blood boil, grabbing my phone I dial Lorenzo's number "Xavier's got Vincenzo" I throw the polaroid in the car and make my way back to the estate.

X

Jumping out of the car I usher for the men to grab Dante, "his asleep be gentle and don't let him out of your sight!" I order charging my way through the men to get inside.

"Get me Garcia now!" I shout pointing at Hacker also ushering him to follow me, if we are going to get him back, we are gonna need all the help we can get. Making my way inside the house I point at Lorenzo, bullseye, Fico, and Luca.

Opening the door to the meeting room we all gather around as everyone stands around, I throw the crumbled polaroid on the table for everyone to see. Everyone bows their heads. Lorenzo slammed his fist on the table while the rest exchanged frustrated sighs.

"How is it possible for someone to kidnap Vincenzo? He has the reflexes of a cat if someone sneaks up on him, he senses it" Lorenzo spits throwing his hands in the air.

"Maybe he was distracted" Hacker points out, I shake my head. "Whatever happened, happened. What we need now is to get him back God knows what Xavier is doing to him in there." My jaw locking in place just thinking about it, the photo shows Vincenzo tied up with a gag in his mouth and needles sticking out of him, "I don't know what his giving him, but I know it won't end well".

"I'll kill him. This man needs to burn in flames with his skin peeled off, this ends now" I grunt through my teeth.

"How do we know its Xavier?" Lorenzo chirps up, I shake my head "the building the photo was taken in is the very place he would take me during our trips to New York … to interrogate someone it's perfect, secluded and a lot of space to work. Besides who else would do this? Vincenzo has many enemies, but none bold enough to kidnap him. Xavier is many things, but I'll give him this he has guts." I hear the haul of cars outside, poking my head out the window I see Garcia and his men step out of the car.

"Hacker grab our guests" I nod, he rushes out following orders. "What's the plan?"

"All we can do is ambush, but the risky part is they're probably expecting an ambush, we need to be careful but the only way to get him back is to go there." I shake my head running my fingers through my hair "I have no fucking clue what we're going to do" I shout frustrated and angry at the universe, "maybe I can help" Garcia speaks up from the door with his signature reassuring smile.

I sigh relieved rushing over to him. He opens his arms waiting for me as I crash into him holding on tight. Immediately embracing me in his arms he soothes me rubbing circles on my back "It's okay Isabella … remember **you are as fierce, as brave, as dangerous, and as majestic as a dragon … el dragón**" the sound of his voice brought me so much peace it immediately calmed me down, I couldn't pin point where I heard that phrase, it was like someone always use to whisper that to me when I was scared, my head was fuzzy with everything going on I couldn't focus on anything except on getting Vincenzo back.

I stepped back and nodded my head taking in a deep breath. "Okay let's get to work" Garcia claps as we all stand around the table.

I shake my head feeling my nerves worsening, I need Vincenzo, please dear god let him be okay I just got him back. I looked over at Garcia who sees the panic on my face, his face dropped from my expression as if he remembered something, he quickly recovered and smiled nodding his head "Isabella you're okay, you got this tap into that fire" he nodded giving me a reassuring smile, letting a similar smile overtake my features I nod my head. "Here's the plan."

"No one knows this building as well as me, we need surveillance around the area, we won't have any near the building for miles, but it's a one road and the building is on a dead-end street so however many cars go in the area is how many men we need to consider. Hacker, you think you can get me the footage now?" I ask putting urgency on the matter, "five minutes" he rushes out getting to work, looking around I continue "if the count of men is more than his usual amount, we will need to get Garcia's men involved to outnumber and surround the building without losing both our and Garcia's men. He has Vincenzo King tied up vulnerable but not entirely contained, he wouldn't risk having the appropriate manpower knowing Vincenzo's capability he would have armed it to the teeth to ensure his own safety and Vincenzo's vulnerable state."

I move over to the computer and pull up a 3D visual of the building, projecting it on the screen, I move over zooming in the image turning it into a 3D blueprint.

"We kept the interrogations mainly on the third floor" I point.

"It was the most spacious, meaning there is a lot of room and in his eyes a lot can go wrong, the more space means more room for error and if something happens, he won't be able to control it, if he got loose in such a spacious room full of knifes and needles as we saw in the polaroid. Vincenzo would kill all of them but have fun with Xavier and he knows that which is why he put Vincenzo in here" I zoomed into the first floor and tapped the room to the far left.

"This is a supply closest big enough to fit two people but not big enough to allow any errors." I added turning back around to face the group. "Let's go" I ushered everyone while ushering for Garcia to hang back. "Are you okay?" he whispered as everyone rushed out, I smiled weakly and nodded "Isabella I think I know you well enough to know that you're one hundred percent not okay" he grabbed my hands holding them tightly in his own smiling gently at me. I let out a sigh before breaking down crying, he pulls me in immediately for a hug holding me tight while I sobbed in his chest.

"Shh, it's going to be okay I promise you" he whispered reassuringly in my ear, I nodded my head in his chest not ready to let go just yet, "I just … I'm so tired. Oh my god, I'm so tired." I cried feeling so exhausted, in a matter of a year I lost my sister, I was kidnapped and hunted down again by Xavier, I was in hospital, I lost Vincenzo more times than I can count and now I lost my parents again … but this time it hurts more than it did when I thought they were dead.

"I know Bella, I know. Listen, life if tough, but so are you. I have never known a girl who has gone through as much as you and is still going out kicking and swinging. Looking for the good in the bleak of all the darkness she had to endure and continues to endure. Choosing to be here and be present when the universe gave her little reason to be, you possess so much power in your pinkie then most do in their entire bodies. Take a moment marvel at your life, at the grief that softened you. The heartache that wisened you, and at the suffering that strengthed you. Despite everything, you're still here healing and growing. Be proud of that because I sure am so proud of you" I stepped back poking my head up looking at Garcia as the tears weld up in my eyes and my bottom lip quivered hearing him speak, something about his voice resonated with me it settled in my heart a soft warm feeling a feeling id only ever felt with Vincenzo ... a feeling of safety.

"Thank you, Garcia." I whispered softly hugging him one more time, "I'm not ready to let go yet" I softly muttered in his chest, he let out a relieved sigh "good because neither am I".

We stayed like that for another twenty or so minutes before we finally pulled apart and agreed It was time for me to wipe my tears and gear up. However not before he went and saw his baby, laughing I smiled and got Lorenzo to take him to Dante while I got ready.

X

Pulling up at the building I scanned the area, "there's no men guarding the place" I muttered out looking over at Lorenzo, who had the same puzzled expression on his face. "Either Xavier wanted us to get him, or he didn't plan on me knowing the location… I think he wanted us to get him but why?" I questioned, getting out of the car I waved out and sent everyone back home leaving only Lorenzo and Bullseye with me in case.

Everyone cleared out while we entered the building through the side window, just as we entered the room the noise of Vincenzo's groaning, I signalled for the men to split up and find him, each one of us going our own way I made my way to the top floor while Lorenzo and Bullseye scanned the bottom.

Pulling out my gun I walk keeping my guard up expecting anything as I got closer to Vincenzo's groaning.

"Come on boy one more" I heard a man's voice, alarmed I bent over the staircase and ushered for Lorenzo and Bullseye to come. Storming in the very dark room all I could see was a dark silhouette standing over a very dazed Vincenzo, the second he saw us standing he dropped the needle and ran. The boys ran after him, he jumped out the window. "Fuck go around!" Lorenzo shouted going down the staircase chasing after him while Bullseye jumped out the window.

"Vincenzo baby" I rushed out, running up to him. I pulled the blindfold from his eyes, "Isabella?" he called out squinting.

"It's me, baby I'm here" I untied him and wrapped my arms around his neck holding him tight, he wrapped his arms around my waist weakly "I'm okay" he reassured me his voice still groggy even after being poked with needles and on the brink of passing out he was trying to calm me down, so I don't stress. This man right here is my person.

I took a second to scan him making sure he was as okay as he claimed to be, he didn't look like he was beaten or tortured nothing expect for those small needle holes in his arms.

"Come on" I helped him up pulling his arm over my shoulder, aiding him as we walked down the stairs and into the car, "careful" I whispered laying him down in the back of the car.

"We fucking lost him" Lorenzo cursed approaching me.

"How?" I asked looking at them both "a car pulled up straight away and he got away. Sneaky bastard" bullseye added, I shook my head "Xavier always had a getaway close and handy, so he did want us to get Vincenzo … but why? I need to know his end game … let's get him home and taken care of then we can talk about all of it." We all got in the car and made our way home.

X

Getting home we got Vincenzo in the shower cleaning him up after we got him checked up at the clinic and some tests done, we have to wait an hour for the results so I figured we should get him cleaned up in the meantime and some food in his system. I sent Lorenzo to get the chef to prepare him some food while I helped him shower.

"Okay, lean on me" wrapping his lower body in a towel, he leans on me as we made our way to the bedroom, he managed to gather enough strength and put on his boxer shorts and his sweats, he looked weak, so I quickly made my way to his side and helped him lay down on the bed.

"Isabella … I need to tell you something".

"I don't remember much, but I do remember him saying Isabella will finally get what she deserves from me." He pointed to himself. "What?" I questioned growing concerned.

"I don't know what he meant, and I don't want to find out. Leave please." He begged looking defenceless.

"Just until I'm back to myself again, one week. I don't want to see you hurt and I rather light myself on fire than be the one to cause your end. Isabella please I don't think I can survive hurting you one more time. If I know I caused you pain it will end me."

I sat next to him and nuzzled into him "I promised to never leave again no matter what. We'll get through it, we always do. I'm not going anywhere and if what he said was true, you would have tried hurting me already." I added, he let out a breath.

"Okay that's true maybe I heard him wrong." He added, wrapping his arms around my waist.

"Do you remember who 'he' was?" I emphasised, looking up at him. He shook his head starring off into the distance "his voice was extremely familiar but he hid himself in the dark then blindfolded me so I wouldn't see him face."

"Xavier has always been one to play in the dark" I added feeling aggravated, I felt Vincenzo's body temperature drop, "do you want a blanket?" I asked getting off him, he looked over at me his entire body shaking, "Vincenzo?" I yelled out officially starting to panic, his eyes rolled back, and foam started falling out of his mouth.

I screamed jumping back calling the nurse, they came rushing in to aid Vincenzo as I ran out not being able to see him like that.

"It's okay Isabella, he was drugged multiple times in a span of a day. I think it's just withdrawals." Lorenzo tried soothing me, I shook my head. "My 'parents' would know exactly what he was given. They worked with Xavier for years if anyone is going to know what's happening it's them".

I stormed away and went down straight to the basement, "what fucking drug did Xavier dose Vincenzo" I burst out, storming up to them.

"What?" Mama blurts out confused and visibly exhausted.

"What. Drug." My voice dropping, while simultaneously my hands balled into a fist.

"How the fuck are we supposed to know that?" Mario shouts insulted.

"You worked with the man for years, probably giving him thousands of new ways to break and torture me. I'm positive you know exactly what this drug is, and im even more sure that you supplied him those drugs. Do you think I forgot all our business meetings you took me along when I was a kid?

Do you think I was so niave I never understood anything? Or are you that stupid you forgot I was the brain behind your empire! So, I will ask one more time. What. Drug" I threatened getting in his face.

"You have some fucking nerve getting in my face and accusing me of such things" he yelled, not blinking a wicked smile overtook my features.

"Really? Are you trying to sound threatening? Do you honestly believe you have the upper hand in this situation? I will and can easily kill you right now and not blink or lose a wink of sleep over it." I threatened.

"Then why haven't you?" he added getting cocky, I smirked "your death won't be quick, I will make sure it stretches for as long as I can, I will use every day for the next two years to invent new ways to torture you, one day for every second I was locked in that basement foolishly calling you for help. I will make your life a living hell, I will take away your ability to sleep, to feel and most of all I will break you until you are nothing but a shell of what you use to be. I won't stop even when your soul tries to leave your body, I'll pull it back and keep going, a soul like yours doesn't deserve rest. Does that answer your question 'papa'?" I snickered watching the colour drain from his face.

I take a step back wanting to go check on Vincenzo, I hear the tear of the ropes that bounded him lunging towards me he swings the chair over my head "I'll kill you first" he yelled, going in for a second swing I faintly hear him struggle against someone.

"Don't you dare touch my daughter" I hazily heard before collapsing on the floor everything around me turned black.

THE PARANOIA

Isabella's POV

Opening my eyes my vision was still blurry looking around the room, I fixated my gaze on Lorenzo who was hovering over me worried, "are you okay?" he asked seeing me waking up. I nodded my head slowly still feeling groggy, "what happened?" I breathed out coughing immediately my throat was as dry at the desert. He hands me a glass of water helping me sit up right, taking a sip he elaborates further. "You passed out in the basement. I think your dad knocked you out I'm not sure." My body tensed up hearing him use the term 'dad' my grip around the glass cup tightened causing it to shatter in my hands.

"His not my father" I spat feeling the rage in me grow the more I think about him and what he did. "The guards carried you out and called the nurse" he cautiously continued explaining while tending to my hand. "I'm fine" I uttered wanting him to stop, "clearly" he rolled his eyes ignoring me.

'Don't you dare touch my daughter' a voiced echoed in my head. "Who else was in the basement with me?" I blurted out looking intensely at Lorenzo "I'm not sure honestly with all the chaos I wasn't exactly fixated on my surroundings, between you and Vincenzo the estate has never been this much havoc."

My eyes widened remembering Vincenzo, I jumped up out of the bed and started running towards our bedroom, looking to make sure Vincenzo was okay. Upon entering our room, I saw him laying peacefully on the bed asleep, Lorenzo catching up to me stops behind me catching his breath "why!" he gasps out of breath, rolling my eyes sheepishly I turned around.

"His, okay?" I asked needing reassurance, he nodded his head "his fine, but Mia wanted to talk to both of us and Ariana." I bit my bottom lip nodding my head slowly, something telling me it wasn't going to be good news.

We made our way to Mia who was in her office at the clinic clearly waiting for us to arrive anxiously, fuck me. I mentally cursed knowing the news we are about to get was going to be anything but positive, "please sit" she ushered for the three of us to sit down, "is my brother, okay?" Ariana asked nervously. Mia bites her lip nervous making it clear the answer was no. "Your brother ... Boss was dosed with heavy drugs and it's going to cause a lot of damage unless we treat it as soon as possible but the effects of what he was dosed with is going to make it very hard." She rushed out clearly scared to tell us the full extent of the issue.

"Mia, what did they dose him with?" Lorenzo blurted sitting on the edge of his seat, taking in a deep breath she starts explaining the extent of everything.

"We found traces of crystal, methamphetamine but high doses of amphetamines and cocaine. All of which are stimulants that speed up the messages traveling between the brain and the body, it can increase energy and concentration and reduce hunger and the need to sleep ... the phycological harms it can cause are depression, extreme anxiety, aggression, and violence but one trait not needed in a mafia boss who has thousands of enemies ... extreme paranoia".

Panicked I felt my throat closing, I put my hand on my chest trying to take steady and deep breaths, Ariana coming around trying to help me, but no one was able to handle or help my panic attacks better than Vincenzo.

"It's okay" she whispered trying to sooth me, I nodded my head feeling my breathing getting back to normal slowly I squeezed her hand reassuring her as she sat next to me making sure to keep an eye on me. "There are treatments regular exercise, healthy diet, and sleep. The withdrawal symptoms will not aid his treatment because after the drug we gave him to help him sleep wears off that's when the true fight begins. We need someone or something that his willing to fight for to push through everything someone he trusts." Everyone's heads turned to me.

I shook my head viscously "he trusted me! When he remembered me before his memory loss, but now I'm the first person he would suspect, like he did when he faked my death. It can't be me if his memory was back, it would be a different story." I rushed to explain, shaking their heads Ariana and Lorenzo turn to face me. Mia excuses herself letting us have a private discussion as she clocks out, "you are the one person on this planet he trusts, even with his memory loss he didn't kill you … the person he was when that happened would have disposed of you immediately. Vincenzo has this nagging voice in the back of his head he knows you're special to him and there's a deeper meaning and connection to you than he is fully aware of. That's why your perfect for this, if anyone can help him in his most vulnerable its you." Ariana added.

I let out a sigh still unsure, "when we saved him, he held your hand the whole way home. He calmed down straight away as soon as you squeezed his hand. Vincenzo... he went through a lot growing up and we might not know what he went through but that scared little boy in him trusts you." Lorenzo spoke softly, both staring at me waiting for my answer. Nodding my head regardless of Vincenzo's concern from before and regardless of my own, I promised to always be there for him and never leave and I'm keeping that promise, he wouldn't have gotten drugged if he didn't go to get his memory back.

X

We all left and made our way back to the house, I walked up the stairs slowly into our bedroom I saw Dante fast asleep in his little bed and Vincenzo was still asleep, but he looked like he was about to wake up soon. Moving and groaning, "Vincenzo?" I whispered softly kneeling next to his bedside. "Vincenzo?" I repeated he opened his eyes with a terrified expression. He jumped back and sat up, making me jump I took a step back my hand on my chest trying to regain my composure.

"Vincenzo baby are you okay?" I whispered trying to reach out for him but instead he jumped back. "Sorry, just a little jumpy" he breathed out keeping his distance. Unsure of what to do I respect his wishes keeping the distance visible between us to calm him down, "how are you feeling?" I breathed out watching his behaviour he was visibly anxious and fidgety. "Fine" he nodded looking down picking at his arm, "do you want to feel better?" I asked softly, he nodded his head looking cautiously at me "how?" he softly spoke.

"I went and spoke to Mia, she let us know what was injected into you and thankfully there's a way to fix it." I explained briefly.

"How do you know something was injected into me?" he asked looking suspicious.

Stuttering I looked up fearing his already starting to get paranoid, "I was there with you-" cutting me off he jumps out of the bed and puts his hand out "you where there?" he shouts. My head darts to Dante, making sure Vincenzo's outbursts didn't wake him up.

"No, no. Vincenzo baby I was there to save you, I wasn't there when it was happening." I tried explaining moving towards him, but he abruptly pushed me away, backing himself up against the wall. Shaking his head like he has a million thoughts rummaging in his head, "Vincenzo, let me help you. There's a simple remedy you don't even need to take anything to-"

"YOU WAN'T ME GONE! YOU WAN'T TO KILL ME! THIS WHOLE THING WAS YOUR IDEA, I DON'T EVEN KNOW WHO YOU ARE!" He started screaming and shouting. Dante started crying visibly startled by Vincenzo's outburst, my heart about to burst out of my chest. I rush to my baby Vincenzo still screaming "DON'T TOUCH MY SON!" he shouts throwing a glass cup into the window behind us, I duck down feeling my heart in my throat my breathing increasing rapidly fearing for what he is going to do next as he starred at me with that sadistic look in his eyes, grinning at me. ***"You grin was always halfway a smile halfway a threat"*** I observed aloud, my breathing heavy.

About to lunge towards me before Lorenzo and Bullseye rush into the room pinning him down before he could reach me. No number of men was about to keep Vincenzo down and it was visibly obvious they were losing their hold on him. He manged to easily get out of their grip and took one look at me "I'll kill you before you kill me" he threatened. Turning around and running out.

"WHAT ARE YOU ALL STARING AT GO GET HIM!" I shouted feeling all my emotions boiling up to tipping point. They all ran out trying to get him before he left the estate or hurt himself. Dante clung to my shirt screaming his little lungs out, "It's okay baby, it's okay" I soothed him softly bouncing him up and down rubbing circles on his back keeping him close to my chest. After a few minutes he calmed down focusing on my chest rising and falling, "Isabella? Are you okay?" Ariana walked in looking the same way I felt on the inside "I'm okay" I whispered softly, I looked around seeing the glass shattered on the floor replaying the events in my head.

Ariana probably seeing the distress on my face, she grabs my arm and guides me towards her bedroom. Slowly taking Dante from my arms she places him on her bed, I wanted to object and keep him in my arms, but I feel so checked out that it was probably the best thing for him if he wasn't in my arms right now. "Can you make sure his laying on his back and his sleep sack is zipped up. Oh, and that his little heart stopped racing" I called out for her to check on him because even though I was talking I couldn't move I was practically frozen in place while my mind relived the events that just happened.

"I always knew Vincenzo had a dark side but that smile he did was the most terrifying thing I've ever seen" she shook her head slightly shaken up, I nodded my head "his always been so gentle with me, making sure I was never exposed to anything more than I needed to be. I never knew he had such a monster in him" she teared up, I snapped my head up and looked at her defensively.

Despite everything I knew what he was going through, and I have never understood anyone as well as I understood him. "If you've never been a monster, you will never understand the strength necessary to command so much power and be gentle".

"I didn't know I'm sorry" she whispered, I shook my head "it's an inner battle every single day to be able to calm down those inner demons that you've grown accompanied to that you relied on to help and aid you through every decision you ever made, to allow them to consume you into the monster that was hiding deep inside you. To completely abandon all that you know and fight them every single step of the way, the amount of strength it takes physically and mentally drains you every single day until one day you just snap, or something forces the snap to happen." I gestured towards my room and the situation that just happened. Just as she was about to speak a shadowy figure slams a note on her glass, Ariana lets out a shriek, jumping up I run out of the room trying to catch up to him in the rain. "Xavier!" I shouted standing outside the window no longer seeing anyone except for our men, "What the fuck are you standing around here for? Huh! Just for show? How could no one have seen a man standing outside the bosses' sister's room? DID NO ONE SEE A SUSPICIOUS MAN FUCKING LURKING AROUND THE ESTATE? NO ONE!" My voice getting louder and louder. I turn ripping the letter off the window my shock and sadness now replaced with pure anger.

The letter was written on thick poster paper he wanted to make sure I could still read it even if it got wet.

'Dear Isabella, naive Isabella.

Did you enjoy the handy work I did on Vincenzo? I really hope you take as much appreciation as I do. He was a very nice guest, I hope you love seeing the hate in his eyes when he looks at you, the hate and paranoia he feels deep in his soul every time he looks at you, I'll admit I was scared it would be aimed at someone else but I knew you would be the first in his face and the first to try and 'fix' him. I watched the show that went down

I must say it was worth standing out in the rain the highlight of it all was him breaking the glass, being the man, I always knew he was. Finally, you see it now the man I always saw in him, I can't wait for this to escalate because my dear Isabella, I know it will, it will sneak up on you and do much more damage than I ever could and what worse than having your life taken from you by someone you love? His paranoia will increase, and it will lead to your death and inevitably lead to his own, after all why would he trust a person, he doesn't remember? I killed two birds with one stone and everything that was his will be mine, everything that was yours will be mine. I will be the one who took down the most feared man in New York and I will be the one who slayed the dragon.

Until we meet again my dear Isabella, I guarantee it will be soon."

I crumbled the note balling it my fists, tensing my jaw staring off into the distance as the rain poured absolutely drenching me. A sane person would run, cower, be scared, cry, not run after a psychotic man or maybe simply just get out of the rain but I couldn't move I couldn't think and as cliché as this may sound, I couldn't feel anything. All that I could think of was how badly I could never catch a break how we could never catch a break.

"I'm so tired, so bloody tired it felt like the universe had been against me all my life and the split second it was on my side, and you gave me a seed of light it was merely a fluke to keep me alive, a cruel fucking joke. Have I not suffered enough? Have I not endured enough torture? Is it not good enough for you! Have I not done enough! What more are you going to put me through do you enjoy watching me crumble do you enjoy watching my soul burn? Watching the life fully be sucked out of me! I've tried so fucking hard, so, so, so hard. I dealt with every trial every situation you made me go through and I never complained not once! I took it on the chin and figured out a way to keep going but the one time you finally smiled on me and gave a crumb you took it away! Please! Please! Enough! ENOUGH!" I screamed allowing every single emotion that bubbled inside me to finally come out, straining my throat my voice boomed through the estate looking up I kept a deep breath in and shook my head.

"You gave me a seed. I'll make it blossom no matter how heavy the rain and thunder you send on me become. I am going to take the situation in my hands now. Fuck your crumbs I'm going to make a 6-foot tier cake. I had enough!" I nodded my head feeling determined, "this isn't the end I won't let it be the end".

X

I wanted to focus on the search for Vincenzo I had our soldiers out looking for him, once they spot him, they are to keep a close eye on him but under no circumstances to approach.

The second he feels like he is being followed he won't hesitate to eliminate what he perceives to be a threat, and the soldiers are not ready nor able to handle Vincenzo on full rage. I wasn't entirely sure if I was ready myself but that doesn't mean I wasn't going to try.

I had Lorenzo mapping out areas he thinks Vincenzo may go in his current state, Ariana was tending to Dante knowing full well I was not mentally able to do anything, even this search for Vincenzo, I find myself constantly mentally checking out not being able to focus no matter how much I wanted to.

My head was scattered all over the place in denial that this really is my life, that this is the hand I was dealt. **"Life can throw a million hurdles at you Isabella, but depending on how you handle those hurdles will determine the outcome of your life. The hand you are dealt isn't necessarily your only fate. Choose your own fate don't let the hand do it for you."** His voice echoed in my head, an imaginary friend I dreamt up amid all the darkness, but something about the way his voice echoed in my head it kept nagging at me … I know this voice was my 'imaginary friend' really imaginary? I couldn't have imagined up an imaginary friend that felt so real. If he was a real person, who was he?

And why me out of all the little girls and all the people going through worse than I was, why did he stick by me? It's like he saw how badly everything would spiral out of control, or that he knew I wasn't given any hope from the moment I was born like he wanted to protect me because he knew no one else will.

Like a personal guardian angel until one day poof, he wasn't there anymore, I chewed on my lip fading further away from the situation at hand. Standing up I start pacing back and forth fiddling with my thumb getting agitated at everything, how did it all come to this! To make it worse if my head wasn't full enough, I heard my real dad's voice and I couldn't see his face, I can't put a name to the voice, he came and declared for no one to harm his daughter but won't show his fucking face? Won't take me in his arms? Won't offer an explanation? Am I so unworthy of love that my own father won't come forward? I grabbed the hourglass from Vincenzo's desk and smashed it on the floor watching as the sand scattered all over the floor a visual representation of my mental state. "Time's up" I muttered to myself.

"Isabella" Lorenzo slowly approached me, "maybe you should sit this one out?" he whispered cautiously to not tip me off, I let out a sigh and took my arm out of his grasp and stormed out, I wasn't mad at him I was just mad at the universe and made at myself for allowing myself to make every bad decision, if I stayed put my parents game to get me kidnap would not have worked and id be rid of them, Maria would still be here and who knows maybe Vincenzo and I would have met under better circumstances.

The only decision I'm proud of is my baby boy, who I can't even face right now. I ran out into the garden sitting under the pergola taking in the fresh air, listening to the sound of the pouring rain hit the roof, trying to re-focus my mind and stop feeling sorry for myself, I knew what I was doing when I did everything I knew what going after Xavier meant, I knew what agreeing to work for him would intel and I knew what torturing and killing would get me. I had no right to victimise myself I may have been dealt a bad hand, but I'd be dammed if I allowed it to send me into a mental spiral that I can't rescue myself from. Not now, not again, not ever.

"Isabella?" I looked up seeing Garcia call out running in the rain, I couldn't help but smile a little. His efforts to constantly make sure I'm okay made me feel warm, a foreign feeling. I laughed looking at him as he stood in front of me visibly annoyed at how drenched he is "this was my favourite suit" he whined shaking his head.

"Thank you" I smiled shaking my head as he sat next to me. "What for?" he whispered.

"For making me laugh when I really didn't want to" I answered.

"It's my pleasure" he smiled putting his arm over me pulling me into his side.

"I thought you left?" I asked recalling him and his men leaving. I felt his body visibly tense up for a second. "No, I sent most of my men off, but I thought you could use some emotional support given the circumstances" nodding my head along as he explained briefly.

"So, tell my dragón are you okay?" he asked softly his voice was so sincere anyone who heard his voice could easily pick up how much he genuinely cared, and how protective he is. I smiled sadly leaning my head on his shoulder letting out a drained sigh. How am I? A question I don't think even I could answer properly, "honestly I don't know" I shook my head still deep in thought, he nodded his head giving me space to get my thoughts together.

"I just feel like I've been through enough traumatic events to last me a thousand lifetimes and every time I look around all I can think is why me? Why is it every bad thing only seems to happen to me, I was the one kidnapped and punished for my mum's infidelity, I was the one who had to work for the man who tortured me because no one was there to save me I had to save myself, kidnapped again and stabbed multiple time in the leg over a man I didn't even know. Hunted again by the man who broke me, the one man who I really cared about forgot I existed and faked my death, my twin sister was murdered, and now when the world was smiling at me for a split-second Vincenzo gets kidnapped and drugged and it was because of me. Now he is God knows where and I can't seem to catch my breath." I ranted running out of breath, taking in a moment I took a deep breath trying to calm myself down.

"I just want a normal life" my voice cracking under so much pressure I felt the tears weal up in my eyes while my bottom lip kept quivering.

"Can I tell you something?" Garcia whispered softly, nodding my head he pulls me off his shoulder and turns me to face him. Looking into his eyes he smiled, "Normality is a paved road, it's comfortable to walk, but no flowers grow." Smiling I shake my head as a tear rolls down my face, I wipe it away letting out a small chuckle "did you just quote Van Goh?" I laughed watching him break character and let out a laugh with me.

"Yes, and I stand by it" I shake my head "should we really trust the man who cut off his ears?" he paused for a second looking at me "you have an answer for everything don't you?" he rolled his eyes sarcastically.

Laughing I smile shaking my head "how is it only you can make me laugh and smile in a moment where nothing, but absolute chaos is erupting around us?" I shake my head always feeling a special bond with Garcia. "Call it a special touch" he smiled.

"Come on let's go" he stands up extending his hand out for me to take, I sigh standing on my feet taking his hand. We made a run for it in the rain trying not to get drenched and back to the estate.

X

Feeling much calmer, I went back into the office where Lorenzo and the men were trying to pinpoint a location, I walked inside looking around everyone was scattered I was so busy focusing on the chaos happening in my head that I didn't see the chaos happening around me. I took in a deep breath. Taking control of the situation before everyone further spirals out of control.

"MEN!" I shout everyone stopped talking shooting their heads towards me, "everyone needs to take in a deep breath, and stop shouting over each other." I instruct watching calmly as they do as I said taking in a deep breath and waiting for my next order.

"We are never going to find him if we don't calm down, now Vincenzo has been through a lot in a short amount of time. We need to think like he would, we can assume he went to the various hideouts he has." I spoke up observing the map they had on the wall, grabbing a marker circling all ten hideouts before continuing. "Or we can assume he circled back to the old estate, something familiar and something he can trust" I circled our old estate on the opposite side of where we are currently. Taking a step back I look at the map feeling all eyes on me while I think everything through in my head.

Then just like that with my clear head it finally came to me the horse ranch, where it all started remembering he told me it was the one place he always went to calm down his safe heaven.

I dropped the marker and turned around "I know where he is" I rushed running out of the room, hearing Lorenzo tell everyone not to follow me, he knew it would be less confrontational if it was just me.

I rushed outside the estate taking my time before I got to the ranch trying to come up with some game plan, and walking in the rain was always therapeutic to me, something about the freezing cold and how the rain fell on me forcing me to feel something is what I needed. Smiling softly "sometimes all we need is not to run inside from the rainstorm, but-"

Flashback

"But to dance, kiss and walk through the rain. Sometimes the rain will make things far more beautiful than before. After all, it takes a little rain to see a rainbow." Maria smiled as she ran and danced in the rain. Laughing to myself I shook my head "On a scale of one to ten how poetic do you feel right now?" I yelled over the noise of the rain "extremely!" she yelled back, looking over at me she waved me down to join her. Rolling my eyes and shaking my head I couldn't help the goofy smile that overtook my previous frown, caving in I ran towards her and joined her dancing. "Sometimes all you need to feel better is to dance in the rain!" She yelled as we danced like children.

End of flashback

I sniffled holding my tears back as much as I could before it came pouring out, how badly I missed her and how badly I need her here. So, I did what I knew she would want me to do I ran to the open field and danced in the rain.

THE KIDNAPPING

Isabella's POV

As I danced in the rain, I felt someone watching me, I froze in my spot and scanned my area, but it was so dark, and the rain made it almost impossible for me to see anyone. I wanted to call out for his name to see if it was him but then I'd be no better than those stupid idiots who scream hello when there's someone in the house like the person whose planning on killing them is going to shout out hey what's up.

I mentally rolled my eyes at the thought and refocused on the task at hand, looking around I let out a frustrated sigh no longer feeling anyone watching, I stomped my feet on the muddy grass and kept walking down the path to the horse ranch. The closer I got the more nervous I became, unsure if it was simply the fact of facing Vincenzo in his current state or just fearing his reaction when he sees me, would he think I was just following him or that I was hunting him down. This whole situation is so fucked that it's making me go insane.

After having a mental battle with myself about if what I'm doing is a smart move, I ultimately decided it was definitely not the right move but when did I ever listen to that rational voice inside my head anyway?

I stood in front of the horse ranch only now dawning on me that what I'd be facing as logic finally hit me in the face that Vincenzo will only grow more suspicious at how I found him so quick at a ranch that he probably thinks he hasn't told anyone about, even though he took me here on the first day at the estate … and our first date.

I heard a branch snap making my body jump, my heart racing as I looked around trying to spot him. I know it's him but fuck when he wasn't paranoid, he was hard to track now it's almost impossible, if he didn't want to be found nothing and no one can find him. I exhaled feeling my nerves worsen the closer I got. Approaching the horses in their stall my horse started to visibly panic moving further back into her stall neighing on her feet, like she didn't recognise me. "Hey girl it's okay" I tried to sooth her reaching my hand out to her, but she only seemed to get more and more panicked.

That was when I felt a presence behind me, spinning around my eyes widen as he slammed a piece of wood over my head. My body hit the floor hard and once again the darkness consumed me.

X

I slowly opened my eyes, but wherever I am it was dark extremely dark. I went to move feeling my panic begin to worsen realising I was handcuffed to a metal pipe, no, no, no.

Not again, "NO!" I screeched fighting against the pipe trying to desperately look for light something! Anything. Feeling the panic in my chest begin to rise my throat slowly started closing up the worse I panicked, I can't survive this again, I won't make it out of here I know I won't. I screamed hot tears rushing down my face as I desperately tried to free myself just as the light suddenly turned on, my breath caught in my throat as Vincenzo looked down at me with a concerned expression "Vincenzo please!" I begged looking up at him, but his concerned expression was immediately replaced with anger.

"Who the fuck are you? Who sent you!" he yelled bending down to my level hatred radiating off every word he spoke as he sat there accusing me once again of betraying him and once again because of his memory loss. Xavier knew exactly what he was doing, he knew it would make him do this to me … again.

For the first time in forever I was petrified of the man standing in front of me, his eyes were unreadable his next move unpredictable, a man with as much power as the mafia king was scary enough but now with his cynical smile as he thought of ways to punish me was enough to send anyone into cardiac arrest.

"Vincenzo, you know me. It's Isabella, the girl who wanted nothing to do with you then suddenly couldn't breathe when you were far from her. The girl that tried to escape and run from you but always seemed to run back to you. The girl you sing to and the shoulder you rest your head on. Isabella the only girl you can be vulnerable with, it's me! I know you're still in there Vincenzo King, I need you to fight like you never fought before."

I tried to reason with him as the tears flowed down my face which he probably presumed as a guilty conscious.

"I don't like repeating myself" he warned his voice dropped to a dangerous low.

I inched back hitting the metal pipe burning my bare back, I yelled out in pain as I jumped forward.

His face softened as he reached out to aid me before catching himself and shooting up, he backed away slowly from me before he shut the lights and ran out. "Vincenzo no! Please! Don't leave me in the dark, I can't survive this! I won't be alive when you get back!" I yelled starting to find it hard to breath.

"Please, not again" I cried softly to myself before looking up seeing him in the door frame putting the light on and leaving once more.

I let out a relieved sigh closing my eyes softly as I regained my composure, I don't know what to think or what to feel. I want to scream, I want to cry, I want to throw a rock at someone. I can't seem to wrap my head around how quickly everything went south, just the moment we finally get back together get back to a comfortable sync this happens.

Was it a sign? Is it the universe once again telling me that I'm just not destined to be happy? That I'm not destined to fall in love? My breathing hitched when I mentally said the word love. I didn't even say it out loud and it made my throat close shut.

Did I love Vincenzo? Did I even know what love felt like? I chewed on my bottom lip as if my head wasn't already in chaos, I just had to make it worse. Although, I never really thought about it before sitting here right now, I have no idea how I feel, I mean given the situation I'm in you can guess why it's hard for me to really get a clear view on my feelings, but one thing is for sure I don't hate him. No matter what he does, I can't seem to fuel the hate that should have been there from the moment we meet. Nothing he does makes me hate him. In a twisted way it only makes me understand him.

Understand why he does what he does, why he thinks the way he thinks, why he behaves the way he behaves. People can call it Stockholm syndrome, but I went through it, I know how he is because I was him, I am him.

I know there's more to it than me just simply being able to relate to him, I know what this feeling is as much as I want to deny it, I know deep down what the answer to my question is.

Within a second, I see Vincenzo standing in front of the doorway staring me down holding a knife in his hand, my eyes widen my breath caught in my throat as I try to speak but no words were coming out other than random heavy puffs of air, "Vincenzo what are you doing?" I blurt out anxiously feeling my heart about to burst out of my chest my eyes keep wandering down to the tight grip he has on the knife.

As a drop of rain glides down the blade stopping at the tip before dropping to floor. "If you know me, then you know exactly what I do to traitors." He breathes out coming closer to me, "I do know you! And this isn't you!" I shouted desperately trying to get him to stop and think for a second. He stopped in front of me cocking his head to the side, that same smile came on his face. The smile before the kill.

I took in a deep breath accepting my fate as I watched him

stop in front of me, the smile never leaving his face "this is my favourite part, watching them beg for mercy" he mocks placing the tip of the knife under my chin forcing me to look up at him. Our eyes locked and I felt all my worries disappear I know it's weird and screwed up, but if I had to die under someone's hands I rather it be him than someone who will benefit from my death. Forgetting everything I sighed, "I don't beg for mercy" I stated feeling calm ... too calm.

He looked slightly taken back but didn't say a word. I exhaled softly and continued needing to get everything off my chest, "When you recover and start to recall these events, I want you to forgive yourself because I forgive you." He takes a step back looking down at me, "I never asked for your forgiveness" he spat looking disgusted.

Rolling my eyes, I shook my head annoyed, "well tough I'm giving it to you anyway." I sassed rolling my eyes again, hey I was going to die no use in being polite now.

"When you remember, you are going to switch and go into full self-destruction just like I know you will, you won't leave anything or anyone in your path and eventually it will result in you loosing everyone and yourself. I need you to take care of yourself after I'm gone because I won't be around to pull you out of it anymore and I need you to okay for everyone's sake. Especially our sons." Once Vincenzo set his mind to something there was no turning back, so I needed to make sure once he regains himself, he remembers my words and knows I forgive him because I know this isn't him.

"Make sure my baby doesn't forget me." I chocked out trying to regain my composure. It took everything in me to imagine a life where my son doesn't have me, if I could fight my way out of this I would, it's bad enough he won't have me I can't leave him without a dad as well.

I know I should fight, I know I should do something and not just sit here and accept my fate, to fight to the death until I kill everyone standing in the way of me and my son, but I just can't imagine a scenario where I kill him. Even if I'm able to escape he will come back and kill me, a life on the run again.

As much as I say how tired I am no one will understand just how tired I truly am, people might think I'm being selfish choosing to die and accept what's to come instead of fighting it, but Dante will be better off with his dad once his better.

He won't even need to run or hide, and he will live a happy life unlike his mum because one thing I know for a fact is Vincenzo sane or not won't ever let anything happen to Dante.

"Dante is my son, I will protect him with my life" Vincenzo muttered out, I nodded my head slowly. "Then go ahead and do it" I spoke up waiting for him to stab me. "You would really accept your death instead of fight?" he speaks up looking at me full of disgust, I let out an exhale and nodded my head "If I fight and escape will you leave me to raise my son peacefully?" I snapped looking at the judgement in his eyes, "will you leave me and not hunt me down until you eventually kill me? Potentially scarring your son for life leaving him without a mum and a dad? Tell me Vincenzo would you!" I shouted getting fed up with the judgement and with my own maternal guilt trying to justify it all, but I know I sound crazy, and I know I'm being selfish and it's eating me up inside. I just don't want to hurt him. I rather let him kill me then kill him.

"That's not good enough" he spat shaking his head, "what's the real reason?" He probed like he was interrogating me, "wh-" I went to speak before he cut me off coming back down to my level placing the knife on my lip. "If you lie ill slice those pretty lips right off. So, tell me what's the real reason you won't fight? The reason you're so ready to accept your fate."

"I'm just tired" I answered half truthfully.

"Say the real reason" he warned,

"I did" I shouted.

"Say it!" he shouted back our faces inches from one another.

"I DID VINCENZO I'M FUCKING TIRED IM SICK OF IT ALL!"

He shook his head unconvinced, "Say. It."

I yelled frustrated feeling myself about to burst "I DON'T WANT TO FUCKING HURT YOU! IF I FIGHT, I KNOW THE ONLY WAY OUT FOR ME IS TO KILL YOU AND I DON'T WANT TO FUCKING KILL YOU!" I yelled reaching boiling point. As soon as the words left my lips, I regretted it instantly. His face twisted into annoyance he stormed out of the room, and I kicked my legs out and screamed "FUCK!" I was beyond frustrated and annoyed I need to get out of here.

I need to get to my son, and I need to help Vincenzo get back on his two feet, I won't let Dante grow up without his parents no matter what I have to endure. I felt like I was all over the place, one-minute I'm ready to die the next I'm ready to fight, but look at the state I'm in who would have a clear head?

I have never accepted my fate and always fought it tooth and fucking nail. I won't stop now either finally coming to my senses I take a deep breath and look down at my hands in the stupid handcuffs. Taking in a deep breath I feel a surge of frustration and panic rising in my chest, like I'm running out of time. I tried thinking of way to free myself looking around Vincenzo wasn't dumb there was absolutely nothing in this room that could help me escape, fucking horse ranch. I mentally cursed rolling my eyes.

I could break my thumb and squeeze my hands out, but it causes more damage than people realise and it's not always successful, besides something tells me if I'm going to make it out alive, I need my hands functional. I look over at the metal pipe and notice a rusted bolt, its barely noticeable but it gave me an idea. I twisted my body trying to position myself so I can reach the bolt with my teeth.

I bend down moving my hands closer to the bolt leaning down I start twisting the bolt with my teeth it took several tries, but finally, I manage to finally get a good grip on the bolt and start twisting it loose.

I can feel it getting loose and I mentally cheer myself on, the bolt comes free I spit it out of my mouth. Feeling the metal pipe loosen I sit back up and start tugging on my handcuffs to break the pipe in two. One more tug and I hear the end of the pipe hit the floor, standing up I look around "I need to get out here before he gets back" I mentally remind myself and I run out of the room. I ran as fast as my legs can carry me, not turning back. I sprinted past the horses I was so close to the estate.

The closer I got to the estate the more my heart pounded, the adrenaline was pumping through my veins like he was running behind me. I could see the estate in the near distance and ran even faster, I need to make sure Dante is safe and send him to Italy with Ariana while I and Lorenzo get Vincenzo back. Deep in thought I didn't notice the tree branch on the floor, tripping over it I hit the ground hard I hissed feeling the fresh scratches on my legs, arms and face. "Fuck!" I cursed trying to stand back on my feet before someone flips me on my back, his tall body towering over me as he pins my hands above my head. I take a sharp inhale, my body kicking into fight or flight as the nerves settled in the pit of my stomach.

Under other circumstances this would turn me on so much, his face was stone as he tensed his jaw and in those grey eyes all you could read from it was anger, he was ready to lose his shit. He hated making mistakes and he just made the biggest one, he underestimated me.

"You okay there Italy?" I mocked winking at him, he let out a low growl and pulled me up throwing me over his shoulder as he made his way back to the dumb ranch. I kicked and punched him as he walked back but it was like he was getting a massage he was so unphased it was starting to piss me off. He threw me down on the hay and I winced the scratches and bruises were still fresh, his face softened as he went to check on me before he abruptly shot back up like he caught onto himself. My hands still handcuffed I slowly stood up facing him "what's the plan here Mafia?" I probed him, was it the smartest idea? No, but I'm known for always picking the wrong moments to piss him off.

Given his newfound paranoia nothing I say or do is going to help him so why change, might as well make the most out of whatever I have left. "Why'd you run?" he questioned looking at me, I walked closer to him until I stood directly in front of him. He didn't move back instead he stood his ground looking down at me as his tall frame towered over me. "I thought it was pretty obvious?" I questioned arching my eyebrow, "I want to send my son far away from you" I spoke through my teeth knowing it's going to set him off. He slammed me back into the wall, my back hitting the back I collapse on my knees. Ugh that fucking hurt.

"Bitch" I hissed feeling the sharp pain travel through my back right to my head, "who are you to take my son away from me?" He shouted.

I rolled my eyes looking up at him "I'm his mother! Until

you're better and clean, you won't go near my son" I breathed out feeling the air being knocked out of me. He griped me by my neck pulling me up, I gasped for air my hands gripping his as he lifted me off the ground. "My son" he reminded me.

My eyes rolled to the back of my head as I felt my airways close up, with all my energy I pushed my thumbs in his eyes wanting him to let go. It worked. I landed flat on my ass gasping for air. I quickly stood up "our son" I corrected his earlier statement. "Vincenzo, look at me you don't have to do all of this let me fucking help you damit" I shouted my tone coming off desperate because I was.

If I die, I want only Vincenzo to take care of our son, but not in this state, and when I'm gone how will I know what kind of state he will be in.

"What makes you think I need any help?" he shouted rubbing his eyes before making eye contact with me.

"This isn't you! Even with your memory loss you couldn't hurt me, you never left me. You protected me no matter what, you never left me even when fate gave you every opportunity too. Now it's my turn, you can stab me, you can punch me. Fuck you can throw me against the wall a hundred times. I won't leave you, even when I ran, I was planning on coming back. You were always in my corner now it's my fucking turn! So, kill me, don't kill me, I'm not leaving". I cried fighting back the tears, I lowered my head feeling the hot tears fall down my face, "when you were in that accident, and everyone thought you were dead. It felt like I died with you, I couldn't eat, I couldn't breathe I drowned myself in Vodka just to numb myself from the pain I was going through" I wince recalling the event's, thankfully I wasn't pregnant yet. I found out two weeks later and thank God it takes 2-3 weeks after sex to officially become pregnant.

If I was drowning myself in vodka and had Dante growing inside of me, I would have hit a new level of guilt. I shake my head refocusing on Vincenzo.

"Why did you do that? Why not start a new life? Why suffer?" he asked confused, I shook my head "unbelievable after everything we've been through you still don't get it do you?" I spoke out in disbelief. I wanted to scream so badly how I felt but there was something stopping me so instead I looked at him as the tears rolled down my cheeks. "Vodka was easier to swallow than the fact that you weren't coming back" I admitted truthfully. "I promised to never leave you, no matter what. I don't intend on breaking that promise. If you want me gone, if you really think I'm capable of doing whatever it is that your brain is telling you than you have to kill me. Otherwise, I'm never leaving".

He hesitated looking me up and down, "I want to believe you. So, tell me why I can't".

I exhaled taking in a deep breath "the drugs he injected in you is causing many side effects but the main one is paranoia, me being the first in sight and the first person to try and help you. It triggered you to think I was behind it all and just wanted to cover my tracks." I answered honestly waiting for his reply. "Do you remember anything?" I asked softly not wanting to trigger him, he runs his fingers through his hair tugging at it, the veins in his neck popping out as he tensed up, he looked like he was about to explode.

He let out a scream so loud and powerful I heard the horses start to panic. I took in a deep breath and walked up to him slowly lifting my arms up and placing it over his neck pulling him closer to me. At first, he tried resisting but every time he tried to push me away, I held him tighter until he eventually relaxed. "Isabella?" he whispered softly in my ear. "Yes" I answered, "It's me baby" I whispered holding him tight. "I'm so sorry" he whispered holding me tight. "NO!" he yelled and pushed me off him switching up as fast as a switch being turned on and off, "Vincenzo" I called out for him, but he shook his head hand out "stop with the mind games! I know what you're trying to do. You want to kill me, to finish off the job. I won't let you I'll kill you first" he stepped back "I'll be back to deal with you later. First, I need to get my son".

My eyes widened as the fear finally settled "No!" I shouted running towards him, but he ran out and locked the door behind him, making sure there was no way out. "FUCK! VINCENZO DON'T TOUCH HIM! LET ME OUT OF HERE MY SON NEED'S ME" I screamed banging on the door, falling down on my knees feeling a mix of vulnerability and rage. If one hair on my son's head is out of place, I will burn down anything and everything in my path.

"I CAN'T LOSE MY SON! VINCENZO OPEN THIS FUCKING DOOR."

My head snapped hearing the door unlock, but nothing prepared me for who I saw on the other side of it.

THE I LOVE YOU

Isabella's POV

"Now you know the feeling of losing a son my dear Isabella" my eyes widened still in shock at who was standing in front of me, never in a million years did I ever think I'd be seeing him in front of me again. Especially after the betrayal, "Giovani?" I breathed out. Vincenzo's father stood before me, drenched from the rain, his beard had grown out like he wasn't able to groom himself for months and the smell that came off him made me gag. It was a mix of alcohol, dirt, and cheap cigarettes.

"Would it have killed you to shower?" I coughed out waving my hand in front of my face to save my poor nose.

"Really not in a position to make fun Isabella" he warned me annoyed.

I shrugged my shoulders "I've never been one to read the room in my defence. Plus, you really stink" I took a few steps back, "now I'm going to take a shot in the dark here and say you're working for Xavier … or doing his dirty work. Pun intended" despite the circumstances I was on a roll. I was trying to keep my cool not wanting to tip him off that I desperately wanted to push past him and run after Vincenzo and get my son, the second he senses I'm desperate whatever he has in mind will worsen.

"Xavier just helped me get a room to do what I needed to my dear boy, once I finally had the space, I went out looking for resources. Besides from hearing you talk about Xavier and his tactics in these situations I made sure to mimic it to send you off my trial until I got what I needed from him." I took in a deep breath waiting for him to continue what he was saying instead he stayed quiet probably wanting me to probe him further. I rolled my eyes his exhausting, I can't master up the facial muscles to seem interested in what he had to say now he wants me to add oos and aahs to his dramatic reveal.

I let out a sigh and played along "what exactly did you want from him?" I questioned.

He smirked feeling victorious "you" he answered bluntly. I widened my eyes shocked, what could he possibly need from me. Seeing my confusion, he laughed "don't you get it

Isabella? You are my ticket back into the underworld, besides you're the reason I lost Vincenzo. Before you came into our lives everything was fine! Vincenzo was ruthless making our name the most feared in all of New York. My boy gave me the power I so desperately craved, the power was in my hands then you came along, and he turned his back on me like I was nothing!" he shouted throwing his hands in the air.

"You are nothing" I commented calmly looking him up and down, "you said so yourself" I pointed out.

I know what I was saying was angering him, I know what I was doing was making him furious, but I figured if I bought myself enough time, I could make a swift escape besides I'm sure Lorenzo and the men have the estate on high alert. Vincenzo is smart and resourceful but surly he couldn't get in and even if he did, he wouldn't dare hurt Ariana to get Dante.

Catching myself drift I shake my head and focus back on Giovani, "Vincenzo is ruthless, merciless, and fucking powerful. He managed to make the King's name a name to be feared, a name once heard out loud sent the underworld into a fright. He single handily managed to take over and be the boss of bosses, taking over the underworld and the top mob bosses who now rule beneath him. He did that, not you. You aided him in none of it. As a matter of a fact all you did was piggy ride on his back. The only contribution you could plausibly argue is the fact that you gave him the surname King." I explained and the more I spoke the angrier he became.

"You would think after all he did, how was able to take over the mafia and rise it from the ashes that you would quietly sit and behave. Instead, you worked with his enemy and for what? To get rid of the one good thing in his life!" I felt myself starting to get a little emotional recalling the events that not only lead to Maria's death but my own. The moment I knew she died was the moment I died with her.

I let out a breath calming myself down looking back up at him, "you only created problems for my son! I was doing him a favour" he shouted pointing at me.

Rolling my eyes, he stormed towards me pinning me

against the wall my by throat, "it wasn't his enemy, it was yours. My son was fighting a fight he didn't need all in order to protect you! And for what? All you did was cause problems the moment he grabbed you off the street" he spat. I tensed my jaw grinding down on my teeth, "Xavier may be my enemy, but he was Vincenzo's as well." I spat. He looked at me confused and I let out a throaty laugh. "Oh, you don't know?" I laughed even harder at his oblivious, "I'm sure Vincenzo mentioned it you before, but I think you were too drunk to remember or comprehend what he was saying. You probably just yelled and tried to take ownership of the man Vincenzo became." I laughed shaking my head, he tightened his grip on my neck but that didn't stop me from mocking him. "WE MADE YOU WHO YOU ARE!" I mimicked what I imagined he would have said to Vincenzo.

"I WAS" He yelled.

"Vincenzo made himself the man he is today, because he was sick and tired of his weak father allowing anyone and everyone to walk over them. He became the boss of bosses because you failed to protect your family, he took it upon himself at such a young age to be the man of the house because the supposed man of the house wasn't man enough to do it." I chocked out feeling his grip on my throat finally about to cut my airways. With my last breath I dropped the bomb "Xavier is the one that killed Dante" his eyes widened immediately letting me go as I gasped for air. Breathing in heavily I took a minute to watch him, he was in shock.

His body shaking, his face turning red from the amount of tension his putting on himself, the veins in his neck bulged out finally screaming letting out all his anger.

"You're lying!" he turned to me refusing to believe the man he betrayed his son for was the cause of Dante's death.

I shook my head no, "you didn't just betray Vincenzo you betrayed Dante" I added, just as he was having an episode, he knelt on the floor holding his head in his hands rocking back and forth. I looked at the unlocked door seeing my opportunity and slowly walked around him, my heart was racing it was pounding against my chest so fast I was convinced it was going to burst out. The adrenaline kicked in, and I felt a sudden burst of energy course through my blood.

Without giving it a second thought, I ran as fast as my legs could carry me, this time I wasn't stopping I needed to get to Vincenzo before he got to Dante. I know the men wouldn't be able to detect him and if they did, they wouldn't be able to detain him.

I approached the estate and quickly scanned the area. I couldn't see him anywhere and all the men were still calm. Where the hell are you Italy, I ran around the corner the men were calling my name trying to get my attention, but I was too focused trying to spot Vincenzo in the shadows, if he didn't want to be found he won't be found. I looked up at my bedroom and saw Ariana holding Dante while she grabbed him some clothes, I looked around my bedroom window and saw a shadow climbing up the window. "Ariana take Dante and run!" I shouted as loud as I could, she looked out the window and saw me screaming. I gestured her to run, Vincenzo turned around facing me even in the dark I could tell he was furious.

I ran inside the house and met Ariana on the staircase "Vincenzo is coming to take Dante. Take him get in the car and don't stop until I call you" I ordered her quickly kissing my son I whispered in his ear "prometon amarte y protegerte por siempre hijo mio" (I promise to love and protect you forever my son. Ariana looked up at me worried, I gave her a reassuring nod giving her a quick hug watching her run past me to the car parked outside, "Ariana!" Vincenzo's voice boomed through the house, Ariana stopped dead in her tracks terrified she turned around looking at her brother "Amo tuo fratello" (I love you brother) the pain in her eyes made my soul ache, turning her back on her brother she takes off. He jumps over the stair railing running after her, I chased after him tackling him to the ground we rolled over the rubble for a few minutes I finally pinned him down both of our heads turning to watch Ariana's car speed off. I let out a sigh of relief knowing his safe. I turn back to face Vincenzo, I was met with his cold, calculating sate. His eyes bored into mine, piercing my emerald, green eyes with his grey eyes intensely. I could see the anger simmering just beneath the surface, the fury that was vibrating off him.

"Don't" I warned him, he lets out a grunt and flips us over. Hovering above me he pins my hands above my head. My hands still in cuffs he shakes his head mockingly "stop me".

He got off me and looked around while I tried getting up, he stopped staring dead straight at something in front of him. I stood up and tried looking over his shoulder to see what he was looking at before my eyes got sight of it, it was an axe that was on a tree stump. He turns to me a wicked glare in his eyes.

"You want a fight Italy? That's exactly what you're going to get." I threatened.

He stormed towards me axe in the air, I push kicked him in the stomach once he got close enough, he stumbled back slightly bending over I took the opportunity to kick him in the face. I smirked feeling proud of myself he stood up snapping his jaw in place he looked me dead in the eye anger evidently radiating off him.

He swung the axe aiming for my head I moved back pulling against the chains putting it in direct line of the hit. The blade made contact with the chains snapping it in half, "finally" I breathed out. He looked at me even more furious than before because I outsmarted him.

"You made a mistake" I mocked. He smirked at me, I can feel the tension in my muscles, as they prepared themselves for the fight that was about to come. We circled around each other, both of us waiting for the perfect moment to strike. "Isabella!" I heard Lorenzo yell from a distance as everyone huddled around us wanting to take Vincenzo down. I yelled for everyone to stay in place, Vincenzo looked at me like a lion looking at its prey waiting for the perfect moment to pounce.

"These are my men" he reminds me, I let out a throaty chuckle "then lead them" I retort.

He charges for me again swinging the axe, I duck down and uppercut him in the ribs and hooking him in the jaw as I stood up slightly. He fell to the ground before quickly getting back up again. Upon his second attempt to hit my head dead on with the axe I catch his arm halfway, bringing it down I twist it outwards until he drops the axe screaming out in pain. I grab the axe from the ground throwing it behind me at the tree.

"ENOIGH!" I shout! "Vincenzo enough" I spoke exhausted staring at him, but it was like talking to a stranger it was worse than the moment at the hospital where he asked who I was, the moment he forgot me at least then he still had that little voice in the back of his head who was telling him to trust me, that little voice from his old self.

Looking at him right now it was clear that, that little voice no longer knew me either. I felt my throat close up as I choked back tears reality sinking in that this time I might of really lost him, looking at how much hatred and fury was beaming from him how much hatred filled his eyes as they pierced through me I knew he was gone, I knew no matter what I did now he was gone for good and it will all be in vain. I lost him for the third time … you know what they say three strikes and its game over, and I finally accepted it.

Its game over for Isabella knight.

I looked over at Lorenzo who was looking at me with concern and anger he knew exactly what I was thinking, and he knew it was game over, no matter how much he pleaded with his eyes … he knew I was tapping out for good.

"Take care of my son, and when his dad gets better take care of both of them. Never let Dante forget his mum, tell him stories about how loca I was, how much of a fighter I use to be and teach him to never give up no matter what. You better make sure he knows how much his mum loves him, and how badly I wish I was here for him. Dead or alive I will always watch over him, so if he does anything bad, I'll haunt him and if anyone messes with my boy I don't care if I'm dead or alive ill unleash a dragon on them." I sniffled a laugh I looked between both Lorenzo and Vincenzo "take care of my boys and make sure Dante knows how much I love him. You tell him that every day!"

Lorenzo shook his head refusing to allow me to simply give up, "you can tell him yourself, make this fair" he pulls something out of his boot "Isabella catch" Lorenzo throws me my knife, well technically its Vincenzo's knife.

I didn't even flinch or reach for it, but Vincenzo did. Swiftly catching his knife, he charges for me, and I take a deep breath and stay put.

He pins me against the side of the house the tip of the knife on my chest one push and it goes through my heart, normally I would fight back. I would scream and cry and do everything in my power to kill whoever dared to put a knife on me.

Never in a million years did I ever think I would simply surrender, and some might think I surrendered because I knew I couldn't win but that wasn't the case, I could easily get out of this especially with his current state he may be paranoid and a ticking time bomb, but he was physically weaker. Plus, his men stand ready for my signal to assist me, but as I stared into his eyes those beautiful grey eyes, that hypnotised me from the moment I saw them I knew deep in my heart I would rather die than see him dead or hurt.

He stared at me not moving a muscle confusion glanced over his eyes as he probably wondered why I wasn't doing anything why I wasn't fighting back. I didn't clarify nor did I move I took my last few moments to look at him, behind those eyes I saw Vincenzo ... my Vincenzo.

The man who sings to me, who forces me to have water when I get too drunk, the man who reads me Greek mythology, the one who on our first date organised lanterns because he knows how much I love tangled, the man who cares for me, the man that knows my soul, the father of my child ... and the man who truly owns my heart.

He stood there the tip of the blade pointed at my chest. Lorenzo ordered for the men to help me, but I put my hand up keeping them in place despite Lorenzo's pleas. Vincenzo's face was emotionless as he asked, "any last words?" My eyes filled with tears as I couldn't bring myself to open my mouth. The sting of the blade being pushed harder against my chest made my cry out in pain, it broke skin and he was going extremely slow to torture me he wanted me to feel this. I knew this was it and I was never going to get another chance I blinked back the tears that filled my eyes as I whispered three words to him. "I love you".

THE YOU'RE MY?

Isabella's POV

He dropped the knife the minute those three words left my mouth. He took a step back shutting his eyes as he gripped his head. He groaned out in pain dropping to his knees. I gasped watching him in so much pain, Lorenzo and the men immediately rushing to their brother and leader, trying to support him in whatever way they can. I stayed put observing him for the first time not knowing exactly what to do, so I did the only logical thing a woman in shock could do … I froze.

"MOVE" He shouted trying to stand up on his feet, he shoves everyone off and away from him as he catches his breath, he was still blinking rapidly his hands gripping the sides of his head like he was trying to supress something, trying to stop the headache that was suddenly coming on, "Vincenzo?" I called out for him softly, the men made way letting me walk up to him. He finally let go his head looking up at me slowly, tears welling up in his eyes he lets out a relived sigh.

"Leonessa?" he whispered softly. My gasp caught in my throat as I looked at him a million and one emotions rushing through me, shock, relief, excitement, confusion … happiness? I stepped closer to him letting out soft laugh "what did you say?" I questioned looking him up and down carefully not wanting to get my hopes up.

He stood up straightening his posture looking me up and down "Isabella?" He called out but this time he was scared. "You're bleeding" he points at my chest before his eyes went wide, dawning on him that he was the reason why. "You remember me?" I called out running towards him.

"Leonessa, I promised you id be back it took me a while but … I'm back" I jumped into his arms feeling a burst of emotion as I held onto him for dear life.

"I missed you" I whispered into his neck, he let out a soft chuckle nuzzling his head into the crook of my neck letting out a relieved sigh "I missed you too Isabella".

I laughed "I don't like it when you call me Isabella" I whispered. He let out a laugh "Leonessa" I moved back stilling keeping my arms wrapped around his neck "that's better" I pulled him in for a kiss, a soft and tender moment before I turned seeing a bright light heading towards us. Breaking the kiss, I see one of the men in the car charging towards us, before I had time to process Vincenzo threw me out of the way. I rolled on the grovel on impact, I felt the rocks tearing my skin the sting making me wince. I looked up towards Vincenzo and saw him ahead lying on his face, "no" I whispered.

I stood up seeing the men gather around Vincenzo while the man behind the wheel goes to run, I grabbed the knife from the floor and run after him. Feeling so much anger at the world, at the universe at everything.

I stopped running and threw the knife aiming for his back thigh, he rolls over and falls to his knees then on his face. I stood over him swiftly taking the knife out of his thigh and turn him over, I rolled my eyes furious to see him. "Giovani" I call out looking at him squirming around in pain, "I would kill you and make you suffer for what you did ... but you're lucky you're not my dad ... and this isn't my place." I spoke up, pulling him up by his hair I throw him to the men "throw him in confinement" I gave them orders quickly obeying they take him away. I watch as the men put Vincenzo in a car and rush him to the hospital, Lorenzo grabs me by the hand and drives off while Vincenzo's car stays close behind us.

X

We got to the hospital and the doctors rushed Vincenzo into the emergency room, turns out they ended up buying the hospital and everyone who works here are on his payroll. The wound on my chest and the cuts on my arms made Lorenzo worry so he forced me to get checked up and stitched up before going to Vincenzo. I eventually caved in and got checked out because I could feel my wound worsen.

The doctor asked routine questions but avoided the one question about how I was stabbed for obvious reasons, after he finished stitching me up, I jumped off the bed walked towards Vincenzo's room before I heard screaming it was Vincenzo calling out my name, panicked I ran towards the screaming. Stopping a few doors back when I saw Lorenzo comforting his brother, "She's okay. She's just getting a few stitches fratello" I smiled watching how concerned he was "it's my fault. I did so much to her fuck! I need to go to her" he cursed trying to get out the bed and find me, Lorenzo pushed him back into the bed "you can't look for her, she's fine and you need to get that wound stitched up before the blood loss is too severe and we go from a simple procedure to a life threatening one" He ushered for the nurses and the reeled him in the room, "Lorenzo ... come here" he calls for his brother.

I slowly make my way to the door wanting to listen in before I went inside, they started setting him up to different machines, and he started looking very drugged. "If I don't make it you need to take better care of Isabella better than I have." He starts off, Lorenzo shakes his head. "No, you can take care of her when you're better and make up for everything you did. Besides it's Isabella she won't let anyone take care of her" he rolled his eyes exhausted.

I mimicked him from behind the door and rolled my eyes, "Fratello, I need you to listen to me. I know if I go there's going to come a time where she might find another man" he speaks through his teeth, I sniffle a laugh at his jealousy. "If I'm dead I need you to kill him for me" he mutters under his breath making Lorenzo laugh under his breath "don't worry I was planning on it … if Dante doesn't beat me to it. For a little man his very protective over his mum" Lorenzo states. Nodding my head in agreement I continue listening in.

"Regardless, if one day a man comes and he passes your test, Isabella's test, and my sons. I need you to tell him word for word what I'm about to say." He takes a deep breath closing his eyes the drugs starting to take effect.

"Make sure he knows she's terrified of spiders. So, if she screams or calls him freaking out for help and his not home, make sure he rushes home and kills it please … otherwise she wont sleep. She is a total textbook extrovert, but she has her moments where she shuts off and she will ignore him on occasion. He will take it personally, tell him not too she's simply taking care of herself, and she'll tell you how much she missed you while she was away but never force her out of that mental shut off, she will bite your head off." I rolled my eyes trying to not smile, he takes a few deep breaths before continuing.

"Isabella is a very jealous person. My god, she gets so jealous. Those emerald, green eyes will turn dark black. Don't make it worse, reassure her and give her forehead kisses … actually don't kiss her at all" he growled annoyed, taking it back making Lorenzo chuckle.

"On that topic though, she needs constant reassurance. If he can't do that, leave. She deserves more than that. She's been through enough her whole life, if he is going to add to that list kill him. She is the most independent woman I know, so sure of herself but also so insecure, it still breaks my heart. How she feels like a burden because of all the torment she went through. She will believe she deserves all the bad in her life but reassure her she doesn't, hold her tight and calm her down. The way I do it is I sing to her. Do. Not. Upset. Her" he warned Lorenzo to warn the guy.

"By the way the Dobermans, the dogs. Plus, her wolves, they come first. Always. Don't let him think otherwise." I could see his eyeroll, making me roll my eyes playfully.

"I chose to hang out with them one damn time" I whispered to myself, knowing that was a blunt lie id pick those dogs and my wolves every time. "Remind him that losing her is a pain you will never shake. Your world will come crashing down on you and those pieces won't ever fit the way they used to. Don't let her go, she will love you with all she's got, but if she lets go, she will ice you out like you never existed. If you can't give her the same love back leave because she deserves the same love back." He nods his head, and his eyelids starts getting heavier.

"Lorenzo tell him that" he whispers unable to keep his eyes open. "There won't be a reason to, you're going to be fine and then you can be that man for her" Lorenzo spoke up, the nurses asked for him to leave. As Lorenzo was about to make his way-out Vincenzo grips his arm "I am begging you don't let anyone hurt her. She is gold and the most precious thing to ever happen to me. I am begging you don't let that shine in her die out. I beg you … protect her with everything you have. Protect her and Dante because if I'm gone, I will divide my heart and give it to the both of them protect them and what's left of me in them." Those were the last things I heard before it went quiet and Lorenzo walked up in front of me "ease dropping?" he questioned with a sly smile, I chewed on the inside of my cheek while a playful smile overtook my features "maybe just a little" I shrugged.

I looked into the window and saw them working on Vincenzo "his going to be fine" Lorenzo reassured me holding me close, I nodded my head "I know" I whispered back.

Lorenzo went to speak up before my phone started buzzing, "Hello?" I answered not looking at the ID "Isabella, someone is at the estate, and he said its urgent he speaks to you" I look up at Lorenzo confusion visible on my face "who is it?" Lorenzo looked at me waiting for me to explain what's happening on the other line. "He doesn't want me to say it over the phone, but don't worry its nothing bad but he looks really serious I think you should come down as soon as you can" with all the chaos that's been happening lately I was trying to clear my mind and refocus on what and who it could be.

"Okay I'm on my way" I hang up my phone Lorenzo looking at me concerned "what's happening?"

I let out a sigh and shrug my shoulders "I have no idea that's why I need to go check. Listen while I go deal with whatever is happening, I need you to call Ariana tell her to stay wherever she is with Dante I have a gut feeling this is the calm before the storm. When Vincenzo is back on his feet and has his full strength back, we'll get Dante back, just make sure Ariana knows her brothers back so she can relax comfortably and well send out a plane when it's time for them to come back home." He nods his head getting his phone out to call his sister while I made my way out of the hospital with a few of our men, I racked my head on who could possibly be waiting for me back at the estate. So much has happened in the past couple of hours, and even more in the last week. I finally reached the car while one of the men drove me back.

x

Jumping out of the car I make my way to hacker seeing him sitting alone around his security system.

"Hacker?" I called out for him trying to get his attention away from the screen, "Oh Isabella, his waiting for you in the basement. He wanted to talk to your parents first." I looked at him beyond confused "who and why on earth would he want to talk to them?" Hacker simply shrugged his shoulders and anxiously turned back around to his screens "you are either going to be happy about what you find out or furious …" he informed me anxiously letting out a deep breath "but regardless of what emotion you end up with I'm here for you" He assured me I smiled giving him a tight hug.

"You have no idea how scared I was when Vincenzo had that knife to your chest" He confessed holding me tighter "I could only imagine how you felt" I let out a sigh and broke the hug looking at him. "I wasn't scared at all. In this world the one and only thing we are promised is death and if I had to die … I genuinely didn't mind dying looking into his eyes. I was dealt worse ways to die in my 25 years but dying looking deep into his silver eyes the same eyes that brought me back to life I don't know it's undeniably a bittersweet and ironic way to go.

The eyes that brought me back to life were the eyes that got to take it away. A full circle moment" I shrugged my shoulders.

Hacker looked at me like I was crazy and maybe I was,

maybe I am. "I just wish to experience a love as crazy and deep as the one you two share." I smile looking away feeling myself blush. "Did you?" he looks at me piecing it together, "Oh my god you did!" he shouts excited. "You sound a lot like Lorenzo right now" I rolled my eyes. "You told him you love him? That's what brought back his memories! To think if you weren't so in denial about your love for him and told him you loved him before he would've remembered you a lot sooner and you could have avoided all of this" he explains looking at me with a smug look. "I'm going to pretend that's not true and go see who is with my parents and what they want from me" I turn around and walk out before I go down a rabbit hole with Hacker.

"Good luck Isabella" he shouts out.

"Thank you!" I shout back waving my hand.

Running inside I spotted Vincenzo's knife on the floor on my way I grabbed it taking it with me never know it might come in handy. I reached the door to the basement and made my down feeling unprepared of what I was about to face, down there. I took a deep breath and usher the men who were gaurding the door to step aside, I could already hear yelling and screaming from both my parents and another voice I couldn't quite pin.

"The two of you need to stop yelling!" Mum shouts, I stop dead in my tracks on the stairs not wanting them to see me I hang back my gut telling me to wait this out.

"I will not stop yelling you hid my daughters from me for years! Then this hijo de puta (son of a bitch) went and got my little girl kidnapped and tortured with no sight of mercy because his ego got hurt." He shouted, I put my hand over my mouth. Whoever was down there was my dad … my real dad and he was fucking mad. I felt the tears starting to well up, I took in a deep breath not ready to see who was down there.

"I killed two birds with one stone" Mario laughed out. I balled my hands into a fist feeling disgusted at the man I looked up too.

"Hijo de puta te voy a matar" (you son of a bitch I will kill you)

"You put my daughter through hell, but in the end, she came out without a burn. She literally rose from the ashes and was stronger, ruthless, and consumed more power than your little brain could even begin to comprehend. This wasn't revenge you knew how powerful she is, how much authority she had over anyone and everyone and it terrified you, when you found out she wasn't yours you were scared. Scared she would kick you to the side while she searched for her dad for me! You didn't care she wasn't yours all you cared about was that her power wasn't yours. You took my innocent little girl and threw her to the wolves all because you feared her." He shouted throwing something against the room, I felt my heart tug listening to every word he said.

Every word, every sentence was filled with so much emotion so much love, anger and the one that radiated most guilt. Guilt he didn't know about us earlier, guilt he couldn't find us, guilt he couldn't save me. "You! Anna, if I didn't see you with the girls at the park, would you have ever told me?"

"No" Mum whispered back.

I rolled my eyes feeling my throat closing. I tried taking in some deep breaths, but nothing was helping, "the day I saw my girls, Isabella, and Maria they were only four years old. You wouldn't let me see them so I would do it behind your back, I snuck into their bedroom and went by 'Marcel' the friendly imaginary friend." I let out a gasp quickly covering my mouth, so he was real, and why does that name sound so familiar do I know a Marcel? My imaginary friend was my dad, he did try to be a part of our lives tried to be there for us when we needed it. Even before my dad knew he wasn't my dad he never once did anything like my real dad.

Never tried to comfort me, never tried to be there with me, never told us bedtime stories, Maria and I loved our imaginary friend he was our escape from our parents, and he always knew when to make an appearance, until one day he stopped.

When we turned 15 years-old, Maria and I always wondered where he was and why he stopped appearing.

"The day my wife died, and I was in a coma was the perfect moment for you to pick up and move my girls away, and it was the time where all hell broke loose! By the time I regained strength and went looking for them, the both of you were dead and dragon was already born. Trying to find Dragon was like trying to find a specific grain of sand at the beach. She was good at hiding her tracks, I managed to find Maria, but she was only concerned with finding her sister, and I would never tell them the truth at an already tough time. She was mourning the two of you and her sister, I couldn't tell her without Isabella, so I went on the hunt for her, until she vanished."

That was when me and Maria were shipped off to that abusive asshole, "do you want a trophy?" Mario laughed out "you cracked the code. I couldn't use her power for my own when I found out my blood wasn't running in her veins. When I found out she was yours I knew it was a matter of time before you took her, and Maria. If they went to you, I lost everything and I was fucking mad, mad at Sophia mad at you and mad at them. If I couldn't have her power no one could, but Xavier misled me the bastard. He was never going to kill her. He wanted her power as much as he feared it, he knew he could use it to his advantage so long as she was working for him. What I didn't know was how much he feared losing her. The son of a bitch is in love with her and only gave her a reason to unleash her inner demons. She grew more powerful every day and when I knew he fell for her I went to kill her myself."

"You did enough. Both of you! None of you deserve my

angel, you had one fucking job protect her! Instead, what do you do? Instead of being the ones who scare away the monsters under the bed you became the monsters. I will make sure she sees the real you, the one who wanted to kill her because his ego was getting threatened by his daughter." "Who do you think our daughter will side with? If she wanted us dead, she would have killed us by now. Isabella has never been one to show mercy the second someone wrongs her they die in the same breath. But we are still here which means one thing, she's no longer as powerful as she used to be, and her emotions are getting in the way. Besides who would kill their own parents?" Both Mario and Sophia laughed. "I would" I spoke up confidently making my presence known stepping forward. I looked around the room almost scared at who I was going to find on the opposite end of my parents ... the man who is really my dad is. My eyes widened in shock as I gasped out his name "Garcia?"

THE KILL

(This chapter contains graphic scenes which some readers may find disturbing scenes will be clearly labelled for your convenance)

Isabella's POV

I walked towards him still in shock "You?" I questioned looking at Garcia. Mixed emotions filled me, and it was too much I didn't know what emotion to focus on. I stood in front of him and took in a deep breath was I relieved staring at his face, was I angry he didn't tell me sooner? Or was I just in shock that the man who I grew so close to and started seeing as a father figure turned out to be my dad. "Isabella" he called out softly, I snapped back into reality hearing shuffling from behind me I pulled Vincenzo's knife out of my pocket turning out I threw the knife, it pierced Mario's hand pinning him to the wall. I rolled my eyes and whistled for the men upstairs to shut and lock the door.

Not saying a word, I turned back around and faced Garcia who had a worried expression unsure of how I'm going to react to his news, so I did what I knew needed to be done something he wasn't expecting I leaped into his arms wrapping my arms around him burying my head into his chest. He let out a relieved sigh and returned the hug holding me tight, "My Bella" he whispered softly making me smile I looked up at him and nodded my head calming down my nerves.

He looked behind me probably satisfied at my parent's reaction to how quickly I accepted Garcia as my father, I admit it should have been harder but his been in my life since I was a child even in the gap where we weren't in contact the second, he saw me with Vincenzo, he has done more for me than they did my whole life. So, no it wasn't hard to accept as a matter of a fact if I had to pick anyone to be my dad, I would have picked Garcia in a heartbeat and I'm beyond grateful it's him.

"What do you say? Wanna have some fun?" I smirked immediately knowing where I was going with this, he put his hand out ushering me to lead the way. I spun around on the heel on my foot a wicked grin overtaking my features never feeling more justified and prouder of what I'm about to do.

(TW torture/killing)

"So, you think I lost my touch? Do you think I lost my power? Well dear father of mine, how about I show you personally just how wrong you are. You want to see Dragon in action? You got it" I winked.

"You!" I snapped my heard towards mother, "just because you didn't talk as much does not mean you get to leave here alive." I smiled looking at her, was this heartless? Yes. If any normal person was in my position, would they kill the women that gave them life? Probably not but what if that same person who gave you life was the one that tried to take it from you?

Was I going to punish her for all she put me through? Yes, yes, I was. Am I going to kill my parents? Yes, yes, I am.

"You might not have done as much as your husband, but you don't deserve to live."

"Isabella, please. I'm so sorry for everything not a day went by where I didn't regret all I put you through" I huffed rolling my eyes not believing a single word.

"Do you expect me to cave? To cry and make some speech?" I laughed shaking my head.

"Everything that comes out of your mouth is a lie, if that was true you could have freed me from Xavier, you could have made your husband back the fuck off but no, instead you joined in on this punishment to cleanse yourself of your adultery … but the only way for you to truly be cleansed is death." I shrugged my shoulders. "Then Marcel should die too" she yelled, rolling my eyes I shook my head. "Oh mother, I know you all too well. I knew how much you despised dad and just how many men I saw leave your room in the middle of the night when Mario was on a 'business trip' and coincidentally your wedding ring was nowhere to be found." I shot a look over to Mario who was furious beyond belief.

"What about his wife?" She smiled trying to call my bluff, I rolled my eyes "please, they were split up because she couldn't have kids and was heartbroken the day Garcia hooked up with you was probably the day, he was heartbroken you were nothing but a rebound. One that ended with his dreams coming true having kids, too bad you didn't have the decency or the heart to tell him. What's worse is you knew the man Mario was and how he would react when he found out we weren't his, and you thought you didn't owe it to the two girls who had no choice but to be born into this world a dad who would love them? No, instead you were selfish and condemned us to live a life without our dad and a world where I singly handily had to be tortured and raped over and over again." I yelled feeling livid, not realising just how much hate I was bottling up how much resentment I had for not just Mario but for Sophia as well.

I could feel Garcia's death stare without even having to turn around, "so, you will have to excuse my manners today. I will not leave this basement until your blood covers every inch of these walls, until your so dismembered that people would assume it was nothing but a pile of chewed up meat. I will not leave you both alone until there is literally nothing else for me to stab, shoot, break or tear." I let out a laugh feeling giddy like a child at a candy store whose been told they can get whatever they want.

"Your eyes" Mario snapped me out of my train of thoughts, I tore my eyes from Sophia and looked at him.

"It's heartless, proud and … animalistic." I stuck my tongue out licking the edge of my lip smiling wide as I slowly made my way towards him.

I stopped dead in front of him and took a moment to take in his features, his eyes were so wide I could see the whites of his eyes, his pupils dilated making him appear much larger than usual. His eyebrows were raised so high it was causing his forehead to crease, creating deep furrows that showed clear signs of worry and distress. His mouth hung open slightly, with the lips pressed tightly together, as if trying to suppress a scream. His cheeks puff out as he takes shallow, rapid breaths.

"I like this" I whispered finally breaking the silence.

He looked at me confused.

"You scared, the fear and utter powerlessness you're displaying. It's my favourite thing, you should know that already dad" I put emphasis on the word 'dad' lacing every word with such power that it made him even more nervous.

"Right now, what you're experiencing is what all my victims experienced, because they knew the end was coming … when it was coming? That's one thing they didn't know and that's what made the kill so much more fun" I smiled taking the knife out of his hand in a swift motion. Watching him fall to the floor, I towered over him smiling.

"I always tried so much to prove myself to you growing up, so let me prove myself to you now. That I haven't lost myself, my touch, or my power" I picked him up by his throat and slammed his head against the metal wall.

I turned around and examined Garcia's expressions, unsure of how he was going to look at me he was watching me at my worst, but to my surprise he had a very satisfying smile on his features. "That's my girl" he laughed out, giving me his sealing nod of approval.

Like he was finally at peace watching me slay my demons, I looked back at them their faces white like a ghost, it made me think for a second would I finally be at peace? Would killing them mean killing my inner demons? I smiled softly shrugging my shoulders I guess I'm about to find out.

I looked between the two of them as Sophia rushed to Mario's side. I pulled her up by her hair pinning her against the wall I put the knife against her throat, "you could have prevented all this. You may not have done as much evil as your husband, but you still don't deserve to live" she looked into my eyes mentally pleading me to let go and spare her life, but that was never going to happen.

I looked down at Mario who looked up at me with genuine fear watching and anticipating my next move. "Sophia." He called out for her, she looked at him waiting for him to reassure her.

"This is all your fault … but I love you so much" He spoke up, I rolled my eyes disgusted.

"Before you go, I just wanted to get my peace out-" with one swift move I slit open her throat cutting him off mid-sentence, her blood splattered all over me, I licked my lips maintaining eye contact with Mario, I let go of her throwing her on the floor, as Mario lets out a scream rushing to her side. "You don't deserve peace … none of you do". He looked up at me fury in his eyes "you killed her!" he shouted.

I laughed rolling my eyes at his obvious statement. "No, I didn't she's just asleep" I pointed at her with my knife as the blood dripped from the tip of the blade. "Oh, don't worry Mario. You can see her soon" I innocently piped up with a huge smile on my face.

"You're fucking insane" he yelled his body still hovering over her body.

"Did it take you 25 years to figure that out?" I questioned mocking him.

"For someone who watched me throughout everything, the torture, then me becoming dragon. I would have assumed you knew exactly what kind of grave you dug yourself into." I approached him but he scampered back terrified, I smiled in pure satisfaction watching him so terrified about what his I have installed for him.

I looked at him in pity "If you didn't do what you did to me, you know what if you had a small amount of genuine remorse, I would take pity on you. I would feel sorry for you I probably wouldn't touch you Id just banish you from New York. However, time has proven time and time again that given the opportunity you would stab me in the back and if you could, you would send me back to Xavier and make sure I stay there until I die."

I went to approach him but stopped dead in my tracks, my eyes transforming into a dark, evil glare. The depths of my eyes now held a cold and calculated stare, as if they become windows into the abyss of my soul. I premeditated the perfect plan to torture Mario in the most wicked and thought-out way I could ever come up with. A wicked smile curls upon my lips, slowly spreading unnaturally across my face. It is a smile filled with a twisted satisfaction and anticipation.

The corners of my mouth stretch wide, revealing a perverse delight in the imminent chaos that is about to unfold. In that moment, my eyes and smile align, merging to create a terrifying image. One that made Mario shake in pure fear, "w-w-what are you going to do to me?" he stuttered out. "Nothing I do with my own hands will scar or hurt you as much as your own personal phobia" I laughed out watching his eyes widen with realisation, I whistled out calling the men at the door, I saw them open the door cautiously poking their head scared what they might see.

I rolled my eyes you would think having Vincenzo as a boss they would be used to these sights and having me here for years they should definitely be used to my 'methods'.

"Get my wolves ready" I instructed him, "wolves?" he

questioned shocked. I laughed, remembering I special instructed professionals to gather my three Gysinge wolfs, man-eating wolves to be specific, no better guard dogs than that. My wolves are my babies, if they get hurt, I'll tear anything to shreds but my pure baby wolves, they were my pride and joy.

I remember having them when I worked for Xavier, of course he didn't know I had them under my possession and control however, I always planned on using them on Xavier but now they serve a much stronger purpose.

"You're going to use my Vorarephilia against me!" he shouted. I laughed out loud feeling genuine joy coursing through my veins, the man who left me for dead, the man who willingly sat by and watched another man rape and abuse me deserved nothing less than an equally painful end.

"You're a smart pup, figure it out" I dismissed the men to wake up my wolves, they are due for a feed.

"Isabella are you sure about this? They're dangerous" Garcia broke my train of thought, I spun on my heel facing him.

"I saved them from death as pups, wolves are a lot of things, but they are extremely loyal. I saved and cared for them. They are only loyal to me." I reassured him, tucking Vincenzo's knife in my waistband. I pulled Mario up by his throat and instructed Lucas to also grab Sophia's body and follow me.

We walked for what felt like half an hour, I had to keep my babies away from any living creature. Like I said they're loyal, but only to me. If they see or sense another scent that isn't my own, they will not hesitate but to go for the kill. Finally approaching the big metal barn house. On occasion I would come for training, feeding, and letting them loose to run and stretch but I tended to keep that to myself not wanting to explain why I have them in the first place.

"Stay far away!" I instructed the men along with Garcia.

"No one is to come any closer under any circumstances, my wolves will attack any unknown predator and I want to enjoy watching this kill." I tightened my grip on Mario's hair as he tried running away.

I could already hear my babies howling and banding

against the metal doors, they sensed unknown scents near me, and they are in kill mode. I smiled feeling so much pride at how ready they are to protect me, one thing I learnt a long time ago was I could never trust humans, but my animals? I trusted with my life.

"ISABELLA PLEASE!" Mario shouted. I could hear in his voice how petrified he was getting. His whole body was getting ready to shut down.

"When Xavier was touching me, and I screamed out for you. What did you do behind closed doors?" I questioned.

Not getting any answers I nodded my head knowingly, "it brings me so much peace knowing that the last thing you will hear before your death is my mocking laughter." I turned around and instructed for the men to leave.

Without another word they could see by my face I was serious, turning around they all ran off. I smirked taking the knife from my waistband I stabbed him in his legs multiple times, making it almost impossible for him to run for long. "Run little puppy" I whispered in his ear letting go. He tried to stand on his feet but failed falling to the floor after every couple of steps. I laughed taking the lock off the door opening it wide they bowed in front of me turning their heads to Mario limping. They turned around anxiously waiting for my command, "matar!" (KILL).

I gave them permission and without a second to waste they chased after him.

His screams filled my ears as I stood there watching in absolute bliss, my babies pounced on him tearing him limb by limb. I laughed watching it all happen, some may say I lost touch with humanity, or that I'm just psychotic because no normal person would ever allow this to happen, what I'd say is I didn't have a normal upbringing, nor did I lead a normal life so ... who is to say what's normal anymore?

X

After my babies finished their dinner, they left no traces of neither Sophia or Mario, I looked up at the sky and smiled softly "there all yours Maria, I hope you finish them for everything they put us both through." I started imagining what Maria would do if she was still here with me. Would she understand why I did what I did? Would she be okay with me killing them? Would she look at me differently for how unbothered I was? How would you react knowing our real father was under our noses this whole time? I took in a deep breath trying to calm down, I need to stop thinking before I lose my mind. I whistled for my wolves to come back, I sat and played with them for a little bit before putting them back inside letting them rest after their full meal. I need to get my trainers back from Spain so they can take care of my babies while I'm busy.

THE ULTIMATUM

Isabella's POV

I ran back to the estate, only one thing was on my mind right now ... okay I had a lot of things on my mind right now but the main one was Dante, I needed to hear his little squeal. His getting so big seems like yesterday when we came to the new estate and Vincenzo took us on the horses, he was only four months now his almost six months and my god so much has happened in that short amount of time.

I reached the estate huffing and puffing feeling out of breath, I rushed to get my phone from my upstairs room. I stopped dead in my tracks seeing the maids cleaned up after Vincenzo and I's 'fight' to put it lightly. I let out a sigh and grabbed my phone called Ariana, I waited patiently as the phone rang.

"Hello? Isabella?" I could hear Ariana's excitement in her voice, I chuckled softly "Ariana?" I laughed out trying to get her to calm down.

"Is it true? Does my brother remember you? Is he okay?

Are you okay? Can we come back? Oh my god how excited are you? Oh, wait OH MY GOD HOW ARE YOU!" she was ranting not being able to restrain herself.

"Ariana!" I yelled hoping it would make her calm down, she took a deep breath indicating that it worked.

"Yes, it's true Vincenzo remembers everything including me, his memory coming back really helped with him trusting me to help him deal with his withdrawals. He is okay and so am I, no you can't come back. I'm on cloud nine and I'm just peachy" I answered all her questions taking in a deep breath.

"Now can I please talk to my son if that's possible."

I heard shuffling before I heard the cutest babbling and noises coming out of my baby's little mouth, I felt my heart jump out of my throat.

"Oh, my baby hi my precious boy" I softly sang out imaging his hands trying to reach the phone and his curious grey eyes looking frantically around the room trying to find me.

"I promise as soon as daddy is back on his feet, and I kill the bad man that hurt me and daddy then the both of us will bring you and your aunty back home." I heard his laughing, and I shook my head "only my and Vincenzo's son will laugh at killing another man" I commented after hearing Ariana's laugh, "at least you know for a fact there's no need for a DNA test" she joked.

I laughed rolling my eyes "I'll call you with updates, okay? Take care of my baby and more importantly take care of yourself. Missing you already crazy" I smiled hearing her giggle "will do keep me updated and love you Bella" she whispered I let out a sigh and smiled "love you too" hanging up the phone.

I felt a weight lift off my shoulders knowing my son and Ariana were okay. I walked out of my room and saw Garcia waiting patiently in the living room downstairs, I smiled and made my way down to him.

"Garcia?" I smiled calling out for him, he turned around with the biggest smile on his face "Isabella" he walked towards me unsure of how I'm going to react now that I was out of such a high-pressure environment. I smiled reassuringly he let out a sigh of relief and pulled me in for a hug, "how long did you know?" I asked him. He let out a sigh not letting go of me "the second I was introduced to you, your emerald-green eyes were never easy to forget. It always made you stand out and the first time I saw your sister It just confirmed my suspicion I couldn't forget those Bambi eyes." He joked reminiscing about the first time he saw Maria, how much I miss her and her innocent Bambi eyes staring back at me.

"I just hope she's finally at peace wherever she is weather its up in the sky or down at the sea. I just hope she's finally at peace".

Maria's POV

I looked around trying to find where I was but everything around me looks like a dream, like what I'm experiencing right not isn't really what I'm experiencing "Maria?" I spun around feeling very light am I dead? I questioned.

"Maria!" a voice yelled out forcing me to focus my attention on the voice that sounded so familiar. I stood in front of a man who looked awfully like Vincenzo, as realisation began to dawn on me, I realised who it was standing in front of me "Dante?" I questioned breathlessly.

Smiling he pulls me in a tight hug, shocked I freeze before

easing in the hug, "am I dead?" I whispered. He chuckled and pulled away looking at me, his features were much softer than Vincenzo. He had a clean look, no beard but his jawline was so sharp I think it would give you a papercut and his, black hair fell at the perfect medium length seemingly shaping his face.

"No, you're not dead. You're in a coma … your soul is caught between the dead and living. You can only see me because of that, otherwise you'd just be going insane" he laughed, his laugh was contagious drawing you in making your insides fly with butterflies giving you a feeling so pure you feel it in your core. I smiled and shook my head "okay, so where are we?" I asked looking around, looking down at my feet we stood in sand, as I looked up the white surrounding area suddenly was filled with the sound and view of a beautiful blue water, I gasped watching myself be completely transported to the beach Isabella and I would visit as kids, "what's happening?" I asked completely mesmerised.

"Since we are technically in your subconscious the place is transforming to a spot your brain feels most safe. I guess it's the beach?" He laughed looking around taking in the view. I nodded my head as it all sunk in, "so is this really happening? Or is it like a dream?" I asked needing conformation if I was going insane. "Oh, it's real. You did say you couldn't wait to meet me" He winked, I looked at him confused before recalling the hospital.

"Wait you were there!" I yelled. He looks taken back by my sudden outburst laughing he shrugs.

"I'm always around, I have been since the day I died. I watch over my siblings all the time and I always watched after Isabella. You my dear were added to the list when you meet my siblings, given the fact that I'm dead I only watch and get attracted to those I'm connected too, so whenever anything happens to anyone of use it's like a gust of wind I get sent there I walk around and watch everything like I'm really in the room, I can't talk or touch anyone but I can make my presence known in other ways." He explains softly.

I nodded my head trying to keep up "if you were in this state like me couldn't you go back to your body?" I questioned softly not sure if I was out of line.

His face dropped as a sad expression took over, "my body

and soul weren't strong enough to fight … I tried so hard. Isabella's cries over my body and then my brothers' cries were what really woke me up, it was his voice that put me in this state. I watched as he hugged me, cried over me, and spoke to me it was the most painful experience I ever had to endure. I ran to him trying to tell him I was okay. That I was right next to him, but he couldn't hear me, I tried to touch my body but to come back I needed strength and I just … I didn't have it." He exhaled softly recalling his death.

"So instead, as he promised to avenge and never forget me or his promise to me. I swore and promised to never leave his side to watch and protect him until he meets me here only then will I cross over." I wrapped my arms around him pulling in for a tight hug "I'm so sorry" I whispered my heart aching hearing him speak, he hugged me back holding me tight as he exhaled a sigh.

"I miss him" he whispered staring off watching the wave's crashing against the water, "he misses you so much" I whispered knowing Vincenzo's deep love for his twin, he chuckled and nods his head "Oh I know, I feel everything he feels, I know what he thinks and whenever he says my name,

I'm right there in front of him. My brother was never good at showing emotions but that changed when he met Isabella just like I knew it would" he laughed.

"I still remember when she stormed into his room to kill him".

I pulled back abruptly shocked "what!" I gasp out, he laughs nodding "oh yeah" I shake my head "if Isabella wants someone dead, they always die" I point out he nods his head "I know that believe me why do you think I woke him up?" he added, I laugh shaking my head "you woke him up? How!" I laughed looking up at him.

"I may be dead but when the person is sleeping because they are in a state of vulnerability and not being ignorant to the endless possibilities of this world and the next. A barrier is lowered why do you think many people dream of their loved ones or when they wake up screaming, they swore they heard a loved one's voice while they slept it's because they did. I stood next to him and whispered 'codice vipera' which means code viper a deadly threat" I smiled nodding my head oh that pretty much sums up Isabella in a nutshell "that's my sister" I say proudly.

He laughs and nods his head in agreement when suddenly, a gush of wind snaps me out of my thoughts suddenly being transported into a hospital room, "what's happening?" he nods his head to the person laying on the bed … Isabella?

"What are you going to name him?" Lorenzo whispers, him? Oh, I gasped placing my hands over my mouth, my handsome nephew "he looks just like his dad" Dante whispered standing near the bed admiring our nephew, "Maria you got to see this" he whispers breath taken. I rush beside him and choke back tears looking at his innocent face as his tiny hands wrapped around Isabella's finger. "Lorenzo, Sebastián, and Alex meet …" she pauses for dramatic effect everyone on the edge of their seats waiting for her to continue include myself and Dante.

"Dante King" she finally announces, my gasp subconsciously lifting my hands in the air as the widest grin overtook my features and pride settled over my whole body. I looked over at Dante who was crying as he looked at both his nephew who carries his name and my sister with so much love, I think he would combust in any moment.

"Hey Dante, look bud you got a cool name, so you're set for life! You're gonna be the coolest kid ever and I will make sure you're safe your whole life. You uncle Dante has your back covered, so you just enjoy life and don't worry about anything." He whispered in the baby's ear as tears continued to escape his down his face, I look over at the window and see Vincenzo with the exact same expressions as Dante, it's scary how much they resemble one another and how connected they are every emotion was exact and judging from his face he just made the same promise to his son as Dante did too his nephew.

"Dante" I whispered for him getting his attention on the glass, he looked up and exhaled softly. He walked over to his brother and wrapped his arms around him, "you're a dad bro! You're going to be the best dad ever. I can feel your panic and fear, but I can also feel your love for that little boy. You'll be a better father than ours ever was to us, I love you Vincenzo" he spoke into his shoulder knowing he can't hear him, but I watched as Vincenzo stature calmed down as though Dante was really with him.

"Come on, you've been in a coma for very long there is still more you haven't seen." Dante called out and as he spoke another gust of wind blew through transporting me to Isabella and Vincenzo in a car.

"What-" I spoke but Dante cut me off, "these events have all occurred in a past time, you're playing catch up" he smiled and nodded his head to the scene unfolding in front of us. Isabella pounds her fist against the car seat "oh she mad" I involuntary spoke up. It was like watching a movie nothing felt real. "Who gave you the right to protect me, Vincenzo?! The moment you forgot me I died! I no longer belong to you!" She hissed, visibly hurt and gutted. He leapt towards her his hands on the edge of the seat closing Isabella in, leaning closer to her face. "WELL, I BELONG TO YOU!"

The veins in his neck bulged as he shouted … "I belong to you," he whispered.

I looked at Dante who shared the same reaction as me "even though I already witnessed this situation unfold … it gets me every time" he speaks up shocked at Vincenzo's revelation. I nod my head and look back at the two of them missing a little bit of the conversation. Isabella sighed deeply ushering Vincenzo to come in and meet the baby officially, as they walked in Lorenzo was furious. I shook my head "his thinks with Vincenzo back in the picture that he will be pushed aside and his last tie to me will be severed, doesn't he?" I whispered, Dante nodded his head softly "you know him better than anyone" Dante confirmed I smiled and looked at him ... really looked at him. I felt so far away from him yet so close in the same breath, I could reach out to touch him, but the feeling felt so empty. Dante was crying and wouldn't stop even when Isabella held him ... until Vincenzo held him in his arms, he calmed down.

"That's my brother" Dante cheered him on softly, I smiled and leaned my head on his shoulder watching the tender moment unfold before me, "I knew he would be an amazing dad, I just knew it" I whispered smiling.

Another gush occurs and suddenly we are all in a bedroom as Vincenzo, my sister, Lorenzo, Ariana and Vincenzo's men huddled in the room forming a circle screaming and chanting for Dante. I laughed feeling the excitement from the room absorb into me as both myself and Dante started screaming and cheering Dante on. He rolled over, as soon as he rolled over the room erupted in cheers and applaud me and Dante include.

"THAT'S MY BIG BOY LOOK AT HIM GO" I yelled.

"THAT'S MY STRONG BOY" Dante cheered by my side, I laughed and watched Dante clap along with the room. Everyone wanting to hold and kiss him, "can you imagine what they'll do when he starts walking?" I laughed looking at Dante.

"I think a grand ball would be an appropriate form of celebration" Dante seriously spoke, I looked over him with an eyebrow raised he kept his features serious before a grin cracked through.

I rolled my eyes, and another gush gets blown through and suddenly we are in a room like a clinic Isabella sits she had her interrogation face on, oh no. I followed her eyes and landed on my parents I gasped shocked as fear settled in my stomach. "What's happening?" I whispered. he shook his head with a pained expression "watch" he pointed to the scene.

"Let's have a peek, shall we?" Isabella piped up smiling about to open the file before mum snatched it out of her hands.

"If you do not pass the file back I promise you that before you won't be Isabella but dragon and she hasn't been woken up to her full extent since Spain, unless you want me to literally unleash all hell on the two of you I suggest that file be in my hand in the next ten seconds" my sisters tone cold and stern, she was daring them to disobey her. I nervously chewed on my lip feeling a mix of emotion from the room. Anger, frustration, anxiousness, fear, and an ounce of guilt. She counted down and immediately they caved handing her the file.

She opened the file her expression never changing, and I knew whatever she read in the file did not shock her, whatever my sister's hunch was she was proven right, and I can't tell if it devastated her or if she was numb to the disappointment.

"So, Mario, Sophia ... or should I say Luna Gonzalez and Romano Gonzalez" she smiled looking up at their terrified expressions, my eyes grew wide ... their alias?

"Isabella" she put her hand up silencing them "No! You don't get the right to Isabella me, you as a matter of fact get no rights what's so ever, you have officially lowered your rank from fucked up parents to scum! You deserve nothing and will be shown no mercy" She made their fate crystal clear. "Do not expect the slightest kindness from me because I will show you none! I much rather show Xavier kindness than you in this moment."

"How could she say such a thing! He held my parent's captive he held my sister!" I yelled feeling angry and confused. Dante sighed and pointed with his eyes back at Isabella.

"The man who tortured and raped you?!" Mum shouted.

"Yes, Sophia that man, because if not thanks to you and your husband than he would not have been able to do any of that, if not for the two of you handing me over to him. None of this would have happened, so expect the same mercy you have showed me." My eyes grew wide as my confusion know was replaced with anger and betrayal.

"WHAT!" I shouted my blood boiling; how could they do such a thing to her! Why? "Isabella you can't kill your own mother" Sophia shouted desperation laced every word and she pleaded for her life. "Why?" Isabella cocked her head.

"It's inhumane!" she shouted failing miserably to plea her case.

"Just as throwing your daughter into the hands of a man who will deliberately torture her both emotionally and mentally! Forcing her to feel so numb and desperate to any kind of human touch and affection that she works side by side for the very man who broke her. All because of some stupid revenge that began long before they were born. That's. Inhumane." Wincing at her words my heart twisted in agony for my sister.

"You both were never emotionally scarred or sick ... but you will be."

"Oh, they're dead" I shook my head knowing once Isabella threatens, she will always uphold her threat, "make them rot in hell hermona" I whispered in her ear.

X

Isabella's POV

Lorenzo and I were making our way to the elevators going to the private sector of the hospital reserved for the Kings, the elevator doors dinged and immediately I had an unsettling feeling settle in my gut, and I knew something is off. "Lorenzo" I called out and he nodded his head "I know I have a bad feeling as well." We walked out of the elevator not seeing anyone on the floor, nor seeing any of our men outside Vincenzo's room. Without even thinking I ran straight towards Vincenzo's room, freezing in my spot I see Xavier looming over him as he laid sound asleep unaware of what's happening around him.

"Isabella, how kind of you to finally join us." He smiled analyzing me from top to bottom, I cringed watching his hungry eyes rank my body.

"How did you get up here?" I gritted through my teeth, he chuckles shaking his head "the usual way, with guns and threats" he winks getting closer to me.

I tense up but was glad he moved away from Vincenzo, I sigh and prey my eyes away from Vincenzo and look at Xavier who was a lot closer than I wanted him to be. "What is it you want Xavier?" I sigh out exhausted of this constant battle wanting everything to just be over, but I knew it was never going to end until one of us is dead.

"I want you Isabella how is that still so unclear to you" he exclaims holding my arms.

I shook my head "why?" I never understood his fascination with me, why he wanted me so desperately, why he can't just let me live in peace.

"Because I'm in love with you, from the very first moment I saw you Isabella you caught my attention, and you haven't let it go since. Even when you were in that basement, I never wanted to hurt you, but I needed you to submit to me, I don't know why it's so hard for you to see how much I crave you. How much I want you!" I cringed thinking back to my time in the basement.

"That's not love Xavier."

"I will be better. I'll show you how much I love you. I promise to prove it to you just come with me" he begged holding my hands to his chest, I sighed and yanked my hands out of his grasp.

"I will never willingly go with you Xavier." He let out a sigh and nodded his head.

"Then I'm sorry for what's about to come, but ill prove it to you that I'm the only man who will put you first even against my own brother" and as if a light bulb just went off in my head and realization just kicked in.

"Lorenzo" I gasped out and ran out of the room, seeing Lorenzo knocked out on the floor being dragged by Xavier's men.

"What did you do" I spun around and watched one of his men hit me with their gun knocking me unconscious.

"He be given the ultimate ultimatum he will have to choose between the two of you and I guarantee he won't be choosing you Isabella."

X

I slowly opened my eyes, adjusting to the dim light in the room. "What … what's happening?" I feel this roaring headache when suddenly everything that happened last night hit me like a ton of bricks. I looked around the room furious, my hands clearly chained down to the chair I was sitting in a chair that was bolted to the floor, I rolled my eyes clearly Xavier took precautions because he knew if I got out, I was going to be furious. If he thinks this is going to be a repeat of him trying to break me, he has another thing coming, "XAVIER!" I screamed on the top of my lungs waiting for him to appear like a demon.

"XAVIER GET DOWN HERE YOU COWARD!"

"Calm down amore I'm here" he rolls his eyes standing in front of me, clenching my jaw it takes every ounce of self-control not to explode.

"Where's Lorenzo?" I question he looked at me amused.

"Alive" he vaguely answers.

"Where?"

"Somewhere"

"Xavier, I don't care how secure you feel right now I will tear these chains off my hands and this chair off its bolts and strangle you if you don't start talking" I warn not in the mood for his stupid games. He exhales a nervous sigh, regaining composure he rolls his eyes and huffs like a child.

"Xavier!" I snap losing my patience.

"He is at another location across town" he answers me. I nod my head slowly eyeing him trying to get a read on him. He was never good at hiding his emotions and I know he has a twisted game planned.

"Go on" I lean back in my chair. He looks at me skeptically not sure what I'm referring to.

"Gloat about your flawless plan, what you're planning on doing and how you know this will be the time I chose you" I elaborate further, he huffs "you will choose me" he sounds so confident that it makes me involuntary roll my eyes.

"You see Vincenzo is faced with two options. He has the chance to save one of you not both. He will be given the location of one person upon his choice, and he can go save whoever it may be. You know Vincenzo already lost one sibling do you think he can go through it all over again? Even if that meant he had to sacrifice you to save his brother. I will sacrifice the world to save you and only you, but he will sacrifice the world to protect his family, and you know when it comes down to it, he will choose his own blood over your life." I looked at the ground and winced, knowing he was right.

I flicked the hair out of my eyes and took in a deep breath, "good" he moves his head back clearly not expecting my response. "If I was given the same ultimatum, I would choose my sister over anyone, given the chance to save her life or another I would always choose her. So, I don't expect any less from Vincenzo or anyone else for that matter, but that won't prove anything for me.

It doesn't prove he doesn't love me, no matter how deep your love runs for someone it's never as strong as a sibling bond." I clarify meaning every single word, but I know one way or another he will save me. Vincenzo just got his memories back; he just got his life back … we just got each other back and we will be dammed if Xavier is going to try and ruin that. His going to come for me … I mean he can't leave me here. Can he?

Vincenzo's POV

I look around the hospital room hoping to see Isabella waiting for me, but I was met with an empty room … to empty. I look around seeing no guards or any of my men outside either. An unsettling feeling decides to settle deep in my gut, "Lorenzo?" I call out but am meet with silence.

"Fuck" I hiss sitting up slowly the stitches still fresh. I look over my shoulder and see a note resting on the table next to my bed. I groan reaching for it seeing my name written in cursive handwriting signed with an X.

My jaw automatically tensed knowing that whatever was in this letter was going to drive me insane, without waiting another second, I tear the envelope open mentally preparing myself for what I was about to read but nothing could have prepared me for this.

Vincenzo,

A little birdy told me you managed to somehow survive the drugs and a car accident. I must say you have more lives than a cat, nonetheless I intended to make sure that this is your last life. As I sit here next to you watching you sleep, I realize just how easy it is to end your life right now, but once I tell you what you must face you will wish I just ended it all. I'll stop toying with you now, as we both know Isabella is the reason for all of this, from our first encounter I told you my only reason for coming to New York was to reclaim what is rightfully mine, with your help I will get her back and show her no one, not even you will love her more than me or choose her over everyone even if that means choosing her over my own brother.

Will you? I have both Lorenzo and Isabella tucked away they are both alive and well for now.

You now have a choice to save only one of them. Behind this letter I give you the address for both locations, Isabella and Lorenzo but remember this is my game and you can only choose one person to save, whoever you pick you can take and the other will face the same fate as Dante, they will be killed by my hands with the same knife. Just keep in mind, in my game I hate cheaters, if you send men to both locations, they will both be killed.

So, choose your next move wisely King, I'll see you soon.
Xavier.

I flipped the letter around seeing two locations each one labeled with their names, my frustration built up like an intense pressure within me, threatening to burst in every direction. I felt the veins in my neck bulge out as I tensed up curling the note in my fist, my knuckles turning white as I tried to hold myself together.

It was useless, the pain and anger that was boiling inside me demanded release, I felt my throat contract, and my voice quivered for the first time with such raw emotion as I let out a scream that seemed to echo through the depths of my soul. My voice cracked and strained under the weight of my emotions, revealing the depths of my agony.

It was as if every hurt, every disappointment, and every failure in my life were all packed into this one cry for help. The intensity of my scream made my body tremble uncontrollably, it wasn't just a scream of anger, or pain it was a desperate cry for help, a plea for relief from the relentless torment that seemed to follow me my whole life, and now it followed the two people I loved the most. I was just thankful Ariana, and my son were somewhere safe.

The sound of my scream was deafening, drowning out everything else around me. My throat felt raw and hoarse, as if I had swallowed a piece of broken glass, but I didn't stop. I couldn't stop the pain in my voice was too real, too raw, and too profound to be silenced.

Gradually, my scream begins to drop, leaving me gasping for breath, my chest heaving. My head is scattered for the first time in my life I had no idea what to do. Nurses and doctors rushed in as I stood up needing to get dressed and back at the house immediately. I grabbed my phone and called Hacker telling him to get men to pick me up, and to get everyone ready for what is about to come. I pushed past the staff who were trying to force me back in bed but at this point I didn't care if death was staring me in the face I needed to go, Grimm reaper can wait I have shit to do.

X

I got into the car as my head went through a million scenarios, I could just send men to both locations but if I cheat, he will kill them both. For the first time in my life, I just … I have no idea what the right move is. I cannot imagine a life without either one of them, trying to fathom a life without my brother the person I vowed to protect until my last breath and who has never left my side or the one person who breaths life back into my soul, the only one who saw my demons and didn't run away instead she kissed each and every one of them. We are two broken souls, scarred with the wounds from our demons, playing a dangerous game of trust and love … and look where it led us. A dangerous love ended with a life-or-death situation and impossible decision.

I stormed out of the car and went straight up to the office, I looked around and saw my men anxiously waiting for me including Garcia and his men, he nods his head at me I return the gesture looking around the room.

"Lorenzo and Isabella have been taken and are being held hostage" I announce, everyone in the room shared gasps, anger and one emotion that stood out most was the need for blood, we want revenge.

"I have a plan" I announced getting them all to quiet down, I sighed knowing whichever decision I was going to make would end with blood, "I need you all to trust me on this one. I'm making the only decision there is, I can't live without-"

Lorenzo's POV

I've been stewing for hours trying to get anyone to come down and fucking speak but no one's showing their fucking faces. I let out a reckless yell feeling hopeless, I've been banging on the door for hours, but it won't budge, and no one will come, I curse under my breath holding my head it's still spinning from whatever they did to knock me out.

"I see you finally woke up. Poor Isabella is still knocked out cold."

I looked up immediately matching the voice to a face, "Xavier!" I shouted looking for him, "where is she!" I yelled out.

"She's safe with me" he responds.

"Count your days Xavier, they're numbered" I threatened him, growing agitated as he laughed.

"You truly believe you're getting out of there? By the time he saves you, Isabella and I will be long gone" he laughs a laugh that made my blood boil.

"Isabella should have killed you when she had the chance." I spat still looking around the dark room not seeing his silhouette only hearing his unbearable voice.

"And yet she didn't, Lorenzo stop looking around you are stuck in a room all by yourself, and I get the privilege to watch you go insane."

I yelled banging on the doors wanting to get out, but I then slowly calmed down as if someone was standing behind me … as if she was standing behind me. I took in a deep breath not wanting to give him the satisfaction of me losing my temper, its exactly what he wants to see me go insane.

I let out a sigh and sat down waiting for the inevitable, it was clear he had both myself and Isabella in confinement he will force Vincenzo to pick between the two of us and I pray with every fiber in my soul that he chooses Isabella.

I don't know what neither he nor I will do without her in our lives, I know just how much he loves her and how much she loves him, watching the two of them the past year and a half was torment how much they both yearned and wanted one another but neither of them knew it, or knew how to show it.

I don't think neither of them truly knew how to love the other, I sigh sadly remembering the conversation Maria and I had.

"Do you think he ever loved her?" Maria's voice rings through my head recalling our conversation I smiled leaning my head back, "Yeah. He loves her so, so much" I whispered to the empty room, I know he did and still does. She was all he ever talked about and the only one he ever saw.

"Then why did he break her heart?" Maria whispered sadly for her sister.

I sighed **"he loves her"** I pause to swallow, **"he just wasn't ready for it to hit him that hard."**

Since I can remember I've known my brother to carry more anger and pain than a thousand armies could ever bear, his childhood was full of 'training' that's what dad liked to call it, it was just torture.

To save his brother from the same fate he took it all on himself not wanting to expose his brother to the same torture. He was betrayed, deceived, hurt. Believe me when I say he has already been to hell and the ones who took him there were the ones who were supposed to protect him from it … and the only time I ever saw peace in my brother's eyes was when he was looking at Isabella.

She's the only reason his still alive and after all the years of my brother protecting us it was finally our turn to protect him. So please choose her.

There is nothing left for me anyway, all I could think about was finally being with Maria again. When I first laid eyes on her, I just knew she was the one for me, her big, beautiful Bambi eyes and how her dimples highlighted her face whenever she would laugh and how much she hated how her eyes always gave her away. I wish she was here so I can say how in love I am with her, and how much I miss holding her in my arms.

I sighed looking straight ahead, "I'll be with you soon Bambi."

THE CHOICE

Isabella's POV

I've been sitting here for hours, feeling my insides shutting down. All I wanted to do was run into Vincenzo's arms and cuddle up to him and breath in his scent, I wanted my son to grow up with both of us.

I smiled sadly as a tear fell out of my eye, I wasn't going to see my son grow up, but I knew my baby had the most amazing support system around, Ariana is the best aunty so caring and loving always ready to spoil and care for him knowing exactly what to do.

Lorenzo is such an amazing uncle, the perfect balance, teaching Dante kindness, love and most importantly how to navigate our world and still enjoy life.

Then he has his dad with Vincenzo watching over him I knew he will always be protected and loved. He would be taught how to be tough but vulnerable, and most importantly how to love, whether he knew it or not he loved me and our son with every single bit of his heart.

I never felt so loved and protected in my whole life not even from my parents. I sighed accepting my fate knowing he better not let Lorenzo die, even if that meant me dying.

I heard footsteps slowly approaching me I lifted my head up my eyes meeting Xavier's.

I could scream, I could try to set myself free, I can even attempt to get under his skin, but I was so tired I just chose to look up at him lifeless a blank expression as I stared into his soul.

"Isabella are you okay?" he questioned softly looking concerned.

I huffed nodding my head "just peachy" I replied with a monotone.

"Are you hungry?" he questioned staying quiet he stands up frustrated.

"Isabella, you can't just starve yourself" he huffs.

I roll my eyes trying to control myself from lashing out knowing it won't get my anywhere anyway.

"Xavier what is it you want?" I asked exhausted.

"You! Isabella, I want you! How can you not see that. Every breath, every heartbeat is all for you! I do everything to get your attention, to get you to look at me with the same admiration but I just … what do I have to do?" he asks desperation laced his question as he looked at me with pleading eyes. I flicked the hair out of my eyes and leaned forward.

"Die" I spat coldly.

My choice of words clearly didn't amuse Xavier, he slapped me across my face and started punching me he wouldn't stop until one of his men pulled him off me, I looked up at him feeling my insides bruised and broken as his men held him back.

"Screw you" I hissed.

He looked at me with wide eyes realizing what he did, and just how unphased I was.

"Why do you push me to do these terrible things? Why can't you just love me?" He yelled frustrated, I narrowed my eyes and kept quiet not in the physical or mental mindset to be able to fight back. He huffed and stepped closer towards me getting out of his man's grasp.

"I love you. Mark my words Isabella … one day you will love me too." Not breathing a word, he sighs and walks off clearly feeling defeated, I rolled my eyes and slumped back into the chair. I drift off into space thinking about my son, I sigh deeply thinking about all the time I'm going to miss with him. His first steps, his first words, him growing up, him going to school, graduating, I won't even be there to help him with his first heartache … or see him with his true love. I'm going to miss it all and it's killing me slowly.

My baby boy will grow up not knowing or having his mum by his side and that's all I ever wanted to do be by his side watch him grow up and just beam with pride and joy that my baby boy is growing up to be a respectful man a future mafia leader but still a man a deadly one in fact. I couldn't help but imagine who he would grow up to be, he has the perfect bits from both me and Vincenzo. I pray he gets the good in both of us and not the parts we wish weren't there, I pray for my son that he goes through his life happiness and grace no torture no pain and no trauma. He doesn't deserve what happened to me and his dad to ever happen to him in fact no one deserves it.

He deserves to grow up happy and with nothing left in his eye, knowing Vincenzo he wouldn't let our son go without getting him everything he wanted anyway, thankfully Ariana will be around to balance Vincenzo out, so my son doesn't grow up to be a spoilt pompous ass. My mind fixated on my son picturing how he'll turn out when he gets older, I may not be physically with him, but I will be there watching over him, myself, Maria, and Dante a supernatural forcefield.

I sighed closing my eyes as though talking to Vincenzo right now, I know you are spiraling and have no clue what to do you're caught between two halves of your heart but know whatever decision you make it will be the right one. Lorenzo is your brother, you watched him grow up and practically raised him I don't expect you to ever pick me or anyone over him. Please don't spiral and don't torment yourself. I love you now and forever it's funny because I fell in love with him from first interaction, but I never knew my only regret is I wish I knew earlier, and my god do I wish I told you sooner.

I felt a tear drop roll down my cheek taking in a deep breath I continue feeling like this is the only way I can feel closure he may not really be here or in front of me but if we are as connected as I think he should know what I'm thinking and feeling, even without knowing. I don't know if I was just losing my mind or if what I thought made any sense, nonetheless I love him so much and I need him to be strong, strong for himself, our family and most importantly strong for our son. You and me forever Italy.

X

I jolted awake hearing the door slam shut, I looked at Xavier who was standing way to close to me, I huffed annoyed he woke me up, "are you freaking stupid? Or do you just have a death wish?" I hissed, he rolled his eyes and smirked amused.

"I kidnap you and the first time you threaten death on me is when I wake you up?" He laughed finding the situation all too amusing. "Oh, because this is the first time you've kidnapped me. Honestly, it's becoming a bad joke at this point" I shrugged still annoyed he woke me up.

"You need to watch your attitude love" he warned smiling, I rolled my eyes.

"What are you gonna do? Kidnap me?" I mocked.

He pulls out a machete from I don't even fucking know where, "seriously Isabella I have a few new toys I was hoping you could try out when you start work, but I don't mind testing it out on you" I laughed hysterically which did not amuse him one bit.

I tried catching my breath my abs starting to hurt the harder I laughed.

"Yeah sure, maybe learn how to hold it before you cut yourself" I laughed and laughed until it felt like I was about to pass out, I finally settled down looking up at Xavier who was still holding the machete in an awkward position not knowing who knew getting kidnapped could be so much fun?

"You don't know what to do or how to handle something so big and long" I smiled innocently up at him knowing full well even if he attempted to do anything with it, it would immediately backfire and result in him hurting himself.

"You're on very thin ice Isabella" he warned.

"I don't mind going for a swim" I smiled.

"Isabella, you are playing a dangerous game."

"That's because I'm the only one who knows how to play it just right." I winked feeling my confidence at a new height.

He dropped the machete and pulled out his gun and pointed it at my thigh, proving me right.

"See small and stubby that's your strong suit" I nodded my head approvingly.

"I'm serious" he takes the safety off. I shrugged my shoulders.

"It won't be the first time I get shot, go for it."

Pulling the trigger the bullet grazes the side of my thigh, my eyes swell up as I bit down on my jaw refusing to let out a sound of pain. Taking in a few deep breaths I push the pain away and stare Xavier down who looked more petrified by what he did than I was about being shot at.

"Your thigh ... it's bleeding" he stutters out like it was his first time pulling a trigger, I knew he didn't mean to shoot me, and he knew. This wasn't about trying to hurt me more so about proving a point.

"Oh really? I hadn't fucking noticed that half of my goddamned blood was flowing out of my fucking thigh but thank you for letting me know I truly appreciate it you fucking pathetic excuse for man!" I sarcastically yelled out at his utter stupidity.

"I was going to offer you help-" I cut him off swiftly.

"I never asked for your help, nor do I want it."

I hissed feeling the sting on my thigh, "don't be stubborn"

he stepped closer, and I kicked him in the face "I said no"

I warned.

"You are outnumbered and injured do not forget that your

life is literally in my hands" he yelled rubbing his jaw

clearly enraged, "just because I'm outnumbered doesn't

mean I can't kill you all one by one if I wanted to" I

warned, and he knew full good and well that I could easily

live up to my threat.

He backed away and nodded his head knowing the only

reason I was behaving was because to keep Lorenzo safe at

least until Vincenzo grabs him. Nodding his head slowly he

exited the room quietly, I looked down at my thigh and

saw the blood fall down my thigh, I hissed as I bent my

leg, I couldn't even aid myself because my hands where still

fucking chained up.

I close my eyes softly and let out a sigh, knowing I was

about to meet my end.

"I'll see you soon hermosa" I whispered softly imagining my sister standing right in front of me.

Vincenzo's POV

I told the men the plan and dismissed everyone, they all ran out of my office scrambling to get to ready, I knew this wasn't going to be easy. As cowardly and pathetic Xavier is, he isn't to be underestimated when you are that gutless you learn to be very cunning slithering out of every confronting situation his spineless attitude is the only reason he is still alive.

Always having an escape plan ready in case things so south not caring to sacrifice his men as long as he is safe, he sees those who work for him as pons in his life always standing in front of the barrel and easily replaceable. One thing Xavier doesn't realize is hungry dogs are never loyal.

I gather my things and rush out of the office, feeling a grip on my arm I turn to see a worried Garcia.

"Vincenzo" he calls my name broken.

"I need you to bring my daughter back to me" taken back I

shake my head "daughter?" I question. His face changes as he calculates what to say next in his head.

"I'm Isabella and Maria's biological father" he clarifies leaving me even more stunned than before, everything slowly falling into place I look at Garcia with mixed emotions. Happiness, confusion, and sorrow, he just got his daughter back and now she's in the hands of a maniac and I'm caught between two rocks and a hard place no matter who I save it will lead to an explosion and I knew it.

I sighed nodding my head "I can't imagine the chaos going on in your head right now, but I just got my daughter back. Please don't let me loose her now ... not again. I'm with you till death Vincenzo just say the word" I gave him a sharp nod to which he returned as though reading my mind before I rushed out jumping in my car. I turned the note around staring at the two locations scribbled on the paper, I bit down my entire body tensing up not being able to look away from the scribble and my body not allowing me to start the car and drive off.

I know what I have to do that doesn't mean I want to do it, I hit the dashboard screaming out in pain, cursing I yelled until my throat became raw.

What I would do for Dante to be with me right now, to reassure me that what I'm doing is the right decision. What I would do to be the one facing death just so I can see my brother, I laughed at the irony I have been so occupied this past year I haven't allowed myself to really sit and remember my brother, fuck I haven't even been out to visit his grave. I felt tears welling up in my eyes letting out a deep breath I nod my head knowing exactly what I needed to do.

Suddenly feeling a sense of calm rush over me the same feeling I use to get when I had Dante standing right next to me, I looked over my shoulder at the empty seat and smiled.

"You weren't born to be soft and quiet. You were born to make the world shatter and shake at your fingertips" I whispered repeating his famous phrase imagining him sitting right next to me saying it at the exact time reassuring me that I knew what I needed to do.

I took in a deep breath turning the car on as the engine roared to life, I felt like someone wrapped their arms around me, or two people. I shook my head shaking the feeling off looking out my window I gesture to my men along with

Garcia and drive off.

My mind drifted off to my brother as I drove down the quiet road, Lorenzo who I raised. I watched him go from a newborn baby to a man. A man I'm so fucking proud of, a man I couldn't become myself. Someone with the purest heart and innocent mind, a real man not a boy who throws a few punches and claims to be a man, no Lorenzo was everything everyone wanted to become.

I remember when they brought him home from the hospital Dante and I were so excited seeing our baby brother, I remember we kept fighting trying to get to him first. Dante would jump over me, and I would throw a Tv remote at his head. I laughed at the distant memory.

I remember when Dante died. Lorenzo was only ten I got him dressed in him tux trying to hold my own emotions back I looked at my brother who was crying his eyes out.

'Why did he have to die Cenzo' he cried out, I had to bite the inside of my cheek to stop myself from crying. *'The angels needed him back Enzo. He has a much higher purpose now; he is living with the stars'* I whispered. *'Tell the angels to give him back! We need him here as well ... I need him'* he whispered. I took in a deep breath feeling as though my heart was being crushed from the inside. *'Why do you need him buddy?'*

He chewed down on his bottom lip before looking me in the eye.

'I need him to help me keep you safe ... I love Dante so much I just want him back' he jumps into my chest hugging me as he cries into my shirt. I hold him tight letting a few tears fall from my eyes.

'My job is to keep you safe not the other way around. I promise you this Lorenzo as long as there is a soul in my body, I will always protect you and Dante will be doing the exact same thing but from the skies.' I kissed his forehead as he looked up at me *'you promise?'*

'I promise.' I nodded my head smiling.

I did just that as the years went by, I spent every second making sure Lorenzo was safe, that his pure heart never darkened that he was never exposed to my father's training. I lived for the sake of my brother and sister, watching them grow up was the most life fulling thing.

It was the only reason I was still alive, watching Lorenzo be a mini version of Dante with his own unique twist is something I would never wish to miss out on, in this life we all have one person who's willing to die for the other. Like I was willing to die for him, I knew he was ready to do the same. Every mission, every meeting, every fight, everything I had to encounter he refused to leave my side always ready to stand in front of me if he saw fit. My dream for him is for him to grow up find that epic love Dante and I dreamed about, have a family, and live a long happy life.

It's my dream for both my siblings and a dream I have for my son.

Rolling down my window I let the air wake me up, confirming that all of this is a reality. Looking out onto the road I smile remembering how me and Isabella met.

I was so angry that I had to do a driver's job and go to the airport to pick up my father's client, but looking back I thank whoever is up there managing everything that it worked out like that. From the moment my eyes landed on her my heart claimed her as mine and so did my ego, I remember being so enchanted with her how powerful she is and how she never backed down even faced with a man double her size. She kept her stance squared ready to attack and when she did attack my heart did a flip.

The time I knew I wanted her the time I really knew I loved her; was the night she came to stab me. I laughed recalling the events of the night, how she straddled me our fight afterwards and how she cut herself and the last thing on my mind was my own life … all I could think about was stopping the bleeding a surging urge to stop the pain never wanting to hear that painful hiss coming from her beautiful lips.

Then when she nursed me back to health it just deepened my feelings, and I knew I was screwed that she was my going to drive me to insanity that she would unleash all hell and chaos leaving nothing in her path, but as long as I saw her smiling, I didn't mind bleeding out in the chaos or listening to my skin sizzle.

The sound of a horn beeping drew me out of my daydream, and I realized I reached the intersection.

Right took me to Lorenzo and the left took me to Isabella. Taking in a deep breath I turned the indictor on and turned, I parked the car in front of the building getting out of my car I stared at the building in front of me my body frozen in place knowing as soon as I walked in the building sealing my choice the other will facing Xavier and whatever fate he had instore.

Feeling like someone was giving me a push, I ran inside the building breaking down the door, I froze looking at a silhouette sitting up lifeless. "No! you didn't … you didn't choose me! Vincenzo, please tell me you didn't do this to yourself!"

"Lorenzo" I called his name rushing to his side. He jumped in my arms holding on for dear life. "I love you brother" he moved back holding my arms "so much that I was ready to die for you. Why did you pick me?"

I bite my tongue nodding my head "I promised you."

Isabella's POV

I spent the next hour trying to figure a way to get out, but I knew there was no use, I knew that I better start getting use to this basement the same feeling I got the first time he did this. The only thing that changed about this time is I'm grown I won't break so easy, and he should be ready for an even bigger fight because this wasn't the same Isabella in front of him.

The door flies open, and storming inside was Xavier his laptop, grabbing a chair he set it in front of me along with the laptop that showed security footage inside was Lorenzo, sitting peacefully almost as if he accepted his fate.

"What is this?" I questioned growing concerned; he smirked and told me to continue watching. Within the next second the door flew open Vincenzo rushing in, I let out a breath I didn't realize I was holding. A sense of relief watched over me knowing he was safe, but as happy as I was, I couldn't help but feel a little disappointed I knew he would save his brother and I would do the same it just finally sunk in that this was it.

"No! you didn't … you didn't choose me! Vincenzo, please tell me you didn't do this to yourself!" Lorenzo yelled in disbelief; I took in a trembling breath feeling my eyes water.

"Lorenzo" Vincenzo called out his name rushing to his side trying to calm him down. I knew Lorenzo was relieved and I knew that If I was chosen, he would have to suffer a worser fate than me.

I couldn't explain how thankful I felt knowing he was going to be safe. He jumped Vincenzo's arms holding on for dear life like any baby brother would and it warmed my heart to watch.

"I love you brother" I heard him whisper "so much that I was ready to die for you. Why did you pick me?"

"I promised you." Was all Vincenzo responded.

"Whatever you think you're gaining from showing me this isn't working. I'm not mad, the opposite actually" I watched Xavier take him eyes from the screen, yelling at me from my frustration if I wasn't paying attention, I would have missed it. That word … he had a plan "did you think I was some sort of *serpente*?" My breathing hitched hearing him while my eyes stayed fixated on Xavier praying, he didn't hear him.

"You should have saved her. You are going to die a million deaths every second for the rest of your life and you just sentenced me to watch you for the rest of our lives dying every second without her." He cried.

"Isabella! I won't let you go without a fight baby. I'm coming" they both run out of the room sending Xavier in a panic.

"Grab her let's go!" he called out for his men; they unchain me and quickly chain me up not taking any risks of me getting free. Xavier holds his hand up his men halt as they help keeping me balanced with an evil twinkle in his eyes, he bends down scraping my wound so fresh blood pours, I hissed kicking him away from me. "What the fuck!" I yelled feeling the pain all over again.

Sitting up he walks over to the wall using my blood he writes 'I warned you! I hate cheaters.' I rolled my eyes at his obnoxious behavior as he snapped his fingers, and his men held me steady as they lead me out of the room and into a car.

"For the mafia king his game plans are very basic" he

comments at Vincenzo's attempt to save me, I roll my eyes knowing there was more to the game Vincenzo was playing but he needed to be smart about it, so smart I honestly don't even know how it's going to play out.

"I told you Isabella, no one will put you first except me. No one will constantly put you first like me." I felt both men who were holding me tense up hearing Xavier speak.

I remained calm and looked Xavier in the eye.

"I promise you, one thing. I won't let you kill me until I kill you first." He smiled getting closer.

"If you leave this earth, I'm leaving it with you love." I rolled my eyes trying to swallow the puke that was threatening to come out. "I'll see you in hell Isabella."

I smiled turning to him "Oh indeed, but why don't you get a head start?"

I let out a heavy sigh wondering what was going through Vincenzo's head, what he was planning on doing how he was planning on playing this game that Xavier started but one thing I didn't have to wonder was how determined he was, he got himself back mixed with his old self. The mafia king was fully unleashed, and he was coming for blood, I looked over at Xavier in pity knowing his days were finally numbered.

I can't wait to watch his soul leave his body, to watch his eyes become halo and his body lifeless. To watch the blood drain from him, one thing was guaranteed we were going to make him pay for every single sin he did, and his death will not be quick. I started feeling sleepy, so I slowly drifted off taking the advantage of the situation and sleep.

X

"Isabella, wake up you're missing the show" Xavier shook me awake directing my attention to the screen. My eyes finally focusing I see Vincenzo and Lorenzo staring at the wall.

"Is that her blood?" Lorenzo shouts running his hand through his hair. Vincenzo nodded looking stressed.

"He killed her!" Lorenzo throws the chair I was previously chained to against the wall.

"He would never kill her Lorenzo. That's the only thing we can trust he will never kill her." I nodded my head slowly, as much as Xavier tortured me, he always stopped when he felt like my body was giving out. He was a sadistic idiot.

I serve a bigger purpose for him alive than dead and according to him he is in love with me. So, Vincenzo is right, he knew that Xavier would easily kill Lorenzo, but he would never kill me.

"It's her blood on the wall Vincenzo, there's a bullet on the floor and you're putting your trust in the hand of a sadistic asshat!" Lorenzo yelled.

I couldn't help but giggle, Xavier looked at me offended

"I'm enjoying the show" I smiled sarcastically.

He rolled his eyes we all resumed focusing back on the screen, "What are we going to do?" Lorenzo shouts. Vincenzo bobs his head letting out a defeated sigh "I have no idea."

Xavier lets out a laugh feeling victorious.

"We have to find her" Vincenzo nods his head I let out a soft breath I can sense his frustration from here, and I hate that he was feeling so defeated.

"You don't think I know that? I finally got her back, all of her and she gets taken from me. You don't think I know we have to find her? Do you think I'm going to spend any waking moment not looking for her? My mind is going a thousand miles an hour trying to figure a way out to find her." Vincenzo ranted his desperation and frustration reaching a new level.

"Boss we need to get out of the city" one of men stated looking at him, I looked at the man and shot him a glare.

"No, no, no. We won't be doing that" I stated shaking my head,

"No, his right we need to leave, Vincenzo might be defeated now but that feeling is going to turn into anger and his going to find you. Don't forget Vincenzo owns this city everyone fears him and if he puts a hit on your head boss. No one is going to protect you against the king." My eyes going wide, I knew what he said was true, but I was beyond frustrated that he made sense. Since when did Xavier hire smart people.

"Where should we go?" Xavier thinks out loud.

"Spain" I suggested.

"No, that's the first place Vincenzo would think of, plus you own Spain. That's the worst place you can go" I elbowed the man in his ribs growing frustrated with the both of them, seriously need to straighten them out when I get a chance. "We can go to Italy?" I shot the other man a look, seriously? Vincenzo's hometown? I take back calling them smart. Xavier looked hesitant as he stared at the men.

"It's the last place he would think of, considering his Italian and has connections there. He wouldn't even expect it" I nodded my head unconsciously Xavier seeing me agree smirked gaining full confidence in the man's suggestion in going to Italy. Something in my gut told me he was going to regret going to Italy, but I wasn't going to fight him. As long as my loved ones were safe, I didn't even care nor dare make a move, like I said Xavier may be cowardly, but he was sneaky he knew how to be threatening without putting himself in danger which is why he lasted this long. It's the only quality that makes him dangerous, I knew if I made a fuss his first move will be to find Dante and silence me by threatening my son, and I'll be damned if I was going to let anyone look at my son the wrong way let alone threaten my baby. I'll escape eventually, everything in life has a way of happening at the right time, my escape will be one of those things but this time it won't take me a year ... hopefully.

I settled into my seat and allowed sleep to consume for me.

ABOUT THE AUTHOR

Hey guy's I'm a twenty-one-year-old self-published author, so please keep in mind that I'm not experienced and am doing the best I can with whatever knowledge I have. I proofread and edited as well as submitted the book to a beta reader. If there are errors just keep in mind, we are still human and might have overlooked it without realizing.

I hope you enjoyed the book! See you Dragons in Book 3!

Printed in Great Britain
by Amazon

35729228R00324